The
Blue
Dragon

The

Blue

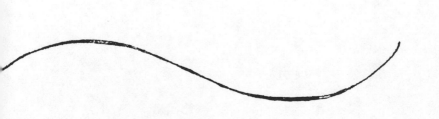

St. Martin's Press

New York

Dragon

Diana
Brown

The following poems reprinted by permission of the University of California Press: "It rained during the night . . ."; "O moon, O shining round moon . . ."; "Love, it is a lying word . . ." from *The Bamboo Grove: An Introduction to Sijo*, edited and translated by Richard Rutt © 1971 The Regents of the University of California. Poem by Song Song-nin from *Anthology of Korean Literature, From Early Times to the Nineteenth Century*, compiled and edited by Peter H. Lee, © 1981 by University of Hawaii Press.

DESIGN BY KAY LEE

LIBRARY OF CONGRESS
Library of Congress Cataloging-in-Publication Data

Brown, Diana.
  The blue dragon/by Diana Brown.
    p. cm.
  ISBN 0-312-01393-0
  I. Title.
  PR6052.R58943B55   1988   87-27473
  823'.914—dc19   CIP

10 9 8 7 6 5 4 3 2

For Kathleen C. Ruddy

In memory of an inestimable friend

Previous Novels by Diana Brown:

The Hand of a Woman
The Sandalwood Fan
St. Martin's Summer
A Debt of Honour
Come Be My Love
The Emerald Necklace

In the Yang-Um (light-dark, masculine-feminine, flux-flow) symbolism developed long before the birth of Confucius, the Koreans adopted four protective symbols to dispel attack by evil forces from any of the four cardinal points of the compass.

The White Tiger of the West

The evil-repelling symbol, the supreme Um, guarding the doorway of Korea from the West.

The Black Turtle of the North

Symbol of long life. The most honored direction. Imperial palaces were always built to the north of the city.

The Red Phoenix of the South

The queen's symbol, the sunbird whose arrival presages an exemplary reign.

The Blue Dragon of the East

The king's symbol, the supreme Yang.
Every religion in the Far East lays claim
to the dragon. It is widely used in Korean art
and is said to be so splendid that no mortal being
should look on the whole figure at once.
That is why it writhes around vases and bowls.

The fusing of the Blue Dragon of the East, the supreme Yang, with the White Tiger of the West, the supreme Um, is said to produce supernatural powers.

THE

WHITE

TIGER

OF THE WEST

1

"Do you think it could possibly be an emerald?"

Primrose Wilder's whisper was clearly audible in the front pews of St. Swithin's. Even the new curate, Algernon Reid-Banning, assisting her father at the altar, heard her question and glanced around. But her sister, Marigold, did not look up.

Eyebrows would have been raised if Marigold had spoken; she had a habit of blurting out disconcerting things. But Primrose was forgiven, since, as usual, she had merely echoed the thoughts of everyone who had turned at the entrance of the stranger.

He was not from Barleigh; in fact, he did not look English at all. His hair was dark, his complexion bronzed. His already considerable height was emphasized by a pair of brown boots—gentlemen wore only black—with almost three-inch heels! His coat was brown, too, and made of leather instead of cloth. He carried a felt hat with a wide brim. But what caught and held Primrose's attention was the pin on his widely knotted maroon tie, an enormous green stone that glittered in the light from the candles as he approached the altar.

The stranger seemed oblivious to the stir he was creating. He walked slowly, occasionally stopping to assess the fourteenth century stained-glass windows, advancing a few steps before stopping again to examine the carved wooden screens before the altar and the brass candelabrum above. He scrutinized the perpendicular style of church architecture as though he were a buyer considering purchase.

Then his eyes fell and remained fixed on the splendid figure of Algernon Reid-Banning, whose displeasure at this interruption was heightened by the obvious diversion of Primrose Wilder. Even her elder sister, whose remarks he often considered irreverent, seemed to be showing greater piety.

"O God the Father of Heaven: have mercy upon us miserable sinners." Marigold Wilder responded automatically to her father's chant, her head bowed low between clasped hands to hide her disbelief. She wished desperately that in her heart she could believe this was something more than a lot of hocus-pocus.

"From all evil and mischief; from sin, from the crafts and assaults of the devil; from thy wrath, and from everlasting damnation." Her father might have been speaking directly to her, Marigold thought. She had always taken great care to conceal her lack of belief in his God, or any other god for that matter. She cared for him deeply and had never breathed a word in her father's presence that might cause him to question her faith. She only wished she'd never told Primrose that she didn't believe anything happened to the water and wine at the altar.

"It would be pretty horrible if it did when you think about it," she had said. "We'd be gulping down body and blood like those heathen cannibals they're always trying to save."

"Maggie, how can you say such things!" Primrose's blue eyes widened in amazement and horror. "How can you even think them? I shall have to tell Father."

"Don't, please don't," Marigold had quickly urged her. "You know Father's heart is weak. John has warned us never to upset him."

"Of course I won't say anything, Maggie, not if you don't want me to," Prim replied. Yet her arch look indicated that Primrose was setting aside a piece of information that might, one day, be useful.

Marigold didn't envy her younger sister, but she often wished she were more like her, able to accept life without questioning everything.

"From all blindness of heart; from pride, vainglory, and hypocrisy; from envy, hatred, and malice, and all uncharitableness.

"Good Lord deliver us."

People often remarked how aptly the Wilder girls had been named.

Marigold, born at summer's end, had fiery orange-red hair with a temper to match. Her features were as defined as the petals of her flower; her constitution was as hardy. Although her duties as her father's housekeeper kept her confined to the house a great deal, she got out on her bicycle whenever she could, not minding when her fair complexion freckled in the sun. Marigold was without guile; if people did not always agree with her bold assertions, they certainly noticed her.

Primrose, on the other hand, was soft and lovable. Born in the dawning months of the year, she had the exquisite coloring of the flower for which she was named and a complexion as delicate as its petals. Her yellow-gold hair was held back in a low chignon and fell in loose waves around her face, a style she had copied from Lily Langtry as pictured in the *London Illustrated News*. Primrose rarely said anything of particular merit, but her manner was charming and she invariably voiced generally held opinions in a soft, melodious voice.

"Do you suppose it could be an emerald, Maggie?" Primrose repeated. This time Marigold heard her sister's whisper and looked up. The stranger had reached the end of the pew, where he stood, staring at the curate. Marigold thought his profile looked slightly familiar, but almost immediately his gaze shifted as his eyes followed Algernon's to remain fixed on the same object—the soft, pink and white complexion beneath the yellow silk roses on the brim of Primrose's hat.

"It looks like glass," Marigold whispered back as Primrose blushed prettily. The newcomer, making no attempt to hide the reason for his choice of seat, caused a general reshuffling in their already full pew. John Keane moved to close the gap between him-

self and his wife, Harriet, in order to accommodate the stranger
with a place at the end.

*"That it may please thee to preserve all that travel by land or by water,
all women laboring of child, all sick persons and young children; and to
show thy pity upon all prisoners and captives."*

Despite the tartness of her response, Marigold eyed the stranger
with curiosity, her interest aroused as much by his behavior as by
his appearance. He didn't bow his head, and though John passed
him a prayer book and indicated the place, he deliberately closed it
and made no attempt to join in the responses. Instead he continued
his examination of the church, noting the carving of Father Time
below the pulpit—one reminder that the vicar of Barleigh studiously disregarded when preaching on his favorite topic, keeping the
sabbath holy. He then considered the silver chalice and paten on
the altar. Last of all, with a flitter of amusement of his lips, the
newcomer turned his attention once again to Algernon, who had
thrust his hands beneath his chasuble and was fluttering them in
disapproval, like an angry gull. Algernon returned a glance guaranteed to kill a lesser mortal. But that only caused the stranger to
smile more broadly. It seemed as if at any moment he might burst
into laughter at the absurdity of it all—a feeling Marigold could
understand all too well.

*"From fornication, and all other deadly sin; and from all the deceits
of the world, the flesh, and the devil."*

Marigold sensed, from the marked emphasis of this chant, that
her father was about to embark once again upon his Fourth Commandment sermon; she groaned inwardly. The topic went down
perfectly well with the manufacturers around Barleigh whose fac-
tories were closed on Sunday, but it aroused wrath among the
farmers whose cows needed milking on the Sabbath just as much
as any other day.

*"In all time of our tribulation; in all time of our wealth; in the hour of
our death,"* Reverend Wilder paused to offer his usual silent prayer
for his departed wife and for his sister, Lucy, who had gone as a

missionary to India only to perish in a climate to which she was totally unsuited. *"And in the day of judgment,"* he concluded at last.

Marigold had once said she thought the saving of souls an odd occupation and that, given her Aunt Lucy's delicate health, she should never have been sent off to India for such an unrewarding task.

"It's a good and useful life for a single person—one that even a lady can undertake," her father pointed out. "My greatest regret was that I was unable to follow my dear friend Herbert Farquhar to the Far East—but alas, that would have been impossible for a married man with a family. However, when I am gone, it is something I wish you to consider, Maggie. You need have no fear—you are robust, not like my dear little Primrose."

"Please don't talk about that, Father," Marigold pleaded.

"We must face facts, Maggie. Eventually I will die, as we all must, and when I do, you will no longer be required to keep house here at the rectory. Your inheritance will be small, so you'll have to do something."

"What about Primrose?" she asked.

"Primrose," her father responded with that note of infinite affection he always adopted when speaking of his younger child. "My little Primrose must have a good husband to take care of her."

"That it may please thee to keep and strengthen in the true worshipping of thee in righteousness and holiness of life, thy Servant Victoria, our most gracious Queen and Governor.

"We beseech thee to hear us Good Lord." The curate's obsequious response led all others in deference to Her Majesty. Marigold sensed that her father had chosen his new curate with Primrose's future in mind. Besides being young, good-looking, and ambitious, Algernon Reid-Banning came from a good family. His grandfather had been bishop of Wells and, after graduating with honors from Oxford's Christ Church, Algernon had set his own sights on the purple. He had been instantly attracted to Primrose; she was not only lovely but her delicacy brought out a protective instinct that

made even the weakest of men feel like a Hercules. The curate had been heard to say that Miss Primrose Wilder was the only thing that made Barleigh livable. Primrose, who adored jewelry, fashionable clothes, and admiration from the opposite sex, in that order, was pleased by such sentiments. Although she looked beyond having a man of the cloth as a husband, the possibility of purple was a consideration not to be ignored.

"That it may please thee to rule her heart in thy faith, fear, and love and that she may ever more have affiance in thee, and ever seek thy honor and glory."

The litany seemed longer than ever this morning. Overhearing John Keane's sigh, which he quickly converted into a cough, Marigold turned to smile at him over his wife's head. Harriet's eyes were tightly closed. All of Barleigh had expected John Keane to offer for Marigold once he finished his medical studies; no one knew that he had done so but that Marigold had refused him in favor of staying with her father. So John returned to his father's medical practice with a new wife, leaving people to surmise that Miss Wilder hid her disappointment well and showed good sportsmanship in befriending the new Mrs. Keane. No one would have believed that a woman like Marigold Wilder, facing a life of spinsterhood, could prefer to have John Keane as a friend instead of a husband.

John Keane reached into his pocket for a handkerchief at the moment she turned to him, and Marigold found herself smiling at the stranger. That was embarrassing enough, but Marigold was dumbfounded when the stranger solemnly winked at her!

"That it may please thee to be her defender and keeper, giving her the victory over all her enemies.

"We beseech thee to hear us, good Lord."

At long last the congregation fell to its knees to repeat the Apostles' Creed—all but the newcomer, who leaned back, seating himself as though he were a spectator about to witness some strange native rite. Marigold felt a flash of envy at this open refusal to participate in a ritual she particularly despised. Yet with her father leading the declaration of faith, she had no choice but to join in.

The Creed ended with the usual creaking of bones as worshippers rose from their kneelers and the sudden rustle of heads turning to examine the newcomer.

"Who can he be?" Primrose whispered. "And why is he staring at Algernon that way?"

"I have no idea. Maybe he finds him handsome."

"Don't be silly, Maggie. Men don't find other men handsome."

"Don't they?" Marigold decided against reminding Primrose of certain biblical stories. Her father often said you could find everything in the Bible if you looked for it; her curiosity always seemed to lead her to find the wrong things.

She forgot the stranger momentarily as the vicar mounted the pulpit and began: "Today is Sunday, a holy day, but a day, alas, that far too many do not keep in accordance with the holy law."

From the corner of her eye, Marigold could see the newcomer cross his arms and, cramped by the pew in front, extend his long legs out into the aisle. Algernon frowned, but to no avail, for the stranger remained in that position for the next forty-eight minutes.

And the expression of pained displeasure remained on Algernon's face, even after the service as he took his usual place in the doorway beside Reverend Wilder. He seemed ill at ease, greeting parishioners in a perfunctory manner, without his usual little jokes and obsequious remarks.

Reverend Wilder's position and age tended to preclude any direct reproach from parishioners about his sermon, and no one ever thought of saying anything unpleasant to his lovely younger daughter, so Marigold had to bear the brunt of the criticism.

"To listen to the way your good father talks, he don't seem to understand there's cows to be milked. Leave them alone on the Sabbath and their udders'll burst; then he'll be up there preaching to us about cruelty to animals. Besides, all this talk of his is giving

our lads ideas. Next thing they'll be wanting the day off Sunday,
worse yet, more money for working it. And if they do, you'd best
warn him . . ."

"I shall, I shall," Marigold promised distractedly. She had just
caught sight of the stranger approaching Algernon.

The farmer's wife who had been speaking glanced at the stranger.
"I've never seen a man wearing high-heeled boots before. Sissified,
I call it. Besides, a man of his size don't even need them. Now if it
were our Will . . ."

But Marigold, giving up any pretense of listening, drew closer to
the doorway.

"Algie! It's great meeting you at long last." The stranger gripped
Algernon's limp hand, his wide smile revealing strong white teeth
against the bronzed complexion of his face. "I recognized you right
away. No, no. Don't apologize." He raised a hand, though Algernon's expression showed no inclination to apology. "You didn't recognize me, but I had the advantage. You see, I made the journey
here expressly to see you. I'm Mark Banning."

Since Algernon remained unmoved by this disclosure, Mark
Banning began shaking his hand even more heartily, repeating,
"Your cousin Mark Banning—from California."

Recognition swept across Algernon's features, though the disparagement remained. "You mean you're—you're the son of my
uncle John Reid-Banning?"

"You got it, Algie—on the nose," he replied with a laugh. "My
father was your uncle, and yours is mine. Of course, a gold pros-
pector wouldn't dare go around with a high-falutin', double-bar-
relled name—the other miners would've made his life hell if he
had. He married my mother as plain old Jack Banning."

"Ah, yes, of course, of course." Algernon looked mortified by this
whole turn of events, especially when he realized half the parish
was listening intently. "We know very little of your mother."

"I'll bet she could help out these hymns of yours—they're a bit
slow, aren't they? You know, she was singing in a Frisco barroom

when Dad met her. He said she had a voice pretty enough to live
with, and he did just that." Algernon took out a handkerchief and
wiped his brow, making Banning laugh. "No need to worry, Algie.
He married her, as you know. Though maybe you don't—Dad
wrote the family but he never did get an answer."

"Indeed." The deep flush of embarrassment that had suffused
Algernon's cheeks now extended as far as the tips of his ears.

"Sorry she couldn't have made the journey here with me. I'll bet
she'd find all of this kind of quaint. She was always asking about
meeting your family. She couldn't understand why she never did
hear from any of you—even when she wrote you about Dad's
death."

"The post," Algernon mumbled, running a hand along the rim of
his collar as though it were too tight. "It's unreliable."

"Of course," Banning conceded. "Terrible, isn't it. Sixteen years
and letters are still in the mail. The system's a disaster." He shook
his head, pursing his lips before going on. "Anyway, since she's
always been curious about your side of the family—and since either her letters or your replies never seemed to get delivered—I
promised her I'd stop by and check up on you next time I was over
here. She'd much prefer to be here herself, of course; says she
can't count on when she'll next see me. I'm always roaming. Guess
I take after Dad."

Algernon, embarrassed by the way everyone was hanging on the
stranger's words as he filled in his life story, was even more perturbed to see Primrose press forward to join them. Mark Banning
turned to her with unconcealed pleasure.

"This, if you'll pardon my saying so, is the prettiest litle lady
here today. I'd go further than that, though. I'd say she's the finest
specimen of English womanhood I've run across since coming to
this picturesque little country—and if I say so myself, I'm quite a
judge. I guess you must think so, too, Algie, the way you've been
eyeing her all through the service." Algernon shut his eyes, perhaps hoping that might make his cousin disappear. But he couldn't

remove himself from the sound of Banning's voice prompting, "Well, Algie, how about it? Are you going to introduce us or aren't you?"

Primrose, blushing and looking even prettier, also turned to prompt Algernon, leaving him no choice.

"Miss Primrose Wilder—Mark Banning. He's my . . . my cousin, from America," he concluded with evident distaste.

"Algernon, you never told me you had a cousin in America." Primrose looked on the newcomer with even greater interest. "You've really come all the way across the Atlantic, Mr. Banning?"

"More than once, Miss Wilder. Though this time I haven't come directly from America. I've journeyed around the globe—Japan, Korea, India, Persia, Africa, and now here I am in . . ." He laughed. "Now I forgot." He turned to the crowd around him. "What do you call this cute little burg?"

"Barleigh," was the chorused response.

"That's it—Barleigh."

"You mean you've been all the way around the whole world, Mr. Banning! How daring of you! I've always longed to travel. I've never known anyone who's been beyond the English Channel, except for my Aunt Lucy who went to India as a missionary—but that's different." Primrose breathed, fluttering her long eyelashes in adoring tribute until a sudden and obviously unpleasant thought struck her. "I hope you're not one, Mr. Banning."

"Not one what, Miss Wilder?"

"A missionary."

Mark Banning threw back his head and laughed. It was the sort of laugh that made other people want to laugh, too, and many of those present joined in without knowing quite why. Algernon shuddered in dismay at what was definitely not the laugh of an English gentleman.

"You may take it, Primrose, that my cousin's calling is not the church," he reproved.

"You're damn right," Banning said, slapping his cousin on the back. "Sorry, no offense, Algie, but I've never fancied wearing a dress. And I must apologize to you for my language, Miss Wilder. It's just that I can't think of anything less likely than having a calling to the church. I think Dad would toss in his grave at the idea. He always claimed there were enough collared dogs in the family." Again he laughed outright before repeating, "No offense intended, Algie."

"None taken, dear boy." Algernon responded frigidly.

And there again was that laugh. "It's years since I've been called a boy—and frankly I can't ever remember being called a *dear* boy. But then, I didn't go to any of your public schools where a lot of that sort of thing goes on, or so I hear."

"What sort of thing are you referring to?" Algernon demanded testily.

"Now, now, calm down," Banning said soothingly. "I didn't come here to upset you, Algie."

"Why did you come then?" Algernon snapped.

Reverend Wilder, freed from duty after shaking the hand of the last parishoner to straggle from the church, hurried over to meet the newcomer.

"I noticed you, sir, as soon as you came in," he said to Banning. "There's a man who recognizes fine church architecture, I thought to myself."

"I'm no authority on churches, but this is a fine building, sir." Banning said politely. His manner changed as he extended his hand without waiting for an introduction. "I'm Algie's cousin from California. His father and mine were brothers."

Reverend Wilder turned to his curate. "I didn't realize you had an uncle in America, Algernon."

"Perhaps that was because my father was rather the black sheep of the family." There was a steely note as Banning added, "Even striking it rich in the Gold Rush didn't manage to redeem him in his family's eyes."

"Gold goes in at any gate except Heaven's," Algernon quoted sententiously.

"Still, as one of our fine American writers puts it, there's nothing quite as habit-forming as money, is there?" Banning responded genially.

"I didn't realize there were any fine American writers, but the idea is certainly American," Algernon said haughtily.

"The parish can't afford to turn up its nose at money," Mr. Wilder reminded his curate. Then, perhaps prompted by this thought, he asked, "Where are you staying, Mr. Reid-Banning?"

"Name's Banning—just Banning. I left my overnight bag at the station. I wasn't sure whether I'd stay on or return to London."

"Not sure of your welcome? Dear me! We must show this relative of yours what English hospitality is, mustn't we, Algernon."

Algernon seemed a lot less ready than his rector to oblige. Mr. Wilder may have sensed this, for he added, "I know your quarters are cramped, but there's plenty of room at the rectory. Your bag shall be sent for, sir, and Maggie will arrange for a room to be prepared for you."

"I've no wish to trouble your housekeeper—especially on a Sunday when she should be resting." There was a glint of amusement in Mark Banning's eyes.

"My daughter takes care of the household. Filial duties can scarcely be looked upon as work," Mr. Wilder said, carefully extricating himself from this dilemma. "Have you met my elder daughter, Maggie, Mr. Banning?"

"I don't believe I've had the pleasure, but if she's anything like the Miss Wilder I've just met, I can hardly wait."

He looked around eagerly, and Marigold, who had never had a man wink at her before, stepped forward eagerly. But as her father introduced her, she sensed Banning's interest diminish. It was obvious that he found her as little like her sister as she found him like his cousin.

2

"You see, I was right. It really is an emerald," Primrose said dreamily, putting aside her needlework. "Just think of it—an emerald that big!"

The rectory living room seemed quiet after the lively conversation they'd had at the dinner table. Primrose, Marigold, and Harriet Keane were all busy embroidering orphreys for the chasubles of the new vestments to be worn by the clergy at Easter. In the nearby dining room, the gentlemen were drinking the vicar's best port.

It was unusual for Reverend Wilder to take port after dinner, and even more unusual for him to suggest that the ladies leave the gentlemen alone. The Wilders lived a quiet life; they rarely moved in high society. But the arrival of Mark Banning seemed to have brought out an unsuspected gregarious side of the vicar.

Her father had not raised his usual objections to working on the Sabbath when Marigold instructed the maid to dust and put out clean linen in the spare room. Nor did he protest when she suggested that the cook roast a loin of beef instead of serving up their usual cold Lenten fare. She would have probably taken these same steps, discreetly, for any visitor—but in this instance, she had employed no subterfuge, rather hoping her father would step in. She was intrigued by Banning in spite of herself, but the special treatment he was receiving rankled her.

Marigold hurried through her tasks, anxious for the chance to escape to the one place where she was never disturbed: her darkroom. She wanted to print the portraits she had recently taken of

Primrose. Her sister's poses had lacked realism, but during the session Marigold had managed to take some without Prim realizing she was being photographed. Those were the ones Marigold was eager to see. But as she approached the basement door, Mr. Wilder interceded.

"*Not* on Sunday, Maggie," he said firmly.

"But, Father, photography is not work, it's my . . . my . . ." passion, she thought, would be too strong a word to use. "It's my hobby," she concluded weakly, knowing it meant far more to her than that.

Ever since Aunt Lucy had given her a choice between a watch and a camera on her eighteenth birthday—Marigold had the uncanny gift of knowing the time without having to consult a timepiece, so the choice had been an easy one—the camera lens had become the window through which she saw the world.

"We don't amuse ourselves with our hobbies on the Sabbath, Maggie," her father cautioned, "particularly when we have a special visitor to attend to."

Marigold nodded and tried not to appear resentful. Still, she ruminated on their visitor throughout the afternoon, as she went about the rest of her chores. Marigold compared Mark Banning's visible pleasure at meeting Primrose with the perfunctory manner in which he had greeted her. Primrose couldn't help being sweet and lovely, and Marigold didn't blame him for liking her best. But she did blame him for arousing her interest by winking at her in church, as though they shared a secret, and then merely greeting her perfunctorily when they met.

By the time they sat down to dinner that evening, though still vexed, Marigold resolved not to side with Algernon, whom she disliked almost as much as he seemed to dislike his new cousin. He poked malicious fun at Mark Banning's manner of speech, his swagger, the way he examined everything as though it were for sale. An obvious cause for Algernon's dislike of Mark Banning was the way Banning openly admired and paid court to Primrose—and the way she revelled in his attentions.

But Marigold's resolve and Algernon's gibes were wasted on Banning, who seemed oblivious to everyone except Primrose and Reverend Wilder. Prompted by his host, he talked at length about his travels in Japan, Russia, Egypt, and Africa—places that had been no more than names on the map to Marigold, places she could only dream about.

As he talked, Marigold found herself studying him as a subject for her camera—he had Algernon's profile, yet his features were stronger, his expression much livelier. Yet her fascination with Banning was mixed with annoyance as he held center stage, telling one tall, flamboyant tale after another.

In Japan the emperor had presented him with a magnificent string of matched pearls—big as mockingbirds' eggs, he said they were; in Russia he had hunted wild boar with the czar and received sables as a parting gift; in the land of the Pharaohs he had sailed the Nile on the sultan's yacht and picnicked in the shade of the pyramids; in South Africa he had discovered diamond mines; and he had dined from gold plate with the Shah of Persia in his marble palace surrounded by peacocks and emeralds. His tiepin, he pointed out, was a token of that event. Prim nodded knowingly at Marigold to indicate the correctness of her earlier conjecture. Marigold silently concluded that Mark Banning was the greatest braggart she'd ever met.

Even so, it was no small feat to make up these stories and she couldn't help but be swept away by the descriptions of all Banning claimed to have seen. She thought how lucky this man was to be free to go to the ends of the earth, while she was confined to the distance her bicycle could carry her within the constraints of time and her household duties.

"Of course it isn't an emerald, Prim," Marigold exclaimed in exasperation when the ladies were finally alone. "Anyone can see it's just a lump of green glass. All he did throughout dinner was boast and brag about who he knew and what they were supposed to have given him—and I'll bet the whole thing's a pack of lies."

"I suppose you must be right about the stone, Maggie," Harriet Keane agreed reluctantly. "I don't think there could really be an emerald that big. If there were, it would be worth a fortune and would have to be kept in a vault. Anyone who owned such a jewel would hardly be sitting at a rectory table here in Barleigh, would they? Of course, I don't mean to imply . . ."

"I know you don't, Harriet. But that's just what I meant."

"But Mr. Banning said it was an emerald," Prim insisted. "Why would he say it was an emerald, if it wasn't?"

"I strongly doubt he knows what truth is. All those stories about kings and emperors and peacocks and pearls—can't you see, all he wants to do is to impress us."

"But why would he want to do that? What would be the point of it?" Harriet asked with a logic Marigold found hard to refute. "I do think you're being a little severe in your criticism of Mr. Banning."

"I'm not criticizing, Harriet. I'm just stating an opinion."

"You only talk about him like that because he hasn't so much as looked at *you*." Primrose had assumed her most appealing pose, blonde head tilted capriciously forward, one eyebrow slightly raised. It was an artful pose no man could resist, but one that completely failed to move Marigold.

"Men never make up to me," she said flatly. "I don't expect them to. Nor would I want that sort of thing from someone like this American. I should think you'd be tired of his boasting by now, Prim. I'll grant you he's crossed the Atlantic, but that's no great feat, with the newly designed steamships. Anyone who can afford the passage can do as much. I'd heard that Americans were materialistic and that they showed off, but I had no idea how true that was until I met Mark Banning. Spare me any more encounters with New York charlatans."

"He's from San Francisco," Prim corrected. "The city by the Golden Gate, he called it."

"Being a San Francisco charlatan makes him no better," Marigold said, taking up her needlework again.

"I must admit I found his tales entertaining—even though they did seem far-fetched. And they had the ring of truth. I know Dr. Keane would have been the first to point out any obvious inconsistencies." Harriet always referred to her husband as Dr. Keane while Marigold continued to call him John; this was, Marigold felt, her friend's one affectation. "Mr. Banning certainly is taken with you, Prim," Harriet went on. "I can't blame Algernon for being upset." Then she leaned forward conspiratorially. "But have you noticed that the more upset Algernon gets, the stronger Mr. Banning's attentions become?"

Prim's face fell. "Harriet, are you implying Mr. Banning's only being nice to me to annoy Algernon?"

"No, no, my dear. Gentlemen always pay attention to you, and Mr. Banning clearly likes you. It's just that I have a strong impression that he dislikes Algernon as much as he likes you."

Marigold grew thoughtful but said nothing.

"Algernon doesn't seem particularly happy about having his cousin here," Primrose agreed. "Though I must say, if he were my cousin, I'd be delighted."

Privately Marigold wished he were Prim's cousin, in which case he'd be less likely to pay such open court to her. But then she realized that would make Banning her cousin as well. She was brooding over this dilemma when the gentlemen, led by Mark Banning, entered the room. He had apparently just told a joke, and the others, even Algernon, were laughing loudly.

"My dear sir—appearances are deceiving, that's capital, simply capital!" Mr. Wilder said, patting his shoulder.

"What is it that's capital, Dr. Keane?" Harriet asked her husband, possessively patting the cushion on the sofa beside her.

John Keane tugged awkwardly at his moustache. "Nothing, my dear."

"It couldn't have been nothing," his wife pressed. "You were all laughing too heartily for it to have been nothing."

"It was just a little story about China and a . . . a rickshaw and a . . . a rather stout gentleman in a tight . . . tight . . . fit." Here John Keane's face wrinkled up again and he burst into laughter.

Algernon, who had been the first to recover, interceded with a sharp, "It's not a story for the ladies, John."

"No, no, of course. I realize that," he said mournfully.

Harriet sat back in resignation. "Then I shall just have to wheedle it out of you when we're alone, Dr. Keane."

"Do tell us," Primrose cajoled. Despite frowns from the other gentlemen, Banning launched into a story about a pompous Western official in China who had had too much to drink at an official reception.

"He jumped in a rickshaw pulled by a boy one-tenth his size. With superhuman effort the boy managed to carry the weight until a sudden deluge of rain caused the wheels of the rickshaw to get stuck in the mud. Then the rickshaw with its cargo started to sink. The official was stuck inside as the conveyance was stuck in the mud. In his befuddled state, the man decided there was nothing for it but to peel off his clothes, so off they came, decorations and all, until he was naked as the day he was born. At that moment, his superior came by and, responding to his training, the official stood up and saluted."

The picture was an amusing one, even though Marigold suspected they were not being told the whole story. Nevertheless, she said, "I think it served him right," and felt surprised when Mark Banning looked directly at her for the first time that evening as he replied.

"So do I, Miss Wilder."

"Girls! This is no fit subject for comment," Reverend Wilder said hastily, although he was clearly in fine spirits. He waited until

Algernon recovered from a sudden fit of coughing before continuing. "And this was in Shanghai, you said. Years ago my dear friend, Herbert Farquhar, was there with an Anglican mission before he moved on to Korea—I can't quite remember when that was."

"Must have been at least ten years ago, because prior to 1882, Korea was closed to the outside world. That's why foreigners often refer to it as the Hermit Kingdom. Of course, ever since it opened up, everyone's been trying to get a finger into the pie."

"Not Herbert Farquhar," Mr. Wilder asserted. "All he wants is to spread God's word."

"So all the missionaries say," Banning commented wryly, "though it seems that wherever they go, their flags soon follow."

"Herbert's done much good there," Reverend Wilder reiterated. "Much good. In fact he's there to this day in . . . in Sule, is it?"

"Seoul."

"Yes, yes, that's it. He's been instrumental in founding our Church of the Advent there. He asked for my assistance. I sent funds, of course. Had I been able to go myself, I should most certainly have done so, but at that time I had with me the blessed lady who was my wife, God rest her soul, and my two dearest daughters. I could scarcely take them off into the unknown."

Mark Banning nodded. "Quite right, sir. Korea, above all, is no place for a woman—most particularly a Western woman. It's an unsociable land with a miserable climate—so hot and humid in the summer you can scarcely breathe, while in winter, freezing winds whip down from Siberia and freeze the life out of you."

"I can see it wouldn't have done, not for anyone of my wife's delicate constitution, or my dear little Primrose, for that matter. Though I dare say Maggie, being stronger than the rest of us, would probably have been all right."

Banning smiled across the room at Primrose. "All lovely things are delicate. I can see that Miss Wilder is as fragile as the flower whose name she bears."

"I don't see anything wrong with a woman being strong and healthy," Marigold asserted. "Nor a flower for that matter."

"No indeed. But it's the delicacy of a flower that makes it tantalizing," Banning observed. "Don't you agree, Algie?"

"A delicate flower mustn't be handled," Algernon snapped.

Banning laughed. "That's where they fool you, Algie. Most are surprisingly resilient." Then he turned to Mr. Wilder. "You'll be pleased to know that your friend, Mr. Farquhar, appears to be surviving the climate quite well."

"Do you know him?" Mr. Wilder asked in excitement.

"I've met him, though I can't claim to know him. Since there are few foreigners in Seoul, sooner or later everyone meets. Our missions, of course, were quite different."

"I'm not sure fortune hunting can be considered a mission, Mr. Banning," Marigold observed scathingly.

"But fortunes are so elusive—they come and go so quickly—I consider hunting them life's greatest mission," Banning responded amiably.

Mr. Wilder was musing, "If I were younger, and if there were not the need for seeing Primrose settled in marriage, and Maggie—well, who knows. Maggie may follow in the steps of my saintly sister, Lucy, who died for the cause in India . . ."

"I've no intention of dying in India or any other place for a cause," Marigold said.

"Again we agree," Banning said. "It would be foolish to die for a cause you don't believe in." At Marigold's sudden anxious look, he went on, "I was speaking of myself, naturally."

"Not believe," Mr. Wilder frowned. "But everyone must believe, Mr. Banning."

"Ultimately, I suppose, everyone does believe in something. We just don't all believe in the same way—and that, in my opinion, is all to the good. I have a friend in Japan—a fine writer by the name of Lafcadio Hearn—who believes in an Unknowable Power."

Primrose took that opportunity to comment innocently, "I don't think that everyone *does* believe. Do you, Maggie?"

Marigold laid the blame for her sister's jibe on Mark Banning, who had started the discussion, and she turned on him with, "I don't seem to recall, among all those amazing accounts of your travels, that you ever mentioned Korea, Mr. Banning. Can it be you were granted no royal favors there? Is that why it escaped your memory?"

If Banning noticed her sarcasm, he didn't pick up on it. "I did meet with King Kojong. His Kyongbok palace, in the heart of Seoul, is a sprawling conglomeration of buildings. I dare say by English standards you would scarcely consider it a palace at all. But Korea is a poor country that's been held under China's fist until now, when everyone's becoming aware of its potential—the Japanese, the Russians, even your country and mine. But there's one person in the palace they can't afford to ignore."

"This King Kojong, I suppose," John Keane put in.

"Not the king, but his wife, Queen Min."

Mr. Wilder nodded. "That's what Herbert has written, that the queen is most influential. He's not had many favorable words for her, I'm afraid, nor has she shown a willingness to listen to the good news he would like to expound. Indeed, she has shunned every overture he has made. His only inroad into the palace has been to teach English to the gentlemen of the court. He has written that if he could only convert some member of the royal family to our faith, it would augur well for our cause."

"Case of monkey see, monkey do, I suppose," Keane observed with the air of a great wit. Only his wife laughed.

Banning ignored the remark, turning to his host. "Members of their royal house do wield power, but it's a house divided against itself. China plays the queen's hand while Japan's aces lie with the king—and Russia looks on, waiting. I think one day the Blue Dragon of the East will lift its head."

"Blue Dragons!" Primrose shuddered.

Banning turned to her. "The Blue Dragon is said to guard the East, while the White Tiger watches over the West. If ever they should fuse, the belief is that they would produce supernatural powers."

"What a lot of mumbo jumbo!" John Keane scoffed.

"Perhaps," Banning replied. "Nevertheless, the situation is quite volatile."

"Herbert seems to feel no qualms," Reverend Wilder said. "Perhaps one day he may be able to turn the queen's heart to our belief. That would be truly magnificent if, as you say, where she goes, her nation follows."

"The queen, like some other women I have known, has no heart," Banning said.

"Everyone has a heart—and a soul," Algernon said bluntly.

"I have very little interest in souls." Banning smiled at Primrose. "But hearts are another matter."

"It would mean a great deal to our Anglican mission to gain one of those royal souls," the vicar pursued the subject. "You see, sir, the Roman Catholics have had an edge over us, since they've been in that sphere for more than a century. Of course, they've been severely persecuted for their efforts."

"Strange, isn't it, how nothing seems to gain converts like persecution." Banning shook his head. "That's hardly something I'd seek out—but then, like Miss Wilder, I'd never put my life on the line for a cause."

Understanding this remark as a deliberate attempt to return to a subject she had been at pains to avoid, Marigold put in caustically, "Since emeralds, diamonds, furs, and precious metals, rather than souls, were the object of your journey, did the queen present you with any token of that sort?"

"Maggie!" her father reprimanded her. "You must excuse Maggie, Mr. Banning. Her tongue is sharp."

"But her meaning is quite plain," Banning observed. "Before I answer your question, Miss Wilder, I should explain that in Korea the sexes live entirely separate lives. They have almost no social intercourse with one another, and apart from that other which is necessary—and also delightful—in the procreation of the race . . ." Algernon suffered another paroxysm of coughing, but his cousin continued undeterred, ". . . there is no mingling of men and women. At all times women must remain concealed. They're only allowed to go out at night, after dark."

"After dark, eh!" John Keane leaned forward with interest. "Doesn't that encourage, even give sanction to promiscuity?"

"Not at all. You see, during those hours no men are allowed on the streets, unless for some emergency—for instance, if they need someone of your profession, Doctor. There are occasional transgressions, but few. Korean justice is swift and exacting. All of which is a long and roundabout way of saying yes, the queen did receive me, but in her husband's presence. It was on the occasion of my departure, and, as a matter of fact, I did receive a gift from her."

"But since it was omitted from your previous litany, I presume the gift was not of any magnitude," Marigold said bitingly.

"Maggie!" her father cautioned again, but Banning intervened, smiling, "Your elder daughter does enjoy teasing." He turned to Marigold. "Queen Min is a strange woman, much influenced by shamanism, the ancient worship of both good and evil spirits, so I doubt that Reverend Farquhar has much hope of winning her for his cause. It is said that the only person who truly has her ear is a mudang who conducts shamanistic rituals, kuts, supposed to allay the evil spirits—a sort of seance on a very grand scale. One of the most powerful spirits she calls on is that White Tiger of the West I mentioned earlier." Mark Banning hesitated before reaching into his waistcoat and pulling out a bright yellow metal chain to which was attached a small green emblem. "This was my gift from Korea's queen."

The green piece dangled, dull, small, insignificant, before the flashing green stone on his tie.

"I was right, then," Marigold concluded. "No rubies or emeralds. What a pity!"

"I've no wish to be at odds with you, Miss Wilder, but in this instance you are wrong. This piece is worth more than rubies or emeralds. It is a jade kokok. These adorned the crowns of the ancient Silla rulers of Korea. They represent the claws of the tiger, the beast's most potent weapon. This is a powerful talisman that is said to carry with it not only the luck, but more important, the power of the White Tiger of the West."

"By George," Algernon sneered derisively, "You really believe that twaddle?"

"I'm not sure, Algie," Banning said, holding up the chain and allowing the kokok to twirl round and round. "The kokok may be a lucky talisman, it may not. But there is one thing I do know, and that is gold. This chain is of the very finest, the very purest gold. And I have discovered that there is more, much more where this came from. It's to be found for the asking along the banks of the Han River."

"And you linger here in England, while there are riches in the East still waiting to be plundered," Algernon commented caustically.

"This is a little family interlude, Algie—a detour, let us say, from my main route. I fully intend to return to Korea." Banning threw his cousin a beatific smile. "Indeed, I would have returned immediately after my meeting with your Prince of Wales, but I was afraid you'd never forgive me, Algie, if you were to discover I'd made yet another visit to your shores and left without seeing you."

3

Mark Banning stayed on all week. Marigold was not certain whether his eventual decision to return to London was the result of his altercation with Algernon, or whether Banning simply could not face another sermon at St. Swithin's. She inclined to the former, since she sensed that Mark Banning possessed a strange sort of honesty that would prevent him from pretending to enjoy something he so obviously had not.

During his week at Barleigh, Banning had befriended Mr. Wilder and had continued to shower Primrose with attention.

Marigold remained aloof, after her father had chastised her for being rude to their guest.

"I'm sorry, Father," Marigold had replied. "But it's Mr. Banning's manner of boasting. He just brings out the worst in me."

"I thought I had brought you up to be courteous and kind to others, not to set yourself up in judgment."

"Mr. Banning has no social conscience." Marigold couldn't restrain this comment.

"If having a social conscience means rushing into poverty-stricken areas and taking wretched photographs, you know my feelings on that. I've had to smooth enough ruffled feathers in the vestry . . ."

"I just wanted to let them see how life was outside their comfortable existence. Hunger, poverty . . ."

"Those were very nasty pictures, Marigold," he reproved. "That's an end to the matter. I expect you to be pleasant to Mr.

Banning as long as he is our guest. I find him amusing, and even if I didn't, any friend of Herbert's is a friend of mine."

Marigold wanted to point out that even Banning hadn't made any claims to friendship with Herbert Farquhar, but she'd already over-stepped her mark. She knew her father mustn't become upset.

Prim saw the opportunity to put in, "And it is a real emerald. I've studied it—glass could never possibly shine like that."

"It may be a real emerald or a fine reproduction," Marigold said, shrugging her shoulders, "but the world he talks about is certainly fake—a world where Mr. Banning can take whatever he fancies, giving nothing in return."

"Who is to judge," her father said, anxious to close the discussion, "excepting God Himself."

Marigold decided to leave well enough alone at the sight of her sister's half-smile. She avoided their visitor as much as possible for the rest of the week, by shutting herself away in her darkroom. But there, one afternoon, Primrose brought Banning. It was unusual for her to visit the basement room with its smelly chemicals, but Marigold guessed she had come to see the portraits of herself.

Marigold sat on a high stool before a rough kitchen table, where her photographic plates and tubs containing solutions of gallic acid and ammonia for development were spread out. She listened as Prim explained the necessity for darkness in the development process, surprised that her sister had retained so much of what Marigold had told her. But the fumes soon made Prim's eyes water; holding a handkerchief to her nose, she mumbled, "Maggie will have to tell you the rest."

"A few ladies of my acquaintance have taken up photography as a hobby, but none I know of develops and prints her own work," Banning put in. "I'm impressed, Miss Wilder."

"The art of photography lies as much in processing the plates as in taking the photographs," she said brusquely, determined not to be won over by Banning's praise.

He picked up a packet of Kennett's Instantaneous Gelatine

Plates and examined them. "Are these what are known as dry collodion?"

"You are a photographer yourself, Mr. Banning?" she asked in surprise.

"No. I just make it my business to know a little about a lot of things."

"These are gelatine-bromide dry plates—much easier to handle than the wet collodion. The sensitivity of the plate depends on the type of gelatine used."

"There's a man by the name of Eastman in New York who has produced photographic film on paper." He weighed the package of plates in his hand as he added, "Much more portable, and the results, they claim, are quite as sharp. For those who are less professional than yourself, he has even invented a camera—a Brownie, I think it is called. After a hundred shots, the whole works, camera and all, can be sent in for processing, printing, and reloading. 'You press the button, we do the rest' is his slogan."

"Another American phenomenon," Marigold sighed.

"We are resourceful, aren't we," Banning agreed blandly. "You have to admit it's one way to help bring photography into general use."

"A long-winded affair, though. I prefer plates, even if they are cumbersome, because I'm able to see the results right away. I couldn't stand having to wait to take a hundred pictures, and then wait goodness knows how long for someone else to develop and print them."

"You're impulsive then, Miss Wilder. I should never have guessed."

She knew he was smiling, though she couldn't clearly see his face by the light of the single candle in its red container.

"Only when I care deeply about something," she responded.

"That is probably true of us all."

He wandered around the room, peering at the prints that covered the wall. He stopped before a photograph she had managed, with some difficulty, to take of herself; it showed long tousled hair and a white face beneath, with an expression of complete vulnerability. As he examined it, Marigold felt uncomfortable, as though she had been seen naked.

"Amazing what the camera is able to reveal," he commented.

She felt a sense of relief when, at last, he moved on.

"I think Eastman must be forgiven the lengthiness of his procedure if it succeeds in popularizing the art, don't you?"

Marigold hid her delight at hearing him refer to photography as an art. "I didn't think you were interested in things that concern ordinary people."

"Nor, I see, are you." He gestured toward a photograph of a child, her body caked with dirt, pleading eyes far too large for her thin face, hands extended in an attitude of supplication.

"I don't understand. That photograph is precisely what the ordinary world is about," Marigold said defensively.

"Poverty, deprivation, hunger should be considered extraordinary rather than ordinary. At least," he went on almost apologetically, "I would suppose that to be your father's view of the world, the view he has shown his children. Surely he wouldn't say Christ had come down to earth so this child could live the sort of life that undoubtedly faces her."

Marigold felt cornered by the cogency of this answer, and she found herself wishing Banning could have pleaded her case to the vestry. All along she'd had the strange impression that he could see through her, that he knew she didn't believe. Was he goading her, she wondered?

"I can scarcely expect a man who visits in courts and palaces, who dines with the Shah of Persia from golden plates and with the Prince of Wales on pheasant and lobster, to be impressed by a glimpse of the real world." She gestured toward the photograph. "But that, for your information, Mr. Banning, is what it looks like."

"I know very well what it looks like, Miss Wilder." It was the first time Marigold had heard that harsh note in his voice. Then he laughed, though it was not the cheerful laugh she had heard so often during the week. "Besides, who's to say what's real and what isn't."

"Unlike people, the camera does not lie."

But now he was smiling. "But in and of itself the camera does nothing. It is merely an instrument. It is the person behind it who chooses the subject and provides the skill to make a good likeness."

"Speaking of good likenesses, Mark," said Primrose to change the subject, "which do you prefer of these?"

She directed the light onto the portraits Marigold had done of her. They hung, like so much washing, from a line stretched across the room.

"Don't touch!" Marigold said, annoyed by the interruption. "They're still wet from the developing solution," she explained, softening her tone.

Banning examined each one closely, before turning to Primrose. "They all portray a very beautiful young lady. How is it possible to make a choice in perfection?"

"But do. You must like one better than the rest. I know I do."

"And which one is that?"

"I shan't say until you have said. Whichever one you choose is yours." Primrose glanced quickly at Marigold. "You did say they were mine."

"Of course, but a photograph is very personal."

Prim tossed her head. "I want to give Mark the one he likes best. Which is it to be?"

He had stopped before the one showing Primrose half turned from the camera, her hair falling forward in some disarray. The expression on her innocent face was puzzled, questioning. It was one of those where Marigold had caught her off-guard.

"That one then."

"Oh!" Prim's face dropped.

"Is there something wrong? I can choose another."

"No, nothing's wrong. It's just that . . . that one is my least favorite. My hair's untidy, and you can't see my face properly."

"Then show me the one you like best," he insisted and she pointed out a careful pose: her heart-shaped chin was clasped pensively between her slender hands, her dewy eyes gazed off dreamily into the distance, her lips pouted alluringly.

"Then that is the one I should like to have," he affirmed. "If I may."

"Of course you may. As soon as it's dry I shall get Maggie to wrap it up for you."

As they left the room together, Marigold glanced over at the portrait Banning had first chosen. Though he'd questioned whether it was possible to tell the real from the unreal, he had chosen the portrait of Prim that showed her exactly as she was: young, beautiful yet untried, unsure. It was the portrait of a girl on the threshold of becoming a woman. It was Marigold's own favorite portrait of her sister.

If Marigold remained aloof throughout the rest of Banning's visit, Algernon was openly hostile. But Banning did nothing to win his cousin over. He showed open admiration for Primrose and Primrose clung to him in a way that eventually made Algernon's precariously curbed temper boil over.

"It could not escape my attention—or anyone else's for that matter," Algernon drawled, glancing pointedly at Reverend Wilder, "that you have little time for our form of worship, Banning. I understand in America they have spirit gods—in the trees and so forth." He smirked, but Banning replied quite seriously.

"The Indians do, that is true. They worship the land and the mountains and the sky as well as the trees."

"Pagans!" Algernon sniffed.

"I've always thought it quite sensible. If I were a worshipping man, I'd be tempted to follow their example."

"Since you scoff at our beliefs, may I ask what you were taught to believe in—that is if you were taught to believe in anything at all."

The curate's tone was peevish as he stood, hand on lapel, as though addressing a catechism class.

"Dear me, Algernon. I don't think this is the time or the place to discuss such things," Mr. Wilder intervened. "Mr. Banning is a guest in our house."

"I do have a particular interest in knowing his background, sir. He is my cousin. I think my father might be interested."

"Your father, interested?" Mark Banning raised an eyebrow. "My father's brother interested in anything that concerns me or my family? Do you really believe that, Algie? I rather thought that when he left my father to die in a penniless state—ignoring all entreaties for what was my father's inheritance by rights, something that might have saved his life—I rather took that as an indication that your father had little or no interest in our family at all."

Despite the scathing derision in his voice, Banning's facial expression remained genial.

Algernon flushed. "Your father . . ."

"Your uncle," Banning reminded.

Algernon paused, then went on, "My uncle left for America against the wishes of his father. He was warned it was foolish to join a mad rush for gold in California. He had a place in the world and he turned his back on it. He chose to be a nobody, marrying a barroom . . ." Algernon broke off as Banning's face clouded over. "Marrying beneath him. Why should family money have been sent halfway around the world to save someone who had already wasted everything he owned? That money would only have dwindled away along with the rest. Don't forget, your father was the one who had deserted his own."

That was the first time Marigold saw that a barb from Algernon had struck home. But almost immediately, as though he realized he had shown vulnerability, the cloud lifted from Banning's face.

"Algie! You're forgetting one of the most important lessons you preach. What about the prodigal son—though maybe that's not a lesson you learned much about at home."

"I was taught at Oxford—Christ Church," Algernon replied haughtily.

"Ah, well, that must be the difference."

"Please excuse this airing of family affairs, sir," Algernon apologized to Mr. Wilder. "It's not at all in good taste, but I didn't bring it up."

"In America we speak openly," Banning put in.

"You Americans are a lot of prating fools," Algernon retorted savagely.

"Algernon!" Primrose cautioned sharply. "That's not nice."

"My dear Miss Wilder," Banning smiled. "You mustn't correct Algie for voicing his opinion. We Americans prize frankness above all else."

"I don't need you to champion my cause," Algernon growled.

Banning looked from Algernon to Primrose and smiled. "Last thing I intended, Algie."

"You should be thrilled to have someone like Mark as your cousin," Primrose went on. "He's been everywhere, met everyone. He's actually dined with the Prince of Wales."

"Pimped for him more like. That is, if he's had anything to do with him at all," Algernon burst out.

"Algernon!" Reverend Wilder was clearly shocked. "That is uncalled for, especially in front of my daughters!"

"It's all right, Father," Marigold put in, afraid her father was becoming upset.

"Thank you, Miss Wilder, for coming to my aid," Algernon said, "I know it was wrong of me—I shouldn't have said it—but no one stopped Banning from telling his off-color stories."

"Those were amusing. Your remark was not," Reverend Wilder censured.

"I'm sorry, sir. I forgot myself, I forgot where I was. I most humbly beg your pardon." Algernon rose, his face a picture of confusion and abject apology as he ran a hand around his stiff clerical collar. "I would never have said such a thing if I hadn't been provoked.

You were perfectly justified in rebuking me. Even though I'm not the only one deserving of censure, perhaps I should leave in an attempt to relieve this charged atmosphere."

"That should do it, Algie," Banning agreed cheerfully. "Though you mustn't let me drive you off your own turf."

"What else have you been doing all week?" Algernon began and then stopped himself. "I'll go."

"No, no, my boy." Reverend Wilder had recovered his composure. "No need to go. A slip of the tongue, no doubt. It's entirely overlooked. You mustn't be unkind to your cousin, though. He's a man of many controversial ideas and beliefs. Still, he's been a breath of fresh air. I've found him stimulating company."

"Not the only one," Algernon muttered under his breath, his eyes on Primrose.

"I'm very glad I came," Banning said, as much to Primrose as to her father. As Primrose threw him another adoring look, Algernon stuck his hands behind the black tails of his frock, agitating them like an infuriated cat, nodded to the assembled company, and strode to the door. "You're really retiring from the field then, Algie," his cousin drawled.

"I wouldn't put it that way, but I am leaving." For emphasis, Algernon clapped his clerical hat upon his head.

Banning arose, hand extended.

"Then we must say good-bye. I'm off in the morning. Miss Wilder kindly left the timetable on my dressing table. I see there's an 11:15 London express."

Primrose paled. "Oh, no, Mark, don't go. Don't leave just because Algernon and Maggie are such spoilsports. I want you to stay."

"Primrose!" It was rare for Mr. Wilder to rebuke his younger daughter, but her emotional plea obviously embarrassed him. "Our guest has his own plans. We have no right to press him to stay . . ." He glanced over at Marigold. "Or to go."

"If I did not have to go, sir," Banning said, looking from Mr.

Wilder to Primrose, "wild horses couldn't drag me away from such delightful company. But the fact is, I have to be in London. I have an appointment that can't be postponed."

"The queen, no doubt," Marigold muttered, stung by her father's reproachful look.

"No, Miss Wilder, not with the queen, but with Mr. Gladstone."

"My second guess would have been the prime minister," Marigold commented dryly, folding away her embroidery with swift, deliberate motions.

"Really, Maggie! I don't know what's got into you—and Primrose, too. Both of you are behaving badly tonight."

"Maggie's behaved badly all week," Primrose said tearfully.

Banning shot Primrose a sympathetic look and then turned to Mr. Wilder. "I shan't forget your kindness to me this past week. I've put you," he glanced over at Marigold, "all of you to such trouble, you must give me a chance to repay your hospitality. Come to London as my guests. I'll arrange for a suite at Claridge's." He turned his gaze on Primrose. "There are so many amusing things to do—Barnum and Bailey's circus is in town. Patti is singing *Aida*, a rare performance according to the *Observer* critic who's supposed to know about these things. And we could dine at the Cafe Royale. I might be able to present you to His Royal Highness—he dines there often."

Primrose's eyes were shining. "Oh, Father, please! Please! May we go? Please, I beg you!"

But Reverend Wilder shook his head. "Thank you, sir. It is kind, very kind of you, but I fear that's not possible. London is a long way away. And there's the matter of parish business; you see, that doesn't only occur on Sunday."

"You have a curate," Banning pointed out.

"I'm afraid we aren't like you Americans, up and off without thinking anything about it. I've only been to London twice in my life. A journey like that would have to be carefully undertaken, planned well in advance. I thank you, but no, it's not possible."

Algernon gave an audible sigh of relief at Mr. Wilder's final refusal.

"Pity," Banning said, studying Primrose's crestfallen face. "A great pity. I should so have enjoyed seeing that London scene through fresh eyes."

Primrose insisted on seeing Mark Banning off at the station, so Marigold trudged along with them and waited for the train. She tried to keep the relief from her voice as she said good-bye but then had to witness the embarrassing spectacle of Primrose's tears as Banning swung his tall frame into a first-class carriage. He lowered the window with a resounding thump, much to the annoyance of a gentleman already seated in the compartment, and leaned out to take her hands.

"I shan't forget our talks," he said.

"Never?" she whispered.

"Never," he affirmed.

"When do you leave London?"

"In a week. I'll send you a postcard from my first port of call."

"How I wish Father had accepted your sweet, kind, generous invitation," she said, her tears falling in earnest. That statement, without the adjectives, was repeated over and over again after she had watched the last puff of smoke from the departing train.

"I've never been anywhere, never done anything," she wailed. "I'll never get to see the world."

"I didn't realize that was what you wanted, Prim." Marigold's surprise was genuine. "I always thought your aim in life was to marry well and settle down."

"Well, so it is. But that doesn't mean I don't want to see the world as well, does it?"

"I suppose they're not mutually exclusive," Marigold agreed dubiously. "Not if you were to find the sort of husband who . . ." she stopped abruptly, looking askance at Primrose's tears. "Prim!

Surely you weren't so taken by that braggart that you were thinking of him as a husband."

"Mark's not a braggart," Primrose asserted fiercely, her tears momentarily stemmed by her anger. "He's done everything he told us about. I know he has. Just the way I knew that tiepin was a real emerald."

"Whether he has or not is of little consequence. I don't believe he was serious about anything—or anyone. Anyway, he's gone now," Marigold said decisively, causing Primrose to burst into another flood of tears.

Algernon was cheered by his cousin's departure, but not by Primrose's tearful face.

"He's a trickster, just like his father," Algernon fumed. "You'll not hear a good word about any of them in my house. There was never any love lost between his father and mine, just as there's none lost between him and me. Thank God he's gone at last. Why he ever came here in the first place is something I'll never understand."

That was something Marigold couldn't understand either. Especially when Banning had stayed on, ostensibly to get to know his cousin, yet making no attempt to do so.

"If he plans to call on my family, he'll get short shrift there after the letter I've written. I only wish yours had done the same."

But Mr. Wilder missed Banning's company. Primrose moped, and even Marigold noticed how quiet the house was after he'd gone. To her surprise, she actually felt something akin to a twinge of regret. That was before she found Primrose's note.

I've gone to London to join Mark Banning. I shall write to you from there. I've no wish to cause you pain. I love you, but I love Mark more.
                                          Your own, Primrose.

Marigold's first feeling as she read the note was panic, pure panic. Her sister gone off, alone, to a huge city to meet with an unscrupulous man they barely knew. Then she felt anger. How could Primrose do such a thing! Couldn't she see the sort of rolling stone Banning was, gathering up whatever moss took his fancy, using it as he saw fit and then dispensing with it when new pastures were at hand. He'd paid a great deal of attention to Prim, but never, for one moment, had Marigold thought him to be sincere. Yet why had he done it? Even someone of his calibre must know Prim came from a respectable family, that he couldn't expect to have his way with her.

Marigold's initial reaction had been to run to her father with the note, but halfway down the stairs cooler reasoning had prevailed. To involve her father in this would force him to go to London and confront Mark Banning. He would try to persuade Banning—or exert whatever pressure he could—to make him marry Primrose. Such a confrontation might kill him.

Marigold thought of Algernon. Banning was his cousin, after all. But what if this were simply a prank, something Primrose might already be regretting? She could imagine Algernon's scorn. Primrose would quickly replace his cousin as an object for his contempt.

Marigold was relieved to find Harriet had arrived downstairs and was already at work on the orphreys. Her friend looked up, smiling, but her smile faded at the sight of Marigold's face.

"Oh, I can't believe it," Harriet cried out in stupefaction when Marigold told her what had happened. "The man's a . . . a . . . a blackguard!"

It was the worst thing Marigold had ever heard Harriet say about anyone.

"I must go to London and bring her home at once," Marigold said firmly.

"But you can't go alone," Harriet insisted. "Dr. Keane will go and bring her back."

"Harriet, you and I alone know what has happened. If it is within my power, I intend to keep this just between us. I certainly don't want Father involved. I don't want John to know."

"I've never kept a secret from Dr. Keane," Harriet said dubiously.

"But it's not your secret, Harriet, it's mine. I'm asking your help as a favor and part of that help means keeping this a secret. If it were ever to come out, I'd make sure no one ever knew you were involved in any way. I plan to tell Father that you asked Primrose to stay with you, that the two of you are working to complete the vestments in time for Easter. Then I want you to send me a note saying that you're short of silk—the red, no, no, the gold—that you need it urgently."

"But the gold is only available from Whipple's in London," Harriet exclaimed. Then her expression changed. "Oh, I see."

"Exactly."

"But your father would never let you go so far."

"My father is becoming used to my coming and going. Besides, I shall take care of that."

"What about Algernon?" Harriet asked.

"I'd prefer to let Primrose decide if he's going to know of this. At the moment I don't believe she's responsible for her actions. That braggart has filled her head with wild ideas. She's young, easily swayed. She likes to be indulged. It's not her fault. It's his. He must have known she was susceptible, that she was likely to be attracted to . . ." Marigold stopped suddenly. "I think I'm beginning to see why he stayed on, why he paid such open court to Primrose."

Harriet looked puzzled. "I suppose because he liked her."

"Perhaps. But I have an idea it goes beyond that. I don't know for sure, not yet. But I'm going to find out."

4

Not until Marigold Wilder stood outside the elegant exterior of Claridge's on Brook Street did she even consider that her sister and the man she now thought of as Primrose's abductor might not be there. Nor, until that moment, did she consider what she would say. Throughout the journey she had been so filled with a combination of anger and indignation that she had literally been carried along with her own sense of purpose.

Marigold looked up at the myriad sparkling windows on the hotel's stone facade, wondering which might conceal the illicit pair. In her handbag was the trite telegram she had intercepted from Primrose. "Having a wonderful time," it read. "Wish you were at Claridge's with us." But was Primrose there?

Marigold stood, suddenly hesitant to enter that august establishment. She wondered whom she should ask for. Brushed by passersby who seemed not to see her and sneered at by barrow boys who did, Marigold lifted her chin. She jammed her boater hat firmly atop her head and sailed past the huge gold-braided doorman, pushing the polished brass handles of the doors for herself.

Once in the lobby she immediately espied the long mahogany reception desk, behind which stood several imperious gentlemen in immaculate frock coats. Tapping her gloved hand on the gleaming surface of the desk, she announced, in as strong a voice as she could summon: "I am Miss Wilder, Miss Marigold Wilder, here to see Mr. Mark Banning."

Like a high priest disturbed at his altar, one of the gentlemen approached the desk. For an instant his lips quivered, as if to say "Not another one," but no word escaped; perhaps the gleam of anger and determination in Marigold's eye silenced the words, or perhaps it would have been beneath his dignity to utter them.

"Mr. Banning is out," he intoned in distinct, plum-shaped tones. Marigold's sigh of relief that he was still staying there was drowned out by the disapproving addition, "with a young lady."

"Excellent!" Marigold's muttered comment caused the man to raise his eyebrows.

"I will wait," she said, and proceeded to ensconce herself in a leather armchair, where she had an unobstructed view of the entrance.

It was not in the tradition of Claridge's for single young ladies to occupy the chairs in the lobby, but something about Marigold's determined attitude made the hotel clerk hesitate to tell her so. Although several gentlemen guests eyed her inquisitively, none was so bold as to approach her.

Marigold sat almost without moving. She had left by the earliest train without eating breakfast. Indeed, she had scarcely eaten since she had discovered Primrose's note. Carried along by the energy of anxiety, she had thought of nothing but finding her sister. Having all but reached her goal, she now realized she was famished and quite exhausted. She would have given her soul—had she believed she possessed one—for a comforting cup of tea, but she dared not leave her post. At any moment the guilty pair might return. The grandfather clock in the corner struck three, then four. Marigold closed her eyes briefly; the clock was chiming five before she opened them. Unable to believe another hour had passed, she turned to consult the clock face.

It was very definitely five o'clock. And it was at that moment that her efforts were rewarded. She saw the uniformed doorman sweep open the door with a flourish to admit Mark Banning and Primrose.

The first thing Marigold noticed was how happy they seemed as they strode into the lobby, arm in arm. Next she noticed the intimacy with which Banning's head inclined toward Primrose. Marigold took in the unfamiliar silk bolero suit her sister was wearing, and the brand-new matching osprey feathers on her wide-brimmed hat.

As Banning approached the desk for the key, Marigold straightened her boater, brushed off her dark skirts, and stood up. But the ground under her feet seemed less firm than usual. She reached down for the arm of the chair to steady her.

Just then Primrose caught sight of her and attempted to cover her gasped "Maggie" with a pink kid-leather-gloved hand. Marigold's inclination was to take that hand and march her sister out of the hotel, but as she stepped forward she discovered her knees had a disconcerting tendency to buckle under her. So, she remained where she was, holding fast to the chair.

The clerks behind the hotel reception desk turned at Primrose's cry. So, too, did Banning. Following the direction of Primrose's frozen stare, he caught sight of Marigold with what she considered an odd expression akin to relief. He came over to her immediately, and Primrose followed reluctantly.

"I've come to take Primrose home," Marigold announced in as firm a voice as she could muster.

She heard Primrose's cry, "I'm not going. I'm never going home." She was aware of astonished glances from the hotel guests and members of the staff who were watching them. Then Marigold's eyes closed. When next she opened them, she was lying on a bed in a sumptuously furnished room.

There was thick pale blue carpeting on the floor and matched draped satin at the windows. A number of boxes, bearing labels from Whiteley's, Asprey's Jeweler and Silversmith, and Brettell's Linens in the Royal Arcade, had been carelessly opened and were strewn about the room. Flung over the arm of a chair were the only things Marigold recognized: the dress Prim had been wearing on the day she left home and, resting on top of it, her own boater hat. On the floor beneath were her high-buttoned shoes.

Her head felt heavy on the pillow; her long hair must have been loosened for she could feel strands falling across her forehead and cheek. Her neck felt bare. She reached up and realized her high starched collar had been unbuttoned.

At her movement someone held a glass to her lips.

"Sip," a voice commanded. "Don't drink. Just a sip."

Recognizing the voice as Mark Banning's, Marigold's immediate response was to refuse, but the glass was placed against her lips in such a way that she had no recourse but to do as she was told. The liquid was fiery; she choked as she swallowed it and, for a moment, struggled for breath.

"I told you not to drink it," Banning said without apology, taking her hands and rubbing them till warmth returned. "That's better. Your color's coming back. Your sister's going to be all right, Primrose."

"That's good," Primrose responded without enthusiasm. "But she shouldn't have come."

"Of course I should have come," Marigold said, attempting to sit up. A hand on her shoulder prevented her from doing so. She felt uneasy, realizing it was Mark Banning's hand—especially since she was lying on a bed in what she considered an advanced state of undress.

"Let go," she said, looking at him directly for the first time. He did not respond immediately to the note of warning in her voice. When he seemed satisfied that she had fully regained consciousness, he moved away and she sat up.

"Leave me and my sister alone," Marigold ordered, struggling with the buttons on her collar.

"I've never known anyone—man or boy, and certainly no female—to wear such a stranglehold as you have around your neck, Miss Wilder. If you'll take my advice, you won't rebutton that thing until you're completely over your fainting fit."

"I don't faint," she said coldly. "I never faint. You can ask Primrose."

"It's true. Maggie doesn't faint," Prim concurred.

"She may not, but she certainly did just now. I should know, since I had the unenviable task of carrying her all the way up here."

Marigold flushed scarlet. "Would you do us the kindness of leaving us alone to talk, or do you wish us to vacate the room?" she asked with exaggerated politeness.

She felt a surge of relief when he said, "This is Primrose's room. Maybe you should ask her." Then, without waiting for Marigold's response, he turned to Primrose. "Do you want me to leave?"

"I most certainly do not," Primrose said firmly.

So Banning stepped back. Leaning against an armoire, he folded his arms across his chest, waiting.

"You really have no right . . ." Marigold began.

"Since what you have to say undoubtedly concerns me, Miss Wilder, I think perhaps it *is* my right to stay and protect my good name," he drawled.

"*Your* good name! You've got a bloody cheek," Marigold exploded.

He raised his eyebrows. "Such language from a parson's daughter."

"Marigold!" Primrose concurred. "You have no right to speak to Mark in that manner. He is a . . . a gentleman."

"Gentleman! Gentleman of fortune, perhaps. I don't doubt he's done his share of pirating in his time," Marigold fumed, trying unsuccessfully to pin up her fallen hair.

"A century ago pirating might have been the way to go. Today, I assure you there are many easier ways of finding a fortune, Miss Wilder."

Banning's laughter infuriated Marigold. "No fortune goes along with my sister, if that's what you had in mind."

"Maggie" Primrose was far more shocked than Banning by this

remark. "I'm not going home, Maggie, and no one's going to make me."

"You most certainly are," Marigold asserted, swinging her feet to the floor. She made an attempt to stand up, but then sat back down on the bed abruptly.

"No one, I think, is going anywhere—at least not for the time being," Banning said decisively.

Primrose pouted. Then her upper lip began to quiver. Marigold recognized the signs. Soon her sister's eyes would begin to fill with tears. Then she would weep uncontrollably.

"But I thought this was to be a special evening—dinner at the Cafe Royale and then *Lady Windermere's Fan* at the Drury Lane. I've been so looking forward to it. You said it was the best play you had seen in years." Her eyes glistened dangerously. "It would have been such a wonderful evening." A note of wrath crept into her voice as she added, "If Maggie hadn't come to spoil everything."

"I've come to take you home, Primrose," Marigold said, half rising again.

"I don't want to go. I don't intend to go." Primrose's voice grew thin and strained as it rose uncontrollably.

Mark Banning stepped between them. "There's nothing I loathe more than hysterics."

"Primrose can have hysterics if she wants to," Marigold interceded hotly.

"I'm not going to have hysterics," Primrose wailed, tears streaming down her face. "And even if I were, I don't need to have your permission."

Banning thrust his handkerchief at her. "You'll not only look conspicuous at the theater but be far less attractive if you don't stop crying."

Primrose seized the proffered handkerchief and mopped up her tears, faltering, "We . . . we are going, then?" She directed a glance of malevolent triumph at her sister before covering her face.

"*You* most certainly are. I wouldn't have you miss it for the world. We were to join the Wyndhams. I'll arrange for them to pick you up. Dotty Wyndham is the greatest fun, but you must promise not to flirt with her husband or she'll never speak to me again."

"You're not coming with me, then?" Primrose said, her upper lip beginning to tremble again.

"I think it's time your sister and I had a serious discussion concerning your welfare. You know I have only your best interests at heart," he added quickly, in an effort to stave off another flood of tears. Unclasping the emerald on his tie, he pressed the huge gem into her hand as though it were a consolation prize. "This will look very pretty in your lapel."

5

"I'm not hungry," Marigold repeated as they crossed the lobby in the direction of the dining room. She could sense Mark Banning at her elbow, guiding her without so much as laying a finger on her arm. The imperious reception clerk glanced in their direction, then turned discreetly away.

"When did you last eat?"

"At lunchtime," she responded hesitantly.

"You once told me you didn't appreciate untruths. I don't either," Banning said firmly, pausing before the glass door to the dining room. Marigold could see elegantly clad diners seated at tables covered in white damask, set with gleaming crystal and silver.

Her fingers traveled awkwardly to the high collar that was no longer stiff and fresh. She brushed at the dust on her dark traveling skirt. When she had washed before coming down, the bathroom mirror had reflected a fatigued, wan face beneath clumsily rearranged red hair.

"Everyone's dressed up. I can't go in there like this." Glancing over at Banning, she added, "Nor can you in that brown suit."

"Since you refused to dine upstairs, I don't see any other alternative. Besides, I doubt anyone's going to care as long as the color of our money is right."

The formidable major domo greeted them with obvious reluctance. But whatever Banning whispered to him and whatever it was that smoothly passed from one hand to another seemed to overcome his disapprobation with alacrity.

With a flourish, he led them to a corner table, secluded behind a palm and banked ferns.

"Is this to your liking, sir? If not . . ." he paused expectantly.

"This'll do fine."

"I trust you will enjoy your dinner, madame," he said, laying a menu before Marigold. To Banning he said, "Call me immediately, sir, if I may be of assistance."

"What did it cost to buy such servility?" Marigold inquired tartly as she studied the cover of the menu.

"That's not the sort of thing a lady asks."

"It's the sort of thing a lady ought to know if she wants to negotiate her way in the world."

"I rather thought you confined your getting around to bicycling. Tipping waiters correctly should hardly matter much to you."

"It's unfair that the world is open to you and closed to me—and even more unfair of you to rub it in."

"I'm sorry, Miss Wilder," he said with genuine regret. "I hadn't thought of it in that light. If you must know, I gave him a ten-pound note."

"Ten pounds!" she exclaimed. "That's absolutely ridiculous!"

He sighed, then turned to study the menu. "I can't recommend the beef; it's tough and stringy and has no flavor. Back home we have beefsteaks you can cut with a fork. However, the roast squab is quite exceptional. They also found a very interesting white burgundy, La Pucelle, last evening. We might see if they can rustle up another bottle. What would you like?"

"I'll take a Welsh rarebit and a glass of warm milk," she said calmly.

"For God's sake! It's quite obvious you're starving. Can't you forget it's Lent and eat a decent meal?"

Her lips pursed for a moment. "You asked what I would like. What I would like—and what my body needs at this moment is Welsh rarebit and a glass of warm milk."

He studied her without saying anything for so long that Marigold could feel herself beginning to flush. She felt her cheeks grow hot as he said, "I doubt you have any idea what your body really needs."

"That's quite uncalled for," she said stiffly.

"Merely an opinion," he said, closing his menu. "I don't believe you have any idea of how to provide proper sustenance, care, amusement, and rest for your body."

With that, he summoned the waiter and added to her discomfort and annoyance by ordering Welsh rarebit and warm milk for both of them.

"Why did you do that?" she demanded.

"Do what?" he asked innocently.

"Order the same thing. You already said you wanted squab and white wine."

"I was curious. I've never had Welsh rarebit and warm milk. I wanted to see whether it could possibly be the thing my body requires at this moment." He raised an eyebrow. "It might, perhaps, have aphrodisiac effects, although I suspect I'll find it's only soporific."

"You really have no redeeming features, Mr. Banning."

He raised his eyebrows. "You think not? Wait till we're better acquainted, then decide."

"I don't intend to become better acquainted with a man who has run off with my sister."

"Ah, ah, ah!" He shook a finger in dissent. "I have to differ with you there. Your sister ran off on her own."

"She ran away to London at your invitation."

"I invited the whole family—your father, yourself too. It seems he is the only one who so far hasn't put in an appearance. I hope he'll show up. I enjoy his company very much. I'm even able to forgive him for being a parson. He's much too good a man for that."

He smiled, and that observation, for a moment, made Marigold sway in his favor. But only for a moment.

"When my sister arrived here—a young lady, completely alone—any true gentleman would have taken immediate steps to find her a chaperone and return her to the bosom of her family without an instant's delay. Instead, we received a telegram saying, 'Having a wonderful time. Wish you were here,' or words to that effect. I suppose that was your idea."

"Possibly." His response was noncommital.

"I'm quite sure it was. Even Primrose wouldn't be that trite."

"The telegram may not have been particularly original, but it seems to have covered the matter. She *has* been having a wonderful time."

"But did either of you really wish we were here?" Marigold scoffed. "I find that hard to believe."

"You find most of what I say hard to believe," he smiled.

"Why did you send it?" she demanded.

"I didn't say that I had," he said evenly. "But I'm glad that you knew she was all right. And I'm glad she came here to enjoy herself for once in her life. She's young, she's vital, she had every right to see musicals and circuses, to shop for fashionable clothes, to dine on fine food in elegant surroundings, to dance . . ."

"Did you ever—for one minute—consider what it might mean to a young lady's reputation to stay alone in London with a man of questionable character, to have him buy her expensive clothes, give her priceless jewels, take her . . ."

"Primrose told me you thought the emerald a fake," he interrupted.

"Don't change the subject," Marigold snapped.

"I don't believe I did."

"Buying her clothes . . . ," she went on.

"I had to buy her clothes. She came with nothing, not even a toothbrush. Do be sensible."

"All of this—clothes, jewelry, amusements—they're all the accoutrements of a kept woman, and it's my sister who . . ."

He broke in, "You don't like her very much, do you?"

Marigold was stunned. "How can you say such a thing!"

"Sorry, perhaps that was a bit strong. I know you've been genuinely worried about her. It's just that I couldn't help but notice your father's marked preference for Primrose, even though you're the one who does everything for him. It seemed quite natural that you might not like her."

"You have no right, absolutely no right to speak in such a way." All color had fled from her cheeks and for one awful moment Marigold was afraid she might cry. "She's my sister, my younger sister."

Mark Banning's face softened. "What I really meant to say was, if I were in your position, I probably wouldn't like her very much, either."

"But you do."

"Excessively. She's delightful, a joy to be with—except when she cries. I can't stand women who cry."

"So you indicated earlier." Marigold swallowed at the lump that was forming in her throat. "She didn't cry until I came on the scene."

"No, she didn't. She enjoyed every minute of everything, and I'm delighted I was able to do this for her before I move on."

Marigold was aghast. "You mean your intentions are . . ."

"I have no intentions," he said simply.

"But you ran off with my sister."

"I must correct you again. I did not run off with your sister. Your sister ran off, in a quite unpremeditated fashion, to join me. I have taken care of her while she was here. I'm glad that you've arrived to see her home."

"You're an absolute cad!"

His brows wrinkled in puzzlement. "But I thought that was what you came for, what you wanted—to take Primrose home."

For a moment, Marigold was nonplussed. By the time she regained her composure, the waiter arrived, bearing an enormous silver tray. From beneath huge silver covering dishes he produced, with the flourish of a magician, two large china plates each containing a tiny portion of Welsh rarebit. The warm milk, served in Russian tea glasses, was delivered with equal flair.

Mark Banning looked down dubiously at the fare.

"I trust it is all right, sir. Our French chef hasn't had a great deal of practice with this particular dish. He conveys his apologies if it is not exactly the way you like it."

"I'm no connoisseur. The young lady, however, is. Perhaps you would try it, Miss Wilder, to put the chef's mind at ease."

Under the watchful gaze of Banning and the waiter, Marigold took a mouthful and solemnly ate it.

"Well?" Banning asked, "May we put the chef out of his misery?"

"It's—it's very good."

The waiter breathed a sigh of relief and Banning said, "You may convey the young lady's compliments to the chef."

"Will there be anything else, sir?"

Banning looked down at the meager meal. "Can you suggest a wine that might make this more palatable? A Moselle, do you think?"

The waiter shrugged. "We have a fine Vouvray, sir, or a Barsac, but I couldn't promise that either one would make a difference."

Marigold finished everything, not saying a word. Banning tasted the rarebit, then pushed it aside. He looked at the milk for a moment, before reaching for the Vouvray the waiter had brought.

"If you didn't want it, you shouldn't have ordered it," Marigold said unkindly, wiping her mouth with her napkin.

"Wherever I am in the world, it's often useful to try the native dishes. Some are beneficial to the body, though I can't think I'd derive much stimulation from these."

"I always thought food provided nourishment, not stimulation," Marigold observed.

"Not necessarily. While I was in Korea, I discovered that the root of the ginseng plant has some quite amazing properties. It can cure almost everything. It is nourishing, but it also has the ability to produce delightful effects—well, I guess you asked me not to mention that again."

Marigold shook her head in disapprobation. Now that she had

eaten, she felt stronger. She decided to ask Banning what had been on her mind all evening. "Tell me, quite honestly, why did you come to Barleigh?"

"Quite honestly? Quite honestly, I came to search out my long-lost cousin Algernon."

"But why? There was obviously no love lost between you."

"That is exactly why—because there was no love lost. I wanted to assure myself that he was every bit the sort of lunkhead I'd always imagined him to be. And he was."

Marigold leaned forward. "And that's why you pressed your attentions on Primrose. You knew Algernon liked her and you wanted to prove you could take her away from him. That was it, wasn't it?" When Banning said nothing, she went on angrily, "You're even worse than I thought you were."

"Is that possible?" he asked, then he shrugged. "Actually, when you stop and think about it, I did Primrose a favor if by coming to London she's got rid of that prating numbskull. And I don't think you care for Algie any more than I do."

"If my father knew that Primrose had stayed here alone with you, he'd never forgive you." Then she added quickly, "But he can't ever be told. At his age, with his weak heart, it could kill him. Not that you'd care about having that on your conscience any more than you do about ruining my sister."

"Don't keep repeating that silly refrain." Banning lifted the wine bottle and, when Marigold refused, poured himself another glass of wine. "I've done nothing at all to your sister except show her a good time and give her a few things that she enjoys. And I really think if your father were here now, he'd understand all of this a great deal better than you."

Marigold refused to respond to this observation.

"Primrose is coming home with me," she said.

For reply, Banning beckoned to the major domo. "I shall see to it that train reservations are made."

6

It really did not matter after all that the embroidered orphreys were not finished in time for Easter, for by then the parish of St. Swithin's was in deepest mourning for its rector.

Marigold and Primrose Wilder found little joy in the cry, "He is risen," when their father's body, clad in his new chasuble, was ready to be confined to the ground. Each sister blamed the other for his death, though Marigold felt the greatest share of the blame lay with Mark Banning.

She had not thought the return from London could possibly be as dismal as the journey there, particularly since the trip's outcome had been successful. But every glimpse of the drawn, bitter expression on her sister's face had filled her with despair.

Primrose was far from happy about being rescued.

"Just because no one ever admired you—just because you don't care about feeling fine silk next to your skin—just because you don't want to move in society, to hear Patti sing—I do!" Primrose had stormed when Marigold announced they were to return to Barleigh. "I want to stay with Mark. I intend to stay with him."

"But he has no intention of staying with you," Marigold said, immediately regretting her bluntness. She remembered that look of relief that had crossed Mark Banning's face when he first saw her in the hotel lobby. She hadn't understood it then. Now she did. She was doing his dirty work—telling Primrose that he didn't want her, that it had all been merely a diversion.

"I don't believe you," Primrose whispered.

"Think, Prim, think! Has he made you any promises? Has he done anything to demand that he make promises?" It was the closest that Marigold dared come to asking whether he had made love to her.

"I don't know what you mean. I don't understand you." Prim was crying. "All I know is that before you came, everything was perfect and now it's all ruined. I hate you! I hate you!"

"It's Mark Banning you should hate," Marigold argued, but to no avail.

"I love him, whatever you say, and I shan't believe any of this until I hear it from him."

Marigold should have known when her sister returned from her talk with Mark Banning that he was even more devious than she had believed, though at the time it hardly seemed possible. Her sister was glum, despairing, but she agreed to return home. However, she absolutely refused to attach any blame to Mark Banning. It was still Marigold who had spoiled everything.

Banning took them to the station. He withstood Primrose's tears and Marigold's icy demeanor with equal forbearance.

On the way, they stopped at Whipple's to pick up the gold couching thread, the ostensible reason for this abortive London visit. Banning went in to get it, purchasing far more than the ladies of the Altar Guild could use in a decade. Marigold was certain he insisted on going because he was a coward and didn't want to be left alone in the hackney carriage with Primrose.

He made only one remark to Marigold in the course of the journey, and it came as a complete surprise. "It was brave of you to come."

"I do whatever has to be done," she said.

He studied her for a moment. "I expect you do."

As the station master walked along the platform, slamming doors, Banning helped them into their carriage. Then, he pressed an object into Marigold's hand. It was the small jade piece he had said was a present from the queen of Korea.

"It's the kokok—a good luck piece, a sort of Korean rabbit's foot—or perhaps I should say tiger's foot." He smiled. "I have a feeling you may need it more than I."

He closed Marigold's fingers around the kokok. Then the train began to move. Primrose hung out of the window, waving and crying as the engine chugged along the platform and out of the station, picking up speed as it passed dingy, narrow back lots and row upon row of miserable smoke-begrimed dwellings. Then she slammed the window shut, flung herself into the seat opposite Marigold, and began to cry in earnest.

Throughout the journey Marigold endured Primrose's sobs. Knowing her sister's anger was directed at her and not at Banning, Marigold had plenty of time to consider the unfairness of it all.

Her arm grew cramped, and she realized it was because she had been clenching her fist. Opening her fingers, she saw she was still holding on fast to the jade talisman Banning had given her. She studied the comma-shaped piece with its hole like an eye at one end, and wondered what it meant. She didn't believe it had been part of a crown, or that it had ever belonged to a queen, but it was an interesting piece, too unusual to throw away.

"Nobody knows anything about this . . . adventure," Marigold reminded her sister as the train drew into the station. Ignoring her sister's muttered, "I don't care who does," she went on, "And Father must never find out about it. If he did, he would probably feel he should have taken care of this himself."

"I only wish he had come. Father would have been more understanding than you," Primrose burst out.

Marigold took hold of her sister's arm. "Don't ever tell him. Promise me you won't. The shock might kill him."

"It's always Father, Father with you—what's right for him, what's good for him. What about me? If Father had come to London, as he should—he's responsible for me, not you—then he would have demanded that Mark marry me. Mark liked him, he wouldn't have been able to refuse him. I know he wouldn't."

Marigold dropped her sister's arm and stepped back. "You mean you *wanted* Father to know! You would have accepted a man who was forced to marry you!"

"Mark may not think he wants to marry, but he would have if Father asked him to. And I know if Father had come, that would have been his solution."

"So it was you, after all, who sent that silly telegram."

"Of course it was me. Who else?" Primrose looked at her sister in disgust. "Who did you think sent it? Mark?"

"How could you, Primrose! How could you!" Only Primrose could have ignored the reproach in Marigold's voice. "I'm ashamed that a sister of mine could scheme to entrap a man, particularly someone like Mark Banning. I am truly ashamed."

Primrose flushed at the rebuke, but Marigold was soon sorry she had spoken so harshly. She was sure that rebuke lay behind Primrose's outburst to their father as soon as they reached home. That, and the lingering hope of forcing Mr. Wilder to demand that Mark Banning make an honest woman of her.

Throwing aside the gold couching thread Marigold had conspicuously produced, along with the story she had carefully concocted to explain their absence, Primrose flung her arms around her father, crying out, "Maggie's lying to you. I ran away with Mark Banning. She forced me to come back, even though he ruined me and should marry me."

"Primrose!" Marigold was horrified. "That's not true. He didn't . . . at least you both said he didn't."

"I'm telling you he did," Primrose said, stamping her foot. "I should know whether I'm ruined or not."

Reverend Wilder's face was deathly pale. He half rose from his chair, but Marigold put an arm on his shoulder. "Sit down, Father. It was all a prank, an escapade, that's all. Don't excite yourself."

"But if Banning has done this terrible thing, Maggie, he must be forced to make an honest woman of Primrose."

Marigold saw his hands begin to shake. She took them between her own and, finding them cold, began to rub them.

"You see, what did I tell you!" Primrose said in triumph. "Mark Banning's still in London, Father. If you go to him, he'll listen to you. He wouldn't listen to Maggie, and why should he? She's nothing but a canting hypocrite, who pretends to believe in God when she really thinks it's all just a lot of hocus-pocus."

Reverend Wilder's expression changed from one of dismay to stark horror. He turned a stunned gaze on his elder daughter. "The world's gone mad, utterly mad. Tell me this is more of its madness, Maggie. Tell me this is not so. Tell me you believe just as you've been taught, just as I do."

Marigold was silent, her fists clenched. In the palm of one hand she could still feel the jade piece. Her father and sister waited, one shaking with horrified despair, the other trembling with reproachful anger.

"I . . . I . . ." she began.

"Tell Father what you told me," Primrose taunted. "Tell him it's nothing but an old story." She turned to her father. "Maggie says no matter what you say at the altar, it is only bread and wine, nothing happens in the tabernacle. She says if it did become body and blood, you'd be a magician and we'd be cannibals for eating it."

"Maggie! Maggie! It's not possible—it can't be . . ." Roughly, Reverend Wilder pulled his hands away from his daughter's hold. His face was ashen, his breathing was shallow. His entire body shook as he spoke in a faint voice. "Tell me it's not so, Maggie. Tell me none of what Primrose has said is true."

She would have gladly lied, if Primrose had not been there. She would have done anything in her power to soothe his distress and calm his wrought nerves. But all she could say was, "Father, I love you more than anything in the world."

His voice suddenly grew strong as he shouted angrily, "Love me!

Love me, you say! How can you love me if you dismiss my life's work as nothing more than magic?"

He started to rise from his chair, then fell back and slumped forward.

"Get John," Marigold commanded, tears streaming down her face as she put her arms around him.

"Don't touch me," he whispered. "Don't touch me. You, Marigold, you of all people. I never thought you'd break my heart."

"Father, I don't want to hurt you, not for anything."

"I think you've hurt all of us quite enough," Primrose put in. "Leave him alone."

"That's it. That's my little Primrose. Come here beside me."

"Very well." Marigold drew herself up, wiping the tears from her face with the back of her hand. "I'll get the doctor."

When the Reverend Wilder died that night, both his daughters were with him, but it was Primrose who sat by his bed, holding his hand. Marigold stayed at the foot of the bed, in the half-light, watching over her father but unable to touch him. Although hers was the last name he spoke before he died, he did not speak it in forgiveness but in deepest disappointment.

"You killed him," Primrose said flatly.

Marigold had cried all her tears, yet she could not speak for the lump in her throat.

"You killed him," Primrose repeated. "And you've ruined my chances of marriage."

But that, as it turned out, was not so.

Algernon Reid-Banning, finding Primrose pale and lifeless, was comfort itself to her in the days that followed. He saw to her every need, kept people away from her whom she did not wish to see, saw that she ate properly and that she rested. He read to her and walked with her—he brought her back to life.

With no further opportunity to gain Mark Banning as a husband, Primrose began to think that his cousin might be a satisfactory substitute. He wasn't flamboyant or daring, but he cut a fine figure in his vestments and his chances of future fortune were already on the rise, for he was certain to be the next rector of Barleigh.

Primrose could think of only one thing that might spoil it—if he were ever to learn of her London adventure. She knew she had to swear Marigold to secrecy, but Marigold had been unapproachable since the funeral.

Once she had written to inform friends and relatives of her father's death, Marigold spent her days out on her bicycle, her evenings in the basement dark room. She hadn't so much as a word for Primrose, who thought her most unkind. After all, she was the younger; everyone else realized she needed to be comforted. The more she thought about Marigold's hard and unreasonable attitude, the angrier she became, until at last she burst out, "You seem to think you're the only one who has suffered. What about me! Can't you see that I need sympathy? Can't you see I need you, Maggie!"

Without a moment's hesitation, Marigold held out her arms. "Forgive me, Prim. I'm sorry. I've been so selfish."

Primrose waited a day or so to let matters heal before reminding Marigold, "That little London escapade—it was only a prank. I'm glad now it worked out as it did. Algernon need never know about it. He might not understand that it was all in fun."

"He might not," Marigold said dryly. Then, as her sister's eyes remained fixed on her, she promised, "He'll never hear of it from me."

Primrose breathed a sigh of relief.

The wedding was announced a week later. The announcement might have been delayed in respect for their mourning, but there was the difficulty of the rectory, which no longer belonged to the Wilders but was, by rights, the residence of Algernon Reid-Banning. Their haste, therefore, was understood and forgiven.

Primrose, busy preparing her trousseau, complained, "I don't see why everything has to be black, do you, Maggie?" It fell to

Marigold, once again, to write the news of the wedding to friends
and relatives. She had grown pensive again, and she wrote one
letter in particular with difficulty, but with a sense of purpose.

One event did threaten the planned wedding. Algernon found
his cousin's emerald tiepin. Unable to wear it, Primrose kept it
hidden, sometimes in her pocket where she delighted in feeling it.
One day she sneezed and as she pulled out a handkerchief, the
huge emerald fell to the floor. She quickly bent down to retrieve it,
as did an overly courteous Algernon. His smile faded when he saw
what it was.

"Where did this come from?" he demanded.

"It . . . it . . . I didn't want to tell you . . ." Primrose burst into
tears.

"What on earth didn't you want to tell me?"

Marigold stood up and put her arm around her sister. "Primrose
didn't want to tell you that your cousin sent that to you as a wedding present. Since you disliked him, she was afraid you would
refuse the gift. I suggested she keep it until she found the right
moment to talk to you about it. She didn't want to keep it from you;
it was my fault."

Algernon eyed the gem in the palm of his hand. He weighed it
thoughtfully.

"She shouldn't have listened to you," he said, pocketing it. "She
should have come directly to me."

"You're not going to send it back, are you, Algernon?" Primrose
asked timidly.

"I shall have it appraised and then make a decision."

Primrose threw a grateful glance at her sister. "Maggie must stay
on with us, mustn't she Algernon?"

"Of course," Algernon agreed perfunctorily, not realizing Marigold was as reluctant to remain as he was to have her stay on in his
household.

Marigold saw the newly married pair off on their wedding trip in
a new carriage, purchased with part of the proceeds from the sale

of the emerald. Then she waited impatiently for the post to arrive each day, anxiously going through the letters that came.

The day that the awaited letter finally came was the day she came across the jade good luck charm. Good luck indeed, Marigold thought as she held it, along with that wafer-thin letter bearing the strange, foreign stamp. She tore the letter open and her eyes raced over its contents. Then she folded the sheet, held it to her heart, and vowed, "Father, I'll make you proud of me. I promise I will." Afterwards, she threaded a chain through the eye of the jade piece and fastened it around her neck.

By the time the Reverend and Mrs. Reid-Banning had returned from Somerset, Marigold was packed, her ticket already procured.

"But you can't go, Maggie. It just isn't right," Primrose wailed, the thought of keeping house suddenly overwhelming her.

"I don't see why not." Algernon was obviously relieved. "It's a fine calling."

"Maggie knows very well why she should not become a missionary and go off to Korea," Primrose asserted angrily. "And I believe you'd agree with me, Algernon, if you knew. You must write to Mr. Farquhar. In fact, if you don't, I believe I must."

"If I knew what, Primrose?" Algernon asked with a touch of acerbity. His wife was threatening to spoil this perfect solution to the problem of his sister-in-law. "You're speaking in riddles."

"Yes, Primrose," Marigold prompted boldly. "Tell us both what you mean. And when you're finished, maybe I'll have something of interest to tell Algernon too."

Primrose swallowed, looking from her sister to her husband, then back again. "I just don't want Maggie to leave, that's all."

"No more do I, my sweet," her husband seconded, "but we must put our own selfish wishes aside. Our mission in Korea needs Maggie. I'm sure she's going to make a fine missionary."

THE
BLUE DRAGON
OF THE EAST

1

If only I could believe it meant something more than a lot of hocus-pocus, Lady Chu-sun thought. Her hands were clasped tightly together, her head was bowed to hide her skepticism, rather than in reverence, as the mudang continued her incantation.

"A book of gold too huge to embrace. A brush of gold too huge to grasp."

The throbbing of Chilyongun's voice and the increased velocity of her gyrations were signs that Queen Min's favorite mudang and confidante would soon enter into a state of possession by the queen's symbol—the Red Phoenix of the South—sign of an exemplary reign. Chilyongun was now supplicating the Red Phoenix to spare Crown Prince Sunjong, the queen's only child, during this most recent outbreak of smallpox.

The shamanist kut had begun with Chilyongun calling upon the Blue Dragon of the East, chief among the four evil-repelling forces. To complete the cycle of the protectors of the Four Directions, Chilyongun still had to invoke the Black Turtle of the North and the White Tiger of the West. Already Lady Chu-sun was weary. Still, she suspected she was not half as weary as her sister, Princess Chun-mae. She longed to look up and see how her sister was bearing the fatigue, but she dared not. It could only bring harm to attract Chilyongun's notice in any way, particularly now, when no special attention should be drawn to her sister. Chu-sun was convinced the mudang possessed no spiritual powers, but she did possess a great deal of political power. That was why she was to be feared. So Chu-sun kept her eyes down and her hands clasped as the mudang cried out:

"All things created, of use may be."

"All things destroyed, of no use can be," responded the kidae, her chief assistant.

If only the queen would pray to the one and only God, the Christian God, some good might be accomplished, Chu-sun thought. But these repetitious, interminable kuts with their chanting and dancing, their incantations and offerings to spirit gods—offerings that Chilyongun pocketed for herself when everyone had gone— were no good to anyone, except the mudang and her cohorts. Yet Chilyongun had the ear of Queen Min and, therefore, of all the ladies at her court. What fools they all were, Chu-sun thought.

Her own background was much the same as that of the other five hundred palace ladies and royal princesses assembled in the Kyonghoe-ru, the pleasure pavilion by the lotus pond, for the kut. Even this shamanist rite was not unknown to her, though no mudang had ever crossed the threshold of her family home in Korea's northeastern corner. Her father would never have allowed that. And because of her father, Chu-sun had been exposed to another message. Christian missionaries had found their way deep into the Diamond Mountains where she grew up, and her father had allowed them to preach their message. Though no more than a child, Chu-sun had been deeply affected by the Christian words of love and hope. But most particularly she remembered their promises of equality to all, men and women, rich and poor. *For the last shall be first, the first last, and the meek shall inherit the earth.* That phrase she remembered, long after the missionaries had departed.

It was an unlikely gospel to preach in a land where Confucian order of precedence was everything and remained unchanged generation after generation, where women were no more than appendages, first to their fathers, then to their husbands. The Christian doctrine of equality could never be a popular message among the yangban, noble families such as her own. Even her father, wise man though he was, had listened and then dismissed it. Chu-sun, too, might have dismissed the Christian doctrine had she not learned that after their departure, the missionaries had been hunted down and crucified at the orders of Min Tae-jon, Wonsan's ruthless yangban magistrate, the brother of Queen Min. Crucifixion was not an uncommon punishment for thieves and murderers, but in view of the stories the missionaries had told of the death of their Christ, this manner of dying seemed a sign; it had affected Chu-sun deeply. Another sign had been their Bible, translated into Korean. She had discovered it after hearing of their death. She had hidden it—the first secret she ever kept—and read it secretly. The more she read its words of hope and love, the more she believed.

Chu-sun had another secret, too, that was hers alone: her love for Kim Tuk-so, son of a neighboring yangban family. He had had free run of Chu-sun's house throughout his childhood; they had been as brother and sister. Then one day she had beaten him at a game of chang-gi, a form of chess.

"You've no right to win," Tuk-so had cried out angrily.

"Why not? I won fairly."

"That's not it. You're a girl." Then he had looked at her as though seeing her for the first time.

"Eppuni," he murmured reluctantly, as though the compliment were forced from him.

And she flushed. "Am I really pretty?"

He shrugged, then ran off, but from that day on they never played chang-gi again. Their relationship had irrevocably changed. Chu-sun knew then that she was extraordinarily glad Tuk-so was not her brother.

She began to study herself in the ancient mirror, not an easy feat since so much of the silver backing had been scraped away by previous owners. Swallowing the lead contained in mirrors was a facile means women chose to escape from an oppressive existence.

"Oh, but how could they!" Chu-sun mentally censored these past unfortunate suicides, as the mirror reflected her own happiness. How could anyone ever choose to die, when life had so much to offer, she wondered.

When Tuk-so was sent to Seoul to study for the civil service examinations, she waited patiently, sure that he would come back to claim her as his wife.

But then a black cloud had descended on her happiness, one she had no power to dispel.

It had been decreed that a wife was to be selected from among daughters of yangban families for Prince Yi Kang, King Kojong's son by Lady Chang, a favorite secondary wife. Clearly, the king expected the royal line to pass through this son, as evidenced by the way he personally directed the selection process.

Chu-sun had been disturbed when the Board of Rites issued an edict refusing to allow any girl of the noble class to marry until after the initial selection of twelve girls for consideration by the king, as wife for his son. This would be a long process, for first the Killye Togam, a group of special judges, had to be established to investigate the ancestry of each candidate before a name could be put forward to the king.

At an earlier time, the signal honor of being amongst the chosen might have thrilled Chu-sun. But when her father was informed that not one but two of his daughters were to be included in the final twelve candidates, and the neighboring yangban families descended upon them to cheer the great fortune that had fallen upon their house, Chu-sun wept. There was nothing she could do, however. Neither she nor her sister, Chun-mae, could consider marriage to anyone else until eliminated as a possible consort to the prince.

In turn she cried, grew angry, then cried again. She fell into the depths of despair and even thought of the lead backing to her mirror, before she reasserted herself. There was really only one thing to do and she did it. She prayed. Not to the Blue Dragon of the East, nor to the White Tiger of the West, but to the only God in whom she had faith.

Her spirits rose as her father teased Chun-mae, "It will be you, I'm sure of it. That mole on the top of your head means you are to marry a high yangban official. And who could be higher than Prince Yi Kang, our king's favorite son?"

Chun-mae giggled, covering her mouth with a delicate white hand in a vain attempt to hide her mirth, and her father smiled at her affectionately.

People often said that Chu-sun, Autumn Nymph, and Chun-mae, Spring Plum, had been aptly named. Apart from the fact that the elder had been born in the year's fall, the younger at its awakening, there was a delicate burgeoning quality to Chun-mae that Chu-sun had sometimes resented, particularly when she felt it gave her sister preference in their father's eyes. Chu-sun had been taught to read and write, but it was Chun-mae their father always called upon when he was dispirited, to sing to him, to make him laugh. Now Chu-sun was glad that her younger sister was so pretty and held such appealing promise.

"It should be Chun-mae, Father," Chu-sun urged. "She looks like a princess. I don't."

"She does, that is true," her father replied, with a doting glance at his younger daughter.

"Then I don't see why I have to go on with this at all."

"But of course you must go on, Chu-sun. Don't talk foolishly. It is not for you to decide, it is for the Killye Togam to make recommendations, and then for the final decision to be made by His Royal Majesty." Chu-sun's father bowed his head. No one ever called the king by name.

But Chu-sun decided she would rather swallow the lead backing from her mirror than be forced to renounce her love for Tuk-so and become a royal princess. Her fate became even more uncertain when both sisters remained in the running after two elimination ceremonies that whittled the number of candidates from twelve to six, from six to three.

Not until the final kantaek were Chu-sun, Chun-mae, and a

certain Miss Chun from Yonan province presented to the members of the royal family for their scrutiny. Identically dressed in the dark blue silk chima (long skirt) and pale blue chogori (short jacket), the usual attire of ladies of the court with the bows of their chogori tied right to left to indicate their yangban class, and their long black hair bound into single braids to denote their unmarried status, they paraded before King Kojong and Queen Min in the Kunjong-jon, the main throne room. Each wore a ribbon stretched across her breast, bearing her name and clan seat.

"Let it be Chun-mae; she would make a good queen. Let it be Miss Chun, even. But please God, let it not be me," Chu-sun prayed over and over again as they posed and twirled on command.

"Keep your eyes lowered," they had been warned. "Do not look up at their majesties. To do so will cause your immediate dismissal from the Kunjong-jon."

Chu-sun was afraid of the royal pair—the evil reputation of the queen was whispered throughout the land—but she was even more afraid that she might be the chosen one. That fate, which would condemn her never to look upon Kim Tuk-so again, decided her. Heart pounding, she deliberately raised her eyes.

And there, fixed upon her in scrutiny, was Queen Min's piercing gaze. The king, too, saw her look up, and frowned. He had turned away, toward Chun-mae, but the queen stared at Chu-sun, willing her to lower her eyes. Chu-sun did not.

The moment passed. Though it seemed like hours, it was no more than an instant. She heard the king commanding her sister, who had dutifully kept her eyes lowered, to raise them. Chun-mae had to be asked more than once, but at last she looked up."

"This," King Kojong announced, "is the one for my son."

Chu-sun breathed a sigh of relief. But her relief was short-lived.

The selection complete, Queen Min said, "Then I shall take the sister to wait upon me. I understand she can write. I am in need of a personal scribe."

So Chun-mae was given to Prince Yi Kang with her eyes sealed shut, as was the custom; she was not allowed to look upon his face until after the ceremony. She went willingly, and it was her good fortune that he had turned out to be a handsome, virile young man, making Chun-mae the envy of nearly every woman in the land.

At the same time, with great reluctance, her sister, Chu-sun, took up the position of scribe to Queen Min at the Yi court. It would not be forever, she vowed. And at least she was still unmarried. Eventually Kim Tuk-so would find some way to come and claim her. In the meantime, while being instructed in court procedures, Chu-sun never mentioned his name. Kim Tuk-so was related to the Andong Kims, a clan highly regarded by the king and, perhaps for that reason as much as any other, hated by the queen.

But she thought and dreamed of Tuk-so constantly, of his fearless courage—at the age of fourteen, he had killed a tiger—and of his superior powers of learning. Chu-sun had proof of that in the sijo he had composed and written out in the finest hand on hearing she was to go to court.

> *If my tears were made of pearls,*
> *   I would catch them all and save them.*
> *When you came back a decade later,*
> *   A jeweled castle would enthrone you.*
> *But these tears leave no trace at all*
> *   So I am left desolate.*

He had hidden the sijo in a vial intended for perfume that her family had given her. But instead of perfume Chu-sun had filled the vial with her tears. Tuk-so's sijo and her Bible were the only personal possessions that meant anything to Chu-sun. And both she kept secret.

However, Kim Tuk-so had brought himself to the king's attention by gaining highest honors in the civil service examination. He had been recommended as a scholar worthy of watching. When his appointment as fifth counselor to the king's court was announced,

Chu-sun thanked God for answering her prayers while the queen's curses could be heard throughout the court.

The quarrel that ensued between the royal pair was overheard by courtiers and relayed with relish, to be whispered about long afterwards.

"I won't have a Kim of the Andong clan here!" The queen's voice had risen to a scream. "And nor would you, if you had any sense. They all but killed my nephew and sent me into exile. They made a puppet of you and brought back that evil father of yours."

"Taewon-gun is your uncle as well as my father," her husband reminded her.

Towering over her husband, like a raven hovering above its prey, the queen declared, "He seeks only power for himself. He chose me for your wife, thinking he could continue to rule the country as he had while you played with your women. But there he made a mistake. I've a mind of my own. I know what I want and what I don't want. I don't want the Andong Kims around, and I've disowned that worthless uncle of mine."

"I rather think it's he who has disowned you," the king responded mildly, half to himself.

"His pro-Japanese plot failed only because of my loyal Chinese support. You'd do well not to forget that."

The king rose with an air of finality. "Kim Tuk-so is appointed to my court and not to yours. That's an end to the matter," he announced, sweeping from the hall with as much dignity as his small stature could afford.

But all who knew Queen Min doubted that. She knew how to bide her time. She would sleep, like a spider in its web, and, when the time was right, she would strike.

Though Chu-sun was elated at the news, the separation of the king's court from the queen's meant that Chu-sun and Tuk-so rarely saw one another. Still, knowing they were both within the same walls was happiness enough for lovers who had expected far less.

The rhythmic beating of the changgu, an hour-glass–shaped drum, played by the kidae, awoke Chu-sun from her dreaming:

> *Before the shrine of the gods,*
> *The Blue Dragon of the East,*
> *The Red Phoenix of the South,*
> *The Black Turtle of the North,*
> *The White Tiger of the West,*
> *I command them one and all to protect our prince.*

"Ahwa chesok," the mudang wailed.

"Ahwa chesok," her assistant, the kidae, echoed.

At long last, the initial prayer ended and Chu-sun could raise her eyes. The first person she looked for was her sister. She stood alongside the other royal princesses, clearly distinguishable by their bright red embroidered chima and yellow chogori. Unlike Chu-sun, whose braided hair hung down her back almost to the floor, Chun-mae had the hairstyle of a married woman: her hair was formed into a chignon held in place by a pinyo, a long pin made of bone. Perhaps that is what makes her look so much more grown up, Chu-sun thought, even though I'm older. Chun-mae's eyes met hers but no spark of recognition passed between them. Chun-mae belonged to the king's court and exchanges, even between the women of the two courts, were limited.

"Mansin momju."

"Mansin momju," came the kidae's response.

It would be hours before the kut was over, Chu-sun realized. These superstitious rituals were generally interminable, but the sight of her sister's pale face, the knowledge of her delicate state of health made this event seem even more insufferable than most.

If only Chun-mae could have avoided attendance, but that would have been impossible. The only acceptable excuse any lady of the court could offer for missing a kut called by the queen would be to have the pox itself. Pregnancy would have been the last reason the queen would accept, especially from the wife of handsome, energetic Prince Yi Kang, who threatened her own sickly son, Prince Sunjong, as heir to the throne. Both sisters knew the necessity for concealing from the queen the fact that Chun-mae was with child. Terrible tales were told of women who were beaten, even poisoned by the queen for conceiving a child. What might be the fate of a child fathered by the son of Lady Chang, the king's favored secondary wife? No, the queen must not know.

Thank goodness that the high-waisted chogori concealed telltale bulges. It had been designed centuries ago, in an effort to save Korean women from marauding soldiers. Pregnant women were usually spared from rape; in this dress all appeared to be with child. Now it could conceal a royal pregnancy, Chu-sun realized, until the very moment of birth.

Chu-sun watched as the mudang donned a black mask and, above it, a red hat with horns held in place by a chin strap. The long striped sleeves of her chogori flounced back and forth as she rattled her hazel wand with its five bells in her left hand. In her right was her fan of the Three Spirits. Grinning mercilessly, she had become the Black Turtle of the North. It was a scene of evil, Chu-sun felt, shivering inwardly.

Chilyongun paused before the altar, which was laden with offerings of rice cakes, pears, persimmons, fish, bean curd, and golden jewelry. Behind the altar was an array of icons depicting the pantheon of shaman spirits. As she waited for possession by the next spirit, a hush fell. Queen Min appeared almost as transfixed as her mudang, her eyes never moving. Her fat son, the only male present, barely stifled a yawn. At the end of the platform where they were seated, Chu-sun caught sight of her sister's white, drawn face.

Suddenly, with a piercing cry, the mudang tore off the black mask and donned a white one, with bared fangs and staring, sightless eyes. The red hat was gone, replaced by a white wig which extended into a long, shaggy mane. Over it all, she wore a white chima with long sleeves that swept the floor.

A whisper went around the room. "The White Tiger of the West."

Of all the symbols to shield against evil, the White Tiger, preventing invasion from the West, stood paramount. Tigers were greatly feared; they roamed throughout the Korean countryside, selecting their victims at random and carrying them off at will. But this symbolic beast, who had lived for five hundred years until the hair on his coat had turned white, ranked among the immortals, the star of great whiteness in the Milky Way.

Now possessed by this White Tiger of the West, Chilyongun began to gyrate faster and faster, moving in ever diminishing circles. As she did, the music rose to a crescendo, the changgu beating wildly, the chegum clashing, and the haegum, a single-stringed fiddle, along with the piri, a flute, wailing in the background. Then, when it seemed the noise could grow no louder, came a thunderous clashing of gongs.

At this moment, Chilyongun threw up one arm. The long wide sleeve of her gown fell, revealing a pale arm and clenched fist. The fingers opened one by one, and there, in the palm of her hand, lay a curved bone, about an inch in length. Innocent enough in appearance, its portent was ominous. In this tiny bone lay the infinite power of the White Tiger, all of which was now in Chilyongun's possession.

Hotun-sori, Chu-sun told herself, hocus-pocus, nothing more. Yet she couldn't shake a sense of foreboding as Chilyongun spun around, pointing the bone at first one, then the other, slower and slower until at last she stopped before Princess Chun-mae. Chilyongun stood still, not moving a muscle. The bone pointed like an accusing finger. The music had stopped. No one moved. No one spoke. It seemed that no one so much as breathed.

Chun-mae's pallor was deathlike. She was convulsed by tremors. She lifted a hand to cover her mouth, perhaps to prevent herself from screaming. Then she fell to the ground in a dead faint.

All present turned away from Chun-mae, as though she had become infected with the pox that the kut was designed to prevent.

Had this been the true purpose of the kut, Chu-sun wondered. Had Queen Min known of her sister's pregnancy all along? Had she called this kut not so much to prevent her worthless son from falling victim to smallpox as to prevent him from falling victim to a stronger aspirant for the throne? Prince Yi Kang, beloved as he was, would be loved still more if he became father to a son. Was that it, Chu-sun wondered, her heart pounding, her hands growing clammy with fear.

"Let this be a lesson!" The queen had risen to her full height. Her piercing eyes surveyed her court, all five hundred ladies, then came to rest on Chu-sun. "Let no one try to conceal anything from me. There can be no secrets in this court."

2

The first sight of Korea on landing at Chemulpo, Seoul's seaport, was dismal. Slimy mud almost as far as the eye could see and, beyond, low hills and a mud-brown town. Hardly a town at all, really, but a collection of mean wooden houses. It was hot, and a drizzling rain began to fall as the vessel that had steamed so majestically out from Southampton inched its way through a narrow channel in the shallows.

A chair with six bearers carried Marigold Wilder along the twenty-five miles of undefined path that served as the road to Seoul. They dodged loaded bullock carts and men carrying equal loads on their backs. Taciturn foot passengers, wearing hats that looked like small umbrellas, cursed as the chair bearers splashed black mud on their white clothes in passing. The mud holes on either side of the path grew larger as the rain continued to fall.

This grim arrival had no adverse effect on Marigold, however. She would have been affronted to find herself in a colorful, exotic land, or to encounter friendly, happy people. Her own thoughts were gray and barren; she felt strangely comforted by a hostile landscape that reflected her mood.

During the journey from England, at the sight of her mourning, fellow travelers had attempted to lighten her mood. The captain had insisted she dine at his table; she had dined there, but her conversation had been minimal, causing the captain to regret his gesture of goodwill. A missionary and his wife had attached themselves to her; even though they were Methodist, they too, were occupied with God's work, as they constantly reminded her. For some unaccountable reason, this seemed of little comfort to Miss Wilder. They had the distinct impression that she went to some pains to avoid them, dodging into passageways at their approach, and even, they had been shocked to discover, going below and mixing with the passengers on the third-class decks and goodness knew who else instead of playing bridge in the saloon. They had spoken to her about this, praising her Christian endeavors but warning her that she must always remember she was not only a representative of her church but, even more importantly, an Englishwoman. Her terse reply that she was only too aware of that fact had seemed enigmatic. So, too, had her almost audible sigh of relief when they left the ship at Hong Kong. After all their kindness and attention, they had expected tears—they could have coped with anything but that enigmatic sigh.

"You have our address. You must write often, Miss Wilder. Let us know how you're getting on. We Christians must stick together. And don't forget to send along the photograph you took of us," they called out, referring to the occasion when they had inveigled her to turn her lens upon them rather than upon the members of the crew. A cheery wave of farewell and a relieved expression had been her only response.

"I'm not sure how she'll fare among the natives," the missionary said dubiously.

His wife shook her head. "Not quite suitable, I'm afraid. Still," she added, her face brightening at the thought, "she's not the only mistake the Anglicans have made."

Throughout the bumpy journey into Seoul, Marigold was troubled by the thought that Reverend Farquhar's attitude might resemble that of the two Methodists—their terrible zeal to convert, to bring English standards to the uncivilized. She would be no good at that. Primrose must have known or guessed what would be expected. Perhaps that was part of the reason why she had tried so hard to dissuade Marigold from going, while Algernon had been equally insistent that she should.

At one point in the narrow path, they came upon a conveyance coming in the opposite direction. Bearers of neither conveyance would give way to the other and for several minutes of terrible uncertainty, as she was lurched back and forth, Marigold was sure she would end up in the mud. She tried to signal that she didn't mind giving way to the oncomer, that she didn't mind walking. Either her bearers did not understand her, or else conviction that their burden was of greater importance would not allow them to give in. The standoff continued until, at last, with a shout and a tremendous lurch forward, they succeeded in upending the oncoming conveyance, forcing chair, bearers, and passenger into the mud, much to Marigold's horror. She cowered back as her bearers triumphantly sailed on by, oblivious to or else enjoying the hostile shouts in their wake. Marigold disliked being carried around by men to begin with. It was even worse to be party to that sort of senseless, barbarous contretemps without being able to do anything about it. She was thankful that she had insisted on including her bicycle with her shipped luggage; she intended to be as independent in Korea as she had been in England.

Seoul, entered through a deep-roofed gateway in a high wall, consisted of a mass of gray hovels divided by a labyrinth of narrow alleys. To the north was a range of mountains.

"Nam-san, Nam-san," the bearers called out, pointing to the closest mountain. "Han, Han," pointing in the other direction toward the wide brown river with its sandy banks.

The hovels on either side of the main thoroughfare were built so close to one another that their tiled or thatched roofs almost touched. On the bearers trotted, paying no attention to carts laden high with brushwood, white-clad gentlemen with tall, black hats, half-naked, grimy children, mangy dogs, or the vendors of straw shoes, bamboo hats, and bright red persimmons, who crowded the way. Beside the thoroughfare was a wide, open conduit where creatures garbed in changot—voluminous green overcoats that enveloped them so completely that even their eyes were barely visible—were ladling water into pails or squatting down to wash clothes.

While the bearers paid no attention to anyone around them, all activity ceased momentarily as they passed.

Have they never seen a woman before, Marigold wondered in desperation as she was met by what seemed to be less than friendly curiosity. There were, she noticed, no women on the street, with the exception of one or two small girls and those shrouded creatures who, judging from their occupation, had to be female. She attempted a smile, but no smiles were returned until one man, bent almost double beneath the load on his back, made a guttural sound. Marigold thought for one awful moment that he was about to expire beneath the weight of his burden as he cast a sidelong glance at her, pointing repeatedly at his own head and then at her own. Then he guffawed. This brought on a round of cruel laughter from those assembled nearby.

She was glad when they turned toward the mountains, where she had previously noticed a few large, stoutly constructed houses. As they drew closer, she saw that the houses were built in distressingly ugly style—or perhaps it would be more accurate to say they lacked style altogether—and added little to the landscape.

The carriers turned in at the gate of a monstrous red brick establishment where, on the steps, her father's friend stood waiting to greet her. Reverend Herbert Farquhar was far taller than she had imagined, though his long black robes probably accentuated an already considerable height. He had an enormous beak of a nose and a full beard, but twinkling eyes and a mouth with an irrepressible urge to curve upward made him seem less formidable.

"My dear Miss Wilder! But it is Marigold, I believe. May I call you Marigold? It is such a pretty name, and, if I may say, with your lovely red hair it suits you admirably."

Marigold flushed with pleasure.

"Then welcome to Korea, Marigold, but most especially welcome to our Anglican mission." He punctuated the greeting with a decisive sniff of his large nose, a habit he had whenever he especially wished to make a point. Then he took both her hands in his. "I feel truly blessed to have my dearest friend's daughter here to assist our efforts. Your father once mentioned to me that this was his dearest wish, but truly I never thought to see the day it would come about. But here you are. I begin to think you had intended it all along."

"Not all along exactly, sir," Marigold replied awkwardly, not wanting to start out their acquaintance with a lie, yet trying not to dampen his enthusiasm. "But it did seem the right thing to do after Father died."

Reverend Farquhar frowned momentarily. "I do hope you didn't come out of a sense of duty to him. I see you're still in mourning."

"Not exactly, sir," Marigold prevaricated, thinking it awful that he had so quickly surmised her motive.

Having made the decision to pursue her father's wishes and become a missionary, Marigold had been nagged by doubt at the wisdom of her choice. The encounter with the Methodist missionaries on the ship had made her doubt her decision even more. What right had she to spread a word in which she had no firm belief?

Her discomfort must have been mirrored in her face, for Reverend Farquhar squeezed her hands consolingly, "I'm as old as your father, but I wish you wouldn't call me sir. Mr. Farquhar, if you must, though I have no objection to your calling me Herbert." Then he stood aside to allow her to precede him up the steps to the house. "My goodness, what kind of a welcome is this! You must be tired after that awfully bumpy ride from Chemulpo. I know my old bones feel it more and more. What you need is a good cup of tea. I believe I can claim, without fear of being refuted, that there I have succeeded in making a conversion. Halmoni, our cook, may never have mastered the art of Yorkshire pudding, but she can make a

fine cup of tea and may even, judging from the way our tea supply
diminishes, enjoy drinking it herself."

Once inside, they might have been in any English rectory—she
saw the same mahogany umbrella stand, the same mahogany coat
rack and, in the living room, the same sofa with faded chintz
covers, the same glass-covered bookcases, the same upright piano
that, she was to discover, was always out of tune, the same large
tabby cat sleeping in the sun, and even the same potted plant in the
bay window. It was only when she went over to that window and
looked down on the sea of brown roofs that Marigold remembered
she was halfway around the world from that rectory she had once
presided over and had left not three months ago. Now that life was
behind her. Even though continuing her father's work, she was
starting a new life of her own. She must not look back.

She sat down. Immediately the cat jumped into her lap.

"Tiffin's welcoming you, Marigold." Herbert Farquhar beamed
as she stroked Tiffin and the cat arched her back and then settled
down. "We call her Tiffin because she does so enjoy her little
nuncheons. I see she's taken to you. She doesn't like everyone,
which isn't surprising, for she is not at all liked by the people here.
We have to take great care not to let her out."

"I don't see why. She's a lovely creature," Marigold said, rubbing
behind Tiffin's ears, which brought on a paroxysm of purring.

"Koreans have a positive aversion to cats. They'd sooner sit down
and stroke a snake than our Tiffin here. I can't understand why;
they worship the cat's relation, the tiger."

"Are there really tigers here?"

"Indeed there are. They're said to grow up to fifteen feet though
I've never seen a skin more than eleven. Still, very fine skins they
are, with long thick fur. The tiger appears on the Royal standard.
There's a saying that the Korean hunts the tiger one half of the year
and the tiger hunts the Korean the other half. But in my humble
opinion, that noble beast doesn't do half the good of our Tiffin.

She's a fine ratter. Rats are such a plague! The country's overrun by them."

Tigers and rats! It was a less than comforting beginning.

"Ah! Here it is at last!" Reverend Farquhar said, rubbing his hands at the clatter of cups and saucers. "And here, if I am not mistaken, comes Gifford—oh, and Sully's with him. Good show! You'll like Sully." Reverend Farquhar winked at Marigold. "Gifford never misses tea, nor does Sully if he's in the vicinity."

Two young men breezed in, chatting and laughing together; they might have been any two young gentlemen arriving for tea at an English rectory. They both sported large mustaches, Sully's brown against a ruddy complexion, Gifford's dark against his pale skin. Gifford's high, stiff clerical collar seemed to emphasize the thinness of his face, while Sully's—of the high-buttoned butterfly variety, fastened with a widely knotted tie—seemed by contrast as generous as his smile. Both wore shiny black boots, evidence that they had not had to climb the hill on foot.

"Reverend Gifford Partridge and Dr. Timothy Sullivan. Gifford's mine, as you may have guessed," Herbert Farquhar explained, his eyes twinkling, "Sully's fallen away from those benighted Jesuits, but so far I haven't quite been able to convince him to fall my way." Noticing the way Sully's expression had brightened on being introduced to Marigold, Reverend Farquhar sniffed decisively as he concluded, "But perhaps you, Miss Wilder, may succeed where I cannot."

"You're with the mission, Dr. Sullivan?" Marigold asked.

"Medical officer and general factotum with the British consular mission," he explained in a pleasant Irish brogue. "No relation to Sir Arthur Sullivan—people are always asking me," he concluded by way of explanation.

"I'm glad," Marigold smiled. "I must confess I find dear Sullivan's music repetitious, but I suppose that's why it fits Gilbert's lyrics so well."

"I completely agree." Sully returned her smile.

"For my part, I must say I rather enjoy the patter. Nice beat, witty comment, altogether enjoyable—but I suppose I hear too little of it," Reverend Farquhar commented. "I'd rather hoped you'd be bringing along some new verses with you."

"I'm not very musical, I'm afraid. But I'll do my best with those I remember."

"In that case, no doubt I'll find them much more to my taste." This time Sully's smile was more intimate, while Gifford, watching, grew more remote.

"Do you write, Miss Wilder?" he asked coldly.

"My hand is quite clear . . ."

"No, no," Gifford snapped. "I mean *write*, compose, create."

"Only with my camera. I'm just not very gifted, I'm afraid."

"Giff's our poet laureate," Sully explained. "Talented fellow. I'm like you; I just get along with the job to be done."

"Sully's one of those consular chaps who imagines their mission to be superior to ours," Gifford put in. He was beginning to resent his friend's interest in the new arrival. She was just the sort one might expect to go out as a missionary: rather odd-looking, no particular interests, dedicated though, he had no doubt; why else would she have come to the ends of the earth? "When in fact it's the aim of both of us to extend the reaches of the flag where it has never before achieved dominance," he continued, throwing an anxious glance at Reverend Farquhar, concluding quickly. "Each in his own fashion, of course."

"To be sure, Gifford. None of us must ever forget that," Reverend Farquhar pointed out in a way that seemed to indicate he had had to make this reminder more than once before.

"I say, Miss Wilder, it's most awfully good to have an English lady around who's young and unattached," Sully exclaimed.

Deliberately dumping two spoonfuls of sugar into his tea and stirring it vigorously, Gifford said, "You're forgetting Miss Gardner."

"I may be lonely, but I'm not up to robbing cradles, Giff," Sully laughd. "Particularly not the cradle of my superior officer and his good lady."

Gifford seemed annoyed. "You never said anything to me about being lonely," he observed sharply. For some reason, he looked crestfallen. He leaned across and took yet another spoonful of sugar, as though to offset a certain bitterness. Then he stirred his tea even more vigorously and sipped it, grimacing slightly.

"You've just consumed your sugar ration for the entire month, Giff," Sully observed, explaining, "It's one thing in short supply that we all miss."

"I'm lucky then. I don't take sugar in my tea."

"Sweet enough," Sully murmured, then flushed at his forwardness.

Gifford ignored this exchange, sipping with deliberation before continuing. "I've been most anxiously awaiting your arrival, Miss Wilder, planning the duties you can take over from me. Teaching the creed to the young people, for example, and carefully explaining its meaning. They're in need of a firm but pious hand."

"Oh dear," Marigold sighed. "I'm not sure my hands are particularly pious."

"I'm sure they are," Reverend Farquhar interceded. "Anyway, Gifford will be there to help you along in the beginning. And it's Marigold isn't it, not Miss Wilder? We're all one family here."

Gifford did not look particularly overjoyed at this idea, though it seemed to meet with Sully's approval. But then, Marigold observed, the more she seemed to please Sully, the less she pleased Gifford.

"Since we'll be working alongside one another, Miss . . . Marigold," Gifford began. "It's as well that you're not a complete stranger to me."

"You sly dog, Giff! You mean to tell me you've already met and you never said a word," Sully accused.

"Not at all. However," Gifford paused and, with the air of a conjurer, drew from an inner pocket of his coat a letter bearing an English stamp. "I've just had an announcement of marriage from my great and good friend, Algernon Reid-Banning—we were up at Oxford together. And the lucky lady who has ensnared Algernon is, I understand, none other than your sister."

"I'm not sure Primrose ensnared Algernon," Marigold said testily before realizing that after her London debacle, that was precisely what Primrose had done.

"Obviously, from your point of view, I would presume it was he who ensnared your sister." Gifford smiled contemptuously. "Women are never stronger than when supported by their weaknesses."

"That sounds positively Voltairian, Giff. And unnecessarily harsh," Sully protested. "I don't think Miss Wilder . . . Marigold, if I may"—he half-bowed, in her direction—"is deserving of such censure."

"It's not censure," Gifford said angrily. "I'm just stating facts."

"I don't see why there has to be sham in matrimony," Marigold commented, thinking as she spoke that so many of the marriages she had witnessed had been the result of such intricate maneuvering as to amount to entrapment.

"Dr. Johnson maintained that mingled motives of convenience and inclination are behind all marriages. And since Dr. Johnson is a great hero of mine, I can't disagree." Sully glanced shyly in Marigold's direction. "For my part, however, I am quite sure that there is a time to marry."

"'To everything there is a season. . . . A time to love,'" quoted Reverend Farquhar.

With a hard glance at Marigold, Gifford added, "'And a time to hate.'"

"What about 'A time to embrace and a time to refrain from embracing,' Giff," Sully laughed. "I may be a fallen-away Catholic but I haven't forgotten all my scriptures. I could make quite a good showing in your sphere if I chose, and who knows," he added, looking directly at Marigold, "I just might."

3

Chu-sun never remembered seeing the moon quite so full or clear against the indigo sky. Or as close—so close she felt she could touch it. And perhaps, had she tried, she might have, for she believed herself capable of doing anything that night of Chu-sok.

Chu-sok, the festival of thanksgiving for past favors and for the bounteous year's harvest, fell on the fifteenth day of the eighth lunar month. Usually it was Chu-sun's favorite holiday, but that year she had not been looking forward to it. Chu-sok was a time for family gatherings, for paying respects to one's ancestors, for feasting and fun together. Being so far from all that was familiar, she was overcome with homesickness. Yet with the entire court gathered together to celebrate, the realization that she could observe, if not to talk to Tuk-so, had dispelled Chu-sun's nostalgia for home.

Swings with long ropes had been attached to tall, widespread branches of the willows by the lotus pond in the courtyard. There, ladies and princesses of the court swung to and fro like brightly hued swallows. Their clear voices rang out:

> *Not in heaven, not on earth*
> *But in the clear, clear cool sky*
> *Blue hills and green waters*
> *Swim to and fro, back and forth,*
> *Down, down we go like falling petals*
> *Up, up again skimming like swallows.*

Meanwhile the gentlemen courtiers gathered together for a vigorous tug-of-war. From her place on the swing, Chu-sun could watch and admire the prowess of Tuk-so as he took his place at one end of the team dedicated to the king. The fight was furious, in fun yet also in earnest, for pride as much as strength, was waged in the battle. Chu-sun's heart beat quickly as she watched Tuk-so's team being overpowered. Compulsively, she swung higher and higher, longing to yell out encouragement yet not daring to do so. Queen Min sat beside the king, silently satisfied at her team's performance. Not far from the queen, also avidly watching the contest, was Chilyongun, undoubtedly casting whatever spells she could create to bring about the ultimate victory of her mistress's team.

The queen's team, more organized in strength and precision, had gained an early advantage. The king's men were desperately struggling to hold their ground. But with an enormous thrust from the opposition, they were pulled forward. Heels dug in, muscles heaved, but all to no avail. They were not simply losing, they were being routed. Queen Min's face remained expressionless, but she directed an approving nod at Chilyongun.

Though Chu-sun did not believe in Chilyongun's magic, she nevertheless felt it essential to counteract it with a more powerful omen. It became vitally important that Tuk-so should win. The victory of his team would mean as much to her as victory of her team would mean to the queen. She must help. Suddenly, she remembered "Onward Christian Soldiers," the hymn taught her by missionaries, and this she began to sing, aloud and quite militantly, as she soared high in the air, then lowering her voice to a whisper, though losing none of the force, as she neared the ground where she might be overheard.

And as Chu-sun put all her heart and soul into the hymn, the king's men started to hold their own ground. Then at last they began to fight back. Soon, the queen's team was groaning in desperation as the rope was forced from their hands. One by one, they fell by the way. Victory had eluded them. The king's men had won the day!

The queen's face was a mask, but the king rose in excitement, ordering rice wine to be brought out for victors and vanquished alike. Then the uinyo—courtesans trained in the medical arts of acupuncture, nursing, and midwifery—arrived to take away those men who had been injured. They were led by Duk-hwa, the king's own apothecary, her metal case of acupuncture needles clanking from her sash. From her perch on high, it appeared to Chu-sun that far more men were claiming to be injured than had actually fallen. Much was whispered in the women's quarters of the arts employed by these apothecary-kisaeng. When the king sent for Duk-hwa to "massage his legs," as he so often did, she would hear them sneer, "Duk-hwa, Virtuous Flower. Her virtue's long gone along with her flower. But she satisfies the royal needs and gives the king's other concubines a much-needed rest."

"Is that what the concubines do, too?" she asked ingenuously.

"Massage!" They roared with laughter. "You might call it that! You're such an innocent. Don't you yet know what it means when a man and woman who have unbraided their queues meet face to face?"

Flushing, she shook her head, but she clapped her hands over her ears in an effort to shut out their gleeful, coarse explanations.

Because of what she now knew, Chu-sun was relieved to see that Tuk-so, though encouraged to join them, refused to be ushered from the field by the uinyo. Instead he stood alone, looking about him. Surely he must be searching for her! Elated, Chu-sun waved her long, multicolored scarf. Unfortunately, her efforts only succeeded in attracting the very person she would have avoided. Chilyongun looked up in puzzlement, then glanced around to see whom her mistress's court scribe was trying to attract. So Chu-sun leaned forward in her swing, then back, flying higher than ever, hoping that Tuk-so might notice her. At the same time, she hoped to convince the mudang that her excitement had simply been brought on by the game and was not caused by anyone in particular. At last, the mudang moved away. Gradually, Chu-sun brought the swing to rest and stepped off.

The dancer kisaeng were being assembled to perform the Ogwangdae mask dance drama, a comic triangular tale of a commoner husband, his wife, and his concubine, complicated by the seduction of an innocent young girl by a wicked old monk. Chu-sun knew the story well and thought it daring of them to perform this dance in the presence of the queen. But the queen, along with her mudang, had vanished from sight.

Chu-sun felt a touch at her elbow.

"Where were you? Did you see?" Tuk-so demanded, still panting from his efforts in the tug-of-war.

She nodded, flushing. "You were magnificent."

All eyes were on the dancing girls, but Tuk-so and Chu-sun looked only at one another.

"Were you hurt?" she whispered.

"Nothing that can't be quickly healed," he responded.

She glanced up at him anxiously, but he motioned her to keep her eyes on the play.

"Do you know the Chogyong, the pavilion by the thirteen-story pagoda?" he whispered urgently. "The one that remains empty."

Chu-sun nodded.

"Do not move now, but in fifteen minutes make your way there. Not directly, mind, but as though you are going somewhere else." With that, Tuk-so drifted away into the crowd behind her.

They would be alone for the first time. She could think of nothing else. Fifteen minutes suddenly seemed like fifteen hours. But Chu-sun waited, her eyes not seeing, her ears not hearing, before slowly making her way to the Chogyong by a circuitous route.

She had never been inside the pavilion. It had once been a favorite of the queen's until the day a snake fell into the room where she was sitting. Snakes freely inhabited the thick layer of earth under the roof tiles; since they kept down the number of nesting sparrows and killed the rats attracted by the sparrows' eggs, their presence was tolerated. But only outside. A snake dropping into a room was regarded as such an ill omen that it was fit cause for the abandonment of the entire building. Thus, the Chogyong remained unoccupied.

Chu-sun walked around the open veranda that surrounded the pavilion. At the entrance, she removed her upturned, red and blue slippers and entered a dusty, circular inner corridor. The oil-paper-covered ondol floors were cold underfoot, for it was long since the flues beneath them had been lit. The paper at the corridor windows was torn in places and had not been replaced. It was a scene of desolation. Chu-sun shivered. Could the Chogyong really be an unlucky place?

The central hall was empty. She was afraid to call out to Tuk-so, afraid she might be heard, yet even more afraid he might not be there. She stood in the center of the large room, not knowing what to do. The surrounding walls consisted of a series of screens picturing the magnificent scenery of the Diamond Mountains, her home, through which the diffused light of the autumn afternoon shone.

She hesitated, studying each screen before noticing the aperture in one. She carefully slid back this door, then paused before entering a small, dark apartment. The darkness frightened her, but she was even more frightened to find herself seized by two strong arms that grasped her own and pulled her close. She gasped; her breath literally taken away as her lips were covered by other lips. Her immediate impulse was to struggle, but then, realizing whose arms, whose lips these were, she was overcome with joy and abandoned herself to an embrace such as she had never known.

"Tuk-so. My dearest Tuk-so," she murmured over and over again between his kisses.

At last, he let her go. Now that she had become accustomed to the dim light, she could make out his face, the strange glow in his eyes. Holding her at arm's length, his voice thick with excitement, he whispered, "Chu-sun, would you—would you let me see you."

She frowned, puzzled. This was their first opportunity to be alone; looking at one another had been the one thing they had been able to do all along.

"In there." With his head, he indicated the central hall.

"But is this not more quiet, more private?"

"Yes. Except I can't see you here. I mean all of you."

"All of me?"

"Without . . . without . . ." His hands plucked awkwardly at the sleeve of her chogori.

"Without . . ." Chu-sun hesitated, blushing furiously.

"I'm sorry," he said hastily. "I know it is against Confucian precepts for the body ever to be completely exposed. I had no right to ask you. It's just that I have for so long imagined how you must look. Forgive me—you must forgive me."

"There is nothing to forgive. I care nothing for Confucian precepts. Nothing at all. You and you alone have the right," she responded seriously, bravely. "Go in there." She motioned toward the central hall. "I will come to you."

"I should like to stay, if you don't mind."

So he stayed by her as, in the dim light, she untied the bow of her multicolored chogori and slipped it off. She undid the wide silk sash and then pulled over her head the bodice attached to her long yellow chima. Then, lastly and much more slowly, she removed her mujugi, the long white undertrousers.

He took her braid in his hands and began to loosen it. In doing so, from time to time his hands touched her bare skin.

"Are you cold?" he asked, caressing her neck, her shoulders, then cupping her small breasts.

She shook her head. Though the room was cold, her blood pounded through her veins.

He took her hand and led her out into the central room of the pavilion.

The sun was setting, its last rays sending long golden shadows through the silk screens, forming a sunset over the mountains to the west that reminded Chu-sun of her home. She flushed at the thought of what her family would think if they could see her there. She was glad the light was muted as Tuk-so stood back to look at her.

"Would you turn," he asked, sitting down on his heels. He took off his gold-trimmed black horsehair cap, letting the long queue that marked his unmarried status fall down behind him. "And walk, let me see you walk, please."

She was reminded of the official at the final kantaek for the selection of a royal bride and felt awkward, shamed by her nakedness. But this was no official, this was Tuk-so, her Tuk-so, she reminded herself. And she did as she was bid. She walked back and forth, too embarrassed to look at him, though he said nothing. At last she lifted her eyes to find an expression on his face she had never seen before—not on his face or on the face of any man.

What happened next was as sudden and unexpected as that first kiss. He sprung on her, like a tiger on its prey. His strength overwhelmed her as he flung her to the ground. Her bare body was crushed beneath the smooth silk of his chongbok, the stiff long red satin waistcoat he wore over his coatlike turugami; the wide blue belt that marked his official rank dug harshly into her skin. She could scarcely breathe beneath his weight. She felt him struggling to push aside his turugami. Then, unceremoniously, he pushed his hand between her legs, forcing them apart. A sudden hard thrust, and he was inside her. He moved with such precision and such force that although he hurt her, she couldn't cry out. In this way, she and Tuk-so first knew one another face to face.

It was over quickly, quietly. Then he buried his face in her bare shoulder.

"I hadn't meant it to be that way," he murmured, "but I couldn't help it, I couldn't stop. You are too lovely. And now you are mine, forever. You must unbind my braid. That will show that we are truly married in one another's eyes."

Though stunned by what had passed between them, Chu-sun undid his long queue and then stroked his blue-black hair. "I am yours. I always was yours. I always will be yours," she whispered, trying to forget how it had been as they lay quietly together.

When next he took her, he made an attempt to combine tenderness with force. She knew, then, that though this might not have been what she expected, though it had not started as she had dreamed it might, this was the only man she could ever allow to touch her in that way. She had learned from Tuk-so what it was for a man to love a woman. That was enough.

Her sigh, then, was one of satisfaction. Then, alarmed, she clung to him for her sigh seemed to have an echo.

Tuk-so had heard it too. He pushed her aside and jumped up, looking anxiously around. Dusk had fallen and the large room was now quite dark.

"Nothing," he said, leaning over her, touching her bare breast before giving her his hand and helping her to her feet. "But we must be careful. No one must know. No one must see us together. We know beyond all reason, beyond all truth, that we are now one. We have undone one another's hair; we have known one another face to face. Give me time. Eventually, I will find a way to let our married state be known. You must trust me."

"Of course I trust you," she murmured, clinging to him.

He kissed her, but the kiss was hurried. "You must dress carefully. Make sure everything is in place—your hair too." He was readjusting his turugami as he spoke and she began to tightly rebraid his queue. Then he replaced the black cap on his head, warning, "When you are sure all is in order, that there is no sign we were here, go back and rejoin the others. By the same way that you came, mark you. You must never say we were together, for that could lead to my banishment. His Majesty would understand, but the queen is unforgiving. She would blame me."

"I will say nothing. I promise. Can we meet here again?"

"Perhaps. I shall let you know. Good-bye, Chu-sun."

"Please don't say good-bye, Tuk-so. We must see one another alone, like this."

He smiled in triumph. "Now you want me as I wanted you. That is good. I shall arrange for us to meet again. Wait for my sign. Above all, be prudent. Say nothing of this to anyone in the queen's court. If she were ever to learn what has happened, I could be banished forever."

"Don't say that, Tuk-so!"

"Shhhh!" He held his finger to his lips. This time they both heard a distinct creaking of boards outside in the corridor. They stood together, not speaking, scarcely breathing. But all was silent.

"The building is old and unused, that is all. But I must go, and so must you. Don't forget that this must be our secret," he warned before silently making his way from the room into the corridor. She heard his step on the boards; he paused to don his shoes, then his footsteps crunched across the fallen leaves until at last they disappeared. Then she did as she had been told. With great care she dressed and rebraided her hair. Yet she was sure she must look different—that what had happened must show—that without being told, everyone must know.

As she left the Chogyong she looked back, thinking it the most lovely place in the world. How lucky that it had been abandoned as a place of ill omen!

She gazed up at the harvest moon. It hung above her like a yellow ornament, too big, too close to be real, lighting everything including her shining face.

Then she hurried back to the celebration, and only just in time. She could hear her name being called.

"Chu-sun's not here. Where's Chu-sun?"

"But I am here," she cried. Fearful of having already been discovered, she ran toward the brightly lit courtyard where the moon's light was augmented by a thousand torches.

There another game was in progress. The young ladies of the court were arranged in a long line, each holding onto the waist of the one ahead.

Beside the line stood her sister, Princess Chun-mae, a palace lady holding each of her hands. Chun-mae looked very pale. She cast an imploring glance at Chu-sun as she hurried to join them.

"I am sorry. I ask your forgiveness," Chu-sun murmured. She was relieved to see that the queen's attention was fastened upon Prince Sunjong, whose sickly countenance evidenced that he had eaten too much. Perhaps for that reason, her absence had gone unnoticed. It was the mudang who impatiently, though without question, motioned her into place in the line.

"What is this?" she whispered to the girl ahead of her.

"The princess bridge," was the soft reply.

"What is the princess bridge?" Chu-sun asked.

"*We* are, or soon will be. This is a commemoration of the welcome given to the Koryo King Konghim by the villagers of Andong when he took refuge there centuries ago. They made a human bridge for him to walk over, a perpetual bridge."

"You mean the king is going to walk over us," Chu-sun said, her knees buckling at the thought.

There was a giggle. "No."

"Not that fat Prince Sunjong, surely."

There was another giggle.

"No. No. The queen has given your sister the honor of representing the king."

Chu-sun's excitement faded. "What does she have to do?"

"We bend over and she walks along our backs, that's all."

Chu-sun glanced along the line. There must have been well over a hundred assembled there.

"She must be careful; it is such a long walk. But at least it won't last too long."

"It will last as long as the queen finds it amusing. I said this is a perpetual bridge. We hold on to one another's waist and bow down for her to walk along our backs. As soon as she has done so, we must run to the front and join the bridge once more. That way, it never ends."

"But Chun-mae can't . . ." Chu-sun cried out, before being ordered to bow down and hold on.

She turned her head to see Chun-mae being assisted by her two escorts to climb upon the back of the last young lady in the line. Then she could see no more for she was ordered to lower her head and stay down. She felt Chun-mae's feet pass over her and then was able to stand up to move to the front of the line. As she did, she saw that Chun-mae had grown paler still. Chu-sun caught her breath as her sister stumbled.

"You can't be tired already, Princess. The game's only just begun," Chu-sun heard the queen call out.

"Go on. Don't stop," Prince Sunjong ordered, motioning to Chu-sun to bow down at the head of the line. Chu-sun felt the girl behind her clasp her waist. Then, soon after, she felt Chun-mae's feet cross her back and again she was prodded to hurry to the front.

How many times she repeated this maneuver, Chu-sun couldn't say. But she did know that each time she moved to the head of the human bridge, she noticed her sister's increased pallor; each time her sister's step crossed her back, she was aware of her increased unsteadiness. Chun-mae's attendants, whose role it was to steady her, treated the whole thing as a game and were less than vigilant. At any moment she could fall. Chu-sun knew that at this point in her sister's pregnancy, a fall could be fatal to both child and mother. Chun-mae knew this too, for with her eyes she was imploring Chu-sun to help in putting a stop to this torturous journey. Somehow, it had to be stopped.

"Oh God, you were with me earlier today, you helped Tuk-so to win the tug of war. Help me now. This game must be stopped. Chun-mae's life depends on it. Please, show me what to do," Chu-sun prayed. She opened her eyes, looked up, and saw a sign. The prince yawned. He was bored. Wonderful! But his next words were not encouraging.

"Why does the princess need to have all those attendants?" he whined.

"Why indeed, if your royal highness prefers that they step aside, so it shall be," seconded his mother, motioning to the two court ladies.

Princess Chun-mae stopped, petrified.

"Go on," the queen motioned sharply.

"And I'd find it more amusing if she moved faster," Prince Sunjong said, yawning again.

"Faster," the mudang ordered, flicking at Chun-mae's ankles with her hazel wand.

Princess Chun-mae took an unsteady step forward, then another.

"Move, your highness. The prince wants you to move," Queen Min said, and her mudang prodded threateningly at Chun-mae's ankles.

So Chun-mae moved. But not Chu-sun. She stood aside, refusing to join at the head of the bridge. The young lady who had been behind her also hesitated, not knowing what to do. She waited for Chu-sun, and the lady behind her stood waiting in turn. Soon the entire group was in disarray, all waiting for Chu-sun to resume her place. Unless she did, the perpetuity of the bridge would be broken. And Chu-sun made no move.

Queen Min's attention turned from Princess Chun-mae to her sister. Chu-sun knew this was no moment to incur her wrath. Her private union with Tuk-so could never be publicly acknowledged without the queen's consent. Yet she could not be a willing party to an amusement that would mean certain death for her sister's child, if not for her sister herself.

For the first time in her life she felt grateful to Prince Sunjong. "I'm glad it's over," he said. "It was fun at first, but now it's become a big bore."

"Your royal highness must never be bored," said the queen, bowing low to her son as he rose and strode off. When she rose, her expression was inscrutable.

"I have a great many official matters to attend to in the morning. My scribe will need all of her wits about her. She can no longer enjoy her part in our festivities. She will leave us and retire to her room."

Though this was a clear rebuke, the queen could have given no order more certain to please Chu-sun. Still, she took care to appear contrite as she bowed her head and backed away from the assembled throng.

4

Marigold had never known what it was to be courted, what it was to have her company in demand, to have her opinion sought. That sort of thing had always happened to Primrose, never to her. But word of her arrival in Seoul flashed through the tiny, bored Western community like a hot knife through butter, bringing with it a flood of invitations to the mission.

Since the first opening of Korea to foreigners in 1882, the British, Russians, and Americans had established legations. Several foreign companies had sent representatives seeking to build roadways, railways, waterworks, and other improvements of civilization regarded as essential in the West. That the East had survived perfectly well for thousands of years without these amenities was unimportant to Western company representatives and entrepreneurs, convinced, as they were, that the benefits they brought to Korea were of far greater use than the missionaries' pie in the sky. They rarely, if ever, alluded to the not inconsiderable profits they hoped to derive from their efforts.

The foreign community was brought together by virtue of being non-Korean and therefore, in the eyes of its members, obviously superior. But among the foreigners, there were distinct divisions—between members of the diplomatic corps and company representatives, between both of these groups and the missionaries, and finally between the missionaries of different denominations, all striving to shine the light of their particular faith into the darkness of that heathen land. Roman Catholics had held a somewhat tenuous foothold in Korea for over a hundred years, but they were eventually followed by Presbyterians, Methodists, Anglicans, and others. The battle for salvation of souls was waged alongside the battle for lucrative contracts; both were overshadowed by the battle for national sovereignty over a weak and divided nation.

Anxious to preserve a sense of its own superiority, the foreign community in Seoul remained close-knit, at least superficially, holding itself aloof from the natives. Since its members had few outside interests, a constant round of tea parties, soirees, dinners, musical evenings, and impromptu dramatics filled their hours. Occasionally, they undertook carefully arranged excursions to sights on the outskirts of the city, though never venturing too far into the unknown.

No matter what event was planned, Marigold became its center, as a novelty that might stave off boredom for a time. And wherever Marigold was, there was an attentive Sully at her side. And wherever Sully was, there was a long-faced Gifford, clearly upset by this usurpation of his friend's attention.

Marigold could as little understand Gifford's dislike as she did Sully's obvious predilection for her. To prevent Gifford from feeling he had lost a companion, she always tried to include him in whatever they were doing, but he would only sulk. Marigold had no conceit. She realized that she was a newcomer in a small community that, through her, sought momentarily to stay in touch with a world from which it was separated. Moreover, apart from the very young daughter of the British consul, she was the only unattached Western woman there. It was scarcely surprising that she should be sought out, and she had no reason to believe that she had changed from the more ordinary Miss Wilder of Barleigh. At first, she was regarded rather like a lemon, to be squeezed for information until everything about her was common knowledge. She could then be discarded as nothing but a lady missionary, denigrated for not staying at home to do her good works.

People soon learned, however, that Marigold Wilder would not be neatly contained in any box. She was a missionary, but she was also a photographer of some merit. She wasn't particularly accomplished in the arts, but she willingly played the piano so that others might dance. She had an open and inquiring mind; she listened, but she also had ideas of her own. And it wasn't long before the community decided that Miss Wilder might well be worth cultivating.

According to Edith Allen, the wife of Dr. Harold Allen, the United States representative, Marigold Wilder grew on you—no pun intended, for Mrs. Allen was not given to puns. Natasha Waeber, wife of the Russian envoy, stated flatly that Miss Wilder was one of those unusual women whose looks and manner improved on better acquaintance. In Mrs. Waeber's eyes, every woman except herself stood in distinct need of improvement, though few managed to actually achieve it.

Marigold loved Korea and, far more than the rest of the Western community, she enjoyed those few Koreans with whom she came into contact. She learned much more from them than she felt they would ever learn from her, for she was far more anxious to absorb their ways than she was to impart creeds in which she had no belief.

She noticed how clean and strong their teeth were and, after discovering they brushed them each day with salt, she began to do the same so that soon her own even smile sparkled as never before. She washed her hair in rain water that left it shining like polished copper. At first, she stoutly refused halmoni's ginseng tea, remembering Banning's distasteful reference to it as an aphrodisiac. But after watching halmoni steam the mysterious root, peculiarly shaped like a reclining female figure, and listening to this vigorous old woman's claim that a tiny portion infused in hot water could elevate blood circulation, increase energy, and impart a joy in living, Marigold decided to try it. It made her feel alive as never before. Her eyes shone, her cheeks took on color. Soon, a morning cup of ginseng tea became as much of an acquired taste as Ceylon or China—and she came to believe it was much better for her.

At Reverend Farquhar's insistence, she put aside full mourning and fashioned blouses from bolts of gaily colored Korean silk to wear with her dark skirts. The primary colors favored by the Koreans—and eschewed by Western women—became her favorites. And strangely, rather than clashing with her red hair, the combination was strikingly attractive.

Her bicycle had arrived and, despite everyone's remonstrances, Marigold insisted on riding about on her own instead of being carried around in a chair. She raced along in the clear air, free and independent, her glowing countenance contrasting with the pallor of the other ladies of the community who moved about in closed palanquins and avoided native air and natives alike wherever possible.

Marigold Wilder's figure, boater jammed firmly on flying red hair as she streaked down the hill from the mission, soon became a familiar sight in Seoul. Men stopped to stare, and children tore wildly after this new Pied Piper heading for the Han River. Marigold was drawn there by the ceaseless rhythm of the club-shaped laundry sticks being beaten against flat rocks. On the river's bank, women, completely concealed head to toe in the changot that hindered their motions ridiculously, were engaged in the never-ending labor of pounding the dirt from their men's white cotton clothing. The fact that no man was ever to be seen in soiled garments and that their white garb became soiled on first wearing constituted the worst form of forced labor in Marigold's eyes, yet these women carried out their Sisyphean task with considerable good humor. It was no simple business. First the garments had to be partially unsewn, then boiled in lye, rolled into hard bundles, and pounded on flat stones with heavy sticks. After being dried, the garments were beaten once again, this time with wooden sticks on cylinders until the cotton attained the shine of dull satin. Given the city's filth,

keeping their men's white clothing in spotless condition was an
arduous task, but the women labored without complaint, peering
out at Marigold from under their green changot with an avid curiosity, yet assiduously avoiding her. The incessant pounding of their
paddles was usually accompanied by the haunting refrain of
"Arirang," a song of rejected love. The repeated chorus echoed
everywhere:

> *Arirang, arirang, arariyo*
> *Arirang kogaero narul nongyo chuso!*

The women chuckled when they heard Marigold join in, but they
never approached her or allowed her to approach them.

In the end, it was her friendship with their children that won
the women over. Marigold gave the children rides on her bicycle
and allowed them to ring the bell, though she had reservations
about that game when the ringing never ceased. Then one day she
brought a bar of soap and a long Korean pipe down to the river. The
laundresses stopped their work to watch as she divided the soap
into small pieces, put one piece into a bowl of water, stirred it up,
then dipped the pipe into the water and puff—instead of smoke,
bubbles spewed forth!

The bicycle bell was forgotten. Marigold, they decided, was
some kind of magician. At first the children were content to watch
the bubbles gleam in the sun as they floated away in the crisp
autumn sky. Soon they wanted to try. They gathered around, taking
the pipe in turn, sometimes choking as they swallowed soapy water.
But it wasn't long before they learned to blow bubbles of their own,
bigger and bigger. Then it was the women's turn. Shyly, one by
one, they too tried. The soft soap literally eased Marigold into a
place among them. As she became accepted by them, the women
began to teach Marigold Korean words. In this way, they came to
understand one another.

But her greatest feat of magic had been her camera. She had

brought it down to the river one day to record the bubble blowing. The laundresses had immediately feared the contraption, but not so the children, who eagerly posed for her. When Marigold returned to show the results, there was immediate interest and no more resistance when Marigold asked the women to pose for her. But they had refused to remove their changot so that the prints merely showed a group of shapeless, bulky creatures, undistinguished by so much as an eyebrow. But this didn't seem to bother them. They knew exactly who was who, peering, laughing with pleasure, pointing at one, then the other, as though the likenesses were perfect. The pictures were a great disappointment to Marigold, who would have dearly loved to see the women beneath their voluminous coverings. Still, she felt she had gone far in winning their confidence.

So, too, did Reverend Farquhar. Even Gifford, who rarely spoke to her, was moved to comment, "I hope you bear in mind our purpose of moving the line of Christ's church further into pagan territory, and that you tell instructive stories from the Bible while you're doing all this larking around."

Gifford could never hide his dislike. He disapproved of lady missionaries in general and of Marigold Wilder in particular. She might have been somewhat redeemed in his sight had she spent more of her time on her knees, instead of tearing around the city on that awful machine of hers. Her religious observances were perfunctory, her performance among their few converts at the Naktong Community House was uninspiring.

"They wouldn't understand if I did," Marigold said. "They don't speak my language, nor I theirs—not yet, at least, but I hope I soon shall."

"I trust that when you do, you'll not forget why you're here," he scoffed. "Blowing bubbles and taking pictures is all very well, but a little more piety would better serve the cause."

"Come now, Giff," Reverend Farquhar protested. "Marigold's

getting along well, winning their confidence. Neither you nor I have had her success there."

"How could we?" Gifford observed coldly. "We're not allowed to so much as ask after the health of a man's wife, let alone talk to their women directly."

"That's just what I mean," Farquhar said, "That's it exactly." He turned to Marigold. "I'm convinced that hope for the Anglican cause lies in the conversion of women. Women have a natural piety about them, an inescapable wish to believe."

"Perhaps," Marigold agreed, lowering her eyes.

"Most of them accept the word as long as it is properly addressed," said Gifford, throwing an accusing look at her. "But that word must be carefully selected. I don't want my young people at our Nak-tong Community House confused by a discussion of Job's problems, as you did last week. Next thing I know, you'll be immersing them in the quagmire of Revelation."

"As a matter of fact, I was going to. I thought they might enjoy the imagery of Revelation," Marigold maintained.

"Then don't! They're likely to find it reminiscent of their shamanistic rubbish. It's to be avoided at all cost."

"But it might be a useful bridge for that reason," Marigold argued.

"Job and Revelation are the books of the Bible most likely to cause embarrassment. They are discussed, with some difficulty, in theological school. They are certainly not fit fare for heathens undergoing conversion."

"They've always been my favorites," Marigold objected. "I've felt great sympathy for poor Job sitting on his boils among the ashes."

"Only because he so foolishly rewarded his daughters, I'll be bound," Gifford sniffed, his pale hands flicking at an invisible speck on his immaculate black coat.

"But only when he realized their worth . . ."

"Come, come," Herbert Farquhar stepped in to restore the peace. "Perhaps it is best to stick to the simple stories, Marigold.

But that's not the matter at hand. Women are sure to listen to the word, if only they can be approached. And in this country, finding anyone to listen is no easy matter." His bulbous nose quivered. He gave a mighty sniff as he leaned forward to make his point. "I believe that women want to hear what we have to say. That is why I was so excited when you wrote asking to join our efforts. Gifford has done magnificently; I don't mean to slight his efforts for a moment. However, the task has been difficult at best. Korea is," Reverend Farquhar paused thoughtfully, "plagued by too many entrenched ideas and cults. This is a people ripe for conversion, yet conversion from what? Chinese Confucianism has been the backbone of this society for centuries; yet the vestiges of Taoism and Buddhism still remain, even though both have been discredited, and their monks and priests have been driven out into the mountains. And then there is shamanism, a pagan mixture of magic and animal spirits that certainly can't give what Christianity has to offer. Yet even when we explain the virtues of Christianity over other beliefs, we are still confronted with a society that doesn't believe deeply in anything." He shook his head. "After all my years here, our fold is dismally small. Gifford calls this a nation of inveterate nonbelievers, but," he beamed at Marigold, "I am convinced that women are going to be the key and that is where you come in."

"It's very difficult to convert women you can't speak to face to face," Marigold said hesitantly.

"But at least you can approach them," Gifford said. "We can't, even accidentally. They're only allowed on the streets after nightfall when we're prohibited . . ."

"But I've seen white-faced ladies riding in their palanquins in the daytime," Marigold put in.

"Those are not ladies," Gifford corrected.

"They look like ladies to me," Marigold asserted, annoyed by his brusque tone.

"Giff's right," Reverend Farquhar intervened. "Those are not ladies, Marigold. It would be unwise to make any overtures to them."

"Why?"

Reverend Farquhar's face flushed. "They're kisaeng, persons of doubtful virtue."

"They're prostitutes," Gifford stated.

"I'm not sure that's exactly right, Giff." Reverend Farquhar was clearly taken aback by the flatness of Gifford's assertion. "I think entertainers would be a better term. They are trained to please in the way of the geisha in Japan. They have greater freedom than others of their sex and do occasionally travel abroad in the daylight hours. But they are not," he concluded emphatically, "definitely not ladies."

Having disposed of the kisaeng, Reverend Farquhar continued in relieved tones, "So, Marigold, because we are restricted from speaking to women, you are our ace in the hole."

"I'll do whatever I can but . . ." Marigold hesitated, then added carefully, "I'd really like to do something practical, like nursing— or perhaps teaching English to girls."

"Unfortunately, the Presbyterians are already building a hospital, and the Methodists are founding a school for girls. We each have our sphere." He paused, then looked at Marigold. "There is something you can do. As you know, I have gained a foothold in the palace, since the king wants members of his court to learn English."

Marigold smiled in relief. "And you would like me to assist you?"

"Actually, I'd like you to have a special pupil of your own. Queen Min is a most astute woman. Some say—and I don't doubt it—that she rules Korea from behind King Kojong's throne. She has been quite anxious to have her own interpreter."

"The old lady wants to keep tabs on us," Gifford commented knowingly.

"Queen Min may be the queen of a backward, oriental nation,

but I think we should refer to her with greater respect," Reverend Farquhar admonished.

"But I don't speak Korean well enough," Marigold objected. "I doubt I'd be able to interpret anything so complex as negotiations at court."

"No, I didn't mean that," Reverend Farquhar laughed. "They would never trust a foreigner's interpretation."

"These people barely tolerate us," Gifford snorted.

Reverend Farquhar nodded. "Some of us may look down upon Koreans as uncivilized barbarians, but that's nothing compared to the way they feel about us. They call us sangnom—nonpersons."

"Perhaps if we were a little less patronizing, if we showed them that we like them," Marigold began.

Gifford gave a heavy sigh. "Here less than a month and already an authority on where we have failed." He rose with an air of finality.

"That's not it at all, Gifford. I was just making a suggestion—"

"Please, please!" Reverend Farquhar held up his hands to silence them. "We mustn't quarrel among ourselves. We have to work together."

"I'm sorry," Marigold said quickly. "I do want to help, and I still haven't found out what it is you want me to do."

"Allow me to explain. For some time now the queen has been sending one of her ladies to listen while I teach the king's courtiers. She sits behind a screen and is never seen—she enters the chamber before anyone else and leaves after we leave—and she is never allowed to speak to me, let alone see me, though occasionally she has been allowed to send me written examples of English for correction." Reverend Farquhar leaned forward. "The most exciting thing about this is that from her writing, I have the strong suspicion that she has leanings toward our faith. Naturally, I try to encourage these leanings in my response, but I have to be very careful. Both her letters and mine are closely scrutinized in the palace. I want to suggest to the queen that her lady be allowed to have private lessons with you, if you are willing."

"Most certainly," Marigold agreed immediately. "I think I can do it, and I'd enjoy it very much."

Reverend Farquhar rubbed his hands together in delight. "Grand! Grand! What a march we'll steal on the others," he chortled.

Gifford surveyed Marigold with a critical eye. "I hope Marigold can be trusted to ascertain this lady's beliefs and then carefully but consistently present our faith to her."

"I'm quite sure she can, Giff. Aren't I right, Marigold?"

"I promise to do whatever I can," Marigold agreed cautiously.

"And leave Job and Revelation out," Gifford persisted.

"I'll leave out whatever you want," Marigold responded amiably.

"Come now, Giff, I'm quite sure Marigold will do what's expected of her."

"For the Anglican cause," Gifford prompted.

"For the cause," Marigold reiterated. She decided to make an effort to avoid further argument with Gifford. While Sully seemed to enjoy her company more and more, as the days wore on Gifford was liking her less and less.

5

Seated on her imperial throne high on a dais, her dark eyes glowing in a white and impassive face, Queen Min appeared even more ominous and sinister than the two huge stone haet'ae—half beast, half reptile—that stood before the main gate of the walled Imperial City. Marigold had paused before those figures of mythical beasts, remembering Sully's description of them as symbols of justice, able to tell right from wrong, reputed to destroy evil.

"Those haet'ae are also alleged to have the rather fascinating, not to say useful, ability to eat fire," he had told her as they discussed Marigold's forthcoming audience with Queen Min. "They were put there when the palace was built to prevent it from ever catching fire—and at the rate things in this country go up in smoke, I'd say they've done a splendid job."

"Do they really think we're evil?" Marigold asked.

"The haet'ae?" he laughed. "I can't give them that much credit. However, if you mean that odd lot within the palace walls, I'd say they see evil everywhere—in us, of course, that goes without saying—but more especially in one another."

"Still, I suppose we are the interlopers," she mused. "And I wonder if we have that right."

Sully shook his head. "One day in the not so distant future, there won't be a corner of this earth that can be preserved from outside intervention—now that we have the ability to send messages to one another in record time with the telegraph and we have fast liners plying the oceans. The world is growing smaller all the time, don't you see, so what hope has any nation of remaining individual and apart from the rest? What right even?"

"I don't see why they shouldn't have a choice, though, about how they want to live. They shouldn't have change thrust upon them." Marigold's response brought a haughty look from Gifford.

"Anyone would think we were a bad influence, Marigold, instead of attempting to bring light to this benighted people," he said caustically. "You seem to believe that this Hermit Kingdom, as it calls itself, once had a choice and lost it with the coming of ourselves and a few other civilized beings. Nothing could be further from the truth. They've had the Chinese deciding their every move for centuries."

"True enough," Reverend Farquhar concurred. "And it's something you'd do well to remember when you meet the queen, Marigold. She's conservative, her own roots go back to China, so naturally she wants things to remain just as they are—Chinese to the core, governed by the tenets of Confucianism. King Kojong, on the other hand, is not at all opposed to progress, and he sees that as coming from Japan rather than China. They're the ones he encourages, much to his queen's objections."

"I thought he'd learned his lesson once and for all after that attempted coup by Kim Ok-Kyun and his group back in '84. Tried to bring in the Japanese but the whole lot came to a rather horrible end after their abortive uprising. Did it at the inauguration of the new postal service—set back that service another fifty years at least. Brutal business. Wiped the lot of them out, families and friends, sent the women off as slaves. Left the queen and her pro-Chinese faction clearly in the commanding position; at least, that's the way I read it," Gifford stated flatly, glancing over at Sully as if for confirmation.

"They have slaves here?" Marigold was horrified.

"Only women," Gifford said, carefully selecting the largest piece of tea cake.

"What do you mean, *only* women?" Marigold's voice was edged with anger.

"It's true what Giff says," Sully concurred. "Women are sold and used for labor mostly. Usually they come from the lower classes, but in the case of the women Giff mentioned, these were women from yangban—noble—families. One can only guess what use was made of them."

Reverend Farquhar lifted a warning hand. "I really don't think we should discuss this in front of Marigold."

"Sorry," Sully muttered. "It's just that Marigold seems to think we're the bad influence around here, and I rather thought we couldn't leave her with that impression."

"They say a people's civilization is gauged by the treatment accorded its women," Gifford pontificated, holding out his cup to Marigold and waiting expectantly as she poured him another cup of tea. "Two sugars," he reminded. Then, as she went to sit down, he decided, "I believe I will have another piece of teacake after all."

"Slavery," Marigold muttered, half to herself as she passed the plate to Gifford. He helped himself to the last piece. "I suppose every country has its own kind of slavery."

"True, Marigold. Just look at the Americans," Reverend Farquhar commented. "And that was during the so-called age of enlightenment." He sniffed to emphasize his point as he reached into his pocket, then looked around helplessly. "What has that halmoni done with the cigarettes?"

"Probably been smoking all of them," Gifford said without attempting to reach for the cigarette box that was plainly in view. It was Marigold who picked up the box, opened it for Herbert Farquhar to take a cigarette, and then lit it for him.

"There's a dear," he approved, sitting back and puffing contentedly. "I don't know what Giff and I would do without you."

"I rather think halmoni's cooking has improved lately," Gifford agreed with an unusual compliment. "The meat at dinner was quite edible."

"Better not ask what kind of meat it was, then," Sully warned. "I have it on good authority that dog is the only viand here that can be counted on to be halfway decent."

"I can assure you it wasn't dog," Marigold said crossly.

Reverend Farquhar smiled. "It's so good to have Marigold here to take all the problems of the household off our shoulders. It leaves so much more time for the ministry."

"Perhaps you will also have time to help women from being treated as beasts of burden," Marigold said, gathering together the teacups.

"I do what I can by example more than outright preaching," Reverend Farquhar said. "It's far better. You see, they don't think of their way as wrong, but once they are shown the example of how our Western women are treated, they will learn." As Marigold went to pick up the tray, he cautioned. "Now, Marigold, that's too heavy for you. Halmoni will get it."

"I'm a lot younger than she is," Marigold responded, carrying the tray off in high dudgeon. She knew Herbert Farquhar considered himself the kindest of men. He and Gifford were simply acting as they had been taught, which was all very well. Still, it gave them little right to criticize Korean customs as barbarous.

"There's terrible dissension in the palace, and it seems to be getting worse," Reverend Farquhar was saying as she returned. "You don't have to understand what's being said to know that. You sense it immediately. You'll find out," he said to Marigold. "You'll see what I mean when you go."

"I've never met a queen before," Marigold said hesitantly. "I'm not sure I want to—not if she is the one responsible for having her own women sent into slavery."

"They weren't her women," Gifford put in. "They were Kim women—from the Andong Kim clan."

"They were women, still, and she is a woman."

"She hates the Andong Kims with a passion, but there are women she holds in high esteem—like her witch of a mudang, and those she keeps to guard that dimwit son of hers," Sully said. "How they manage to survive—relying on kisaeng apothecaries with no training who use primitive methods of sticking needles into people in a feeble attempt to cure them—is beyond me."

"Don't they ever ask your advice, Sully?" Marigold asked.

"I've been called in to treat gentlemen of the king's court once or twice, but that's only when all else has failed. Makes my work more difficult. If they were to die at that juncture, it would be my fault, no matter what had been done to them previously."

"But if saved, you'd be a hero, Sully," Marigold pointed out.

"Not necessarily. If you save a life in this country, you're responsible for the well-being of that person from then on. That life rests and remains in your hands, so to speak. It's rather a case of damned if you do and damned if you don't, if you'll pardon my language. So I'm just as glad not to be on call at the palace and not so sorry never to be let near, let alone look upon the ladies of the court, especially the queen. Her person is sacred."

"You'll never meet another queen like Queen Min, that I can promise you, Marigold," Reverend Farquhar agreed with another mighty sniff of his beaked nose.

"At least we hope she won't," Sully put in.

"Suppose she doesn't like me," Marigold said doubtfully.

"The queen's nunchi will size you up. Nunchi is a kind of sense, like our common sense or the French *bon sens*. Here people live by their nunchi. Usually, in this structured society, it is the way the weaker take eye measure of the stronger and then proceed accordingly. In our case, it's the way Koreans perceive us. As you can see, it's not particularly logical, which is what makes it so difficult to deal with. And with nunchi there are no second chances, the judgment is final. You'll know right away if Queen Min approves of you."

"You're filling me with trepidation," Marigold responded, but Sully only laughed.

"Anyone who careens through these tumultuous streets and alleys on a bicycle the way you do, weaving your way through A-frames, bullocks, and carts, old men tottering before you, children tearing after you as though you were the Pied Piper, is totally incapable of trepidation."

Marigold had laughed with Sully, but when at last she had passed the huge haet'ae guarding the palace gate, she wasn't so sure. She felt the sweat on her hands, the pounding of her heart as she hurried through the Imperial Gate and into the walled city for her interview with its queen.

"Must I go?" she had pleaded at the last moment, her courage almost deserting her.

"It's absolutely essential," Reverend Farquhar had replied. "Anyone—especially any foreigner—who is to have contact with a member of the court retinue must have the approval of either the king or the queen."

"I don't understand why you or Gifford can't get that approval for me."

"We're men. No man—and certainly no foreign man—may set eyes on the palace ladies. It's one case where you have the advantage over us."

Marigold grew thoughtful. "Is it true that those who live inside the palace never leave it?"

"Quite true, except for very rare occasions such as the Kurdong." Noting Marigold's puzzlement, Reverend Farquhar explained, "That's the grand occasion when the king goes out to sacrifice at the Yi dynasty ancestral tombs."

"Heathen practice," Gifford sniffed. "But necessary, since it's perhaps the only chance his subjects have to see that he really exists."

Reverend Farquhar nodded. "He's surrounded by his thousand bodyguards. Otherwise, he lives in complete seclusion."

Proves how well liked he is," Gifford noted.

"At least the Kur-dong gives people a chance to know their money's not going on a pig in a poke," Sully put in irreverently. Then he leaned forward conspiratorially, "Did you know that they may not so much as pronounce his name! And we talk about Queen Vicky being reticent about coming forward! Kojong could teach her a thing or two."

"You're sounding very disrespectful, Sully," Gifford protested. "You never used to talk like that."

"Only half the lies the Irish tell are true, Giff," Sully commented with a grin and sly wink at Marigold.

She desperately wished that Sully, with his easy manner and broad grin, were beside her as she stood in the Imperial Throne Room gazing up at Queen Min.

From Marigold's vantage point, looking up the flight of carpeted stairs leading to the throne, the queen seemed enormously tall, perhaps in part because her sleek black hair was looped into huge braids raised some twelve inches or more on either side of her head and held in back with an enormous gold hairpin. Through these braids was linked a band of gold. Gold, too, was woven into her bright red *chima* beneath which two small feet clad in white stockings and gold slippers were clearly visible. Her hands, however, were completely hidden under the huge gold cuffs of her green *chogori*. This short coat was held in place by a gold sash bound across her chest.

All of this was awe-inspiring, but it was the queen's face, a mask of pure white relieved only by the dark expressionless slits of her eyes, that was most fearful.

She made no sign to Marigold to advance closer, nor did she indicate she might sit. Indeed, there was no chair to sit on in the enormous hall, nor even a cushion. So Marigold stood and waited, glad that the floor at least was warm under her feet. If this were her queen, she knew she should curtsy, but she was unsure what etiquette demanded. Instead, she bowed, a low bow but not, she hoped, an obsequious one.

This, however, drew an immediate and sharp rebuke. Marigold raised herself immediately, wondering what she could possibly have done wrong. Her alarm was assuaged somewhat by a soft voice that came from someone almost hidden in her post behind the queen. She was clad in the dark blue chima and lighter blue chogori that indicated she was a lady in waiting.

"Only royal princesses permitted to bow to Her Majesty. You not royal princess. Bend head only." The awesome creature on the throne bore entirely too close a resemblance to the Red Queen in *Alice in Wonderland.* As she bowed her head, Marigold hoped that no cry would ensue, demanding it be lopped off.

"Your hair very strange. What happened?" she was next asked.

"Happened to my hair?" Marigold quickly reached up to see whether it had fallen, but all seemed in place. "There seems to be nothing wrong with it."

"Very strange color. We not like women with strange color hair."

Marigold flushed. "There is nothing I can do about it, Your Majesty. Red is the natural color of my hair."

"Spirits not like women with hair color of fire. Very dangerous, I think."

"I cannot see what the color of my hair has to do with my ability to teach English," Marigold said angrily, adding as an afterthought, "Your Majesty."

Marigold knew enough Korean to realize that the translator had considerably softened her words. Even so, the queen had caught her tone and studied her with greater interest.

"What is your name?"

"Marigold Wilder. I am an Anglican missionary . . ." she broke off, feeling this statement was somehow incorrect and finished lamely, "I work with Reverend Farquhar."

Her response was whispered in the queen's ear before the next question was put to her.

"How old you are?"

It was not a question Marigold had expected, but she replied frankly, "Twenty-seven."

"You married woman?"

"No, Your Majesty."

"Why you no marry?"

To say no one had ever asked her would not be correct, Marigold realized, remembering John Keane. She didn't suppose women in Korca waited to be asked; it was probably all arranged. She remembered Sully's remark the first day she had arrived and echoed that in her reply.

"There is a time to marry. Mine has not come."

"You no find husband because of your hair," the queen said in satisfaction.

"Many women in my country have red hair and they marry," Marigold countered.

"You come to Korea to find husband," the queen said knowingly. "Perhaps this reverend not mind you so old and have ugly hair."

Marigold drew herself up angrily. "I came here because Reverend Farquhar was a friend of my father, who was also an Anglican clergyman. When my father died, I . . ." Unexpectedly, Marigold's eyes filled with tears. She swallowed before continuing, "I wanted to continue his work."

The queen made a sharp response. Whereas her previous remarks had been phrased more hesitantly by the translator, this, perhaps because of the peremptory tone in which the queen delivered it, was promptly translated. "You never mention this work if you allowed to come to palace. You give promise to say nothing of this spirit of yours. Christianity, bah! Vulgar superstitions, very false. Not mention ever in my house. You promise that!"

"Gladly," Marigold said with some relief.

Marigold noted the surprise on the translator's face. Then she noticed the first sign of interest on the queen's previously impassive face as her response was translated.

"Why gladly? All missionaries talk nothing else but this . . . this God of theirs."

"I really don't know enough to talk about religious matters," Marigold explained frankly. "In England, women do not become priests. They just do practical, helpful things around the church."

"Like what?"

"Making tea."

It was a simple response, perhaps made all the more impressive by its truth. Quite suddenly, Queen Min laughed, though the sound was more like a short, sharp bark than a laugh. It was evident that she seldom laughed from the astonishment on her translator's face, followed by visible relief as she said, "Queen Min say you may teach English in palace. When you come you ask guard take you Hamhwa-dang. There you give your lessons."

Marigold smiled. She thought she saw a smile flitter across the face of the palace lady who had been translating, but there was no responsive gleam from the queen. Her closing retort was, "Lessons only in English language, not other things."

"I understand," Marigold said, inclining her head. Queen Min's nunchi had examined her and, it seemed, she had passed that crucial test. "May I ask who will be my pupils?"

"Me," said the translator, shyly yet sadly, speaking for herself for the first time.

Marigold wondered how she stood in this lady's nunchi, for while the translator had had ample opportunity to examine her, her position behind the queen had allowed Marigold little more than an occasional glimpse of her.

"You know my name. May I know yours?" Marigold asked, wondering about the sadness in her tone.

"I am the Lady Chu-sun."

6

"How goes it, Marigold?" Reverend Farquhar asked, both hands curled around his breakfast cup of tea.

They sat at the table wearing coats over their warmest clothes, for the icy Siberian winds were sweeping down on Seoul, howling around their Western house on the hill, which was less equipped to protect them from the cold than the hovels below.

"Yes, how *is* it going, Marigold?" Gifford seconded. His nose was red and chafed with a cold he had had all winter and been unable to shake off. His humor was not improved by the fact that Marigold had not caught one. "Do you feel you're getting any results with this Lady—*Lady* . . ." His emphasis was derisive.

"Lady Chu-sun," Marigold supplied. "She's coming along wonderfully well—she's very quick and adept. She speaks quite fluently now. Her reading is good, her writing is improving. Still a few problems with grammar and syntax. But, goodness knows, our language is not the easiest. Its rules are certainly difficult to explain. But I only have to correct her once—she never repeats a mistake. She's remarkable, quite remarkable."

Gifford sneezed violently, took out his handkerchief and blew his nose. "All of that and you still haven't answered the question. Is this *Lady* Chu-chu . . ."

"Lady Chu-sun," Marigold corrected coldly.

He ignored the correction and went on in a muffled voice, "Is this person now fully converted to our faith?"

"I believe that she is," Marigold answered cautiously. "Though if she is, I claim no credit."

"But of course the credit is yours," Reverend Farquhar put in enthusiastically.

"No. We rarely discuss matters of religion so I cannot be sure."

"You mean you've been with her all these months and yet you're not sure of where she stands?" Gifford said disdainfully.

"It could be dangerous for both of us if I were sure of her stand on Christianity, Gifford," Marigold said.

"On Anglicanism," he corrected. "But that, I thought, was the purpose . . ."

"Now, now, Giff, I know how anxious you are, but don't worry," Farquhar intervened. "Marigold's handling this slowly and carefully. I know how it is behind the palace walls on the king's side, and I understand the intrigues are even worse in the queen's court. What counts is that our young colleague has made her presence there accepted. Anything beyond that must be approached cautiously; with no more than a whim or whisper in the right quarter, one can become *persona non grata* overnight."

"I appreciate your support and your faith in me," Marigold said. She looked up at the clock and rose from the table. "I must be going."

"I really think you should take a chair this morning. The weather's quite severe," Reverend Farquhar called after her.

But already the front door was closing. When next they saw Marigold's mufflered figure, she was bicycling past their front window.

"I don't understand why she doesn't get pneumonia," Gifford said savagely, blowing his nose again.

"She shouldn't be bicycling in these winds—shouldn't be out at all. It's odd, though, this dreadful climate almost seems to suit her."

"I hope something is going to come of all of this, for while Marigold's devoting the majority of her time to these English lessons,

I'm unable to properly instruct her in our work," Gifford complained, "or to get the full benefit of her assistance."

"She's the only foreigner who has entry to the queen's court, Giff. It's even been suggested she may photograph the king. That's a coup for us," Farquhar said. "I am quite satisfied something will come of it."

"Has she said anything to you, then?"

"Not in so many words, no. But I've noticed changes in Marigold over these past few months, decided changes."

"They're probably converting her to shamanism."

"Giff! That's unkind."

"Sorry. I just meant that what we want are changes in the people at the palace, not changes in our own people."

"I'm not sure that change in us all, at some point or other, isn't to be sought after. Change is said to be the only thing we can count on," his superior countered gently.

"I should like to be able to count on Marigold's help on my spring trip into the interior, but from the way things are going, I doubt that will be possible. She lacks fervor. You saw that just now in the way she talked of this pupil of hers. If it had been me, as soon as I learned of her positive inclinations toward our faith, I'd have been pounding the lesson home day and night, but Marigold admits she's done nothing." He sighed, though even his sigh was muffled by his cold. "She is such a disappointment. She needs so much training in the proper way to spread the word."

"I appreciate your concern, Giff, but I think you worry too much. I know you're enthusiastic, but sometimes slowly but surely is the way to go."

"I was taught that determination to succeed is the only way." Giff sniffed in aggrievement.

"Of course. But Marigold is determined, too."

"Far too determined in some things," he glowered. "Like the way she hogs Sully's attentions."

"Oh come now," Farquhar laughed, then grew serious. "You

know, I have grave doubts about Marigold accompanying you on this trip of yours, Giff. A journey up the Han by sanpan will be hard. There are few if any resources. I don't know that it's the thing for a young Englishwoman."

"I thought she came over here to make herself useful. She has an abnormally strong constitution," his hoarse voice quivered, as though this were a personal affront. "You said, yourself, that she can withstand the rigors of this climate better than either of us."

"I don't know; it could be dangerous. Apart from the dirt, disease, mosquitoes, lack of conveniences, the people in those parts have never seen a Western woman before. Their reaction would be unpredictable at best. I just don't know. Have you spoken to Marigold about it?"

"I have. And all she said was that it would be a good chance to get some interesting photographs. Photographs! I ask you. As though we're out here to take photographs. The conversion of the heathen is serious work—I've tried to explain that to her time and time again. And this journey into the interior is our chance to reach people who are relatively unspoiled by exposure to the mishmash of other faiths—virgin territory, so to speak."

"Mmmm. I see." Farquhar's expression was reflective. "Tell me, Giff, why do you dislike Marigold so?"

Reverend Farquhar had previously made oblique references to Gifford's hostility, references that had been studiously overlooked. This was the first time he had directly confronted Gifford and, as he did so, his eyes fell on his assistant, measuring him up in Korean nunchi fashion. Gifford may not have recognized that, but he was disquieted nevertheless. He shrugged, awkwardly, not daring to acknowledge the reasons behind his antagonism.

"All I see is that she's making a nuisance of herself—hanging around, not really accomplishing anything. It's not so much that I dislike her as that I consider her inept."

"Come now, of course you do! You're pleasant and charming

with Sully, with me too, for that matter, but with Marigold you're critical and impatient."

"I don't like people who push their way in where they're not wanted. Look at the way she traipses around after Sully. It's unbecoming, to say the least."

"I rather thought it was Sully who was following Marigold around," Farquhar observed mildly. "They're quite a pair. Have you heard the amusing piece Marigold composed based on the rhythm of the laundresses' paddles? Sully's doing the words. Imagine Sully, writing lyrics!" He laughed, then caught sight of Gifford's look of disgust, his eyes narrowing. "Don't tell me you're jealous, Giff?"

Gifford's face paled. "Of course I'm not. How could you even suspect me of such a thing!"

"It wouldn't be so odd. Marigold's not just the only single young woman around but a very attractive one to boot."

"Oh, you mean . . ." Gifford's face cleared. "But I don't care for her in the least, most certainly not in that way."

"That's certainly good to know, for there's the matter of propriety. If you're to be alone in one another's company for weeks at a time . . ."

"Surely you can trust my conduct to be above reproach!"

"If I thought otherwise, I'd never countenance the plan, though for the life of me, I still can't understand your insistence on Marigold's going along with you."

"I shall need someone. Sully had originally agreed to come, as you know, but now he tells me he can't."

"And you don't want Marigold and Sully to be left here alone together, is that it?"

"That's not it, at all. You're twisting my words," Gifford snapped excitedly. He suddenly developed a paroxysm of coughing. Once quelled, it seemed to have a calming effect, for when he went on, his voice was quite steady. "It's simply that she could be useful. She speaks the language fairly well and you, yourself, have said that it is helpful to make contact with women in spreading the word."

Farquhar nodded "She does speak better Korean than either of us, though she's been here only a short time—so I hardly think it just to call her inept. And she has adapted to people, custom, and climate in a way neither of us has. She could be a wonderful representative of the church, if only . . ." he broke off abruptly.

"If only what?" Gifford demanded.

"If only she had come here for that purpose of her own volition. I have the strong suspicion that she's doing all of this for her father."

"But I thought he was dead."

"He is. That's why I'll never get her to admit it. I think she has some notion that this is what he would have expected of her." Reverend Farquhar pushed back his chair and rose from the table. "Ah, well. I suppose I should simply be thankful she is here, rather than questioning her motivation." He stared out at the icy terrain. "This ought to be a good day to stay home and work on my sermon. I just hope halmoni can get a decent fire going. That last batch of wood we got in was awfully green. Marigold's promised to speak to the woodman about it."

Reverend Farquhar wasn't the only one who thought the weather too severe. As she entered the palace grounds, Marigold noticed that even members of the king's bodyguard were huddled together inside the walls, seeking shelter.

She made her way back to the women's quarters, stopping to remove her shoes in the inner courtyard and then gratefully stepping onto the oiled patina of the ondol floor. She admired the Korean system of heating by a series of flues that ran from the brick and stone firebox in the kitchen beneath the floors of an entire building; it was certainly far preferable to the English hearth that roasted one side of the room while leaving the rest draughty and cold. Curiosity led her to thoroughly examine the system; she found the stone flues were covered with a cemented layer of limestone. The floors themselves were overlaid with a covering of strong oiled paper, whose glossy yellow-tan surface gave the impression of well-varnished wood. The result was a tight and virtually draught-proof floor-covering through which no smoke could penetrate to damage and discolor the white-papered room partitions.

Thoughts of the outside world never followed Marigold beyond the orchid door. That was one of the delicate phrases—perfumed screen and jade courtyard were others—Chu-sun used to describe the women's quarters. The strict separation of the sexes had, at first, seemed abhorrent to Marigold, but in a land where women were totally subservient to men, having one's own prescribed living space was an advantage.

As usual, Chu-sun was waiting for her. She sat at a low table, her papers neatly stacked in front of her. With the arrival of winter, they had moved from the great Hamhwa-dang, the audience reception hall for foreigners, to a small room in the rear of the Konchong Villa, the queen's domestic quarters. That Marigold was allowed to enter this building at all was a mark of the trust she had engendered. She much preferred the intimacy of their new quarters to the great hall.

Chu-sun and Marigold had become good friends, but it had not always been so. The lessons had begun stiffly, formally, with frequent interruptions from various and sundry court ladies, especially the mudang in her tall red hat, flashing a false smile from her gold-capped teeth, and on occasion, even the queen herself.

"What are you doing?" she would demand, seeming surprised to find Marigold there at all.

"I was speaking of the different uses for humor, wit, satire, and sarcasm, ma'am."

Noticing the queen's frown as Chu-sun translated, Marigold explained further: "Humor throws light on human nature, wit requires intelligence, satire accentuates morals and manners, and sarcasm, sometimes referred to as the lowest form of wit, is to be avoided for it so often inflicts pain."

"This childish. Lessons are supposed to instruct on serious matters," the queen admonished.

"To understand a people, it is important to know what makes them laugh," Marigold explained.

The queen thought this over for a moment, then waved her hand for them to continue.

"Paksa, even Her Majesty begins to listen to you," Chu-sun whispered in admiration after the queen had departed.

"It is not necessary to call me teacher. Call me Marigold, for we are friends."

Chu-sun nodded. "We are friends. It is good to have a friend. But here we rarely call one another by name but rather by relationship."

"If that is so, then I should call you paksa for I am learning so much from you," Marigold responded.

Still, their friendship had been slow to ripen. At first Chu-sun would not speak except in reply to a direct question and this she did in the fewest words possible. Their meetings were so formal at the beginning that Marigold found English lessons at the palace almost as difficult as scriptural lessons had been at the mission. The ice had been broken when Chu-sun caught sight of the jade ornament Marigold wore around her neck.

"A kokok!" she exclaimed. "Where did you find it?"

Marigold reached to touch the piece Mark Banning had given her for luck. "A friend—an acquaintance—someone I once knew for a very brief time, gave it to me."

"She *gave* it to you!"

"He," Marigold corrected.

"He!" Chu-sun was even more surprised. "Who is this he who gives such a gift?"

"His name is Mark Banning," Marigold replied reluctantly. She hadn't spoken his name since Prim's engagement. She didn't want to now, yet she thought of him more than she wanted to admit, even to herself.

"He must think a great deal of you, this Mark Banning, to give you such a piece. To give a kokok is to give good luck. These decorated the ancient Silla crowns. They are very hard to find. Where did he get it?"

"He said Queen Min gave it to him."

"The queen!" Chu-sun was astonished. "But who is this man that the queen would give him such a piece?"

"I dare say it wasn't true," Marigold said. "He boasted a great deal. He was not an honest man."

"What a shame," Chu-sun said. "I kept hoping . . ." she broke off.

"Hoping what?" Marigold prompted.

"That you, too, would have someone in your life."

"Mark Banning never meant anything to me."

"Yet he gave you the kokok—and you wear it."

"I wear it because it is a pretty piece. I cannot claim that it has given me good luck."

"But it will, I know it will," Chu-sun affirmed.

"We shall see. Now back to our lesson."

In seclusion behind the orchid door as they sat on cushions on the warm ondol floor, their friendship flourished. One day, Marigold brought along her copy of Shakespeare. They began with *Romeo and Juliet,* with Chu-sun as Juliet to her Romeo. Chu-sun, who read quite fluently by this time, experienced great difficulty at certain points in the play. Her many hesitations, Marigold felt, were not brought about so much by problems of pronunciation as by her emotional reaction to the play's content. And from the way Chu-sun shielded her face with the sleeve of her chogori when Marigold questioned her, it was soon obvious that this was an emotion of a personal, even painful nature.

When they reached the parting scene, Chu-sun could no longer hide her tears, and Marigold closed the book.

"I am sorry. I should have chosen something else, a comedy.

When I first saw you, I guessed you had some great sorrow in your life."

"How could you guess?" Chu-sun demanded through her tears. "I try so hard not to show it."

"Because of the sadness in your eyes, in your voice." And though she did not say so, Marigold had long pondered that phrase *you too* when Chu-sun had mistakenly believed that Mark Banning was her lover. "I have known great sadness, though not for the same reason."

"Then this Mark Banning really was . . ."

"No, of course not," she interceded quickly. "I have never suffered from lost love. I have never been in love."

"Never?"

"Never. I was speaking of the loss of my father."

"I think, perhaps, this Mr. Banning who gave you such a gift, I think perhaps he loves you. Now you are far away, lost to him, so it must be he who is sad."

"You're a romantic, Chu-sun, but don't waste your tears on Mark Banning. He would never understand lost love. If he loves anyone, it can only be himself. But your lost love . . ."

"Mine is not a lost love," Chu-sun emphasized. "Though Tuk-so is far from me, he can never be lost to me."

"Where is he, this Tuk-so?"

"He has been sent to the far north, to Wonsan, as assistant to Min Tae-jon, one of the queen's brothers."

"That must be an important posting, then, since I understand the most powerful positions throughout the country are held by the queen's relatives."

"It may be, but Min Tae-jon is a cruel man. He is given to horrible debacles—opium . . ."

"Debaucheries," Marigold corrected gently.

"Horrible debaucheries—opium, drunkenness, women," Chu-sun shuddered. "I hate to think that Tuk-so should be near such a fiend."

"He did not want to go, then?"

"No. Tuk-so did not mind for he thought as you, that this was an important posting, that it would give him a chance of advancement. That was how it was presented to him. I did not agree. I saw that they wanted us parted. But that made no difference. There was nothing either of us could do about it."

"Was it known you were . . ." Marigold broke off. It had been on the point of her tongue to say lovers, for she was sure they must be, but that seemed an unapproachable subject, given the strict separation of the sexes at the court. Instead, she carefully finished, "Was it known that you were friends?"

Chu-sun studied Marigold's face. She found such compassion and kindness there that all the precious secrets she had kept from everyone poured from her lips.

She began with stories of her childhood in the Diamond Mountains, of the impression the missionaries' visit had made upon her.

"You are so fortunate in being able to openly acknowledge your faith," she told Marigold. "I can say nothing, except in my own heart. But I know it is your God who has given me strength. Before I had nothing and no one to turn to. It is He who has seen me through much bitterness. And it is to your Lord of love and justice that I pray to keep Tuk-so from harm and to bring him back to me. That Lord has been beside me in my happiness and in my tears. Though I must keep my faith secret, I would die rather than be forced back to the nothingness of shamanism."

This simple but profound statement of belief, and the fact that Chu-sun was willing to die for something she had turned her back on, filled Marigold with shame. It was not her lack of faith that shamed her, but her hypocrisy in coming to Korea, draped in the trappings of that faith.

"I am not allowed to say anything," Marigold replied, hiding behind her promise to the queen.

"I know. It is good of you. I am often asked whether you try to convert me and I can say with all honesty that you do not."

"And this Tuk-so of yours, does he believe as you do?" Marigold asked.

Chu-sun shook her head. "Not yet, but I believe he is not entirely convinced that the precepts of Confucianism must be followed to the letter. Of that I am glad. It is a beginning which shows a sense of his open mind."

She flushed at the remembrance of the time when she had made that discovery, then went on to describe the kantaek and her sister's selection as the wife of Prince Yi Kang.

"She had never seen him," Marigold questioned in dismay, "and her eyes were actually sealed shut so that she could not?"

"It is the custom," Chu-sun said simply. "Many girls have a terrible shock when the wax sealing is removed, but Chun-mae was lucky. Prince Yi Kang is handsome and very, very . . ." she clenched her fist, thrusting it back and forth, "how do you say it?"

"Virile, I think," Marigold murmured hesitantly, with considerable embarrassment.

"Chun-mae's husband is very virile. She will have a baby."

"You must congratulate her on my behalf," Marigold said.

Chu-sun shook her head. "Not until the baby comes. Queen Min does everything to stop it from happening. I fear greatly for my sister. At the birth she will be attended by Duk-hwa, the king's apothecary kisaeng. It is no good. My sister is small. She will have difficulty. Though I do not like Duk-hwa, I hope she alone is with Chun-mae when her time comes. I greatly fear the queen will offer to send assistance. That could be very dangerous for both my sister and her child."

"But, I don't understand. If the queen offers to assist . . ."

"She assists with poison—she has done it before with the king's concubines who were in labor. Poison in the ginseng sent to give strength."

"Chu-sun! That is a very serious allegation. I can't believe that the queen would . . ."

"She would stop at nothing. She discovered about Tuk-so and me

. . . through Chilyongun, that evil mudang who is with her always. One day, I was summoned to the queen's presence. She told me she would have Tuk-so sent to Wonsan, that I would never see him again. She said I was twice shamed, for allowing a man to . . ." again she made that thrusting motion with her fist, "virile me?"

Marigold flushed. "No—virile is an adjective. *Ravish,* perhaps, or *make love*—those are the verbs."

"I see," Chu-sun said seriously. "Then for allowing a man to ravish me and for being so foolish as to think that I could keep it secret from her. She said she had known about it since the night of Chu-sok, when first it happened at the Chogyong pavilion."

"You met there by prearrangement?"

Chu-sun nodded. "I was overjoyed to be alone with Tuk-so, though I admit that when it happened, I did not like being taken by force . . ."

"You can't mean Tuk-so raped you," Marigold gasped.

"Rape? What is this rape?"

"Rape is an ugly act, when a man gives in to uncontrollable urges and forces himself upon a woman and violates her."

Chu-sun considered for a moment. "Perhaps it was so."

"I don't understand, Chu-sun. How could you possibly love a man who did something like that?" Marigold was thoroughly shocked.

"I loved him before. I loved him after. I didn't like the way it happened that first time, but afterwards, it was different. Then it no longer hurt. I was glad to be, what was it—violated. I proudly admitted that to the queen. I was sure she would not keep at her court a woman who had fallen, but she just smiled. Her smile was far worse than her anger. I waited and then—then she told me this awful thing. . . ." As Chu-sun's shoulders began to shake with sobs, Marigold put her arms around her.

"Chu-sun. Chu-sun. I'm here. I am your friend. Friends help one another. If there is anything I can do, you have only to tell me."

"There is no way anyone can help," Chu-sun sobbed.

"Please, don't cry," Marigold pleaded.

"In Korea everything cries—the streams, the grass, the bells. Even the spinning wheel cries. Tears cover our land. Even love may be told in tears. You must not forbid me to cry."

"I forbid you nothing, you know that. Only tell me, what is this terrible thing? How could it be any worse than being forced to leave home, to hide your faith, to come to a court that is a virtual prison, to be separated from the man whom you love? What can be worse than all this? Has your life been threatened?"

"In a way," Chu-sun said, wiping her eyes. "You see the queen said that Tuk-so and I had been watched each time we met at the Chogyong to . . . to violate each other . . ."

"Make love to each other, Chu-sun," Marigold corrected softly.

"Make love, then. The queen said she knew everything—everything we had done. She said she was . . . she was pleased by my—my performance. I was to be congratulated. I cried out that I was not a kisaeng, and she said she was glad I was not, for otherwise I would be no good to her. She told me she had been searching for a yangban lady with the right blood lines for royalty, one who was pure and yet skilled in the arts of love."

"What on earth can she mean?" Marigold gasped.

"She wants me for her son," Chu-sun said simply. "She told me she had that thought when first she asked me to come to the court as her scribe. She said she liked me. I reminded her of herself when she was young—intelligent and unafraid. She knew with the proper training that I would have the ability to rule through her son, just as she does with the king. Oh, no words could have hurt me more!"

"Prince Sunjong is young."

"He is not so young. But because he is weak in mind, he appears young. He thinks mostly of food, little else. She has been warned he may never have the ability to get a woman with child unless she finds one who can help him with the task. She is determined that the royal line must pass through her son. She told me she has been searching everywhere for the right one for him, one of noble birth yet one who should be able to help him—help him violate, ravish . . ." Dully, Chu-sun shook her head. "I don't know how to say it . . . make love?"

"That would not be making love but helping him to consummate the marriage," Marigold supplied in an equally dull voice. "That is awful, Chu-sun. Simply awful. I will do anything I can to help you, though I don't see what I could . . ."

"Nor do I, unless . . ." Chu-sun looked up, suddenly hopeful. "If I could get a message to Tuk-so, if he could know what is planned, somehow, with God's help, he would stop it. In his eyes, as well as in mine, we are married."

"Then when he hears the announcement of the wedding . . ."

Chu-sun shook her head. "That won't be made until after it has taken place. Chilyongun, the queen's mudang, will hold a kut to decide the auspicious day. But it will probably not be soon. The queen told me she is in no hurry. She must gradually get the crown prince used to the idea, and I . . . I must be trained in the duties of a queen that will one day be mine."

"Is that to make sure there is no possibility that you . . ." Marigold broke off, thinking her question inappropriate. However, Chu-sun divined her thoughts, "I am not pregnant. The queen had me examined by Duk-hwa, the medical kisaeng. She was very rough with me, and very coarse. Now, more than ever, I dread this awful woman bringing Chun-mae's child into the world."

"Perhaps Sully—Dr. Sullivan from the British Consulate— could be called in for his advice, particularly if there may be difficulties. He is a good doctor, kind and gentle, too."

"He makes love to you, this Dr. Sullivan?" Chu-sun asked factually.

"Oh, no! Of course not!" Marigold couldn't hide her shock at the suggestion.

"But if he does not make love to you, how do you know what he is really like? How do you know he is kind and gentle?" The question was put so ingenuously, it made Marigold realize that women in this secluded and segregated society thought nothing of discussing matters that no Englishwoman would ever admit to thinking, let alone mentioning. Chu-sun, whom Marigold had known for only a few months, had raised matters she would never have discussed with her sister, Primrose, or her best friend, Harriet Keane.

Recognizing Chu-sun's sincerity, Marigold tried to be equally frank in her response. "If it were necessary to judge a man by the way he made love, a single woman could never draw any just conclusions about him."

"Just so," Chu-sun agreed. "You seem to have some harsh conclusions about Mark Banning, though he has not made love to you. Perhaps, if he did . . ."

"It serves no purpose to discuss things that will never happen," Marigold interceded swiftly, flushing at the idea. "In the matter of Dr. Sullivan, others have vouched for the fact that he is a good doctor and I have been in his company enough to know that he is also kind and gentle."

"But if we are alone with a man, it is for the purpose of making love. When Tuk-so asked me to meet him alone, I knew what it must mean. Yet you meet this Sully for what reason?"

"We talk or play the piano or go for walks or dine together. We do not ever spend the night together."

"But it is possible to make love in the daytime. And you are alone."

Chu-sun was so clearly intrigued that there was no turning away from the subject.

"Only occasionally. Usually Gifford is with us—Gifford Partridge. He is Reverend Farquhar's assistant."

"Reverend Farquhar has a nice voice," Chu-sun observed. "I never saw him, but I used to listen to his lessons from behind the screen. This Gifford has a nice voice too?"

"His voice is all right, but to be honest, I don't like him at all. However, Sully's a dear. In the matter of your sister's confinement,

I should be glad to ask his advice. I know he would gladly offer his help when her time comes."

But Chu-sun shook her head vehemently. "No man could be there, no man could see a woman at such a time."

Marigold knew it would serve no purpose to point out that some man had already been very much there to produce the condition, or that it made sense to have someone—male or female—with the proper training in attendance. Chu-sun was adamant.

"I would offer to come myself, though I would be of limited help, I'm afraid," Marigold concluded lamely.

"I think no foreigner would be allowed at a royal birth. You are my friend, but, I am sorry to say, you are also sangnom, nonperson." Chu-sun put out her hand to touch Marigold's arm. "I only tell you because I think you understand."

Marigold nodded. "I am very fond of you, Chu-sun. I think you know that I will help you in any way that you want me to."

Pensively, Chu-sun nested her chin in her hands. "Do you think you could get a message to Tuk-so for me, secretly, so no one would know?"

"He is in Wonson, you said. Where is that?"

"It is an important port on the northeast coast, some one hundred and fifty kilometers north of the thirty-eighth parallel. I know for I have studied the map so many times. From my home it is not far, but from here it is a great journey—an impossible journey for me, since I could never get permission to leave the palace."

"Then write a letter. I will send it to him for you."

Chu-sun shook her head. "No letter would ever reach him, even if you sent it. The message must be carried to him, told to him personally, and I know of no one I would trust to do that except you. And even for you it may be impossible."

"Perhaps not," Marigold said slowly. "Gifford has asked me to accompany him on a mission along the north branch of the Han River. Possibly I could persuade him to go as far as the coast."

"Could you? Would you? Oh would you really, paksa?"

Seeing her friend's face light up, Marigold said, "I can't stand by and see you forced to marry that fat, witless prince. One way or another, I promise to get your message to Tuk-so."

"The queen must know nothing."

"She'll learn nothing from me, though there is the matter of obtaining official permission to make the journey." Chu-sun's face fell and Marigold leaned across the table to pat her hand encouragingly. "But we'll find some way around that. Perhaps our planned itinerary need not specifically mention Wonsan."

Chu-sun smiled in relief. "He will come to me. I know Tuk-so will come."

7

Christmas came and went. The consular group joined the missionary community to celebrate the holiday in an appropriately religious manner. After paying homage where it was due, the missionaries were free to join the diplomats in their commemorative feasting and social merrymaking. It was a Christmas like the others that had preceded it; resplendently robed figures celebrating before their respective altars, while resplendently uniformed diplomats presided over the receptions at their respective legations.

As usual, Mrs. Gardner bemoaned the lack of holly for the plum pudding. Her name suited her, for she was an inveterate gardener. Mabel Gardner spent a great deal of time mourning the demise of the plants in her garden, blaming a variety of culprits: rigors of the climate or the clumsiness of her servants in trampling seedlings she had so carefully nurtured. The loss of a plant could never be laid at her own door, for she maintained that plants knew when they were being handled by a true green thumb and flourished accordingly.

When not digging her fingers into the earth, Mabel Gardner was usually to be found with pruning shears in hand. And when reluctantly forced from her garden by consular or social functions, she spent much of her time surveying her surroundings with an intense yet removed look in her pale, watery eyes. Sully confided to Marigold that this was a sure indication of mental pruning; whatever caught her attention as unruly or unkempt provided fodder for the click, click, click of her imaginary shears. The beauty of this pruning was that it did not have to be confined to plants and trees; people, too, could benefit from the trim of her snipping blades.

Happily, not everyone in the community was privy to this habit of hers. It would have infuriated Natasha Waeber, possessor of an extensive wardrobe of large and often quite outrageous headgear, who was under the impression that Mrs. Gardner greatly admired the range of her millinery taste—flowers and fruit in season, nesting robins in the spring, fall foliage, even the holly missing from the pudding; in fact, what Mrs. Waeber vainly mistook for a look of unspoken adoration in the eyes of the drab little wife of the British consul was, to Natasha, Mabel's only endearing quality.

The round of Christmas festivities was invariably followed by a dismal lull when members of the small community, tired of one another's constant company, looked around for a fresh source of amusement to relieve their ennui. This year the solution came from Dr. Allen, the American minister, who announced that he was expecting a group of visitors from the States.

"Who are they and when do they arrive?" Mrs. Waeber demanded. She didn't feel particularly comfortable with the Allens. He had been a missionary before he became the American consular representative and had retained the sort of religious fervor that she detested in that ever-growing community. Diplomatic flair ran counter to missionary zeal in the eyes of the wife of the Russian representative. Trust the Americans with their puritanical streak to choose a zealot, she thought contemptuously. She had only met one American who did not fit the mold. Her heart quickened at the thought of that man, but he traveled alone; he was unlikely to be among Dr. Allen's prospective visitors.

"It's a trade delegation, led by Mr. Andrews of the Department of State, a decent enough fellow and unlike some I've met, a good Christian," Dr. Allen announced.

Natasha Waeber's distinctively beautiful face fell; Mr. Andrews and his delegation did not sound at all promising.

"They still haven't indicated the number," Mrs. Allen complained. "Our home is turning into a hotel. It really is too bad. You can hardly call it a home when, at a moment's notice, you have to put up dozens of people you don't know and often don't even like."

"But where else can they stay?" her husband interposed. "We could hardly expect Americans to stay at those inns run by the Japanese for their own people. Besides, Edith, as diplomatic representatives, it is expected of us to host our traveling countrymen."

"Of course it is. God knows I understand Edith's feelings, but we all have to put up with it. The worst one Boris and I ever had to entertain slept in his boots and drank vodka at breakfast," Natasha put in.

"Ah, yes, but of course that was a Russian," Edith Allen commented decisively, as though that explained the aberration.

"Boris and I are also Russian." Natasha Waeber arched her long, slim neck in high dudgeon. "And I can assure you neither of us sleeps in our boots."

"No, no, of course . . . I didn't mean . . ."

Mrs. Waeber was quite convinced that Edith Allen did mean, but she generously let her off the hook with, "Don't worry, Edith, we always help one another out." A trade delegation sounded less than exciting—a lot of earnest men talking business over meals, all out to grab contracts for the highest dollar. Still, it would be a change, and Mrs. Waeber decided her contribution to their visit would probably be a small supper. In the unlikely event that any among the visiting group should prove either dashingly attractive or disgustingly rich, a dinner party of lavish proportions, easily capable of eclipsing any entertainment Edith could put on, might be in order.

"You know you can always count on me," Natasha purred. "What about you, Mabel?"

Mrs. Gardner's rapt gaze was fixed on Dr. Allen's white hair, which he always allowed to grow beyond his collar in the cold weather. She did not answer.

Edith Allen had noticed Mabel staring at her husband before

with that look of transfixed admiration. She didn't like it. Mousy ones like Mabel Gardner, who were so quick to point a finger at others needed watching themselves. Mabel never stopped talking about the way Natasha Waeber had carried on with that man from San Francisco last year, when she should be looking out for that young daughter of hers, Mrs. Allen thought sententiously. Little Miss Gardner was only fifteen but just look at the way she was making up to that nice Dr. Sullivan. Of course, he only had eyes for Marigold Wilder. Everyone knew it was only a matter of time before he'd propose. She looked forward to that—a wedding would make a nice change.

Of course, poor old Gifford Partridge would feel cut out when that happened; he and Dr. Sullivan had been inseparable. Mrs. Allen wondered whether Marigold Wilder had stolen Gifford's heart as well. His poetry used to be quite pretty; it rhymed and described clouds and trees. Now it didn't sound quite proper, especially the way he uttered it in that dismal, soulful tone. Mrs. Allen didn't altogether approve of Marigold Wilder, finding her something of an exhibitionist—the way she was always rushing around on that bicycle of hers and setting up that infernal camera whenever the mood struck her. It wasn't the sort of behavior to be expected from a lady missionary and a clergyman's daughter to boot. Of course, there were always rebels among the children of the clergy.

While Mrs. Allen was vainly wishing that the trade delegation would consist of men who did not drink liquor, chew tobacco, or smoke those disgusting stogies, Marigold was wishing that she could make the decision on where the king would sit and how he would pose for his portrait.

She walked around the Kunjong-jon, or the Hall of Government by Restraint, as the main throne room of the palace was aptly called, cupping her hands to frame different viewpoints. She had to select her position with care for she would not be allowed to move or utter a word once the king entered the room.

She could hardly complain about these restrictions, for she was fortunate in being allowed to take the photograph at all. Her requests to photograph the palace ladies had been firmly denied by the queen. She was told that no Korean lady had ever had her picture taken; it was considered unseemly. A kisaeng, a professional woman, perhaps, but not a lady. Marigold interpreted this denial as further proof of the nonexistent status of palace ladies, since the queen's repugnance of photographic reproduction did not extend to her husband, or to her son, for that matter.

The queen had asked or, rather, commanded Marigold to take a photograph of the ruler of Korea with the crown prince by his side, but not, as Marigold at first thought, for his Korean subjects; instead the picture was intended for Queen Victoria. This was clearly another of the queen's maneuvers to cement her son's right of succession by announcing it to the world's most powerful monarch. It would have been far more apt, in Marigold's opinion, for Queen Min to have sent a photograph of herself. But she had learned to temper her words with care. Even though Marigold had been ordered to stay beneath the black drape and not reveal herself to the king, this was still a signal honor that might, eventually, put her in a better position to aid Chu-sun.

Selecting a viewpoint at last, Marigold firmly planted the legs of the tripod, unlatched the rosewood camera case, extended the leather bellows of the camera to their fullest, and then fixed the cumbersome piece on top of the tripod. Next she pulled the dark cloth over her head to look through the camera's aperture at the throne where the king would sit for his official portrait. Seen through the lens, the image was upside down and indistinct. Since she would not be allowed to look upon the king in person once he arrived, Marigold carefully adjusted the camera, choosing the top of the throne as her focal point.

Marigold studied her Wynne's infallible actinometer, carefully noting the time the paper sample took to darken before adjusting the lens aperture of her magazine camera. Though she had brought several extra packs of Bennett's instantaneous gelatin dry plates with her, she didn't expect to have the opportunity to use them, since she was unable to leave the black canopy. The six holders in the magazine would have to suffice; each held two plates, allowing for twelve exposures.

Hearing the shout of "His Majesty" and the resulting commotion from the bodyguard and Officers of the Household who preceded him, Marigold pulled the cloth carefully around her. At last the king came into view. She could see his upside-down image through the lens. He seated himself, with a good deal of precision, upon his throne. A sure sign of insecurity, Marigold thought, remembering that it was said Queen Victoria never looked back to see whether there was a chair behind her when she sat down. She knew her royal personage would never be allowed to fall.

Even though his satin slippers barely touched the floor, King Kojong looked regal enough in his rich crimson brocade. The gold embroidered plastrons on his chest and shoulders and the richly ornamented manggon over his topknot, visible through the black tall-crowned horse-hair kat, all contributed to his stature.

As soon as he was seated, a quarrel began as to where Prince Sunjong should stand. The queen pressed for him to be placed by the right side of the throne, while the king insisted he should stand behind it. Marigold far preferred the latter arrangement, but she had been forbidden to speak. The queen won out. The prince's squat form came suddenly into view as he struck a pugnacious pose beside his father.

At a word from the queen, the photography session began. As each plate was used, it had to be reversed, emulsion side out, before the holder could be slipped behind the ground glass of the camera lens; after the exposure, the plate was put back, emulsion side in. The holder was turned over, and the process was repeated with the accompanying plate; then the holder with its exposed plates was replaced in the magazine and the next taken out.

Knowing she was likely to have only one opportunity to photograph the Hermit Kingdom's monarch, Marigold took extra care to avoid exposing the same plate twice. She carefully counted the exposures and the plate holders as she worked.

This maneuver meant she had to reach forward in the dim light beneath the cloth. All went well until the sixth holder got stuck in the wooden grooves of the magazine. Unable to leave her draped covering, Marigold struggled but could not make it budge. Through the lens she could see Prince Sunjong squirming in irritation while the king's eyes were fixed on her groping hand.

She stepped forward in an effort to force the plate holder from the magazine. She was so occupied with releasing it that she was unaware she had trodden on the edge of the black drape. At last, she felt the holder give. She stepped back triumphantly, but that step inadvertently pulled the drape from her head. She stood up to find herself doing the forbidden: looking directly on the person of the king.

He examined her curiously as she grappled to tug the cloth back into place. But it was no good; the damage was done.

"Cover your face," the queen commanded.

One look at the queen's expression as she called an immediate halt to the sitting informed Marigold of her abysmal failure. Her attempts to cover her face with the black draping only produced an even stronger glare of disapproval. The queen swept from the room with her son in tow. His face was a mask of contempt mingled with glee at Marigold's predicament.

Marigold was relieved to hear the king order his courtiers to leave. Then, pointing an imperious finger in her direction, he commanded, "You will stay."

When the courtiers had gone, he signaled her to approach the throne.

Marigold remembered to bow only her head.

"Here, yobo," he commanded.

Her lowly estate emphasized by this form of address, Marigold moved forward hesitantly.

"Your Majesty."

"You are mudang?"

"No, a missionary," she corrected, before realizing this was probably the same thing in his eyes.

"You have husband?" he demanded.

"No, Your Majesty."

"Come. Come."

He beckoned impatiently in quick, irritated motions until she was so close that she could have touched him. Then he leaned forward, grasped a handful of her hair, and tugged it!

She gasped in astonishment and pain. The king was equally astonished.

"It's real!" he exclaimed.

"Of course my hair is real," was her aggrieved response.

"Why you make it that color?" he demanded.

"I didn't make it that color. I was born with red hair."

The king frowned. "I've never seen before. It is strange, very, very strange."

He scrutinized her from the top of her head to her black leather buttoned shoes before pronouncing enigmatically, "Maybe sometime I call on you to come massage my legs."

"Massage your legs?" Marigold was astounded. Had he confused missionary with masseuse?

But the king was unable to expand upon his request, for at that moment an urgent message arrived from the queen, ordering Marigold to the Hamwha-dang. Lady Chu-sun was to perform her first official act as interpreter and her teacher must be there to see that it was properly carried out. Reluctantly, the king dismissed Marigold, and, with great relief, she hurried away.

A screen had been placed behind the queen's throne, at the back of which Marigold found an anxious Chu-sun kneeling. This arrangement indicated that the visitor she was to translate for must be a man.

Marigold fell to her knees beside her friend. She had had little time alone with Chu-sun since the New Year. Then the air had been filled with the odor of burning hair as the clippings and combings of an entire year were burned to prevent demons from entering the palace grounds. The last time she had seen her, Marigold had found Chu-sun stuffing a straw doll with coins.

"It's our custom," Chu-sun explained shyly. "I will throw the doll over the palace wall and whoever picks it up will take away my sorrows. I don't believe, of course, not now I know about your God. Still, habit dies hard. Besides, if I did not do as the others do, I would be called to account."

"May I do one, too," Marigold had asked, to Chu-sun's astonishment.

"You! I thought you would say it was silly. Besides, you never talk of sorrows."

"We all have sorrows. How wonderful it would be if a doll could really carry them away."

Marigold had touched Chu-sun's hands to comfort her then, just as she did now behind the screen.

"I'm so nervous," Chu-sun whispered.

"I'm not. I am satisfied you're quite ready." Marigold pulled a cushion beneath her knees. She still could not kneel for very long on a hard floor. "I seem to be hiding away all day. I really think it ridiculous that men and women can't even look at one another." And she went on to describe the abortive portrait-taking session she had just experienced in the Kunjong-jon. Chu-sun listened with interest until Prince Sunjong's name was mentioned. Then her face fell.

"I don't want to hear about him."

"Don't worry, Chu-sun. We've requested permission to journey up the Han River. I don't see any reason why it won't be granted."

"I see a hundred reasons," Chu-sun mourned. "When the queen hears of it, and she hears of everything, she'll guess the purpose."

"The purpose is for Giff to preach and for me to take photographs. She probably won't appreciate either reason, but it's unlikely she'll suspect anything else." Marigold touched Chu-sun's hand again by way of reassurance. "There's no mention of Wonsan in our request."

"The city lies on the coast, far over the mountains."

"Don't worry. I'll get there somehow and when I do, I'll make sure Tuk-so hears everything from my own lips. You mustn't worry."

"It is selfish of me, I know. My difficulties are small. Chun-mae's time is close, the pains will begin any day. I've warned her to refuse anything that the queen may send to relieve this, but I can't be sure that . . ."

Chu-sun broke off, suddenly lifting a finger to her lips. She had heard the queen's entourage approaching long before they entered the room. Next came the sound of the queen's steps as she climbed the dais to her throne, then that of a chair being pulled forward for the visitor, a signal honor.

Chu-sun knelt forward expectantly, while Marigold leaned back, exhausted from her ordeal in the Kunjong-jon. At the visitor's first words, both their attitudes changed.

"Your Majesty. It is a great honor you do me in granting me this audience. May I say how delighted I am to be back in the Land of the Morning Calm."

Chu-sun nodded. "A good voice, strong and clear," she murmured. Her assurance returned, she sat back on her heels and began to translate. That same voice, however, shattered Marigold's composure. She was now the one who leaned forward, tense and agitated.

"You may sit down, Mr. Banning," said the queen.

Chu-sun threw an astonished glance at Marigold. "Can this be *your* Mr. Banning?" she whispered.

The look of astonishment on Marigold's face confirmed the conjecture as she said under her breath, "It is Mark Banning, but he's by no means mine."

"Before I do, would Your Majesty do me the great honor of accepting this small gift. The box is inlaid with lapis lazuli and comes from Persia. Its contents you may find amusing. Perfume from France that I hope Your Majesty may find as intoxicating as I do. The pearly white face powder is, as I remember it, of the variety you prefer. The small container of black paste is kohl, used by Indian ladies with great effect to emphasize their eyes. The lip rouge is from my own country, as well as a cream developed by Harriet Hubbard Ayer, who claims it has great rejuvenating powers for the complexion. Your Majesty has no need . . ."

"My Majesty has no need of flattery, Mr. Banning."

"It is impossible to flatter so great a personage as Your Highness. The world has two great queens, both of whom I have had the privilege to meet. One possesses an empire on which the sun never sets; however she is but a figurehead. Bills require her signature, but her ministers decide which bills she will sign. There is, however, a queen on the other side of the globe who unobtrusively rules a difficult and divided land with her own power and wisdom. Such a lady it is impossible to flatter."

"It is not I who rules Korea, but my husband." The statement contained no rebuke.

"Modesty is of little use to a beggar, but how it shines in the great, ma'am."

Marigold restrained a contemptuous snort with difficulty.

"We are pleased you have chosen to return to our land." Marigold had never actually heard the queen sound pleased, yet in this instance her tone matched her expression. "Why did you not come with the trade delegation from your country that is expected soon?"

"I travel alone," he said simply.

"You arrive first," she observed. "You wanted to be here before them."

"Your Majesty is astute, as I observed earlier."

"What is the true purpose of your visit?" the queen demanded.

"Gold, ma'am," Banning responded succinctly.

"You flaunt your intention of robbing us of our gold?" she rasped.

"Not robbing you of it, Your Highness, but rather bringing it to light."

"We have a saying that when a family has gold, outsiders come with money scales."

"And it's your good fortune they do, ma'am. Korean gold is rich and pure, but it does no good hidden in the dirt—it cannot be seen, let alone enjoyed. You have power, but power needs wealth behind it. With gold at your disposal as well as brains, who knows what you may accomplish. There, I believe, we can be of great help to one another."

The queen laughed. "Why should I need you? At a word from me, a thousand men, ten thousand will work themselves to death to find gold for me."

"A most unproductive way of going about it, if I may say."

"And what is your *productive* way? Some new American invention, I suppose."

"I have a nose for gold, Your Majesty."

Though the reply was simple, Chu-sun had wrongly translated *nose* as *knows*. Fearing this mistake would cause confusion, Marigold pointed first to her own nose by way of correction and then, when Chu-sun still did not understand, she rephrased it aloud.

"Have a scent for gold."

A pause followed this prompting, before Banning reiterated, "Exactly, I have the scent for gold, an inherited scent. My father came from England to California, following the scent of gold. He found gold, and plenty of it."

"And filled his own pockets."

Banning laughed. "For a time, yes, but only for a time. It was soon taken from him in bars and dance halls. A fool and his gold soon part company."

"But you seem no fool."

"That is why I come to you. Because, Your Majesty, if I may make so bold, is no fool either and can judge the merits of a sound business proposition."

"Which is?"

Banning paused, as though reaching a decision, before going on. "In exchange for exclusive rights to search for gold for one year, after which I may stake a claim, Your Highness will be entitled to forty-five percent of all my findings."

"How can I be sure of my share?"

"Your Majesty's spies are everywhere. I should expect to find them highly placed among the men I select."

She laughed. "I think we understand one another well, Mr. Banning. I think, too, my share is not enough. Fifty-five is preferable."

"Your Majesty drives a hard bargain. The territory, it is true, is yours, but I take all the risks. Tigers abound along the river, I'm told, not to mention other hazards. I think, perhaps, to keep both of us honest, that a fifty-fifty split is in order."

The queen considered for a moment.

"Do you guarantee to make me rich?"

"I guarantee to make you rich as long as I make myself rich. I'm not the sort of man to take on an endeavor that uses my energy and resources without adequate return."

"Then you don't believe in laying up your treasure in this mythical heaven your countrymen are always preaching about?"

"Hell, no!" Banning laughed. "I can't abide that missionary twaddle."

"Neither can I. It corrupts my people. I think we understand one another, Mr. Banning. When do you begin?"

"As soon as the spring thaw ensures the river is navigable, but I'll set about assembling men and equipment immediately."

"I wish you luck."

"Thank you, Your Majesty. Your wish will bring luck to both of us."

Marigold sat motionless after the queen and her visitor had departed from the hall.

Chu-sun looked at Marigold for approval and finally asked timidly, "Was the mistake really bad?"

Marigold aroused herself. "Of course it wasn't. You did well, very well. I should have said nothing."

In truth, Marigold wished she had let that one slip go. When Banning had paused, she feared he had recognized her voice, yet she doubted he would have gone on to reveal his intentions quite as clearly if he had.

"So that is Mark Banning. His voice was nice, but I regret his unkind words about missionaries. He would never have said them had he known you were here."

"Perhaps he would," Marigold said, remembering that Banning had said as much to his cousin in her hearing.

"I fear he is not a believer. That is why you don't like him."

"He is not a believer. But I dislike him for other reasons. He almost ruined my sister."

"What did he do?" Chu-sun asked.

"He made her like him too much. She followed him to London, expecting he would marry her, something he had no intention of doing."

"But you told me she is married and, like my sister, she is to have a child."

"She married Mark Banning's cousin."

"So it was all right in the end."

"No thanks to Mark Banning."

"I think you don't like him the way I don't like the crown prince."

Marigold nodded. "I don't like him, but at least I have no fear of being forced into marriage with him."

"And yet he is not like Prince Sunjong. He seems outspoken, but honest. I wish I could have seen what he looked like. Explain him to me. Is his appearance as formidable as his voice?"

Marigold had to agree. "I suppose so. He has dark hair, his eyes are dark, too. I think his mother is Latin . . ."

"From Rome?" Chu-sun asked.

"I meant she's either Italian or Spanish—not English like his father."

"That is bad?"

"In the eyes of some people," Marigold said, remembering Algernon's unkind remarks.

"In yours?"

"I don't like Mark Banning, but the fact that his mother is not English has nothing to do with it."

"I think he may be tall," Chu-sun hazarded. Marigold nodded.

"It is good for a man to have long legs," Chu-sun approved.

"Speaking of legs," said Marigold, anxious to turn away from the subject of Mark Banning, "what could the king have meant when he said he would call on me to massage his legs? I've heard that he suffers from arthritis, but does he think photographers have some special healing power in their hands?"

Chu-sun giggled, covering her mouth with her hand as she did so. "That is how he calls for his concubine or his kisaeng when he is in the mood for—don't tell me, let me remember." Brows knit, she paused, then finished triumphantly, "when he is in the mood to ravish. But it was naughty to say that to you."

"It was very naughty," Marigold agreed tersely, now that she understood the full import of the remark. "How could he possibly suggest such a thing!"

"You are a foreigner; worse yet, you are a woman, so, in the opinion of the king, you are nobody," Chu-sun explained factually as they slipped on their shoes and left the Hamhwa-dang. And as they walked away together, she observed, "This Mr. Banning is a clever man. He knows the power lies with the queen and he has made her his friend. He must be formidable. I can tell that her nunchi approved of him." Then she asked ingenuously, "I wonder if one day Mr. Banning may call on you to massage his legs."

"Chu-sun!" Marigold reproved. "He wouldn't dare!"

"He seems to me to be the kind of man who would," Chu-sun observed thoughtfully.

8

Natasha Waeber decided to give a large dinner party for the trade delegation after all, replete with whiskey from Scotland, beef from Kobe, and beluga caviar. Speculation was rife among Seoul's foreign community that the real reason behind the planned lavish entertainment was Mark Banning's return to Korea.

"I wonder how that Mr. Banning dares to show his face here," Mrs. Gardner said in disapproval. "The way he carried on with Natasha last time, I fully expected Boris Waeber to put a bullet through his head."

"Through his back, don't you mean?" Her husband commented, not raising his eyes from the papers just delivered in the diplomatic pouch.

"Boris may not be noted for his valor, John, but I still think Mr. Banning is testing his luck."

"Boris is a cuckold and an outright coward. If anyone had made advances to you the way Banning made advances to Natasha, he'd not be around to tell about it, let alone to return to the trough."

Mabel Gardner flushed at the idea of such advances and, too, at the idea of her husband doing anything as gallant as fighting for her honor. However, she found the expression *returning to the trough* a trifle crude, and she told him so.

"Any other way I put it will offend you even more, Mabel," her husband responded dryly. "We all know what they're up to. Boris does, too, but as usual, he's closing his eyes to his wife's peccadilloes. This time, though, he may be making a serious mistake."

"I've never seen Natasha so taken with anyone," his wife agreed with avid interest despite her disapproval. "If Boris doesn't watch out, she'll be leaving the country with him."

"Rumor has it Banning's going to stay on for some time, and what I'd like to know is why."

"For Natasha, of course."

Her husband shook his head. "The man's too shrewd for that. He may act the romantic, he may even be enjoying the fruits, but there's more to his visit than that. I've heard he's had an audience with the queen. I'm sure he didn't discuss Natasha Waeber with her, but what actually passed between them has to be a matter of sheer speculation."

"Or how," Mabel Gardner commented, mentally clipping their tabby cat's bush tail into neat symmetry.

Her husband knew that look and his irritation evidenced itself in a terse, "What do you mean, Mabel, 'or how'?"

Reluctantly she withdrew her gaze from the unkempt feline tail. "I just meant that the queen doesn't speak English and Mark Banning, as far as I know, doesn't speak Korean. I wondered how they discussed anything at all."

John Gardner folded the diplomatic papers with deliberation, got up, and unexpectedly kissed his wife on the cheek, making her jump in agitation.

"What on earth's the matter with you, John."

"Nothing, dear, but you've given me an idea."

"And what is that?" she demanded suspiciously, dreading that all the talk of the romantic involvement between Natasha Waeber and Mark Banning might have given her husband unpleasant notions about exercising his marital rights at that hour of the day. Even the best of men were such animals.

"Marigold Wilder's been teaching some woman at the palace to act as the queen's interpreter. You know how friendly Sully is with her. I'll get him to find out what she knows about all this."

"Excellent idea, John," his wife breathed in relief.

It may have been an excellent idea, but, though Sully ascertained that Marigold was clearly aware of the audience Queen Min had granted the visitor, she refused to disclose more than that.

"I can't betray a confidence," Marigold stated flatly.

"Not even if you know something that could be of value to your country?" Sully eyed her curiously. "Who are you protecting— Mark Banning?"

"Of course not. There's nothing you can say about that man that's any worse than the opinion I already have of him."

"He's a braggart and a Lothario. Leaves nothing but dissension and gossip in his wake. Breaks up families, runs roughshod . . ."

"You don't have to tell me, Sully. I know all about that first hand."

"You *know!*" Sully's face reddened in anger. "But surely he hasn't been making advances to you! Tell me if he has and I'll horsewhip him. I'm no Boris Waeber. If he has the audacity to . . ."

"*I* have absolutely no concern on that score," Marigold interrupted, "so neither should you."

"But you just said you knew about his behavior first hand," he persisted. "You can't blame me for surmising he's been up to some of his shenanigans."

"He was. Not here, though, but in England."

"You knew him in England?"

She nodded and went on to tell him of Mark Banning's visit to Barleigh and, making some effort not to damage her reputation, of her sister's disastrous London visit.

"The man's a blackguard, an absolute blackguard" Sully fumed. "He shouldn't be allowed in civilized drawing rooms, let alone welcomed."

"From all the talk about Natasha Waeber's entertainment tonight, he seems to be the star attracton," Marigold commented acerbically. "They are friends, I take it."

"Friends! She's absolutely besotted by him."

"I'm sorry for that. He uses everyone to his convenience."

"I'm glad you're wise to him, Marigold. Natasha can do as she damned well pleases. All that matters is that I can be sure of you."

Sully was such a dear, it was difficult for Marigold to object to his proprietary attitude toward her. She knew he liked her, but since she never thought of marrying, she was probably the only person in their circle who did not expect him to propose. Even if she had, she certainly did not expect a proposal to come at Natasha Waeber's party.

The reason Sully was able to find the courage to speak lay in the fact that the guest of honor failed to appear at the appointed hour. The group gathered in the drawing room was little perturbed, however, for everyone was growing vociferously merry on generous refills of Scotch, much to Mrs. Allen's chagrin. Only Natasha Waeber, hovering anxiously in the hallway, seemed concerned.

Sully had consumed far more than his usual two glasses before dinner; he was flushed and exceptionally garrulous. Though he joked with the visitors, his eyes remained on Marigold. At last, as though plucking up courage, he came over to her. Gripping her arm, he whispered hoarsely, "I must talk to you."

Alone with him in the dining room, Marigold noticed his flushed cheeks.

"Do you feel all right, Sully?" she asked.

"Never better!" He swayed slightly.

"Maybe you should sit down," Marigold suggested then, glancing at the long table, set with Natasha's finest silver embossed with the czarist crest. "I know Natasha's concerned about the beef being overdone, but I suppose we really shouldn't seat ourselves before the others."

"Damn the beef!" Sully exclaimed, pulling out a chair and unceremoniously seating Marigold there, rather than himself. It was so unlike Sully that just when she realized he must have had too much to drink, to her horror he flung himself down on his knees, took both her hands in his, and looked up at her with a soulful sigh.

"Sully!" She tried to loosen his hold without avail.

"Marigold! Marigold! My dear Marigold. My own Marigold! Marigold for . . . for . . ."

"Marigold's for grief and jealousy and despair, Sully. Take your pick, but do get up off your knees."

But Sully was not to be put off. "My own Marigold!" he repeated. "Marry me, Marigold."

Behind them a voice repeated, "Marry me, Marigold. Mmmmm, that certainly has a nice ring to it."

It was hard to know who was more surprised by the unexpected interruption.

Marigold spun round in her chair, and though Sully still held fast to her hands, perhaps for support, he abruptly sat back on his heels.

"Banning!" Sully bellowed in clear distress. "You haven't the slightest sense of decency."

"Not my strong suit, I must admit," Mark Banning observed, selecting an olive from a dish on the table and popping it into his mouth while he looked from one to the other. His face, as he nodded to Marigold, was completely expressionless.

"Miss Wilder, we meet again."

She returned the merest inclination of her head, her cheeks flushing at the thought of the ridiculous picture they must make. She wished Sully would get to his feet; she wished she could walk away; she wished Mark Banning was at the other end of the earth.

Banning turned his attention to Sully.

"It is Dr. Sullivan, isn't it?"

"It is," Sully's voice now sounded wounded.

"I rarely forget a face, though I had to think for a moment. You're so horribly shrunk since last I met you." Banning smiled. "Or is this a Toulouse-Lautrec impersonation?"

Angrily, Sully scrambled to his feet.

"If you had any decency, you'd realize this isn't the sort of thing a fellow walks in on, or if he does, he makes himself scarce pretty damned quick."

"Apart from having already admitted that I've no great regard for anything as abysmally dull as decency, my hostess asked me to meet her here. I presume she didn't realize you had engaged the room. You left no sign on the door indicating that it was being used for . . . for a proposal of some sort, I take it." He looked from Sully to Marigold. "Given the respectability of both of you, I take it to be one of marriage," he added ingenuously.

"You'd know little enough about respectability," Sully exploded.

"Must admit that does rather stand in my book alongside decency," Banning agreed. "Still, is it known that you two are alone here? Miss Wilder, as I remember, puts great store in single young ladies being chaperoned at all times. I've never been a chaperone, but I'm willing to try anything. Carry on, Dr. Sullivan."

"Your audacity knows no bounds, Mr. Banning. But then, it never did," Marigold snapped.

He smiled. "Now audacity's something I rather like. I don't mind laying claim to that at all, Maggie."

"How dare you!" Sully said to Banning, then he commanded Marigold. "Don't talk to the man. How dare he compare our meeting here together to his own entanglement with our hostess. It's an insult after the way she's been panting all evening, waiting for his arrival like a dog in heat."

"Sully!" Marigold cautioned angrily. "That's unfair to Natasha, as well as unkind."

"And to me, Miss Wilder, but I'm willing to overlook it," Banning affirmed calmly. "Natasha asked me to come in here because we have a lot of catching up to do. She's anxious because I was late, but I'm glad to see you've put the time to good use." Banning carefully selected a triangular piece of toast and spread it with black caviar. "Maybe I'd better go and forewarn Natasha that the room is occcupied."

"I rather think it's her husband who should be forewarned,"

Sully shot back at him. Banning was unperturbed; after savoring the caviar and indicating his approval with a wave of his hand, he responded impassively, "If I may give a word of advice, Dr. Sullivan. Say what you intend to without returning to that uncomfortable and rather ridiculous position. From what I know of Maggie, she's a down-to-earth sort of person who won't object to a straightforward approach. Besides which, it will be a lot easier on your knees."

"You've got a bloody cheek, Yank!" Sully's fists were clenched, his arms upraised menacingly in a boxing stance. "Think you can come in here and tell me what to do and not do, do you! Well, you've got another think coming."

"Don't, Sully!" Marigold had jumped to her feet, anxious to protect Natasha's china rather than Banning's grinning face.

"Natasha would never forgive us for ruining her table, Dr. Sullivan," Banning pointed out. "And it's far too cold outside to engage in fisticuffs."

"You're a bloody coward into the bargain, aren't you!" Sully began advancing menacingly. But just as he was about to swing, the door opened and Natasha rushed in, arms outstretched.

"Mark! My darling one. Here you are at last—or I should say, here we are together at last. I've been waiting for you forever. Where have you been, my darling? What kept you?"

"Natasha!" As though it were the most natural thing in the world, as though no one else were there, Mark Banning took Natasha Waeber into his arms and kissed her. It was a long, fervent kiss, not the sort a guest usually bestows on his hostess.

Sully's belligerence changed to embarrassment. Not knowing what to do, he cleared his throat in a cough of pure censure. Natasha drew back, and, becoming cognizant of other guests present in the room, flushed guiltily. Her guilt, however, was not sufficient to make her release hold of Mark Banning. Rather, she clung to his arm even more possessively.

"Marigold—Sully—what on earth are you doing here?"

"I rather think they came here, as we did, to be alone," Banning put in.

"Not much chance of being alone with the likes of you around, Banning," Sully said haughtily and more than a little pompously. "Come, Marigold. This no place for decent people."

"You're retiring from the field, then, Dr. Sullivan," Banning said, holding the door open.

But before Marigold and Sully could retire, the field at that moment was invaded by a plaintive Boris Waeber.

"Can we not serve dinner now, my love?" he asked. "Unless we get food into our guests, I fear for the consequences. Someone has even spiked Mr. Andrews's coffee. Mrs. Allen is most perturbed. She tells me he never touches alcohol."

"Don't worry, Boris," Banning consoled. "Doug Andrews can drink with the best of us when he's of a mind. If anyone spiked his drink, I'll bet dollars to donuts he did it himself."

"I'll take the dollars, I have no use for the—what was it—donut, a sort of blintz, isn't it?" Boris was the only one to laugh, clutching at the cummerbund girding his expansive waistline as he did so. "But dinner, my love, let us wait no longer for dinner."

"Certainly, Boris. That is exactly what I came in here to arrange, now that our guest is here," Natasha said. "Marigold and Sully were just helping me check the name cards. Everything is in order. You may have our guests come in."

Mark Banning was wandering around the table, examining the place cards as she spoke. But as her husband left the room, Natasha motioned to him, "Your place is to my right, Mark."

Given the amount of vodka and whiskey consumed prior to the meal, conversation at the table was less than brilliant. Sully, still furious, spoke little. His anger had increased when he went to take his seat beside Marigold and found that place now allocated to Mr. Andrews. Somehow his place card had been spirited to the other end of the table, next to Mrs. Allen, with whom he always seemed to talk at cross-purposes. Sure of the culprit, he threw a furious glance at Banning, but in return for his scowl, all he got was a smile and an innocent shrug.

"The man's an incorrigible rogue," he muttered, looking over at Marigold in conversation with Mr. Andrews.

"Mr. Andrews a rogue! Why, Dr. Sullivan, what are you saying! I can assure you that he is the best of men. That little incident before dinner was none of his doing. He has assured me more than once that he never touches a drop of liquor except for medicinal purposes. Because he was the victim of a rather unpleasant prank, you must not call him a rogue, you really mustn't."

"Mrs. Allen, I meant no such thing," Sully attempted to explain as soon as he could get a word in edgewise.

He might have spent the rest of the evening straightening the matter out, had not a note been delivered to Marigold as the main course was about to be served. Seeing her excuse herself and leave the table, he too rose and followed her from the room.

"Not bad news, surely?" he asked. Marigold, her brows drawn, her face pale with worry, was fastening her long wrap.

"It's Princess Chun-mae, Sully. She's been in labor for almost three days. Chu-sun is begging me to come. She has faith that I can be of help. I just don't know what I can do—I have no experience as a nurse, but I must go for Chu-sun's sake."

"If you must go, then you shan't go alone. I shall come with you," Sully said, calling for his coat. "I have to say, though, that I don't think this is at all wise. After three days of labor, I'd say her chances of survival are slim and the baby's are all but nil."

"But Sully, she's alive, and while there's . . ."

"I know. I know. While there's life, there's hope, but that's about all there is. But what matters to me is you—my place is with you."

But Marigold hung back. "It's kind of you to offer to come, Sully, but you know as well as I that men aren't allowed on the streets during the evening hours. Of course, I realize you're the most logical one to be there, but even if you got to the palace, you'd never be allowed into the women's quarters. There's not a chance in the world, unless . . ." She hesitated, sizing him up. "We're about the same height, aren't we." She took off her hooded wrap. "Put this on, perhaps there is a way after all."

"Marigold, I can't go as . . ."

"You just said you wanted to help me."

"I know I did, but . . ."

But Marigold was already fastening her cloak around him and pulling the hook over his head.

"Not bad. It might work."

"But I can't," Sully protested.

"Come on, Sully. Remember your oath. There's a chance that a life can be saved—even two."

"May I be of help?" At the sight of Mark Banning, Sully began to tear himself free of the shroud of Marigold's cloak, but she stopped him.

"You can help by leaving us alone, Mr. Banning," Marigold snapped, afraid of her newly conceived plan failing before it had been attempted.

"Just tell me what's happened," he said tersely.

"Princess Chun-mae is in childbirth. It's not going well. Her sister Chu-sun . . ."

"Chu-sun? Isn't that the queen's interpreter?"

"She's my friend," Marigold put in, not responding to the question. She preferred that he did not know she had been present during his visit to the queen and was glad when Sully interrupted, "If we're going, Marigold, we're going now. Otherwise I'm getting out of this thing."

"No, Sully. You must wear it, for me. Please!"

"Since your friend's all decked out in your things, let's find something for you. Wait here," Banning said, returning moments later with a sable wrap. "Natasha won't mind."

As he wrapped the luxurious fur around her, he held the collar close for a moment, running his fingers along her neck.

"Take care, Maggie," he murmured in her ear. Out loud, he said, "And take care of that comely serving wench."

"Bloody bastard!" Sully swore under his breath as they made their way out into the cold night air.

9

Luck seemed to be with them. Marigold was known at the palace, and they gained admittance with Sully receiving only a cursory glance from the guard. They made their way across the grounds to the women's quarters without arousing undue suspicion, but once there, Marigold feared their difficulties might begin. The obstacle of a male attending a woman in labor had still to be overcome. Telling Sully to wait outside, she went in search of Chu-sun.

She found her friend pacing the floor outside her sister's room.

"You've come. I knew you would," she cried as soon as she caught sight of Marigold. "It's terrible. Duk-hwa is not particularly competent at the best of times, but now she's worse than useless. The queen sent her over a flagon of mokkoli and she's drunk. Somehow I shall get you admitted, but take care. She's in a very aggressive mood."

"Sully's here with me," Marigold whispered.

"Sully?"

"Dr. Sullivan."

Chu-sun's hand flew to her face. "But that's not possible. He can't come. With you it's different. You are known in the palace, you are a woman. But if it were ever discovered that a man had seen a royal princess at such a time—oh, no." She shook her head vehemently. "It's not possible."

"But Chun-mae's your sister. Having Sully here to help may be her only chance," Marigold insisted. "I'm willing to do whatever I can, but I don't have the knowledge to help her. Sully has. He's wearing my cloak, Chu-sun. It's to our advantage that Duk-hwa is drunk. She may not realize who he is. He'll keep the cloak on, I promise. It's Chun-mae's only chance."

Chu-sun shook her head. "You, yes, but Dr. Sullivan . . . if he were found out. . . . I'm not thinking just of myself, but my sister . . ."

"I would swear on a stack of Bibles that you knew nothing about it."

"Paksa, I would never let you do such a thing." Chu-sun stood, wringing her hands. Still, Marigold sensed she was wavering.

"We're wasting time. Sully's freezing outside. Let him come in, at least."

"Very well," Chu-sun whispered reluctantly.

Sully's grip stuck out at an angle beneath the cloak. It was the first thing Chu-sun noticed.

"No more needles," she said. "My sister is half dead from those needles."

"We don't use needles," Sully said tersely. All the way over he had regretted agreeing to Marigold's plan; it could mean nothing but trouble. "Where is she?"

The warm ondol floor creaked occasionally under their stock-inged feet as they followed Chu-sun into a small room where an almost lifeless form lay on a pallet. Slumped in the corner was Duk-hwa, her face bright red. Her eyes glistened oddly as they fell on Marigold.

"Red-hair," she called out. "Dog's dung worm—that's what we call the Marigold."

"To us it's not much better—it stands for jealousy or despair," Marigold responded in as pleasant a tone as she could manage.

"Think I'm jealous of you. Is that it? Just because you're trying to take my place with the king. Now you're moving in here, trying to take my patients from me. Get out! Get out or I'll send word to the queen. And who's that with you? Who is it?"

She got up and advanced threateningly on Sully, who was already kneeling beside Chun-mae, his ear pressed against her swollen belly.

"By God, the child's still alive!" he cried.

Duk-hwa stood stock still, her finger pointing. "It's a man—I swear it's a man," she cried hoarsely.

"Of course it isn't a man. This is Sarah. I brought her with me because she's a midwife. She's seen many babies into the world. She can help Chun-mae. The queen asked me to bring help."

"The queen asked you to bring help!" Duk-hwa cackled. "You expect me to believe that. And you think, because I've had a drink or two, that I don't know a man when I see one. A kisaeng's life depends on men. I can smell them a mile off."

"I believe you, Duk-hwa, but in this case you're mistaken, that's all," Marigold said, drawing Duk-hwa away from Sully. "I know you're clever. The healing arts are where you excel. That is why I came too this evening, as much to talk to you as to see the princess."

"What is it you want to know?" Duk-hwa swayed slightly as she spoke, but nevertheless Marigold had gained her attention. "You have a pain, is that it?"

"That's it. That's it exactly." Behind Duk-hwa, Marigold noticed that Sully, now working desperately at Chun-mae's side, had allowed the hood of the cloak to slip down. There was no longer any denying he was a man.

In desperation, Marigold cried out, "I have a pain, a most awful pain. That's really why I came. I need your help. I brought Sarah with me so she could look after the princess while you examine me. Would you, please! Please!" Her plea grew louder, making Sully turn around for an instant. She tried to signal to him to push up the hood of the cape.

"Where is this pain?" Duk-hwa asked suspiciously.

"It's, it's . . ." In trying to think of the area of her body where the least harm might be done, Marigold mistakenly clutched at her stomach.

"Don't tell me. The stomach. I know. Let me see it."

"Not here, please not here. Let us go somewhere else—your room, perhaps."

"I can't leave the princess," Duk-hwa muttered. "I have my orders."

"Just for a few minutes. It's all I ask. You are the only one who can help me."

Duk-hwa smiled. "In that case, I don't suppose a few minutes will matter. She's done for, anyway."

As Duk-hwa turned back to the patient, Marigold let out a howl of pain that made both Duk-hwa and Sully turn around. Having his attention, she motioned to Sully to pull the hood up and then doubled up as though in agony.

"Come then. There's nothing I can do for this one. Let me take care of that stomach of yours," the kisaeng said, stumbling from the room.

An hour later, Chun-mae delivered a baby girl. If she was conscious of her shame in not having produced a boy, she didn't show it. Perhaps she realized this was the one thing that would save her baby from the queen. For the first time in three days she slept, the child suckling at her breast.

Marigold, however, did not rest as easy. A sullen, drunken Duk-hwa had made her drink a foul liquid, then pushed six-inch needles into her toes, twisting them to the right to increase the yang which was guaranteed to release the stomach tension. Though the opposite occurred, Marigold held back her cries, swearing again and again that she was cured. She might never have been able to get up if Duk-hwa had not at last fallen into a deep, drunken sleep.

Chu-sun brought her the news of Chun-mae's recovery and whispered her gratitude.

"It's a girl, paksa," she said. "Born in the year of the horse, a bad sign for a girl."

"Why?"

"She may be too strong-willed to get a husband. Horse, dragon, and tiger are all bad. Oh, paksa, I'm sorry. I forgot you are born in the year of the tiger. But you see, it is true. You have not married, unless this Dr. Sullivan . . ."

"He's a friend, Chu-sun," Marigold answered quickly, "just a friend." Still, she flushed, remembering the interrupted proposal.

Chu-sun smiled. "It is clear he's a good friend. And you were right, paksa, he is a good doctor. But it must never be known that he saw Chun-mae, that he treated her."

"No one will ever hear of it from me," Marigold promised. "Nor from Sully."

"And no one else knows," Chu-sun breathed a sigh of relief.

"No, except . . . except for Mark Banning."

"That is not good! He is a friend of the queen," Chu-sun murmured fearfully.

"He will say nothing."

"Are you sure?"

"I give you my promise that he will say nothing."

Even this promise did not clear the frown from Chu-sun's face.

"I don't like him. He is brash," Marigold explained. "But I really don't think he . . ."

"It's not Mr. Banning that worries me now, but the difficulty you may have in leaving at this late hour. The gates will be locked for the night. You and Dr. Sullivan could stay in the Chogyong, the abandoned pavilion, until daylight."

"We could not," Marigold said firmly. "Don't worry. I'll find a way."

Outside, a shivering Sully waited.

"You were wonderful, Sully. I'm so very grateful to you."

"That makes it all worthwhile, then," Sully said as they started out across the courtyard. "But let's save all that until we get outside these walls. It went all right, but if she had died, I would have been held reponsible. They would have demanded that I support all her relatives and God knows what, and Mr. Gardner would have been called to account for my having been here at all."

"But no one need ever know, Sully. Only you and I know."

"And that bastard Banning."

"I'll see to it that he'll say nothing."

"I don't want you to even talk to him," Sully said.

"You're a dear man, but you really can't say who I may or may not talk to."

"Not now, perhaps, but if you'll let me finish what I began . . ."

"This is not the time, Sully," Marigold said firmly. "First, as you so rightly observed, we must get outside these walls."

As they approached the massive gates, she saw one was ajar.

"That must be your Irish luck, Sully. Leave the guard to me. What matters is for you to get out unnoticed—I can make some excuse for being here, but you can't."

"I'm not leaving you."

Marigold stopped. "If you argue about this, Chu-sun, her sister, and the baby may all be doomed, not to mention your being dispatched home at the next sailing. Leave the guard to me and slip out as inconspicuously as you can, promise?"

She softened her tone at the last word, and Sully reluctantly promised.

The guard at the gate was talking to a stooped, cloaked washerwoman—he was doing the talking and she was listening—but there was nothing unusual about that. It was unusual that the woman should be there at that hour, but Marigold thanked heaven that she was. There was even a sedan chair waiting in front of the gate. If she'd planned it, it couldn't have been better. As the guard challenged her, she motioned to Sully to take the chair and leave. She was relieved to see that he did.

"Who is it? Who's there? Ah, the red-headed sangnom. And what do you think you are doing here at this time of the night?" the guard demanded in unusually belligerent, thick tones. He was drunk, Marigold realized thankfully, and she knew why as the washerwoman filled a cup with mokkoli—obviously not the first of the evening—and handed it to him. Another piece of luck.

"On a cold night like this a man needs a little something," the guard muttered, draining it. Speculatively, if blearily, he looked from the washerwoman to Marigold as he added, "a little warm brew inside him, warm arms around him, that's what a man needs."

"The queen may be interested in hearing your ideas on the subject, especially while you're on duty," Marigold said coldly. "Perhaps I should go back and tell her about them."

The guard straightened up, unsteadily, but nevertheless he somehow managed to pull himself to his full height. He shoved the cup into the washerwoman's hands and growled, "I told you not to hang around here, old woman! Get a chair for the lady. She can't stand around on a night like this."

"I'll walk," Marigold began, pulling Natasha's sable around her, but, as if miraculously summoned, a chair appeared and she climbed inside.

Sully was standing at the door of the Russian legation as she drew up.

"Thank God you're all right. I was giving you five more minutes. If you hadn't come by then, I was going to throw caution to the winds and come after you. Are you all right?"

"My stomach aches and my toes are burning. That apothecary kisaeng almost murdered me with those needles of hers."

"You should have told me earlier," he consoled. "Anyway, I'll prescribe something for you. Those needles are dangerous. They can introduce bacteria into the body. I've seen cases of osteomyelitis, even arteriovenous fistula that can lead to a heart attack, all because of unsterile needles."

"Don't Sully, I feel bad enough as it is. Anyway, thanks to that old washerwoman feeling sorry for the guard on a cold night, he was quite drunk on mokkoli. I got away with far less trouble than I'd imagined. He even got me a chair."

His eyes searched her face as they entered the hallway. "You look pale."

She was describing the vile drink Duk-hwa had made her swallow when Natasha came out of the drawing room; a look of hauteur crossed her face when she saw Marigold.

"Oh, I almost forgot. Your sable." Marigold started to pull it off.

"Mr. Banning got it for me. He said you wouldn't mind. Thank you . . ."

"You'd better thank Mark since he loaned it to you. Have you seen him?"

"No. But we've been out." Marigold bit her tongue; no one else must know where they'd been. And she had to make sure that Banning said nothing.

Natasha's eyebrows rose. "Together?"

"Of course not. I didn't realize that Mr. Banning had been out too."

"Just taking the air," said a voice behind them.

"There you are, Mark," Natasha said. "I've been looking for you everywhere. Then I realized Marigold was gone . . ."

"And it looked suspiciously as though we'd gone off on a clandestine tryst," Banning finished. "But I'd never choose to go trysting with Sully along—anymore than he'd like having me around at a time like that—right, Sully?"

"You're damned right," Sully agreed angrily, then immediately apologized for swearing in the presence of ladies. "But it's Banning's fault," he concluded.

"He does lead people into doing things they don't intend to," Marigold agreed.

"I never realized I had such power," Banning commented lightly.

"Come on in, all of you. You're spoiling my party," Natasha said in annoyance. Sully followed her, but Marigold lagged behind.

"There's something I must say to you, Mr. Banning," she said urgently. "Alone."

Banning smiled. "This is an unexpected pleasure, Maggie. Maybe you did want a tryst, after all. I'm honored."

"Nothing of the sort," she snapped. "But there's one thing I have

to tell you, and it's important. Sully managed to save the princess—
and the baby, too. He was wonderful. He's courageous. He thinks
of others—not just himself."

"Unlike some you prefer not to mention, is that it?"

"I just meant that if the fact that Sully went to the palace to
attend the princess were ever to come out, it could cause great
harm. Promise me you'll never breathe a word of it. If the queen
should know, the princess would suffer, and her sister, too."

"Not to mention Sully," Banning put in, studying her face. "You
don't want harm to come to Sully, do you Maggie?"

"Of course I don't. Nor should you."

"Probably not. You've picked a good man," he observed rather
wistfully.

"I didn't pick Sully," she said, annoyed by his assumption.

"I rather thought you had after that scene I came in on earlier
this evening."

"I rather think it's to both our advantages to forget what happened there." Without knowing what prompted her, she looked up
at him and blurted out, "Is Natasha Waeber the reason you came
back to Korea?"

"Maggie! What kind of a question is that! You of all people
should know exactly why I came back."

"Should I?" She hesitated, wondering whether he'd been aware
all along that she'd been privy to everything that had passed between him and the queen.

"Warm brew inside him, warm arms around him, that's what a
man's after with no questions asked," he said lightly.

"You . . . that was you?" Marigold spluttered in astonishment.
"Is it possible that washerwoman was you?"

"Me—a washerwoman!" He spread his hands in a gesture of
amazement. "I've been called lots of things, Maggie, but never a
washerwoman."

"But what you just said about . . ."

"I was just about to say that Sully's right, for once. You do look pale. I overheard that drink you described to him, the one the ki-saeng gave you at the palace. I dare say that's what's wrong. I'll just bet it was broth of pig's feces—it's one of their big cure-alls."

"Oh, you . . . you beast!" Marigold gasped. Covering her mouth, she hurried away.

THE
BLACK TURTLE
OF THE NORTH

1

While Marigold spent hours, entire days, plotting and scheming how to extend the planned journey up the Han River, so that she could talk to Tuk-so on Chu-sun's behalf, Gifford fretted about the lack of response to their request for a kwan-ja entitling them to make the journey at all.

"Banning gets to go wherever he wants and have whatever he needs in his search for a base metal, but we can't get permission for a simple sightseeing journey up the river to Ku-munio," he fumed.

"I'm sure it will come eventually." By way of assurance, Farquhar gave a mighty sniff of his beaked nose. "All this talk of another rising of Tong-hak rebels has got them worried—that's probably what's delaying things. I know the Tong-hak are as much opposed to us as they are to the government; still, I can't find them altogether wrong in seeking relief from corrupt officials."

"All the officials here are corrupt, the whole lot from the king down," Gifford said.

"It would be unwise to say that outside this room, Giff," Farquhar cautioned. "Besides, everything's slow in this country. You should know that by now."

"Slow for everyone except Banning. No doubt he's greased plenty of palms. If they think I'm going to resort to bribery in order to get the required chops on my request, they've another think coming."

Farquhar nodded. "Probably he has, though he does seem to have the queen's ear."

"Not to mention what he has of Natasha Waeber," Gifford said caustically, bringing a look of warning to Herbert Farquhar's face as he nodded in Marigold's direction. As usual, where Marigold was concerned, Gifford didn't seem to know that she was there, or, more likely, he simply didn't care.

Sully had repeated his marriage proposal to Marigold and, though she had not accepted him, she had refused in such a way as to make Sully believe there was still hope.

"She's playing fast and loose with you," Gifford had warned his friend. "Take my advice, Sully. Withdraw while you have time. I'm convinced that young woman is unstable."

"That's not so. Giff. All young ladies are taught not to accept proposals with alacrity—they don't want to show too much eagerness, too much anxiety not to be left on the shelf."

"Sully, if you'd open your eyes and come out of this wild infatuation of yours, you'd see Miss Wilder as I do. Her place on the shelf is assured, unless she can find some gullible man to ensnare. She's plain and uninteresting and, I repeat, she's not stable."

"I don't know what makes you say that, Giff. If you really believed she was unstable, why would you want her along on this great trip you're planning?" Sully demanded.

Not daring to admit he feared that if he left Marigold behind, it would be to return and find Sully married to her, Gifford hastily pointed out, "Look at the way she made you go down to the palace in the middle of the night to tend that Korean. Was that the request of a reasonable woman? You could have been expelled from the country for giving medical care to a royal princess—and she knew it. Worse yet, you could have easily put your license to practice medicine in jeopardy. You would have returned to England in disgrace, and undoubtedly the Medical Association would have taken the matter up. Who can tell where an official inquiry by one of those august bodies might lead? And what did you get for all your trouble? That useless little piece of pottery."

"It was a very old piece, according to Marigold," Sully reminded him. "She said it was a signal honor for Princess Chun-mae to send a relic like that by way of thanks. Besides, it couldn't have been so useless, otherwise why would Mark Banning have given me a hundred pounds for it? I thought I made out rather well. Wish I'd got a hundred pounds for every house call I've made."

Sully's face grew glum as he remembered how annoyed Marigold had been when he sold the gray-green celadon bowl with its swirled dragon design. It had led to their first quarrel.

"Celadon is prized above jade, Sully. That piece was particularly rare because of the inlaid dragon decoration. I can't understand why you let Banning steal it from you."

"Paying a hundred pounds for a bit of pottery can hardly be called stealing." His mouth was set in a straight, unyielding line, showing a stubborn side he'd never revealed to Marigold before. However, she seemed undaunted by this display of truculence.

"A hundred pounds is a pittance to someone who'll give ten to a waiter to sit down in a restaurant."

Sully's sharp rejoinder surprised her. "For someone who keeps insisting she detests the man, you certainly seem to know a lot about him. That's all I can say. I'll bet I can make better use of his hundred pounds than he'll make of that pot."

"Perhaps." Marigold paused, then smiled in apology. "Sorry, Sully. It's really none of my business. I have absolutely no right to tell you what to do. Banning's a swaggering blowhard. You're worth a hundred of his kind. I suppose it's because I dislike him so that I objected to what you did. Forgive me."

"No, I'm the one who should apologize," Sully responded. "I should have realized how you feel about old stuff by that odd piece you wear around your neck all the time."

Marigold's hand flew to the kokok Banning had given her and quickly pushed it inside the neckline of her dress. "I just wear it for luck. It's silly to be superstitious."

"Nothing you do is silly, Marigold," Sully said, leaning across to take her hand. "You have every right to tell me what you think.

And, if you must know, I did it for you. I snapped at his offer to buy the bowl so I could send the money to England to get a ring. I just hope the size is going to be right."

"Oh, Sully, you shouldn't have. You know . . ."

"I know it was my money and I'm doing what I wanted with it."

"But you shouldn't," Marigold repeated weakly, hating herself for still hesitating about Sully's offer. The problem was that she couldn't understand why she didn't accept him outright. She was lucky to have met someone like Sully. They got along well together. He was a good doctor, but more important, he was a good man. She knew her father would have approved of Sully, and she liked and respected him. Whether she loved him or not seemed of little account. She knew nothing of love nor had she ever known love to be a criterion for marriage. Compatibility was what mattered, and she and Sully were unquestionably compatible. It certainly wasn't from a sense of coyness that she hesitated. She suspected that underlying her indecision, there might be a desire to frustrate others' expectations. Especially Banning's.

Every time she and Mark Banning met—which, given the size of the foreign community in Seoul, was frequently—he would smile and hold onto her hand in greeting as he asked, "Well, Maggie, have you and Sully named the day yet? I should be the first to know, being, in a sense, family."

It was his familiarity, his use of her father's name for her, that annoyed her the most.

"You assume, Mr. Banning. I really don't see what I do or don't do as being any business of yours," she responded coolly. He reminded her that since her sister was married to his cousin, they were more than just friends.

"I never think of you as a friend," she snapped, drawing a sharp glance from Natasha Waeber, who was never far from Banning.

Since he showed no dismay, she went on, "And I certainly don't consider you family. *My* family, Mr. Banning, has never been given to boasting."

At which, he merely smiled, "Maybe it's about time, then, for you to take credit when credit is due."

Natasha, who had previously supported Marigold, objected to this undercurrent of hostility. "I just don't understand your talking to Mark like that. I don't like it and I won't have it—not in my presence, at least."

And since wherever Mark Banning was, there was Natasha, a woman who always got her way, Marigold tried to hold her tongue. She hated having to give in to Natasha's whims, but she knew that to get on the wrong side of the leader of the Seoul's foreign community could result in harm to Reverend Farquhar's mission. After all his kindness, Marigold did not want that laid at her door.

Though the coming of spring and the warmer weather made it possible for Marigold and Chu-sun to return to the Hamhwa-dang for their lessons, it was a sign of her acceptance at the palace that Marigold was still permitted to see Chu-sun in the private women's quarters of the queen's pavilion.

Chu-sun was even more upset than Gifford that the kwan-ja had not been granted for their journey.

"Every night I pray that you will be able to go and talk to Tuk-so. Every morning I awake in hope. Every night I cry myself to sleep, fearing I will be forced to marry Prince Sunjong."

"That won't happen—not once Tuk-so knows. And he will be told," Marigold repeated, though as time passed, the conviction in her voice grew weaker.

"No. He will never know because you will not be allowed to go," she said flatly one day.

"That's not so, Chu-sun." And, echoing Reverend Farquhar's consoling words to Gifford, she added, "The official wheels move slowly, you know that."

"I know. But that's not the reason in this case. The queen has guessed your intention," she said disconsolately. "That is why there is no response."

"I don't believe that," Marigold averred. "The trip, after all, was planned by Gifford, not by me. She may surmise and object to his intentions, but I'm sure she knows nothing of mine. And anyway, the given purpose of our journey up the Han was ku kyong—pleasure seeking, sight seeing, indulging curiosity in the way of most travelers. It was all perfectly reasonable. There was nothing there to make anyone suspicious. No mention was made of Wonsan as our destination, so how could she possibly know?"

"Paksa, the queen knows everything—everything," Chu-sun emphasized. "Besides my own position, I fear for Tuk-so." She hesitated. "What I tell you is in confidence—promise to say nothing." The promise given, Chu-sun went on, "I know from the queen's correspondence that the rumors of a Tong-hak uprising are more than rumors, and I fear for Tuk-so."

"The Tong-hak are rebels?"

"*Tong-hak* means Eastern learning, as opposed to *Sohak*, the Western learning, that came into Korea with the missionaries."

"Then they are not rebels."

"But they are rebels because they challenge Confucianism just as much as the missionaries—perhaps even more, for they challenge from a position of knowledge. Choe, who started it, was executed some thirty years ago. His followers continue to be persecuted but the movement doesn't die."

"I wonder why," Marigold mused. "What do they believe in?"

"Equality, they say, of poor and rich, noble and humble . . . men and women even."

"It's no wonder, then, that it doesn't die." Sensing hesitance in Chu-sun, Marigold studied her friend's face before commenting, "From all you have said, this seems a good movement."

"In many ways it is," Chu-sun agreed, in a lowered voice.

"Then do you . . ."

Chu-sun shook her head vigorously. "No, I can't."

"I don't see why not," Marigold said in puzzlement. "You've said they believe in ideals you hold dear, equality of men and women, for

instance. I like the sound of the Tong-hak. It seems to be a movement ahead of its time."

"I agree, it sounds attractive. Many of their demands are good,
but I could never espouse their cause, nor could you. As I said,
they oppose Western ways and most of all they oppose our God.
They say they believe in a sort of universal power. For that reason,
no Christian can be a Tong-hak."

"I suppose not," Marigold agreed, though her voice lacked conviction. "But you fear that Tuk-so may be involved with the
movement."

Chu-sun shook her head. "No, no, you misunderstand. In any
Tong-hak uprising, I fear for Tuk-so because of his position in the
government. He has been appointed magistrate under Min Tae-jon.
For a man so young, this is a great honor and proof of his ability.
Nevertheless, it puts him in danger, for the Tong-hak may think he
is cut of the same cloth as other officials. But he is a fine man,
nothing like the corrupt members of the queen's family."

"As magistrate, his virtue will have made itself known," Marigold said in an effort to comfort Chu-sun.

"I am sure that is so. Yet I fear for him." Chu-sun shook her
head, then squared her shoulders and drew Marigold back to the
study of sijo. Now that her English was so fluent, Chu-sun had
suggested it was time to introduce Marigold to Korea's literature.
She had begun with the sijo, concise poems with a standardized
syllabic arrangement originally written to be sung to the kayagum,
the zither, or chanted to the changgu, the hourglass drum.

"The sijo is like a folk song, passed down from generation to
generation; the name of the writer is often forgotten or unknown.
Because they contain the seeds of truth about human emotion, the
songs remain as alive today as at the time they were written. This is
one from the fifteenth century that my mother would sometimes
sing while I accompanied her on the wol kun, the moon harp,"
Chu-sun explained. She furrowed her brow as she recited:

> *It rained during the night,*
> *and pomegranates have all burst into bloom.*
> *I sit in the lotus lake pavilion*
> *with the curtain of crystal beads rolled up.*
> *As ever, my efforts are vain*
> *to forget him who makes me sad.*

Sin Hum, a statesman who rose to be prime minister under King Injo, wrote that one. He is said to be speaking of Li Po, who has been disappointed in love."

"Was it he who disappointed her?"

"I believe it was," Chu-sun said, her face expressionless.

"It is very sad," Marigold said quietly.

"A woman's existence is always one of unquestioning obedience, first to her father, then, when she marries, to her husband and, in due course to her eldest son; but above all she owes obedience to her mother-in-law." Chu-sun shuddered, perhaps thinking of Queen Min in that role. "Poetry about women is full of laments for their plight. It is a happy woman who loves where she must obey— and a rare one."

She looked down at the scroll on the table for some minutes before continuing:

> *O moon, O shining round moon,*
> *O moon that shines in my beloved's room!*
> *Is he sleeping there alone,*
> *Or does he clasp some other girl?*
> *I beg you to tell the truth, moon:*
> *It is life and death to me.*

But this time her voice broke and there was pain in her dark eyes as she raised them despairingly to Marigold. "Oh, paksa, do you think that he . . . is it possible that . . ."

"Chu-sun, my dear friend." Marigold laid a hand on her shoulder. "From all you've told me of Tuk-so, I can't believe for a minute that he has forgotten you or is untrue."

"No, no. Of course not," Chu-sun agreed, but looking back at the poem, she hesitated, "It's just that never being able to have direct news of him, never being able to know that he still feels for me as I feel for him makes me fearful. I fear the influence of the queen's brother. Min Tae-jon is a terrible man. If only you were able to go and talk to Tuk-so for me. If only . . ."

Abruptly she broke off. Though Marigold heard nothing, Chu-sun held a finger to her lips, signaling silence. Long after, there was a creaking of mats in the corridor outside. Then the sliding floor was flung back to allow the entrance of Queen Min, followed by Chilyongun. Immediately Chu-sun rose from the floor. Marigold made to do the same, but the queen imperiously, even graciously, motioned her to remain seated.

"It has been brought to my attention that you and your missionary compatriot are planning a journey," the queen announced, her eyes fixed on the scroll that lay open on the table. The mudang, like a cat watching a mouse, kept her eyes fixed on Marigold.

"That is so, Your Majesty. Some time ago, Reverend Partridge applied through our consulate for a kwan-ja, but to date no approval has been given."

"These things require consideration."

"I understand, Your Majesty. But if permission is not soon received, we are concerned that the upper reaches of the Han will no longer be navigable."

"What is the reason for this journey?" the queen demanded, turning to survey Marigold, who returned her stare unflinchingly.

"Ku kyong—sightseeing. The reason was stated on the application," she replied.

"I want the true reason, not this twaddle about ku kyong given by every nefarious visitor to this county."

Marigold took a deep breath. "The true reason is that Reverend Partridge wants to save souls and I want to take pictures."

They continued to survey one another without comment, then the queen said, "In that case, I think you would find it well worthwhile, since you are going to the upper reaches of the Han, to cross the Diamond Mountains and go on to Wonsan. To see Keum Kang San, the highest peak in the Diamond Mountains, is the experience that distinguishes the true traveler in my country. And beyond is Wonsan, our major eastern port. Under the influence of my brother, who was appointed chief magistrate there and is now governor of the province, the port has grown and prospered. Wonsan has been opened to foreign trade. You'll find the city most attractive, situated as it is in the southwest corner of Yung-hing," Queen Min lifted her nose disdainfully as she added, "referred to by foreigners as Broughton Bay. Few of your fellow missionaries have yet found their way there, so undoubtedly your Reverend Partridge will find this city of some fifteen thousand souls to save much to his liking also."

As she spoke, the queen had turned the suggestion into a decision, Marigold realized. She tried to hide her delight and relief.

"It will add some days to your journey and will entail some difficulty as you will have to cross the Diamond Mountains. Few foreigners have followed the route from Seoul to Wonsan. However, since I see you are studying our sijo, this magnificent range has long been a subject lauded by our poets.

> *Twelve thousand jagged peaks—*
> *Some high, some low.*
> *Observe, I beg, when the sun rises,*
> *Which peak first turns crimson.*

The queen motioned to the mudang to roll up the scroll as she admonished Chu-sun.

"Nature is a far preferable theme to lost love, unless that love be one worthy of such attention. Our Koryo Queen In-mok, much renowned for her great scholarship, has written movingly of her murdered son, Prince Yung-chang. There can be no love as great as maternal love, don't you agree?" the queen demanded of Marigold.

"I . . . I don't know. My mother died when I was young."

"You will know—perhaps—that is, if you are ever able to find a man willing to marry a woman with straight eyebrows and hair like hot coals." After this sally, the queen paused. Her face remained impassive, but there was a break in her voice—perhaps at the thought of maternal love—as she continued, "Centuries cannot lessen a tragedy much as that suffered by this great queen." She turned to Marigold. "I recommend you stop at the Yu-chom Sa Monastery in the Diamond Mountains where Queen In-mok spent her last days copying the sacred Mita Book of the Buddha. It is to be regretted that she devoted so much of her time to a cult since fallen into sad disrepute. But, I am sure that as a queen, with all the responsibilities of that great position, she had honorable intentions. There you may see her final words, written in gold: 'May my parents and my son Prince Yung-chang find eternal blessing in the world beyond by my having copied this.'"

"I should like to do that very much," Marigold replied in all sincerity.

"That is settled then. It will be necessary for you to take ponies from Paik-kui Mi, where you will leave your sampan. Our beasts, though hard of mouth and hide, are sturdy and sure-footed, so you need have no fear. I will arrange it."

As she thanked the queen, Marigold had to restrain herself from glancing triumphantly at Chu-sun.

"Come to me in the morning and I shall dictate a letter of introduction to Min Tae-jon," the queen commanded Chu-sun, before sweeping from the room, her mudang at her heels like an obedient dog.

As their footsteps died away, Marigold smiled, but Chu-sun held her hand to her lips, waiting several minutes before announcing, "Now we may talk. They are gone."

"Isn't that perfect! Absolutely too perfect!" Marigold whooped in delight.

But instead of sharing her joy, Chu-sun seemed unaccountably subdued.

"What's wrong?" Marigold asked. "What's the matter?"

"I don't know, exactly, except I don't understand it. I don't know what she means by it." Chu-sun shook her head. "I don't think I like it."

"Why on earth not?" Marigold demanded in exasperation. "Here we've spent these last months fretting and worrying that the journey would never take place, or if it did, plotting how I'd be able to get to Wonsan to see Tuk-so and now it's fallen into our laps and you don't like it. I really don't understnd you, Chu-sun. I expected you to be jumping with joy. I thought you'd see this as a heaven-sent opportunity." Marigold laughed aloud, shaking her head in elation. "After all my scheming to circumvent authorities and get to Wonsan, suddenly the queen herself was standing in front of me, making the suggestion that I go. I had to restrain myself from jumping up and shouting with joy. I even began to think maybe there actually was a god up there listening to all those prayers of yours."

These last words slipped out unintentionally, causing Chu-sun to start, draw back, and stare at her friend with undisguised dismay.

"Paksa, what has happened! I don't understand! What is this you are saying? How can you say you begin to believe there may be a god in heaven when you, of all people, you who came to spread his word, *know* that God is in His heaven."

When Marigold made no attempt to defend her position, Chu-sun went on in agitation, "Oh, paksa, what has happened to you? What has happened?" She sat cradling her knees in her arms, rocking back and forth as she cried out in bewilderment. "Some terrible thing, I know it, I feel it." Suddenly she sat up, still. "I know what it is. It's that man—the queen's friend. It's Mark Banning. That's it! When you speak of him your face, your voice, they change. He has a great influence on you. I have suspected it from the first."

"That's not true," Marigold cried out. "I don't even like him."

"But you do. I didn't realize how much you felt for him until now. You say you dislike him, yet I see he has crept into your heart and your soul—along with all his blasphemous ideas. He does not believe, I heard him say so. He is the one responsible for this terrible change in you."

"No, that's not so, Chu-sun," Marigold interrupted angrily. "Mark Banning doesn't influence me—except to upset and annoy me. I would like to be able to blame him for all my failures, but I know that would be a lie. You are wrong to believe he has crept into my heart and soul. Nothing could be further from the truth. I have no respect for him—or for anything he stands for."

"Then why?" Chu-sun cried. "Why?"

Marigold shook her head, her eyes filling with tears. "I—I must confess I came to Korea under false pretenses. My purpose was to serve my father's faith, even though I've known for quite a long time that I no longer believe in it. Try to understand. I loved my father more than anyone. He died when he discovered that I did not believe in God—an admission that may have partially caused his death, though I cannot believe it was the only reason. Nevertheless, I wanted to expiate myself and . . . and I felt that by coming here and doing what he would have done I . . ." Marigold threw herself down at her friend's feet, sobbing, "Oh, Chu-sun, if you only knew how difficult it has been for me. I've felt like such a hypocrite . . . such a terrible hypocrite! I think Gifford knows, but I don't care about him. I do care about Herbert Farquhar, though. He is a good man. I would never want to hurt him. But most of all, I care about you. You've made me so ashamed, being with you, seeing your faith shine in your eyes—like sun streaming through a stained-glass window—knowing that you're willing to die for a belief I'm here to spread and yet don't hold in my heart. Chu-sun, if there were any way I could make myself believe, I would. But faith

is either in your heart or it isn't. It's you, not me, who should be
the missionary. So, you see, it's not Mark Banning's fault—it's
mine. I'm glad you know, because pretending to you has been hell
for me, sheer hell."

As the tears ran down Marigold's face, Chu-sun reached over to
draw her friend to her. "Cry, paksa. Cry. It is good to cry. Cry
because you dare not believe in your own emotions, in your own
heart. Cry."

"It's I who should be calling you paksa—teacher."

"You will be my teacher—always." Chu-sun took Marigold's face
between her hands but made no effort to wipe the tears from her
face. "You English say birds sing, we say they cry:

> With cry and moan,
>   The birds fly overhead.
> Great sorrow nests in me,
> I cry and groan even after I wake.

We Koreans are a sorrowful people who find tears everywhere—in
the movement of a branch, in the rustle of a blade of grass, in the
toll of every bell, in the ripple of a stream. We begin and end our
life with tears. We express love more often in tears than in laughter. You can never be a Korean unless you know how to cry. So cry,
paksa, cry."

Marigold's voice, when at last she spoke, was thickened by her
tears. "Crying may help to relieve sorrow, Chu-sun, but it really
doesn't solve anything. Crying won't help me believe in God when
belief is not in my heart."

"It doesn't matter," Chu-sun replied. "It's not important
whether you believe in God or not. What matters is that God believes in you."

2

Mark Banning had proved an attractive addition to Seoul society and his departure called for a number of farewell parties. None was as lavish as that arranged by Natasha Waeber at the Russian legation. High above the legation tower, visible from every section of Seoul—even beyond the high walls of the palace—flags were hoisted to augur a safe return. Inside, the voyager was toasted with a fine Bollinger '85, which according to Gifford, who fancied himself an authority on such things, was a particularly good year.

"Of course, we hardly expected anything else." Gifford eyed the bottle knowledgeably as his glass was refilled. "And as it's for the wine we came, we might as well drink up and leave Banning's mistress to sit at his feet."

Sully frowned, even though he disliked Banning every bit as much as Gifford did. When it came to the toast, however, neither had the temerity to refuse to raise their glasses.

"I'm charmed by Mark's promise of the largest nugget he finds. I shall most certainly cherish it," Natasha's tone was imperious.

"What do you suppose she'll really cherish most, the nugget or the donor?" Gifford whispered to Sully.

Natasha smiled up at Banning, her long, slender fingers resting lightly on his arm. "But what we are gathered for today is to wish him a fair wind at his back speeding his safe return," she said.

"There is nothing as capricious as the wind, Natasha," Banning responded, their eyes meeting over his glass as he raised it in acknowledgment. "Let us drink to caprice."

Sully, taking another glass from the tray, commented, "I'll join in any toast to hasten his departure. As far as I'm concerned, he can stay away forever. His presence is disruptive and I, for one, shan't be sorry to see him gone." And, glancing across the large reception room at the magnificently bemedalled, portly figure of Boris Waeber, he added, "Nor, I should suppose, will Boris."

"Do you think Boris notices—I mean really notices—anything, except what he eats and drinks?" Gifford's caustic comment was hastily covered by a cough from Sully, then a nod of his head indicating that Banning was approaching them.

"I'll bet he thinks Boris is even more a fool than I do," Gifford muttered in a low voice as Banning joined them, remarking blandly, "I agree with you, Partridge, Boris is looking particularly fit, isn't he?" And to Sully, "That's a nasty cough you have there. Surely our great white medicine man isn't coming down with a cold."

"I'm a physician, not a medicine man, Banning," Sully said with a note of annoyance.

"Sorry, *Doctor* Sullivan." Banning turned back to Gifford. "I've heard you, too, have plans to journey up the Han."

"Finally." Gifford sniffed resentfully. "We had to wait forever for our kwan-ja to be approved."

"We? Dr. Sullivan, are you going along with Partridge on this dangerous expedition? From all accounts, the river can be very treacherous."

"You're not afraid to go, so why should I be?" Sully snapped. "However, my duties here won't permit it, otherwise I'd be off in a flash."

"I didn't, for a moment, think an intrepid Irishman would be afraid. And I can quite understand how difficult it would be for someone with your responsibilities to be spared for such a lengthy journey." His voice was light as he added, "Partridge, I know, takes on such risks in the service of a higher cause."

"My journey is certainly not for personal gain." Gifford made no attempt to hide his condemnation. "I really don't think we can compare grubbing for gold with spreading God's word."

"Both have their uses. However, compared with your mission, I suppose mine must seem like something befitting a prodigal son— off to waste his substance in search of precious metal."

That Banning took no offense heightened Gifford's chagrin. "The prodigal son, as I remember, came back with empty hands and an even emptier purse."

"True. So there the analogy fails. I most certainly intend to return with something of value."

"There's no vice like avarice, particularly when it's coupled with audacity," Gifford commented icily.

"How unjust of fortune to favor the audacious!" The smile Banning directed at Partridge was entirely friendly.

Though Sully, too, disliked Banning, he felt uncomfortable with Gifford's gibes and made an attempt at concilation. "We've wished you farewell any number of times, Banning. Do I take it this is really it?"

"You'll be glad to know it is. I'm off from Han Kang at first light."

"Why Han Kang? What's the point of trekking all your supplies over Nam-san ridge to Han Kang when we have the river at our doorstep?" Gifford jeered.

"There's quite a rise and fall in the tide at the river estuary at Chemulpo. That causes a dangerous flux in the river. But once you get beyond the rapids between here and Han Kang, there is smooth passage—for a time at least."

"How long will you be gone?" Sully asked.

"Until the onset of the cold hardens the ground. And you, Partridge, what are your plans?"

"Because of the delay in our kwan-ja, we lost a lot of time. It'll still be a few weeks before we're ready to leave."

"We? Since Dr. Sullivan's duties, and," Banning glanced in Marigold's direction, "I've no doubt, his fair companion, keep him

in Seoul, who'll be making the trip with you? You must realize it's
too arduous for a man of Farquhar's years."

"Reverend Farquhar most certainly cannot be spared, Banning.
Miss Wilder will be accompanying me."

"Maggie!" Banning's angrily raised voice caused heads to turn.
"But it's absolutely impossible for Maggie to go. I won't hear of it.
The Han, for the most part, is uncharted; in certain sections its
rapids are as treacherous as those of the Yangtse. It's out of the
question to take Maggie along. You can't be serious!"

"I really don't see what right you have . . ." Sully began. Though
the sentiment was one he'd echoed any number of times, he was
furious to find Banning adopting his own proprietary stand. Judging from the look on Marigold's face as she hastened across the
room, she, too, was angry.

"Mr. Banning, you have absolutely no right to intervene—even
to voice an opinion in this matter. It's already been decided that I'm
to go with Gifford. The date of our departure was only delayed
because our kwan-ja was not granted as rapidly as your own . . ."

"For obvious reasons," Gifford put in.

"For whatever reason," Marigold snapped, ignoring Gifford's
sneer. "The point is that at long last we can make ready for the
journey and we intend to do so with all haste."

"Maggie! Maggie!" Banning shook his head. "You're taking a terrible risk. Your father would never approve. He might think missionary work is appropriate for women—I dare say he'd applaud
your dedication to the cause, coming here to Korea to spread the
word—but he would certainly not have wanted you to embark on
this sampan trip. The Han is dangerous, difficult for a man to
navigate, let alone a woman. Your father would never have sanc-
tioned the idea."

"How dare you say what my father would or would not have
wanted!" Marigold's hostility toward Banning was never as acute as
when he used her father's name to add strength to his argument.

What made her still angrier was her suspicion that he was right—
her father would very likely have made exactly the same ojections.

"You've really gone too far when you presume to echo my father's
wishes, Mr. Banning. My father was a fine, decent gentleman. You
have absolutely nothing in common with him and you have no right
to tell me what he would or would not have approved." The heat of
their argument had caused all other conversation in the room to
cease.

"Marigold!" Reverend Farquhar hurried over to intervene. "I'm
sure Mr. Banning meant no harm. He is simply expressing his
concern for your safety, a concern we all share, ever since the idea
of your going was proposed. If he considers it impractical for a
woman . . ."

"I do," Banning said flatly.

"I don't give a damn what he thinks," Marigold exploded, "I
won't have him interfering in my life, deciding what I may or may
not do."

Her outburst raised eyebrows and produced disapproving looks
all around the room. Edith Allen found the language and tone entirely unsuitable for a lady—a missionary lady at that! Mrs.
Gardner decided she must take care that her young daughter, who
was inclined to emulate Marigold Wilder, wouldn't attempt to copy
this distasteful display. Natasha Waeber was strangely troubled by
the antagonism that surfaced whenever Marigold was in Mark
Banning's company. The antagonism of Gifford and Sully was cold
and calculated, undoubtedly caused by envy, but Marigold's was
different. It sparked spontaneously, like a match against flint, and
its origin was entirely unclear. Where there were sparks, Natasha
knew flames were likely to follow.

"Maggie, I just want . . ." Banning began.

"Don't call me that!" Marigold exploded again. "Don't ever call
me that!"

"Very well." Banning's sudden laugh relieved the tension. "Miss

Wilder, I apologize. You're right, I shouldn't interfere. Given your faith, your devotion, your desire to serve the cause, who am I to queston the wisdom of your making such a journey? God, of course will be your protector."

No one present, with the exception of Banning, understood why this seemingly graceful apology caused Marigold's anger to erupt beyond heated words. But Banning had touched her at her most vulnerable point, and she knew that he knew that. She struck back in the only way that occurred to her at that moment, lashing out, her hand making an impression on his cheek but not eliminating his smile.

The room became so quiet that, to Marigold, the sound of that slap echoed in the silence. Her immediate impulse was to beg forgiveness. She'd never struck anyone before, never even thought of doing such a thing. But, instead, she bit her lip, and, with head high, she abruptly turned on her heel and left the room. As she closed the door, quite deliberately, taking care not to slam it, the silence broke and a hubbub of voices arose.

Marigold didn't let the tears of shame for her action fall until the door of the legation closed behind her. She could feel them, heavy against her lids. Once alone, however, striding toward the iron gates, she no longer fought to hold them back.

She prided herself on her self-control. What would her father have thought of such abysmal behavior? How ashamed of her he would have been! These recurring thoughts made her even more angry at Banning. His barely veiled inferences made her believe he knew she was missionary in name only, that she was there under false pretenses. She'd always suspected, ever since he winked at her in church, that he had somehow guessed her guilty secret. And now he'd rubbed her nose in it in front of everyone. How despicable of him!

When she heard the footsteps behind her she increased her pace, thinking it was Gifford or, worse yet, Herbert Farquhar, and not feeling capable of facing either of them.

"Maggie . . . Marigold . . . Miss Wilder. It was all my fault. I am sorry. Really, I am."

"Damn you, Mark Banning!" With tears coursing down her cheeks, she lengthened her stride. But he caught up with her, and taking hold of her arm, forced her to turn and face him.

"I really am sorry, Maggie." His eyes searched hers, while hers sought—and found—a slight sign of her blow still visible on his cheek.

"I don't need you to feel sorry for me." Her voice was muffled by tears. She just wished his tone weren't quite as sincere, his expression quite as contrite. She knew her father would have expected her to apologize for hitting him, but his very contrition made her want to strike out again.

"I know you don't. But I can't help how I feel about you, any more than you can help your feelings for me."

"I hate you," she said vehemently.

"Love . . . hate . . . faith. They're all so confusing, aren't they? I goaded you and got what I deserved."

"You knew, didn't you?" she fumed.

"So you have a skeptical nature. It's not the end of the world, Maggie, in fact, I like you all the more because of it. It's one more thing we have in common. I find uncertainty about God's existence a sight more healthy than a lot of pious do-gooders ritualistically repeating things they don't understand but don't care to—or don't even care to question."

Although he was expressing thoughts she'd had a hundred times, Banning's words did nothing to melt her anger.

"You made me do something I've never done before," she raged. "You've made me feel thoroughly ashamed of myself. Now, I suppose, you're satisfied."

"Oh, Maggie! Maggie!" He took both her hands in his and held them fast. "I'd like to be able to make you do any number of things you've never done before. But I'd never want you to be ashamed of them."

"We have nothing, absolutely nothing in common." She tried to wrench her hands free. "Don't talk to me as though I'm Natasha Waeber, because I have as little in common with her as I do with you."

"True. I'm well aware you're not Natasha. I assure you I don't talk to you in the same way at all," he agreed seriously, somehow not making her feel any better at all.

"I imagine not. You obviously know her intimately. She's been everywhere and done everything." Though her tongue, on occasion, was known to be sharp, it was unlike Marigold to malign anyone. She might have little in common with Natasha, but she didn't dislike her. She could not understand why she found herself speaking so caustically about her.

"That's not what I mean and you know it. But don't spoil her party. I apologize. I've explained to everyone it was my fault. Come on back."

"I don't care about her silly party. And I don't need you to apologize on my behalf." She tugged at her hands again, and this time he didn't stop her from wrenching them free.

"You're really serious about going on this trip with Partridge?"

"If you're implying that there's anything wrong about my going with . . ."

"You and Partridge! Not for a minute. There's no fear of danger from that quarter. But you should fear the river. The Han's perilous. Partridge won't be of much help. Besides the river, there are tigers . . ."

"Tigers! I'm sick to death of hearing about tigers," she scoffed. "These scare tactics of yours are despicable! If there were as many tigers in Korea as there are tales about them, the place would be uninhabitable—as infested with them as it is with rats."

"The stories may be exaggerated—I certainly hope they are—but I know there are tigers roaming those hills and you'll need some protection. You can't count on Partridge, you know. He dislikes you as much as you dislike me—probably even more."

His perspicacity was even more annoying. "I don't rely on anyone," she snapped.

"I realize that, but you can't fight a tiger with bare hands. Apart from the big cats, word has it that a Tong-hak uprising is imminent. Do you have a gun?"

"No."

"You'll need one, and you'll need to know how to use it."

"I suppose someone from an uncivilized country like yours would consider using a gun the answer to every dilemma."

"Not every dilemma, but sometimes it can come in mighty handy. Just talking to a hungry tiger or a hostile bandit won't do much good."

"I'd have thought with your glib tongue, you could talk yourself out of anything," Marigold said tartly as she turned on her heel; she could feel his eyes on her as she strode down the path.

"What I'd like to talk you out of is that trip," he called after her.

She swung around "You can't talk me out of—or into—anything."

"Don't challenge me, Maggie!" he warned lightly. "That only brings out the devil in me."

She turned away then, allowing him the last word

Marigold's behavior at the Russian legation was the subject of gossip over teacups for weeks to come. The only apology she made, however, was to Farquhar.

"I should never have struck Banning, but I hope you realize I didn't create that scene. He did."

"So he said. But he's right, Marigold, to be concerned about this trip. And knowing your father, undoubtedly he felt he had to express that concern."

"He barely knew Father. He visited us in Barleigh once, for just a few days, that's all," she said in exasperation.

"Perhaps. Still, Mr. Banning's nunchi seems rather astute in summing people up," Farquhar commented. "I find him a man of unusual understanding."

Why was it, Marigold wondered, that Farquhar seemed as appreciative of Banning as her father had been? But she carefully refrained from carrying the argument any further for fear he might reconsider the wisdom of his decision to allow her to go with Gifford. Now that they had the kwan-ja and the queen's nod of approval, she wasn't about to jeopardize the journey.

As it was, the delay in their departure had caused enough problems. The sampan and boatman they had originally planned to hire for the journey had been taken by someone else. Another sampan, not nearly as stoutly constructed, and far smaller—less than thirty feet, in fact—had been found, but Hong, the boat's owner, was surly and, Marigold suspected, quite lazy. However, at this late date, there was no other option, so she took it. She arranged for a roof of straw mats supported on ridge poles to be constructed over the mid and stern sections. These were divided, for privacy, by yet another wall of matting. Though Gifford was in charge of the operation and nominally made decisions, he found the planning for their day-to-day living arrangements a difficult and unrewarding task, so he left it to Marigold.

Because of the extremely limited space, she kept their supplies to a minimum: trestle beds, bedding, mosquito nets, folding chairs; simple kitchen equipment including a brazier for charcoal, tongs, saucepan and frying pan, a small kettle; and, for the table, metal mugs and plates together with folding eating utensils. Food supplies consisted of flour—any found along the way would likely be full of weevils—curry powder, a few cans of soup and corned beef, and tea. Rice, fruit, and eggs could easily be purchased; before buying meat, however, Marigold would take care to know exactly what it was, for she had no desire to eat dog.

The middle and largest section of the sampan Marigold allocated to Gifford, and there she had placed the metal-lined chest that housed his Bibles, prayer books, vestments, and articles of office.

In the stern, Marigold made up her own quarters, arranging her own chest containing her bulky magazine camera, tripod, a variety of chemicals for developing, and a large supply of glass plates. She was taking only two changes of clothing; into the skirts she had sewn pockets deep enough to carry photographic equipment. Since the rainy season was imminent, she added high rubber boots and an oversized waterproof cape. In her section, too, she kept the saddles they would require for their journey across the Diamond Mountains. The fore section, to be occupied by Hong and his promised crew of three, was filled to capacity with equipment, tools, lines, kitchen utensils, and stores.

But by far the greatest difficulty was finding space in the sampan for the money supply required for the journey. Since there were unlikely to be any banks or money changers en route and since the only acceptable coin was a large copper piece with a hole in the center known as *cash* (exchanged at a rate of over three thousand to the English pound), the ten-pounds worth estimated for the journey made an enormous ballast. The more than thirty thousand coins, strung through the middle on lengths of straw, required six men to load into the sampan, after which the boat settled into the river with water lapping dangerously close to the gunwale.

At long last they neared readiness and the day of their departure loomed before them.

"I shall miss you, paksa." Chu-sun's expression was solemn when Marigold went to the palace to say good-bye. "I didn't realize how very much I would miss you until now. I begged and prayed that you would make this journey and now that you are going, I'm suddenly afraid."

"I'm not afraid, Chu-sun, so you mustn't be. All this talk of tigers and Tong-hak rebels is mostly just that—talk."

"That's not all I am afraid of, paksa," she said, wringing her hands compulsively.

"What is it then, Chu-sun?" Marigold asked quietly.

"I am afraid because the queen has suggested you go to Wonsan, because she has written to her brother there . . ."

"But you, yourself, wrote that letter for her. You know exactly what she said—nothing but kind phrases requesting that he make us welcome. You told me so."

"I know, I know." Chu-sun nodded, but her face did not lighten. "I know what she said, but I don't trust her words. And nor must you. You must be careful. If anything should happen to you, it would be my fault. I could never forgive myself. You are doing this for me."

"I am going on this journey because I want to see the country. And I'm glad that in going, I have the opportunity to do something for you. I'm really looking forward to it. I just wish you could come to Han Kang where the sampan is lying and see us off."

"Hurry back, paksa." Chu-sun held her close, as though to hold her back.

"I shall, and when I do, I shall have news for you," Marigold promised.

Marigold and Gifford's departure was not toasted in champagne, but a tea party was held at the British consulate. Though the tea they drank was Mrs. Gardner's finest Ceylon, and was served with her own jam tarts and a rather heavy Madeira cake, the atmosphere of the afternoon tea was entirely different from that of the jubilant send-off given to Banning. Marigold had been treated with a certain reserve since the incident at the Russian legation. And as she had made no attempt to publicly apologize for her behavior, or to justify it, she scarcely expected to retain her previously favored position in their community. Sully was the only one who had seemed pleased by her angry outburst.

"Good show!" he had whispered to her when next he saw her. "He's had that coming for a long time."

Somehow, Marigold felt more deflated than pleased by Sully's endorsement of her action.

But Sully wasn't there when they arrived at the British consulate, and Marigold was left to her own devices. Natasha hadn't spoken to her since the incident at her reception. Edith Allen remained clearly vexed at "the sorry sight of a missionary lady raising her hand to a gentlemen" as she kept repeating behind Marigold's back. Mabel Gardner went to some pains to prevent her daughter from talking to Marigold on her own, but with her garden now in full bloom, she had her hands full and little time to spare for human foibles. Besides, Marigold had somewhat redeemed herself promising to bring back any unusual plant specimens found along the way.

Rescued from her ostracized position by Sully, Marigold realized she was beginning to find his presence comforting.

"Come outside. I have to talk to you," he whispered, his eyes glowing with excitement.

"What is it Sully?" Marigold asked.

"Not here," he whispered again, drawing her out onto the veranda and closing the door on young Miss Gardner's envious gaze.

"Well?" she asked, but even before he drew the box from his pocket, she knew what his excitement was about. She knew, too, that she could no longer hedge. She had to decide.

"It came, and just in time." He opened the box ceremoniously, like a child savoring a single Christmas gift. "Here, Marigold, it's yours."

He took the ring from the box and proffered it to her.

"It's yours," he repeated.

"It's beautiful, Sully. But . . ."

"It's yours," he said again. "Freely given. You can decide on which finger to wear it."

She looked down at the diamond and sapphire ring in the palm of her hand. Sully was such a fine man, so kind, so patient, so fair . . . so unlike Mark Banning.

She looked up at him and smiled.

"You're really such a dear, Sully, the very nicest man I know," she said, slipping the ring on the third finger of her left hand.

3

The morning before the departure of Marigold and Gifford, an entirely unexpected visitor was shown into the dining room of the Anglican mission on Nam-san.

"Banning! Why it's our Mr. Banning," Reverend Farquhar beamed, getting up to greet the new arrival.

As Banning removed his wide-brimmed hat, Marigold noticed his deeply tanned complexion. He wore the same tall boots he had worn that day he had arrived, just as unexpectedly, in Barleigh. How long ago that seemed! She remembered someone saying, "Never seen a man wearing high-heeled boots before. Sissified I call it. Besides, he don't even need them." Now he stood in the doorway, dressed in a checkered, short-sleeved shirt with leather chaps over his brown trousers, a holstered gun at his belt, his presence overpowering the small room.

"But I thought we weren't to expect you until some time in the autumn," Herbert Farquhar was saying. "What's the matter? Is something wrong?"

"Maybe the gold ran out?" Gifford hazarded. "Or was the supply not quite as bountiful as expected?"

Banning shook his head. "Wrong on both counts, Partridge. There's gold there, and plenty of it. The Koreans don't call the Han the River of Golden Sand for nothing, but the placer deposits are just icing on the cake. I've discovered a real lode in the mountains above Chum-yol. But getting there isn't easy. Are you still planning on making that trip up the north branch of the river?"

"We leave tomorrow," Gifford replied.

Banning looked at Marigold. "And you're still set on going along?"

"There's never been any question in my mind," she said firmly.

"Very well, then." He dug into the pocket of the leather coat he carried over his arm to produce a map that he unfolded and spread out on the dining room table. "Then you'd better know what you're up against—both of you." He looked over at Gifford and waited, refusing to go on until, with obvious reluctance, he joined them.

"Almost as soon as you leave Han Kang, you'll be in mountainous country. Really beautiful. At sunset you'll be able to spot the series of signal beacons that terminate right here above you on Nam-san. It's a system designed to let that poor devil penned up in his palace know all's as well as can be expected in this sorry mess of a kingdom of his.

"The river forks here at Ma'chai. This north branch will take you on to Yo-Ju, birthplace of the beloved queen. You should get there from Ma'chai in a couple of days. Then it's fine going as far as Tan-yang—plan on making around fifteen miles a day if you can. At Tan-yang you'll find a marker indicating you're slap-dab in the middle of this Land of the Morning Calm. There's also a Confucian temple you might want to take a look at or do a few rubbings if you're so inclined. You'll go through a fine cultivated valley after Tan-yang, and the river broadens out as far as To-tam. Look up at this point and you'll see quite a spectacular natural bridge. Then the river narrows with high limestone cliffs on either side. That's where the rapids begin in earnest and where the going gets rough and treacherous. There's a nasty stretch before Yong-chun, and not much relief when you get there. The people, officials and commoners alike, are on edge about the Tong-hak, and they don't welcome strangers of any kind, most especially round-eyed foreigners. I know. I had to beach there for repairs, so let that be a warning to you. There's a fine old pagoda on the cliffs above Chum-yol, where I'm mining. From there to Paik-kui Mi, it's one rapid after another.

You'll have to pole or drag the sampan to make it. After Ut-Kiri, the river's all but impassable." He looked up at Marigold, rather than Gifford, to demand, "Got a good, stout boat?"

"A thirty-footer," she replied, "The best we could find."

"Is the boatman experienced? Does he know the river?"

"He says he does," she answered.

"What's his name?"

"Hong."

"Tied up at Han Kang, is he?"

She nodded.

"How many in the crew?"

"He's promised three."

"Good! Be firm with him. Let him know you aim at making fifteen miles a day. Don't let him get away with rotted lines either, because you'll need good stout rope to get through the rapids."

"The lines are good. I've seen them myself."

Banning looked at Marigold with added respect. "Are you well supplied?"

She nodded.

"As I said, I'm above the rapids at Chum-yol, so if you need anything . . ."

"Look here, Banning," Gifford interrupted. "We're not novices. I've planned this trip down to the last detail. I really resent your barging in with all these high-handed questions and advice we didn't ask for and don't need."

"You are a novice, Partridge. This river is one of the worst I've ever encountered. You'd better listen and you'd better listen good if you're going to make it to Paik-kui Mi and back."

"We're going all the way to Wonsan," Gifford said airily. He hadn't been in favor of the extension of their journey until that moment. But it was all worth it to see that look of disbelief on Banning's face.

"You're crossing the Diamond Mountains! Damn it to hell! You'd better start praying in earnest then." Banning burst out in anger, turning from Gifford to Marigold, then back again. When neither spoke, he demanded, "Just how do you plan to cross them?"

"By pony."

"Then you're even crazier than I thought. There are rebel strongholds all through those mountains. Not to mention tigers."

"I'm sick to death of these constant warnings about tigers," Marigold began, but Farquhar interrupted quickly, "Have you ever encountered any, Mr. Banning?"

"No," Banning admitted. "I can't say I have."

"There! You see," Marigold triumphed.

"But make no mistake about it, they're out there. Even without the tigers, even without the Tong-hak, crossing those mountains is no piece of cake. The paths are practically nonexistent; as soon as the rainy season comes, they disappear altogether. Better not over-load those ponies—you'll have to keep your supplies to the very minimum. What kind of arms are you carrying?"

"I'll have a carbine along, good for a pheasant or two." Sensing the next question on Banning's lips, Gifford stated firmly, "I've taken part in quite a few shooting parties in Scotland." Then, as Banning continued staring at him expectantly, he added loftily, "I fancy myself a rather good shot."

"A carbine's too heavy for Maggie," Banning said.

"Surely you can't expect Marigold to have need of a gun." The frown on Herbert Farquhar's face deepened.

"I'd advise no one to be on the river unarmed," Banning said, "But to travel across those mountains without a gun is sheer madness."

"Oh dear! But Mr. Banning, this is terrible! You really believe it to be that dangerous?" Farquhar was clearly shaken.

"I do," Banning affirmed.

"I'll be there, and I've told you I'll be armed," Gifford said, though a note of diffidence had crept into his voice.

"You are hardly . . ." Banning began, then seemed to change his mind. He unlatched the holster on his belt and reached for his pistol. "You'd better take this, Maggie. Know how to use it?"

She shook her head.

He laid the gun on the table.

"It's a Borchardt, made in Germany. I found it at Purdey's on South Audley Street. It's a real gem—the most powerful pistol I've come across, accurate at both short and long range. Here's the magazine—it holds eight rounds. This—are you listening, Maggie, it's important—this is the safety catch. When it's pressed in, there's no chance of the gun going off accidentally. And here's the trigger." He picked up the gun. "You must carefully align the foresight and backsight to hit your target. Try it."

She took the gun gingerly.

"Hold it steady. It's a weapon, not a fan. Lift it so those two sights are directly in your line of vision." He grinned. "Point it at me if you want a target."

"I really wouldn't care to have the blood of even the dumbest of beasts on my hands," she said, putting the gun down.

"You'd rather be dead yourself, is that it? Martyred for the cause." He was still grinning.

She bit her lip to hold back a retort.

"I'm really getting concerned about this whole thing, Marigold," Farquhar fretted.

Marigold immediately took up the gun. "All right, then. I'll take it."

"Fine, but a gun's no good unless you know how to use it. Let's walk on up the hill and fire a few rounds."

As they went to the door, Gifford smiled fleetingly. "Natasha Waeber's been dismal company since you left, Banning. I suppose now we may expect her humor to improve."

Banning stopped and turned back. He looked at Gifford, then at Farquhar as he said, "I'd count it a great favor if you'd mention to no one—not even Natasha—that I was here."

"You can count on me, Mr. Banning," Farquhar promised. "I'm

only too glad that you came." He looked at Gifford for corroboration and, when none came, he emphasized, "Gifford, Marigold—all of us are grateful to you for your willingness to share your knowledge."

"It's the least I can do, sir."

As Marigold and Banning climbed Nam-san, neither spoke. They passed beyond all places of habitation, but still Banning kept climbing.

"We don't want the shots to be heard in the city," he said at last. "They might get the idea the rebellion's already broken out."

"Do you think it could?" Marigold asked.

He nodded. "It's entirely possible. The Tong-hak have gained a lot of ground. They've been after reform for a long time. Looks like this time they're determined to have it. And who can blame them?"

"You've met them, talked to them?" she asked curiously, sensing he knew far more than he was telling. And when he didn't answer, she asked, "What did you come back for?"

"There was something I had to take care of," he replied without looking at her.

"A secret mission," Marigold said lightly.

"Something like that," he responded. His voice was quite serious.

"Do you think the Tong-hak mean trouble?"

"I think they're only the tip of the iceberg, speaking of which . . ." He had stopped to look down on the city below them, a maze of brown roofs with scarcely a tree visible except within the granite walls of the palace. Banning indicated the main thoroughfare, which was absolutely white, "If you didn't know better, you'd think it was snowing. Though, come to think of it, a flock of sheeps more like it."

She shaded her eyes. "Have you ever thought of all those women, pounding laundry sticks until their arms are ready to fall off, just so their men can appear in spotless garb that gets filthy after the first wearing? It's sheer madness—wearing white in a country like this. It condemns women to forced labor."

"It's not forced. They're doing what they were taught, what their mothers have done before them. I'm not sure I agree with using words like *madness* or *forced labor* to describe something that's their traditional way of doing things."

"But it *is* madness to work day and night as they do—unpicking seams, pounding to wash, pounding to iron, sewing it all up again," Marigold insisted earnestly. Glancing up, she caught his smile and retorted, "I suppose you wouldn't mind having some woman slaving away like that for you."

His eyes twinkled, "Are you making the offer?"

Marigold tossed her head. "I've told you what I think of it—madness! But I don't suppose you'd realize what these women go through . . ." She broke off, remembering the washerwoman at the palace. "Though maybe you do. Where did you get that washerwoman's coverall, the changot you wore the night Sully delivered Chun-mae's baby? We still owe you our thanks."

He shrugged. "Since I so seldom earn your gratitude, Maggie, it's too bad I can't accept it when it's given. But I haven't earned it, not yet at least. And as for that rather snide comment of yours just now, I'd find it degrading to have any woman make a slave of herself for me. Early on, I learned to take care of myself, and I'm damned glad I did. Otherwise I might have turned out as helpless as Partridge or Algie. My background's as different from theirs as yours is from that of these women. To try to impose our standards or ideas too quickly here would be wrong—dead wrong. All you have to do is read history, any country's history, to see that too great a push for reform only brings on a conservative backlash. Not that this place isn't crying out for reform—the government and the yangban are corrupt and tyrannical. They've had their way at the expense of the people for centuries. Reform must come, there's no question about it, but how, when, . . ." he shrugged.

"You really think trouble's brewing?"

He nodded, then looked off in the direction of the coast. "It's not looking good out there, Maggie. This country may be in for a blood-bath before long."

"Is that why you came back?" she asked.

He turned to her, answering her question with a question. "Why are you and Partridge going all the way to Wonsan?"

For a moment, she had an urge to tell him everything but then she remembered his friendship with the queen.

"Gifford thinks it may be fruitful territory for his mission," she lied, thinking how hard she'd had to work to convince him to go.

"He didn't appear to be overly enthusiastic about making the trip, so I thought it must be your idea," Banning observed. He waited and when she said nothing more, he looked around. "Here, I guess this place is as good as any." He pointed toward a rocky incline and stooped down to select several distinctively shaped rocks; these he placed on a ledge. Then he took the gun from its holster, removed the safety, and handed it to her.

"A gun's a lethal instrument. No one should handle one without knowing what they're doing. You must hold it firmly. Never pull the trigger—squeeze back on it—smooth and even. Don't be in a hurry. Even though your life or someone else's may depend on it, take your time. Being trigger-happy doesn't do much except make a lot of racket. It can also hurt people—the wrong people. When you're ready, make sure the gun is properly loaded and the safety's off. Then sight your target carefully and shoot."

He raised the gun, then fired. The middle rock shattered and fell.

"Okay. Now you try."

Gingerly, distastefully, Marigold took the gun from him and raised it impulsively.

"Maggie, for God's sake handle the thing as though you mean business."

She lowered the gun. "But I don't mean business. This idea of shooting at things is abhorrent to me. Guns kill. I'm not a killer."

In exasperation, he yelled, "Maggie, either you shoot that thing or I'm going back down there and put such fear of God into Farquhar he'll forbid you from now till kingdom come to ever go out on that river."

"I'm sick and tired of your scare tactics," she yelled back at him. "First it's me, then Gifford, now Herbert. For some reason, you want us to put off this trip—I don't know why—but it's not going to work."

"Maggie," his voice was filled with quiet fury. "Never, ever yell at anyone and wave a gun in their direction with the safety off unless you really mean it."

"You're making me feel more like meaning it every minute," she railed, but nevertheless, she lowered the gun.

"Okay. Let's get on with it," he ordered.

"All right," she snapped. Raising the gun, she pointed it in the general direction of the targets he had set up.

"Watch for . . ." he began as she fired, "the recoil," he finished as she stumbled back and fell.

"You might have told me," she fumed. Refusing his offer of help, she got to her feet.

"You might have waited. Don't ever fire without properly sighting your target. Then watch for the recoil. Firm hold, remember. Now, do it again."

In quick succession, she shot the remaining six rounds in the magazine, one after the other, jerking the trigger, closing her eyes at each report, not hitting or even coming close to hitting any of the targets he'd set up. He reloaded the magazine without comment.

"Okay. This time, will you just try? And how about keeping your eyes open?"

She shot another round and, though she no longer staggered at the recoil, though she managed to pull the trigger more firmly, she didn't so much as graze the target rocks.

Without a word, he came up behind her, put both his arms around her, his hands over hers, and raised the gun. Then he lined up the sights and, with his finger over hers, pulled the trigger. The rock at the end of the row shattered and fell.

He stood his ground firmly, and the impact of the recoil pressed her back against him. His hands tightened over hers, pressing down hard on the ring on her left hand. She could feel his lips brushing aginst her hair.

"Do you love him, Maggie?" he whispered, "Do you really love him?"

"Sully?" Her voice was unsteady, she didn't trust herself to say more.

"Who else? That's his ring on your finger, isn't it?"

"I . . . I think Sully's the nicest man I know."

"Which doesn't begin to answer my question," he replied softly, his hold around her tightening. His lips were kissing her hair, the nape of her neck as he repeated, "Oh, Maggie, Maggie!"

"Don't!" she said, but the word was drowned by the staccato beat of her heart.

"You should be kissed," he said as he kissed her again, "and you should be touched where a woman wants to be touched." His hands ran lightly across her breasts and a sudden pleasurable surge ran through her. Her stomach quivered as though she were on a merry-go-round. She felt a sense of excitement; she wanted the moment to go on forever. But when she felt herself losing control, excitement was replaced by fear. Mark Banning had a way of making her forget who she was.

As he turned her toward him, she suddenly pushed away.

"Don't!" she cried out. "This isn't right!"

"Maggie," his tone was serious, "Whatever happens between you and me will always be right."

"I'm not like the others. I'm not falling for those glib words of yours." She backed way from him, the gun dangling loosely in her hand. "And you'd better not touch me again, not with this thing in my hand—if you do, I may do something you'll regret."

He laughed. "Maggie, I'll bet you couldn't hit me from where you are right now."

"Don't tempt me," she warned, conscious that she was still trembling.

He shook his head. "Teaching you to hit a target's like teaching a mule to ride a bicycle. I don't think it can be done."

"Here, then." She handed him back the gun.

He took it, put on the safety catch, and handed it back to her.

"I'd rather you hang on to it, even if you can't hit anything with it. Maybe the sight of a gun in your hand will be sufficient to strike terror in the heart of a marauding bandit, or perhaps the noise of an exploding bullet may scare off some hungry tiger."

"You're so . . . so insufferably sure of yourself!"

"From hungry tigers and purposeful women may the good Lord deliver me," he intoned, removing the empty hoster from his waist. But in handing it to her, he held onto her hand for a moment. "I don't think you'd find me so insufferable if you really knew me, Maggie. But in any case, I hope you'll remember everything that happened here this morning. One of these days you may have reason to wish you'd paid more attention."

With his eyes on her, Marigold felt herself falling under his spell again. She turned away with a terse, "One of those days you may have reason to wish you hadn't taunted me so."

4

Arriving at Han Kang early on the morning of their departure, Gifford and Marigold found Hong, the boatman, fast asleep. Marigold felt it was a bad omen, giving proof to the laziness she had earlier suspected. But, even when they discovered that far from having a crew of three, as promised, Hong had only one wiry but very old man to help him—a man who gave every appearance of being both deaf and dumb—even when they saw that though the poles were sturdy, the lines on the boat were not the new stout ropes they had been shown earlier, but ragged, limp pieces of hemp, they felt they had little choice but to embark.

"You should have seen to it, why didn't you? I left it to you, and now look what we're stuck with," Gifford raged. But before Marigold could reply, he held up his hand to silence her. "No, no. I don't want excuses. Besides, it's my fault—all mine."

"It's both our . . ." Marigold began.

"No. No. Mine. It's mine," he insisted with a short laugh. "I should have known by this time that if I wanted anything done right, I'd have to do it all myself, down to the very last detail."

She held back a retort. After all, they would be thrown in one another's company almost exclusively for two, possibly three months. What was the use of beginning with a quarrel? She must learn to guard her temper and keep to her own devices as much as possible.

Despite their close confinement, this was not difficult. Though divided only by a curtain of straw, they set up their separate quarters, employing every inch of space to its fullest in order to accommodate their individual goals. Marigold immediately began going over her photographic supplies and making arrangements for a dark room, using her large waterproof cape and the blankets from her trestle bed. If too much light filtered through, she could always wait for night to provide a natural dark room. She tested the river water and found it too muddy to wash the hypo out of her negatives, but using the fine filter she had brought along for tea seemed to solve that problem; even if it didn't work perfectly, mud particles might make for interesting effects. In her cramped quarters she could find no space to hang her prints up to dry, but then she discovered she could put the print frames over the side and let the wind take care of that. She had decided to keep a journal which, along with the photographs, would provide a useful record of the journey. She was so thoroughly immersed in her own projects that she was quite undisturbed by Gifford, next door, moving his trunk around until he found the exact place for it to serve as a desk, setting out his writing implements, paper, and books. She didn't even mind when he drew aside the curtain, since it was impossible to stand upright under the roof drape.

"Getting all shipshape?" Without waiting for an answer, Gifford moved his folding chair to the side, put his feet up on the gunwale, lit up a cigarette, and drew on it. He gazed out at the passing scenery, dreaming or perhaps seeking inspiration for his writings.

And from that first day, as they pulled out of Han Kang north past the Nam Han fortress, the last familiar landmark, and entered the mountains, the countryside was inspiring. As they moved further north, toward the source of the great river in the Diamond Mountains, they would encounter scene after scene of unsurpassed beauty. But that lay far ahead, not only in distance, but in time. Hong was lazy, and even when the weather was good, even when there were no rapids to encounter, they never made more than ten miles a day. Hong poled in the sampan's bow, while his little assistant plied a pole several times his height and weight at the rear. He would accept Marigold's help, though he never thanked her; in fact, he never spoke at all.

Frequently, sometimes as often as once each hour, Hong would pull over and go off to pick vegetables or fruit, or else he would disappear, possibly for a call of nature, but more likely just for a smoke. Marigold employed these frequent halts to explore the river banks, taking pictures of the scenery and plants, finding huge pink heliotrope and scarlet azaleas, samples of which she dug up to take back to Mrs. Gardner. It was better than grumbling at Hong for stopping so often, as Gifford did, for then the boatman would feign exhaustion and lie down on the bank, his assistant curled at his feet like a dog, to gather his energy. The slow pace might have exasperated Gifford, but Marigold didn't mind. The river was slow-moving but fascinating and she revelled in the languor that gave her time to dwell on the changes in her life.

She might have been still in Barleigh, embroidering orphreys for Primrose's husband to wear before his altar. She might have been a maiden aunt caring for their newly born daughter, christened Esmeralda—an awful name, Marigold thought, sensing that Primrose did also. The child had been named for a rich relative of Algernon's; presumably he cherished hopes of inheritance. Poor Prim, Marigold thought, leaning against the gunwale as she looked out on other sampans plying the river, piled high with sacks of rice and barley bound for the capital. Out beyond was the river bank, with its rows of Spanish chestnuts, orange peels, persimmons, and squid hung out to dry like a Monday wash before walled, thatched huts. She drank it all in, feeling fortunate beyond measure. Here she was, setting out on a journey into the unknown, with a chance of doing a service for her dearest friend, while Prim was immersed in rectory teas and the Women's Altar Guild.

Poor Prim, Marigold thought again, wondering if somewhere Prim was thinking poor Marigold! But she supposed Prim was leading the life she wanted. Or was she? Prim had wanted Mark Banning, knowing that he would never settle down anywhere. Would

·Prim have been happy mining for gold somewhere far to the north on this river? Marigold tried to imagine her sister living for weeks in these cramped quarters—seven by four feet at best—with only one change of clothing, chosen for wear rather than fashion. Her imagination failed her. Remembering Mark Banning's treatment of her sister, reminded her of Mark Banning. Their last meeting had been disquieting, and Marigold tried to get him out of her mind. She set about the business of preparing lunch.

Hong and his assistant cooked their own meals, while Marigold prepared the food for herself and Gifford. The main meal, eaten in the middle of the day, usually consisted of a flat bread, made from flour and water and salt, and cooked on an iron skillet on the charcoal brazier. Rice was always a staple, along with whatever had been found in the way of chicken, fish, or, when Gifford was lucky, game, stewed with carrots and onions. The curry powder was a frequent lifesaver, giving taste to the most unappetizing potage. Meat, of any recognizable kind, was usually in scant supply, so Marigold often substituted chestnuts that she gathered along the way, boiling them and making them into rissoles. She found she enjoyed these as much if not more than a tough, wiry bird or a suspect chop. Fruit was plentiful—persimmons, pears, melons— and always made a refreshing conclusion to the meal. At four, Marigold made tea and served biscuits with it or, when that supply was exhausted, whatever remained of the flat bread. Their evening meal was a simpler variation of their midday repast. Though there was little variety, the diet was quite adequate; even Gifford did not grumble about the food.

His main complaint, however, was directed at Marigold herself, for as her presence on the river became known, it caused excitement and curious crowds all along their route. How word of a foreign woman being aboard spread so quickly was difficult to discover, unless the message had been passed by the same beacon fires lit on the mountain tops at sunset that notified the king that all was well. One way or another, the news was out and it had the neighboring villagers, many of whom had never seen a Westerner, let alone a Western woman, agog with excitement. Inquisitive sightseers from miles into the interior flocked down to the river hours before their sampan came into sight, just to be able to catch a glimpse of her.

"We're a sideshow," Gifford complained. "How can I preach the word and expect to be listened to when they treat us like a circus act?"

"We're different, that's all," Marigold said. "Besides, you have the people gathered together. That's what you wanted."

"But all they want is to gawk at you."

"If you think I find it enjoyable, you're mistaken," Marigold said hotly. She'd caught rumblings from the crowd about her being a "child-eater." Chu-sun had told her of a common superstition that "foreign devils" bought female babies and used them as stew meat; it was one thing to laugh at such a horrible superstition within the safety of the royal palace, another to be accused of it miles from home.

At each magistracy, Gifford and Marigold were obliged to venture out into the crowd to make their way to the yamen where the local magistrate sat to show they had in their possession a valid kwan-ja granting them permission to be there. They could then go on to buy food or else pass out Gifford's missionary tracts, invariably with the huge crowd still in tow, pushing and shoving, reaching out to touch Marigold, or, worse yet, to try to grab a piece of her clothing or a lock of her hair. The magistrates, notoriously highhanded, were of no help whatsoever in providing protection, though Marigold was never molested in their presence. They would sit back—smoking on long, bamboo pipes, lit and relit by anxious assistants who cowered at their beck and call—examining them without speaking a word until, with an imperious wave of the hand, they thrust their visitors back out into the baying crowd.

Worse than the magistrates, though, were the local yangban. These so-called noble gentlemen (they saw only the men, for their women were kept from view) were ill-mannered and obstreperous. They were literally waited on hand and foot by servants, not deigning to carry a book or pipe for themselves, even going so far as to be supported on horseback, with an attendant carrying the bridle and cruelly thrusting aside anyone who crossed their path. Their servants bullied and browbeat the villagers, never paid for anything, and freely borrowed money which they never returned. Hearing of the presence of a foreign woman, the yangban demanded that she be presented, and Marigold was forced to go and exhibit herself to them, then listen to rude, guffawed comments about the ugliness of her hair and features. She soon let it be known that she understood what they said, but this fact did little to curtail their amusement.

"No wonder there's an uprising of the Tong-hak," Marigold fumed, after a visit to a particularly unpleasant yangban who had ordered her to undo her hair and then had his servants snip pieces from it. Her disgust increased on learning he intended to have these snippings mounted into a brooch for his favorite concubine. To make matters worse, on their return to the river, she found their belongings had been removed from their sampan by the yangban's servants, who had confiscated the boat to take a supply of tiles to Seoul. Hong and his assistant, without any reimbursement beyond threats, had begun loading the tiles when Marigold and Gifford arrived.

Hong was in a sorry state. Gone was his former insolence. "Missy, give money, give anything, so they don't take boat," he pleaded.

"But it's ours. We've paid you for it. Why should we pay them?"

"Because they take it," he muttered, shrugging in exasperation at her ignorance.

"They won't take it," Marigold insisted, untying the lines herself, intent on throwing the servants into the river if need be.

But as soon as they saw her, the servants rushed at her, tearing the rope from her hands.

"Yobo!" they yelled. "Stay away!"

"I won't stay away. This is my boat."

"Get out. Go look for your testicles!" They guffawed as they pushed her ashore, then tied the boat up firmly so that the job could be finished.

Gifford was appalled, not at their language, which he did not undertand, but at the situation. "What are we going to do! What are we going to do!" he kept repeating. It was not so much a question as an exclamation of despair. "We can't be stuck here in this no-man's land. Let's give them the money as Hong suggested and be done with it."

"But without money we can't survive on the river," Marigold pointed out, brushing herself off disconsolately, then uprighting the box that contained her photographic equipment.

"We can't survive without a boat," Gifford pointed out. "At least with the boat we can return to Seoul."

"We can't go back now, Gifford," Marigold insisted.

Gifford, watching Hong's assistant staggering on board beneath yet another load of tiles, mourned, "We're fools! We've got no choice. They're going to take both the boat and the money and there's nothing we can do about it."

Marigold began rummaging in her box, pulling out broken photographic plates. She stopped suddenly as her hand closed around something hard and cold. When she stood up, she held Banning's pistol in her hand.

"No, Marigold, you'd better put that back," Gifford said hastily. "Taking justice into your own hands is not wise—not wise at all."

"And what about them?" she waved the pistol in the direction of the servants, engrossed in their task. "Is what they're doing wise?"

"But it's their country—their custom. We could get killed if we argue with them. And don't point that thing at me!" Gifford responded angrily.

"It's daylight robbery," Marigold said, turning to point the gun at the yangban's servants. "That's it!" she yelled. "I've had quite enough. Stop! Stop I say! Do you hear me? Get those tiles off that boat now, this instant or you'll pay for it with your lives."

The yangban's servants looked at the gun in her hand in utter disbelief. There was a guttural muttering, then they shrugged.

"It's only a woman. Even a tiger won't eat the entrails of a woman. Get on with it. Hurry!" They lashed out with a whip at Hong's assistant, who had been watching with obvious relief at being able to pause with his heavy load. He yelped with pain.

"I've found those testicles you sent me to look for," Marigold shouted, using their own language but relieved that Gifford could not understand what she was saying. "You'd better pay attention to what I say now, or else! Stop!" Marigold ordered the little man. He obeyed, looking back and forth in nervous confusion from the whip in the hands of the yangban's servants to the pistol in Marigold's hand.

Marigold turned to the servants. "Now get those tiles off that boat and put our things back. Do it yourselves, don't expect our hired men to do your work for you. I'm going to count to three and if you haven't started unloading those tiles, you," she waved the gun at the head servant, "will go first. One . . ." she clasped the gun firmly in both hands and raised it.

"Oh, my God!" Gifford moaned. "Have you gone mad, Marigold? They'll lock us up. We'll starve in prison or, worse yet, be hanged . . . or tortured . . . or . . ."

"I've just about had enough for one day, Gifford. First that awful man cutting at my hair, now this. I've had enough," Marigold muttered fiercely. "Besides, I can't harm them. I can't hit anything."

"Oh, my God!" Gifford moaned. Whether in prayer or expletive, it was hard to say.

As they made no move, Marigold took another step forward, "Two," she said firmly.

"Oh, my God!" Gifford moaned again, but this time there was no doubt it was an expletive. "You're mad as a hatter."

"I'm mad of heart, not of head!" Marigold took another step forward. This time she unclicked the safety catch on the gun, "Thr . . ."

No!" Marigold heard the cry but couldn't tell whether it was English or Korean, whether it came from Gifford or the servants. But she did see the head servant hold up his hand. "Don't shoot. Stop!" She then saw him motion to Hong's assistant to return the load of tiles to the river bank.

Marigold swallowed her sigh of relief. "Our man's done all he's going to do. It's up to you to unload the rest of the tiles and get our things back on board," Marigold ordered.

"Why split hairs now," Gifford muttered. "The quicker the job's done, the better."

"We've got to show them who's boss."

"I suppose so," Gifford said, attempting to take charge, now that the immediate danger had passed. "I must say, Marigold, that though the high-handed way you handled that seems, momentarily, to have succeeded, I can't say I like it or condone it. I don't think it was at all wise."

"So you said, but I don't think it was at all wise of that yangban to cut my hair," Marigold snapped.

"You realize we'll probably end up having to pay for your heroics," Gifford said after they had cast off, leaving a disconsolate group of servants on the bank looking up and down the river for another boat to commandeer.

"We were going to have to pay whichever way it went," Marigold reminded him. "Anyway, our next stop is Yo-Ju. It's the queen's birthplace."

"So?"

"So there's no harm in letting it be known there that we're in her good graces. We have her letter of introduction to her brother in Wonsan, after all. That should be good for something."

That letter turned out to be good for an invitation from Yo-Ju's leading yangban, a young relative of the queen, to attend a circus he was holding to celebrate his having gained good placement in the civil service examination.

As they entered the courtyard of his large tile-roofed mansion, Marigold was literally set upon and seized by serving women who dragged her off to the women's apartment, where the wife of the yangban, a girl who had barely passed puberty, was decked out in bright red and yellow and covered with jingling silver jewelry, waiting impatiently for the entertainment to begin. She was surrounded by concubines and servants all of whom looked on Marigold with fervent interest, presuming, perhaps, that she was a circus freak sent for their pleasure.

The women gathered around her, unpinning her hair and twisting and untwisting it, examining every article of clothing she wore, even down to her underclothing, all the while shrieking with delight. With forty pairs of hands pawing at her, Marigold found it next to impossible to make herself heard, but when she managed to raise her voice above the din, they were enchanted to find she spoke their language. They then seated her on a cushion and fed her beancakes, dried ginger, persimmons, and a light rice wine. Next they conducted her on a tour through their apartments. An odd attempt had been made to westernize the huge villa. There were huge, gilt-framed mirrors on the walls and French chiming clocks everywhere, all keeping different times. Marigold felt as though she had just stepped through the looking glass.

She was relieved when at last the host sent for her. He had heard she took photographs and demanded one be taken of himself as a gift for the queen. She was only too pleased to get away from the women's overenthusiasm and hastened to set up her camera.

The pink-faced young man, resplendently arrayed in blue and gold brocade, sat stiffly on a velvet-upholstered settee on the veranda. His attention was divided between Marigold's apparatus and events in the courtyard below. A rope had been stretched across, presumably for a high-wire act, and musicians were setting up kettledrums and reed pipes. He was so caught between his youthful desire to cut a dashing figure and his childlike desire to watch the activity below that Marigold had a difficult time getting him to stay still. Just as she was about to take the photograph, the young man jumped up once again, this time to greet arriving guests.

Despondently, Marigold pushed back the dark cloth and found herself face to face with the yangban from the village to the south, whose servants had given them so much trouble. A look of fury crossed his face as soon as he saw her. He immediately began to harangue her treatment of his servants and demanded that the local magistrate, also a guest, take immediate action to show these foreigner devils what happened to those who refused to obey the law of the land.

"I was obeying the law. It's your men who were not," Marigold pointed out. "We've paid for that sampan; it's ours. They had no right to try to take it away from us."

Everyone present, including her host, suddenly looked at her as though she had developed a bad case of leprosy.

"Shut up, Marigold," Gifford hissed. "Can't you see we're in trouble again? Why don't you try a bit of sugar instead of acid."

"Sugar cloys. Acid burns. This yangban deserves to burn." Unwittingly, her reply to Gifford was made in Korean.

"This woman has big hands and a big mouth and hair the color of a rotting chestnut." The yangban drew himself up to his full height. "She looks like a woman born in year of horse."

"Year of tiger," Marigold corrected.

"Even worse. She has done wrong. She must be punished. Respect comes at the end of a great rod—I suggest you have her beaten."

"But she's a foreigner," the youth stuttered awkwardly, in awe of his neighbor and clearly in a dilemma.

The yangban walked around Marigold, looking her up and down. "If this were my jurisdiction, I would have her beaten and then make her a slave. She would make a good slave—she knows how to entertain. But perhaps you are too young to take the responsibility of seeing that justice is done."

"She will be punished," the young host promised hoarsely, though clearly uncertain about what measures to take.

"What are you saying?" Gifford asked,

"They think I would make a good slave, I know how to entertain." Marigold's voice was calm but she was trembling inside. What had once been a great adventure was quickly becoming a nightmare. Suddenly, she began to laugh uncontrollably.

"Shut up?" Gifford whispered fiercely. "This is no laughing matter!"

But though she knew he was right, Marigold couldn't shut up. She looked at the men surrounding her in their high tungkuri headwear, their stiff brocade turugami. They seemed at that minute to be two-dimensional, just like a lot of playing cards. Why be so afraid of a pack of playing cards!

Imperiously, she motioned to the young man to sit back down in his chair. Gifford gazed at her as though she'd gone completely mad.

"A fine looking young man like you could undoubtedly attract high placement if you could be brought to the queen's attention," Marigold found herself saying, "but how will she ever know how handsome and imposing you are if she doesn't have a picture of you? And she won't unless you sit down and keep still."

As her young host moved toward the chair, Marigold, with more than a little pride, took her place behind her camera. But before she could focus, the yangban interceded.

"Huh! The queen has your picture and she likes it, that is good. But what if she does not? What if she gives your likeness to that wicked mudang of hers. She will put a curse on it and then where will you be?"

The young man half arose, but Marigold motioned for him to sit down again.

"Perhaps Min Tae-jon should have a copy. He is influential in finding positions for young men. Kim Tuk-so, who has been with him only a short time, is already a magistrate. Because you have been so hospitable, I shall make an extra print and give it to him when I go to Wonsan. Sit down, now, and don't move until I am finished. I can't delay my journey any longer. Min Tae-jon is awaiting my arrival, and I understand he is not a patient man."

Purposefully, Marigold got back under the black cloth. Through the lens she could see the figure of her young host, still for the first time. She thought it odd that he obeyed so quickly at the mention of Min Tae-jon's name.

"You are going all the way to Wonsan to see Min Tae-jon?" She heard the yangban's awestruck question but made no reply until she had finished taking the photograph.

Then, slowly, she came from beneath the cloth and nodded curtly. "I am to deliver a letter to him from the queen." She deliberately allowed a note of importance to creep into her voice, certain that she had somehow gained the upper hand.

The yangban positively fawned. "Would you carry my good wishes to Min Tae-jon and tell him I would be honored if he would deign to stay at my humble abode when next he is on his way to the capital. I shall move out. He may have the whole estate, tell him, and for as long as he wishes."

"I shall certainly do so," Marigold agreed pleasantly, "after I have told him about my own visit to your village."

The yangban's face darkened. "No. Say nothing of that. It was a joke, nothing more. If anything happened to give you offense, I beg you to forget it. And the invitation to use my humble home is extended to both of you when next you pass this way. I beg you to come to me and stay this time. Your visit was too short, it didn't allow me to make you truly welcome." The man all but grovelled before her. His attitude, which sickened Marigold, dazed Gifford.

"What did you say to him?" he demanded, as they withdrew.

"I told him we'd give the picture to Min Tae-jon." She grew

thoughtful. "He must be quite something, to be able to put the fear of God into these hooligans."

"How like you to call it the fear of God?" Gifford said angrily. "How can it be the fear of God when they don't even know who God is? And here I am, miles from civilization, intent on spreading the word and not able to because you insist on making a sideshow of a journey intended to win converts to our faith. How can my message ever be taken seriously when you make us a laughing stock of the countryside? How can I have the energy to preach the word when I'm constantly having to put out fires that you light?"

Marigold swung to face him. "Very well. If it's all my fault, I shan't go ashore with you. I shan't interfere. That's perfectly all right with me. You go your way and I'll go mine."

But this agreement was no sooner made than it was broken. Up until Yo-Ju, the rapids they encountered had been passable. Even after Yo-Ju, they made it through the rapids at Tan-yang without too much difficulty.

"And Banning made all that fuss," Gifford scoffed as they made their way through a wide valley.

But after they left To-tam, the river narrowed into gorges with great limestone cliffs bordering either side. Compressed between these colossal walls, the river roared and foamed and the sampan bounced madly over its surface, at times leaving it altogether to rise high in the air, then slapping back down to graze and bump the rocks beneath the surface. Sometimes they came to an eddy and spun round and round until they were giddy before Hong managed to get a footing with his pole and push them forward. Then they were off again, leaping madly forward, onward, upward, downward.

The river spray soaked their clothes and bedding. Gifford clung to his box, but Marigold, exhilarated by the encounter with the elements, forgot all about her possessions. She helped Hong, who was for the first time truly exhausted, climbing onto the rocks and pulling the lines to try to guide them forward without smashing on the cliffs on either side. This was no easy job since the rope was rotten and kept on breaking. When the boat landed on a sharp rock and sprung a serious leak, she set to and bailed and managed to temporarily plug the hole with her waterproof cape.

At last they reached a beautiful wide stretch in the river and pulled in to survey the damage. The sun shone on the calm water, the birds sang. The scene surrounding them seemed utterly remote from the mad excitement they'd just been through.

Marigold lay back on the bank, staring up at the endless blue sky, feeling a marvelous sense of contentment.

"We can't go on," Gifford declared, surveying his water-damaged books and tracts.

That damage might be repaired, but not the loss of their money supply, for in unloading the sampan they had discovered the bulk of their cash had been replaced by rocks, carefully concealed beneath a surface layer of bronze coins.

"Bloody bastards" It was the first time Marigold had ever heard Gifford swear, and he startled her into sitting up. "If you hadn't been so free with that gun, we might at least have money enough to get the boat repaired."

"We can't go back," Marigold stated firmly, "not now that we've come this far."

"The boat needs repairs. Hong and that useless old fellow he brought along aren't capable of doing them, and we've no money to pay to get them done, so what do you suggest?"

She didn't pick up on his sarcastic tone, but replied evenly. "The boat will have to be repaired whether we go on or back. Easier to go on, for if we turn back, we'll have to haul her up the rapids we just came down. We'll need good strong lines for that. These are all rotted."

"And how do you propose we get them without money?"

"I don't know." She thought for a while and then asked, "Where's the next place we come to?"

Gifford studied the map.

"Yong-chun."

"I think that's the place where Mark Banning said they don't welcome strangers, so we're likely to get short shrift if we apply for help there. What about further on?"

Gifford ran his finger along the line of the river.

"Looks like Chum-yol."

"Good!" Marigold jumped up. "That's where Banning's camped. He'll have the men and equipment we need. And perhaps he'll be able to exchange the Japanese silver yen I brought along."

"Perhaps—if he's as free with his supplies as he is with his advice." Gifford studied her slowly as he concluded, "We'll go to Banning, if that's what you want."

Since he never deferred to her opinions, she wondered why he did so now, but she was in no mood to try to penetrate the devious crevices of his mind.

"I think it's probably the only thing that can be done."

5

Marigold had never thought it possible that she would be glad to see Mark Banning, but as their sampan rounded the bend in the river and limped into Chum-yol, she found herself scanning the bank for his tall figure and felt her heart jump as she caught sight of him among a swarm of men at the bottom of a long sluice box built into the side of the hill. She had thought he might be high up in the mountains, working on the lode he'd talked about. Now she was unaccountably glad to find him there. She wondered if it was his usual practice to come down to the river at that time of day, or whether, from that mysterious, invisible grapevine that carried news up and down the Han, he had come because he knew they were arriving.

That must have been it, she realized, for he greeted them with a wave of his hand but without any surprise. And she somehow felt cheated. She would have liked to have surprised him. She wanted to make an impression, to astonish him with their having survived the perils of the journey to meet again in this distant spot so far from civilization. But since they hadn't surprised him, she felt he could have at least expressed some pleasure in their arrival.

Instead, he jumped aboard and was immediately all business. Gifford might have noticed that the flutter of Marigold's pulse brought a flush to her cheeks, but not Banning. He was far too busy examining the boat damage, estimating the extent of repairs, shouting out orders to his men in a pidgin Korean that they seemed to have no difficulty understanding.

"They'll get on it right away," he promised. "We should be able to get you out of here tomorow, the next day at the very latest."

His hurry to see them gone was disheartening. Even Gifford demurred that he wouldn't mind spending a few nights on dry land.

"We've had the devil of a job getting Hong to tie up in quiet areas of the river so we can sleep. At nightfall he invariably tries to pull in alongside other sampans; then they keep us awake with their smoking and chattering until dawn and he's quite useless the next day."

"Probably wise not to be alone." Banning looked at Hong's old assistant and demanded, "What happened to your other two men? Lose them in the rapids?"

"Damned man was so cheap he only hired one," Gifford said.

"And your lines—is that all that's left of them?"

"Okay. So he cheated us," Marigold said, annoyed that Banning's only interest was Hong and the boat, and that he was discussing all this with Gifford and not her. "But anyway, we've made it this far."

He looked at her for the first time. "Yes," he said slowly. "At least you've made it this far."

He held out his hand to help her off the boat, and she took it, even though she was well used to jumping ashore on her own. His hand was firm, warm, strong, but he released his hold immediately, and again she felt cheated. As they walked toward his cabin he said, "I thought you might welcome a good meal. I've had beefsteak brought in for dinner."

"You knew we were coming today, then?" she asked.

"There aren't many secrets on the river."

"How could there be," Gifford put in. "What's that old adage— the secret of two is God's secret but the secret of three is everybody's. Got any to share, Banning?"

"If you're trying to find out where I get my beefsteak, I'm afraid you're out of luck."

"I haven't tasted it yet," Gifford replied skeptically.

But after he had dined on the steak served with a fresh salad and a robust Beaujolais, he sat back in satisfaction, drawing on a Havana cigar. "That's a secret worth paying for, Banning."

"What secret?" There was tension in Banning's response. All evening, in fact ever since their arrival, Marigold had felt him to be unusually ill at ease.

"Where you get the beefsteak, old chap—what else?"

Banning's laugh seemed to be one of relief. "I don't think I'd reveal that, even if you made me do the crane's dance. Brandy? It's Courvoisier."

Gifford took the proferred snifter. "Crane's dance?"

"A favorite torture in Korea—I'm surprised you haven't heard of it. The naked victim's hung by his hands from a rafter and then soundly thrashed, first on one leg, then the other. His writhing silhouette resembles the lively movements of a crane—or so it's said. Hence the name. Or else there's the leg screw, where the victim's legs are tied together and two sticks are put between them and slowly twisted until . . ."

Marigold shuddered and got up from the table.

"I didn't mean to drive you away," Banning said and yet she felt sure that he did.

"That's all right. I'm quite tired. I really wish you hadn't insisted on giving up your room to me, though."

"It's the only place where there's any privacy," he explained. That was true, for apart from the room where they now sat, it was the only enclosed space in the peasant's hut he had converted into living quarters. Though his hospitality was flawless, there was an underlying reserve that she had not expected. She found it somehow daunting.

"I dare say we won't need to bother you for more than one night."

"They do seem to have made a good start on the repairs," Banning agreed.

As she lay on his narrow cot, Marigold looked around the bare room, wondering at the enigma of its owner. The furnishings—a chair, table, and chest—were neat and clean, but sparse and without any individual stamp. On the chest was a clock and a pair of binoculars; on the table beside the bed were a few books. But there were no personal items, nothing to give a clue as to the sort of man he was. Perhaps he'd put them away, she thought, when he'd had clean sheets put on the bed for her.

Though she was more comfortable than she'd been since leaving Seoul, Marigold couldn't sleep. Maybe she'd become used to distraction at night—the lapping of the water, the open air, the rustle of the grasses, the croak of frogs in the rice paddies, even the fleas in the straw roofing or Hong's chatter with his fellow boatmen. She lay awake, tossing and turning. She heard Gifford snoring, then she heard Banning get up and go out, quietly closing the door after him. From the window she could make out his figure climbing the path by the sluice. She wanted to get up and follow him, but since he hadn't welcomed her as she had expected when they arrived, she sensed he would welcome her even less now. Where could he be going at that hour? Not digging for gold, that was certain. There was an air of mystery about him.

She no longer pretended to try to sleep. She lit the lamp and examined his books—an odd selection that gave little clue to the personality of their owner. A history of the Far East, heavy and dull; a record of battles and feuds and treaties, quite devoid of social interest, from which a piece of paper fluttered out. The paper bore a consular seal and writing in a script she didn't recognize— Russian, she thought. On the back of the sheet was a series of numbers. The books beneath looked more promising: *Some Chinese Ghosts* and *Glimpses of Unfamiliar Japan,* both by the writer Banning had mentioned in Barleigh, Lafcadio Hearn. Before opening *Glimpses of Unfamiliar Japan* she noticed a tattered copy of *Treasure Island* half hidden at the bottom of the stack. She couldn't imagine Banning reading history or being especially interested in the literary and social aspects of the East, but the uncomplicated, high adventure of *Treasure Island* seemed more in keeping with his taste. She was about to put it back when, remembering that her father had considered *Treasure Island* a boy's book and therefore unsuitable for her, she opened the well-thumbed copy and began to read.

She listened for Banning's return, but the adventures must have lulled her to sleep for she awoke to the cheering smell of bacon and coffee. The sun was high, and although she had lain awake for so long—or perhaps for that reason—when she did sleep, she slept soundly and awoke feeling rested. She hurried to dress, and packed away her things. They would be leaving as soon as the repairs were finished.

Despite his night's ramblings, Banning seemed more relaxed than he had the day before. He and Gifford had already eaten, but he summoned the cook to put on some eggs for her.

"It was almost like home." Gifford wiped his lips with unusual gusto. "I mean England, of course. He's actually managed to get them to feed the chickens on grain instead of fish, so the eggs taste like eggs. You must get halmoni to do that when we get back."

"I don't believe you slept well," Banning remarked as he rose and pulled out a chair for her, an extravagant gesture, given the rustic setting.

"How do you know?" Gifford asked with unusual interest.

"I noticed the light."

"Did you? I don't think you slept well either. I heard you go out." Marigold studied his face. His expression remained unchanged, but she thought she might have learned something had Gifford not intervened with, "You two seem to have been checking up on one another. I'm sure I was too tired to notice anything."

"I went through your books. I hope you don't mind. I didn't realize you were a history buff."

"Is that what those books are? Natasha gave them to me when I left, but I haven't picked them up since I unpacked. They're useful for propping open doors."

That might explain the consular report stuck inside the Far

Eastern history; even the Lafcadio Hearn, perhaps, Marigold thought. "I somehow can't see Natasha immersed in *Treasure Island*," she commented, spreading honey on a hot biscuit. "It just doesn't seem to be her style."

"You'd be more qualified than me to comment on Natasha's style."

"Do you really think so?" Marigold looked at him directly.

Gifford intervened with, "Style's not really Marigold's cup of tea."

"Perhaps she gave it to you thinking it was to your taste," Marigold pursued.

His brows furrowed. "Gave me what?"

"*Treasure Island.*"

"I really don't know. I suppose she may have."

She sensed annoyance in his clipped response, and, perhaps because of it, continued to pursue the subject. "I'd never read it—it's quite a good yarn. Since you don't want it, perhaps I'll take it along and finish it."

His brows remained furrowed. "If it were mine, I'd gladly give it to you. However, since it belongs to Natasha . . ."

"But I thought you said . . ."

"I really think the Hearn books would be more to your liking, anyway," he interposed. "He's a fascinating guy—half-Irish, half-Greek. I met him when I was in Japan. He's married to a Japanese woman and has become a Buddhist of sorts. He's commonsensical, witty, curious. Why don't you take his books along with you?"

"But didn't you say they belonged . . ."

"Marigold, do stop arguing and eat your breakfast," Gifford interrupted, much to Marigold's frustration. "Banning's agreed to take us up to his mine. Did you notice that ancient pavilion high on the mountain top as we came in? He says it's quite close by. He's explored it—and apparently it's worth taking a look at. It supposed to have been built by early Koryo royalty."

"I understood the boat would be ready today," Marigold reminded him.

"My supplications for another day of this civilized food and drink and rest have been granted," Gifford replied airily.

"I won't complain. It will give me the opportunity to finish *Treasure Island* and discover whether good, honest, but headstrong Jim wrests the treasure from crafty Long John Silver." She eyed Banning. "I presume he does."

"Since it's a work of fiction, you may presume so. I wouldn't want to spoil it for you."

"But you have read it?"

"Years ago." The short reply ended the discussion. "Would you like to see the mine?"

"Are you sure our staying on another day won't upset your plans?" she asked.

"What plans?" he demanded.

She hesitated. "I rather felt we intruded."

He neither denied nor agreed with this observation. "I'm not the one with plans. It's you who have these grandiose schemes of crossing the Diamond Mountains. Wouldn't catch me embarking along that precarious route."

"Tigers again?" Marigold couldn't keep the quizzical note from her voice.

"Banning says there's a big one around. He's been having difficulty with the men since it made off with one of them. I'd like to take a shot at it."

"So it *is* tigers." Marigold heaved an exasperated sigh.

Banning responded seriously. "At least one—a big Siberian, very light in color, almost white, in fact. I've only caught a glimpse of it once—magnificent animal, but it's just about wrecked my operation. The men never go anywhere after dark for fear of the beasts, and now it's hard to get them to work at all, even in daylight. They claim because of this tiger's size and color it's a messenger of the

Mountain Spirit, the Sansin. They say the Sansin must be displeased because we're hard rock mining in his territory. As long as
we confine our digging to the placer deposits along the river, it's all
right."

So that was why he'd been down by the river when they arrived,
Marigold realized with some disappointment.

"I don't know who they're more scared of, the Siberian cat or the
Mountain Spirit. Long before sundown they put away their tools
and that's it—no inducements or threats will make them go on.
Even in broad daylight they spend half their time looking behind
them instead of getting on with the job. The foreman's as bad as
any of them."

"It's probably just laziness," Gifford said.

Banning shook his had. "You can smell their fear."

"Why don't you hunt it down? Afraid?"

Gifford studied Banning closely as he answered, "Anyone in his
right mind should feel fear around a beast of that size."

"You could use the men as beaters to drive it out. Might be fun,"
Gifford went on.

"It's not easy to get a good, long shot at the animal up here in
these mountains—we're not in the African bush—the danger of
close range is you may only have one chance. Besides, I'd be willing
to bet half of them would never come back. I'm already far enough
behind in my production schedule as it is."

His concern was quite evident. As they left, he slung his rifle
over his arm and, noticing Marigold wasn't wearing a gun, he insisted she go back for it.

"She can't hit anything," Gifford scoffed, adding quickly, "She
said so herself when she threatened that yangban's servants—that
incident I told you about last night."

"Even if Maggie can't shoot straight, the servants didn't know it.
So the gun came in handy, just as I thought it would."

"Well, they obviously knew enough to be frightened by the sight
of it. But a tiger's another matter."

"A gun makes a lot of noise. Tigers don't like noise unless it's the noise of their own roar. I heard this one the night it made off with its prey—such a damnable sound as I never thought to hear until the gates of Hell swing open on me." Sensing Gifford was about to embark on a sermon, Banning added, "There's no use, I'm quite resigned to my destination."

"Satisfied?" Marigold asked as she returned, the gun strapped to her waist. She swung into the saddle.

"I'd be more satisfied if you hadn't been so obstinate and refused to learn how to use it," he observed.

"Perhaps I've no aptitude," she said as they started off.

"I don't underestimate you, and I don't believe you underestimate yourself."

"I don't think she does, either," Gifford agreed with a touch of asperity.

The trail up to the mine followed the long wooden sluice supported on trestles.

"Water washes the dirt out, leaving the gold trapped in the riffles," Banning explained. "You can tell gold by its heft." He reached into his pocket for a nugget about the size of a walnut and handed it to Marigold. She took it, wondering if this were the nugget he had promised Natasha. "It's heavy. It won't melt easily but it's malleable."

They stopped frequently for Marigold to collect specimens of mountain peonies, gentians, and tiger lilies for Mrs. Gardner, or for Gifford, to take potshots at a hovering bird that he insisted, even after he ran out of ammunition, had been a rare sheldrake, so that it was close to noon before they arrived at the mine site. The men were gathered together, close to one another, sitting on their haunches. Their chopsticks flew in short, rapid motion, back and forth from their mouths to bowls containing fish and rice. The pungent smell of kimchi, the garlic-laced pickled cabbage, filled the air.

Banning greeted the foreman in his form of pidgin Korean. "Work good today, Yu?"

The man shook his head. "They say they smell tiger."

"They smell kimchi, not tiger," Banning said.

Yu shrugged.

Banning walked over to where a mule was turning a wooden post attached to a large stone that crushed rocks brought from the mine. He bent down to touch the ore and pursed his lips. "Not good, Yu."

"I know not good. Kill tiger, then good."

"Queen Min not happy."

"Tell queen send us brigade of tiger hunters, then we dig for gold."

At the palace Marigold had often seen the royal tiger hunters with their loose blue uniforms and brimmed hats with comical crowns. Aside from these symbolic leaders, the main body of the brigade was only called out in the event of emergency.

"Will she send them?" Marigold asked as they walked toward the crevice carved into the side of the mountain.

"I haven't even asked her to. For one tiger, it seems ridiculous. Besides, she'd complain that all her profits had been squandered on their wages."

"And demand your share?" Marigold hazarded.

He laughed. "Probably, unless she were presented with the tiger skin. They're greatly prized, you know."

Marigold nodded. "It's a sign of highest office. The tiger's important enough to appear on the royal standard. Underlings have to be content with wearing leopard."

"I sometimes think it's the tiger that runs this country. The Chinese are well aware it's the Korean preoccupation. You've probably heard it said the Korean hunts the tiger half the year while the tiger hunts the Korean the other half."

"And which half is this?" Gifford asked, a note of caution in his voice.

"I'm not sure."

"This cave would make a perfect lair."

Banning held up an oil lantern and led the way, but it still took their eyes some time to adjust to the darkness of the mine.

"I was lucky to find this crevice in the rock. It saved shafting—that would have meant blasting. We can follow the vein."

He stopped where a gathering of picks and shovels indicated the work place of the men and laid his hand on the rock wall.

"There it is—gold."

Gifford peered forward. "It just looks like plain, old rock to me."

"Feel it."

"It just feels like rock to me," he said again.

Banning took hold of Marigold's hand and ran it along the vein.

"Feel that texture? That's gold, pure gold."

More than the gold under her fingers, she felt Banning's hand on top of hers. His palm had the hardened skin of one who knows what work is; his fingers had the strong and capable grasp of one who knows what he's doing.

"How did you know it was here?" she asked.

"It's as you heard me tell the queen, I have a nose for gold. Remember?"

She was glad of the dark, glad he could not see her face. She'd felt less than honest for never acknowledging to him that she had been present, if concealed, at that interview. He'd hinted before, but she'd never before been sure he knew.

"It's cold in here," she said, awkwardly pulling her hand away.

"I can't stand this feeling of being shut in," Gifford said.

"Lots of people feel like that," Banning said, turning back to lead them out of the mine. "That's until they get gold fever. Then gold's all they can think about. Careful. Watch your step here."

He held out his hand to Marigold. But discomforted by his disclosure, she didn't take it.

After the dark and cool of the mine, the sun's rays were brighter, warmer than ever. The men had finished smoking. As they reluctantly returned to work, they paused to examine Marigold with open curiosity.

"You're causing a sensation, Maggie," Banning remarked.

"It's been like that throughout the journey," Gifford complained. "Almost ruined my mission. If I'd realized Marigold would be regarded as some sort of circus freak, I'd never have agreed to her coming along."

"Come off it, Partridge. You'd never have enjoyed the trip with Maggie amusing Sully back in Seoul, now would you?" Banning said lightly.

The jocular remark was followed by silence. Marigold was still perturbed by the knowledge that Banning had been aware all along that she knew of his conversation with the queen. Now Gifford was sulking. But after a luncheon of cold chicken, with white wine cooled in one of the many streams that cascaded down the mountainside, their spirits were somewhat restored.

"Wish you'd loan us your cook," Gifford commented, leaning back. "Flatbread and chestnuts have become meager fare."

"Can't spare my cook, but I plan to send a man along to help your boatman. And I can spare a few bottles of wine. A good wine makes almost anything palatable."

Gifford examined the label on the bottle. "Valmur Chablis. It sounds expensive."

"It is expensive," Banning agreed. "I'm cursed with expensive taste that, like a good mistress, must be supported."

"Men with taste beyond their means become easy targets for vice of one sort or another."

"It may be the death of me, but without it, life wouldn't be worth living," Banning agreed amiably, unaffected by Gifford's sententiousness. He got up. "We'd better leave now if we're going to tour that pavilion."

Gifford stretched in the sun. "If it's all the same to you, I've changed my mind. I'd rather take a short nap instead."

"You were the one who wanted to come up here," Marigold protested, but Banning intervened, "If he wants to sleep, let him."

"There's nothing to stop you two from running along," Gifford yawned.

Banning took the rifle from his shoulder. "You're out of ammunition. You'd better keep this. We'll have Maggie's gun if we need it," he said. Then he turned to Marigold. "Do you want to go?"

She hesitated, but only for a moment. She felt, rather than saw Gifford studying them through half-closed eyes as Banning led the way. They started off down a narrow path in the direction of the pavilion.

6

They walked, not speaking, through the heat of the sultry afternoon. Once, in a densely wooded area, Banning went to take her hand, but Marigold ignored the gesture, pretending not to have noticed. She had wanted to come, yet now that they were alone together, she felt her decision had been unwise. She remembered Chu-sun saying the only reason for a man and woman to be alone was to make love.

She was glad when at last they reached a grove of gigantic elms, and before them, on the promontory jutting out over the river was the porticoed pavilion. Its fretted, painted woodwork had been sadly neglected and its original opulence had to be imagined. Banning pointed out the symbols on the walls indicating direction: a blue dragon to the east, denoting the power of heaven and symbol of the king; a black turtle to the north, symbol of long life; a red phoenix to the south, a sun-bird and symbol of the queen; and a white tiger to the west, to repel all evil.

"Perhaps you know what the flowers underneath mean. I haven't figured them out."

Marigold nodded. "They're called the Four Gentlemen; they're supposed to symbolize the qualities of the ideal gentleman. Bamboo for refinement and resilience, plum for courage and fortitude, orchid for loyalty and elegance, and chrysanthemum for eternal youth."

"And which would you give me?" he asked. "That is, if you were to give me any."

"The chrysanthemum," she replied unhesitatingly.

"Watch where you step. This time you'd better give me your hand, else you're liable to go right through the floor." Banning pointed to a place where the floor was shattered and held out his hand. This time she took it. "It's safer to walk around the edge than to cross the middle of the building. Come over here and I'll show you a view to take your breath away."

They rested, side by side, on the railing of the portico above the river that sparkled like a silver ribbon miles beneath them. The rapids through which she and Giff had passed the day before looked like no more than trickling waterfalls from that distance. The precarious position of their perch was intimidating but strangely intoxicating.

"It's beautiful, so very beautiful," she murmured.

"I wonder about all the people who stood here before us and what happened to them. Do you suppose it was a lovers' leap?"

"I hope not. I expect they came here seeking inspiration."

He squeezed her hand lightly as he asked, "For what?"

"For their poetry," she said, suddenly withdrawing her hand from his. "They have a special form of poetry called the sijo. It's something like the Japanese haiku." Even to herself she sounded like a schoolteacher.

"Tell me one."

Marigold thought for a moment, looking out at the scene before her. Then she spoke:

> Love. It is a lying word.
> That you love me another lie.
> That my love is seen in dreams,
> Is yet a greater lie.
> How may I, who can never sleep,
> Hope to see you in my dreams?

"That's not a very good translation," she finished awkwardly, wondering why that poem was the one that she had remembered.

"Is that why you didn't sleep?" he asked curiously. "Were you dwelling on some lost love?"

"Of course not!" she snapped, even more annoyed with her choice.

He said nothing for a moment, then demanded, "Have you ever been in love, Maggie?"

Her response was stiff, very proper. "I'm engaged to be married."

"Being engaged, married even, has absolutely nothing to do with being in love. Look at your sister and my cousin. It may be a match made in Heaven—let's hope it is—but in all honesty, do you think either Primrose or Algie knows much about love?"

"They're ideally suited . . ."

"True. They're both selfish, conceited . . ."

"I can't let you insult my sister that way. I shouldn't have thought you'd have mentioned her name, having all but ruined her."

"My dear Maggie, what rot!" he snorted. "You know better than that. Primrose is soft and sweet and charming, but she's not honest. You are. And rather than giving me a direct answer to my question, because you don't want to lie, you're talking about all sorts of inconsequential things like Sully. Come now."

"You'd be the last person I'd be likely to confide in," she said.

He looked hurt. "Surely you don't think I'd talk about it?"

"No," she admitted. "But we're hardly on confiding terms."

"I'd like to be—and you're the only woman I've ever said that to."

"Then tell me—have *you* ever been in love?" she demanded, suddenly wanting very much to know. But he was silent, looking down on the river for so long, that she had all but given up hope of an answer. Suddenly, without looking up he said, "The answer is either hundreds of times or never—and both are true. When I'm with a woman who is special to me, when she looks at me in a certain way, when she says my name—then I'm in love. But when

I leave, though I may carry fond memories of her with me, it's in the past. I meet someone else, it begins again."

"That's not love," Marigold said flatly.

"I suspected you would condemn me—but it's the truth. Now you tell me what is," he grinned mischievously. "Better yet, show me."

"Always the man of action," Marigold replied lightly. "That's why I picked the chrysanthemum for you."

"I rather thought you meant I'd never grown up," Banning said, flustering her once again since that was exactly what she had meant.

He pointed toward the jagged peaks to the north. "Those are the Diamond Mountains, where you're headed."

"They look formidable."

"They are. Sure you really want to go?"

"I have to," she said, then bit her tongue remembering Banning's friendship with the queen. "I don't mean that. It sounds too . . ."

"Ominous," he finished for her. "I've always thought death and taxes were the only irrevocable demands made of us."

"That's cynical. Friendship makes demands."

"So, you're going for a friend."

"I didn't say that," she denied.

He turned to her, his expression grave.

"You didn't, Maggie, but whatever's taking you to Wonsan, for God's sake, take care. I know only too well that the governor there—Min Tae-jon, the queen's brother—is no man to play around with. He's unspeakably cruel and will stop at nothing to get what he wants."

"I have nothing he could want."

"I wouldn't be too sure."

"How do you know so much about him?"

"His reputation as a potentate not to be crossed is no secret. And don't expect Gifford to help if you get in a tight corner. He's jealous of you. I've a strong suspicion he'd just as soon come back without you."

"Mark! What an awful thing to say!"

But instead of an explanation, she got a smile. "You've never called me by name before, Maggie."

Again, she felt that quiver inside—just as she had felt when she first caught sight of him from the river. It made her uneasy, yet excited.

"You always call me Maggie," she pointed out almost shyly.

"And you don't like it?"

"It's a family name. No one uses it here."

"Mind if I do? I feel as though I have known you forever," he said, taking her hand. He turned it, palm up, and leaned over to brush it with his lips. She could no longer ignore that quiver inside; it was making her feel less sure, less certain of herself.

"Maggie, Maggie!" His voice was gruff and tender. "Maggie, I want you. Have you any idea how much I want you."

He put his arms around her and she made no effort to resist him. It was as though it were all a dream, as though time stood still at that moment and would stand still forever. His dark eyes came closer, closer still and she basked in their warmth. She was inside herself, feeling his arms tightening around her, pulling her closer and closer to him until they breathed as one. At the same time she had the strange sensation of being outside and looking on, seeing herself and the man who held her in his arms. But as his lips touched hers, she suddenly saw that same man at the Russian legation, holding Natasha Waeber in much the same way, kissing her then as he was about to kiss her now.

"No!" She pushed him from her. "I suppose you've known Natasha Waeber forever—and my sister, Primrose—you probably said the same thing to her. And to dozens of others. You said so just now, that whoever you're with you find irresistible. Now it's me. Do you know what I think?"

At her rebuff, he drew back and folded his arms across his

chest, his face expressionless. "I suspect I'm going to hear it whether I want to or not."

"I think I'm irresistible to you at this moment not just because I'm the only one around, but because I'm safely engaged to someone else. Primrose was all but engaged to your cousin. Natasha's married. You like women who belong to someone else. You can enjoy them with no fear of ties. That's it, isn't it?"

"You seem to have made up your mind to it," he said coldly.

"You said you'd never grown up . . ."

"I said you probably thought I'd never grown up," he corrected.

"Well, you're right. Anyone who'd base his life on *Treasure Island* . . ."

"Will you shut up about that book," he said fiercely and she sensed, with infinite satisfaction, that at last she'd got under his skin. "Now you've had your say, and I've listened, and it's my turn. Want to know what I think?" She didn't answer, and he went on, "I think you're afraid of me."

"Afraid of you?" she scoffed. "Why on earth would I be afraid of you?"

"Because you're attracted to me. You've had things your own way for so long that you can't bear the thought of losing control. You pull Sully's strings, don't deny it, but with me you know you're not in the driver's seat. That frightens you, doesn't it? Like just now. You don't know what to expect. You don't trust yourself to let go and enjoy. Rapture just isn't something that you understand. You can't bear to be overwhelmed by anything or by anyone. I asked you if you'd ever been in love. I didn't get an answer, but I don't need one. Women like you never fall in love because they'd never allow themselves to."

"Of all the conceited nonsense, that's the worst I've ever heard," Marigold fumed, standing up. "You're talking a lot of rubbish today—not just about me, but about Gifford, too. Like that thing about him preferring to return without me. Gifford and I may not get along, but that's positively slanderous. I've no idea why you'd say such a thing."

"You're so observant about so many things and yet . . ." He hesitated. "And yet there's so much you don't see—or maybe you see and don't know, don't understand."

"What do you mean?"

He, too, stood up. "I really don't feel like explaining it to you, not now, anyway. In the mood you're in, you won't listen, or else you'll deliberately misunderstand."

"I don't know what you're talking about," Marigold said, suddenly flushing, for at that moment she realized what he did mean.

"Don't you?" Suddenly he smiled and held out his hand. "Maggie, let's not part enemies. I like you—besides, who knows when we may need one another."

She stood looking at him for a moment before she extended her hand. Very solemnly, they shook hands as though sealing a pact. Then slowly, deliberately, he pulled her to him once again but this time he kissed her.

It was just as he had said, a loss of self. She felt powerless to resist once his lips had touched hers. She was no longer the reliable, self-controlled Maggie that she knew; instead she had become a pliant, willing creature who gave herself and adored the giving because it brought such pleasure. Even after Mark lifted his lips from hers, she clung to him, burying her face in his shirt.

"I believe there's hope for you after all, Maggie. You may not know rapture, but you're certainly willing to learn." His voice was husky and soft, but not soft enough to preserve the spell she'd fallen under. She suddenly realized who she was, and where she was, and who it was she was clinging to.

She dropped her arms to her sides in defeat. He wasn't the one who had defeated her; she had defeated herself. He had set a trap and she had walked into it, just like Prim, and Natasha, and all the others.

"That's not rapture," she said briskly. "That's lust. You know it and I know it. It's about time we woke up Gifford and got back to camp."

Without waiting for him she started off along the path, deliberately striding, even running so that he wouldn't catch up with her.

"Maggie!" She heard him behind her and hurried even faster It wasn't a sensible thing to do, but then she hadn't been acting sensibly ever since she got there. She was angry with him but even angrier with herself.

Earlier in the afternoon, when they had come by that same path, Mark had led the way. The path had been indistinct even then, but in the lengthening rays of the setting sun, it had all but disappeared. Even so, hearing him call her name again—"Maggie! Not that way! Maggie come back!"—made her perversely hurry on.

She stumbled and ran, pushing through brush and trees. She didn't stop—not until she heard the roar!

It was so loud, so ominous, so close that she froze. She couldn't believe anything could produce such an ear-splitting, blood-curdling sound. It came from somewhere behind her, and her impulse, as soon as she could get her legs to move, was to run on. She began to sob and whimper with fright. The roar came again, but instead of running on she stopped, for even more frightening than the roar was the echoed shout, "Run, Maggie! Run!" Next came a yell of agony.

"My God! Oh my God!" she whimpered.

She must have been quite mad, for she turned back. She was running toward a sound that no one of sound mind would have willingly approached.

"My God! Oh my God!" she repeated. Her breathing was hard, she trembled from head to foot. Her hands shook. Cold sweat poured down her body.

"My God! Oh my God!" she murmured again as she pushed on into a clearing she'd passed through moments before. There she found herself face to face with a beast larger than any she'd ever imagined.

Despite all the talk of tigers, Marigold had never thought of them as anything but oversized cats. Big cats. That's what they were called, after all. That's the way they were depicted in paintings and scrolls—as playful, even cuddly creatures. They hadn't seemed so awful, certainly not the menace that people made of them.

But in one split second, those preconceptions vanished for all time. In front of her was an enormous, striped, shaggy-haired beast, longer than two tall men, of massive weight and girth. It was very light, almost white, in color; sinews bulged from its muscular haunches. This was no big cat. This was a monster!

Marigold saw the tiger before it saw her; it was crouched over Banning, preoccupied with tightening the grip of its powerful jaws on his shoulder. Judging from the broken branches and the amount of blood on the ground surrounding them, quite a fight had taken place. Though clearly weakened, Banning was still struggling in a vain attempt to get free. But even Hercules would have been no match for a beast of that size—especially unarmed.

That was it! Banning was unarmed, Marigold suddenly realized. He had left his rifle with Gifford. "We'll have Maggie's gun if we need it," he'd said—and she'd rushed off and left him!

It wasn't until then that Marigold thought of the gun at her waist. She reached for the holster, tugging to get it open. Her hand closed around the handle. Slowly, cautiously, she drew out the gun, her finger clicking back the safety as she did so.

It was that tiny sound that caught the tiger's attention. Without releasing its hold on Banning, the tiger lifted its head and looked directly at her. Its eyes were light, alert, but incredibly cold.

For the second time that day, time stood still for Marigold Wilder. But there was no euphoria in the moment, unless it was the euphoria of fear. She felt acutely alive yet in a strange nightmarelike trance. She was frozen in place, unable to move, stricken before the menace that confronted her. All around her was still. No wind disturbed the leaves in the trees. Not an insect stirred,

not a bird sang. The tiger's eyes remained fixed on her. Banning's
eyes were fixed on her as well. The blood that soaked his shirt-
front—where her head had so recently nestled—looked less ominous than cochineal; the deadly pallor of his face might have been
smooth carved granite. The gun in her hand was hard and smooth
yet that, too, felt unreal, toylike.

Slowly, very slowly, as though in a trance, she lifted the gun. She
moved as though not moving. She held the gun shoulder-high and
aligned the sights. The tiger raised its head, pulling at Mark's
shoulder as he did so.

"Point it at me if you want a target," Banning had once said.

"I really wouldn't care to have the blood of even the dumbest of
beasts on my hands," had been her retort then. But now she even
called on God, whom she had denied, to give her just one thing and
one only—the white tiger.

Tiger and man were so close together they formed one target in
the aligned sights. Would she kill both? Would she kill either?
What if she killed Banning and not the tiger? What if . . .

The tiger moved and her finger closed on the trigger.

"Oh, God! Help me!" she cried. She closed her eyes.

"Never pull the trigger," he had warned. "Squeeze it back—
smooth and even. Don't be in a hurry. Even though your life or
someone else's may depend on it, take your time."

She opened her eyes and tried to steady her trembling hands.
She saw fear in Banning's eyes.

"God help me!" she whispered as she squeezed the trigger.

7

It had been a miracle. That was the only possible explanation.
With one shot, and one only, Marigold Wilder had dropped that
thirteen-foot tiger. She stared uncomprehendingly, from the cold
hard weapon in her hand to the slumped figure of the massive
beast. She had the proof of her own eyes, yet still she could not
believe it.

Even as a child, when she had paid perfunctory homage to her
father's deity, she had always rejected miracles. To believe in them
was to believe in the supernatural and Marigold spurned miracles
along with witches and elves and fairies; water was water and wine
was wine. And anyone unable to hit a carefully displayed target
under optimum conditions, could not, while terrified, shoot a rampant tiger right between the eyes. And yet that was precisely what
she had just done.

"Oh God, Maggie! You did it!" A badly weakened Mark Banning
pulled himself up to examine the shot. "Incredible! Your aim had to
be perfect to bring down a beast of this size with a handgun. Come
here, see for yourself!" He pointed to the small, virtually bloodless
wound in the tiger's head. "You put it right where it counts. A
champion marksman couldn't have placed the bullet any better."
Then, with a wan grin, "Very frankly, when I saw you pointing
that thing in my direction, all I was hoping for was a quick end to
my misery."

"It was a miracle," she said, looking down at the gun in her
hand, repeating, "a miracle."

"I could hear you calling on God for help."

She nodded. "I did—out of cowardice, helplessness—I didn't know what else to do."

Then, suddenly noticing his deathlike pallor, she realized that the worst might not be over. Unlike the tiger's wound, the enormous gash in his shoulder was bleeding profusely. She tore off the pockets she had sewn into her skirt and used them to help staunch the flow.

"I'll go for help."

"No, I think I can make it. Besides, I know the way."

She helped him to his feet and put his arm around her neck. He swayed and she wondered how she could manage his weight, but with a supreme effort he pulled himself upright, balancing his weight carefully. Slowly, stopping often, they made their way back to the mine. There, the men fashioned a stretcher to carry him back down the mountain. They were soon followed by others who carried the dead tiger strung between two poles, borne high in triumph.

News of the kill spread rapidly, and a great celebration was soon underway. Crowds of people appeared from nowhere to examine with awe the carcass of the magnificent beast before men ripped out its liver and eyeballs. The whiskers, teeth, and nose were handled with special care since they were said to contain medicinal properties. The bones were rendered into hogolji, a fiery liquor that the men passed to one another and drank with reverence. But most magnificent of all was the animal's lush hide, laid out for all to admire.

As they worked, they sang to Sansin, the Great Mountain Spirit, songs that grew less and less distinct as the hogolji vat was stirred and the mokkoli jugs emptied. They also sang to Marigold, the White Tiger who had come from the West in the guise of a goddess. Previously only an oddity, with this kill Marigold had become an idolized oddity.

But the object of their adoration was too busy to celebrate or to enjoy her new status. Inside the hut, Marigold bathed and re-bathed Banning's wound. His face was far too pale, he'd lost too much blood, but his breathing was regular.

"You must get back to Seoul. There's medical help there."

"No." His voice was weak but determined. "No, I'm all right. In a day or two I'll be good as new."

"A doctor should look at this." She found some Friar's balsam to help staunch the flow of blood so she could examine the deep gash in his shoulder. She did so with an audible sigh.

"It has to be stitched. I know it must be stitched. If only Sully were here. Oh, if only Sully were here!"

Banning opened his eyes. "I'm glad he isn't," he said, his voice barely a whisper, indicating where she might find needle and thread.

He lay silent, watching her as she bathed the wound once again, then sterilized the needle in a flame and threaded it. She flinched as the needle passed through his flesh but he kept his eyes un-blinkingly upon her.

She looked around. "I need antiseptic."

"Cigar ashes and spittle will do the trick." He pointed to the ashtray.

"Ashes!"

"It'll do just as well. Believe me."

Against her better judgment, she applied the gray mixture.

"You can't go back to work," she said, rummaging in her photo-graphic supplies for some collodion to seal the wound.

"Work's the best cure. Work's always the best cure." He turned, winced, and turned back. "Still, I wouldn't object to seeing old JC walk in that door right now."

"JC?" Marigold glanced at his face, afraid he was delirious.

"JC's an old guy who taught my father about mining gold—he taught me too. He knows gold and he knows people. He was the only person I could really trust when I was growing up."

Marigold had found the collodion; as she was applying the final covering to the wound, she noticed his eyes close.

"Tell me about what it was like when you were a child." She asked from personal interest but also to keep him awake and alert until she had finished.

"It wasn't the way it was for Algie, or Partridge, or Sully. It wasn't . . ." He winced, and she stopped, unsure whether the cause was the wound or memory of his childhood.

"You weren't happy?"

"No, not so much that. In some ways it was the ideal childhood for a boy—no rules, no regular schooling—but there's always a trade-off."

"And what was that?"

"I don't know—insecurity, I suppose. My father always bore a grudge against his family for cutting him off after his marriage— the Reid-Bannings considered my mother beneath them. The funny thing is that as the daughter of an *alcalde* in California's Salinas valley, her Spanish lineage was far more ancient than theirs—but to them she was just some bar-girl. She'd run away from a strict father—my father did meet her in a bar. I always wanted to make his family pay for the way they snubbed her."

"That's why you sought out Algie, then, and that's why . . ." she stopped.

"Why I made a play for Primrose," he concluded.

So her conjecture had been right.

"I wanted to spite him. Maybe it wasn't right, but I guessed all along that your sister knew how to take care of herself."

That was true, Marigold realized with a sense of surprise.

"Your parents had a happy marriage?" she asked.

"I can't say they did—not a tranquil one at least. They fought a lot—couldn't live with each other but couldn't live without each other either. But they were deeply in love—I often felt like an intruder."

"So JC filled in for you."

"He was always there—still is, for that matter. We were always on the move. Mother complained that Father never gave her the home she deserved. Well, now he's gone, and she has it."

"Thanks to you?"

"I suppose. But now that she has everything she always said she wanted, I know she'd give it all up just to have him back for five minutes." He grew pensive. "It's no good to want anything too much."

"Do you live with her?"

"Hell, no! I live wherever I am. This is all I need." As Marigold surveyed the bare hut, he went on, "I don't believe in accumulating things. Better to give stuff away than carry around a lot of excess baggage."

He closed his eyes. She sat beside him, watching him, thinking him asleep. Suddenly his eyes opened and he looked up at her.

"I owe you my life," he murmured. "Did you know if you save a life in this country, it belongs to you."

She smiled. "Such power!" She ran her hand over his hair, smoothing it back from his face. "I've felt guilty for not telling you before now that I was there when you had that audience with the queen."

"You didn't have to. I knew." He pointed to his nose and she smiled.

"But that washerwoman at the palace . . . ?"

"Fair trade—I should have admitted that was me."

"But how did you get those clothes? Weren't you afraid that the guard would find out?"

But his eyes had closed again. He was asleep.

She went into the main room where Gifford was eating dinner. He indicated her place at the table, but she shook her head.

"I'm not hungry."

"How is he? Is he going to pull through?"

"I think so." She picked up a sleeping bag.

"Where are you taking that?"

"I'm going to stay with him." Gifford looked flabbergasted. "He's been badly wounded, Gifford. He shouldn't be alone. There's nothing wrong . . ."

"No. No, of course not," he replied quickly.

"Sully would understand. He's a doctor."

"Of course," Gifford said again.

Banning was restless. His temperature rose and several times Marigold got up to give him water. But by morning, when at last he was resting comfortably, the door to the room suddenly burst open.

Banning awoke immediately. He raised himself from his pillow, reached beneath it, and, to Marigold's horror, pulled out a gun. He put it away as soon as he caught sight of the newcomer.

"Teuk-sil! What are you doing here?"

She was young, scarcely at the age of puberty, small and slender, with long, loose dark hair reaching to her waist. Her dark almond-shaped eyes were filled with tears.

"Lee just found out what happened. He's so worried. We're both so worried. Are you all right? Tell me you are all right." She twisted a kerchief in her hands as she spoke.

"Thanks to Miss Wilder, everything's all right. Now run along and tell Lee not to worry. All you have to do is to take care of yourself. Run along now."

After she was gone, he looked over at Marigold, making no mention of the interruption.

"You've had no rest."

"I'm quite all right. I can sleep any time."

"But you're leaving today."

"I can stay . . . we can stay on, at least until you're better."

"I am better. Now that I'm awake, I might as well get up. There's a lot to be done. I've got to get production back on schedule."

"But you must stay in bed. You're weak. You've lost a tremendous amount of blood," she protested.

"There's no time for lollygagging. Besides, I want to come down to the river and see you off myself."

"But I thought I'd—we thought we'd stay, at least until you're fully recovered. That wound must be carefully watched and kept clean. The bandages must be changed and . . . and you need . . ."

"I don't need anyone," Banning said firmly.

"Perhaps this young girl, Teuk-sil will . . ."

"I'd rather you didn't mention to anyone that you saw her here."

"I see," she said, though she didn't.

"Don't worry, Maggie. I've known how to take care of myself for a long time."

"But last night you said your life belonged to me. If that's the case . . ."

"Okay, for now it does. But one way or another, I intend to get it back." He sat up and swung his legs over the side of the bed. "Do you want to watch me dress?"

As he pulled a robe around him, she scrambled to her feet and bundled up the sleeping bag.

"I'm sorry," Banning said then. "I must seem ungracious. I appreciate everything you've done for me, Maggie. You saved my life, I'll never forget that. But I'm all right. I'm better. See?" he said, standing for an instant, then almost immediately sitting back down on the bed.

"See!" she reiterated. "I must stay with you."

"No, Maggie," he insisted. "You must go."

"Don't you want me to be here?" she asked.

He leaned forward, taking both her hands in his. "If it were only that simple, a matter of that—you and me, it would be different. But we both have a lot of other things to consider."

"Like what?"

"Like . . ." he hesitated.

"Like your gold production," she supplied crisply, "and Natasha Waeber."

"I was going to say like Sully."

Instinctively she covered the ring on her left hand.

"I just want to help you, "she said, adding, "I'd want to do the same for anyone who'd been as badly injured."

"I expect you would." For a moment he seemed crestfallen. "You always know how to get on with things, do what has to be done, think about others before yourself. Maybe that's why you attract men of the healing profession. Prim said you were once engaged to John Keane—now Sully."

"I was never engaged to John. It was just an understanding."

"They're both dependable, decent men," Banning pointed out.

"And you're not."

"I am not," he affirmed. "I'll never forget all you've done, but I'm used to doing things for myself. I don't think I'd know what to do if I had someone around me all the time. Maybe you hit the nail on the head when you said I deliberately pick women who belong to other men."

She began folding the sleeping bag in precise, rapid motions. "You don't have to worry. I wasn't suggesting any permanent arrangement. I'm used to being helpful."

"Maggie, don't be angry . ."

"I'm not angry," she snapped. She drew a deep breath and repeated with more control, "I'm not angry. I just wanted to help."

"I know. But I'm tough. I'm already on my feet. In a week I won't know it happened. Besides, there's your trip. You keep telling me you have to get to Wonsan—if that's so, you can't afford to lose another day. The rains will soon be here. That's okay for me, washing the gold out of the ground, but it'll be perilous for anyone whose trying to get through those mountains. Come along. I want to go down to the river with you to see you off."

She felt betrayed by her deep desire to stay with him, even in the light of his rejection—ever since they'd arrived there, he'd seemed anxious to see them gone. Engrossed by these deep feelings, she had almost forgotten the object of the journey that still lay ahead.

Mark reached for the copy of Lafcadio Hearn's *Glimpses of Unfamiliar Japan*, saying, "Who knows where our paths may cross again. Japan, perhaps."

She wished now that she and Gifford were returning by way of the Han so she might see him again, to make sure he was all right. But instead they would be returning to Seoul by steamer from Wonsan, journeying around the coastline of Korea.

"Will we see you when we get back to Seoul?"

"I doubt it. The mine's in operation now. That, as you know, is the point of my being here. I'll close it down as soon as the cold sets in. There would be no point in staying in Korea through the winter."

"I suppose not. But next year?" she pressed.

"Maybe. I don't know. I never plan ahead. Nothing in my life is certain."

"What an interesting way to live!"

He studied her for a minute. "I wonder if you really mean that. Adventure, travel are appealing to women up to a point, but eventually all they really want to do is settle down, make a home, have babies, build walls—at least all the women I've ever known. Are you and Sully going to stay on here after you . . ."

"I don't know," she interrupted, not wanting to discuss her marriage. "He's mentioned a practice in Ireland."

"Would you like that?"

"I don't know." There was silence. Then she said awkwardly, "I suppose we must be going."

She waited for some objection to her departure, but none came. He handed her the book and she took it from him. She noticed then that the tattered copy of *Treasure Island* had disappeared from his bedside.

"I was only teasing you about reading *Treasure Island*," she said."You didn't have to get rid of it."

"I'd take it kindly if you'd never mention that book again." Though he laughed as he said it, she had the odd impression that the request was quite seriously made.

Later, at the river, she noticed that the tiger skin had been prepared to be taken aboard the sampan.

Marigold shivered at the sight of it, remembering that scene in the clearing when she had been sure Mark was dying. "Take that thing away. I don't ever want to see it again."

"But it's a great trophy," Gifford insisted, thinking of all the souls that would be attracted to the Nak-tong Community House just to catch a glimpse of that skin—souls he might save. But Marigold never thought about important things like that.

A very pallid Banning slowly approached, leaning on the foreman from the mine who beamed at the sight of Marigold.

"White Tiger." The foreman's voice was filled with awe.

"I don't want it," Marigold said firmly, pointing to the hide." Send it to the queen."

"I thought it might remind you of miracles," Banning said. "But if you really want Queen Min to add it to her trophies, I'll see it gets to her with your compliments."

"I'll bet he takes the credit for it," Gifford muttered sarcastically as he climbed aboard, but if Banning or Marigold heard, neither paid atttention.

Banning took Marigold's arm and held her back for a moment. "Be careful, Maggie—especially where Min Tae-jon is concerned." His voice was low and serious. "Stay away from him—he's cruel. He'll stop at nothing."

She clung to his arm for a moment, then climbed aboard. Mark stood back as Hong pushed off.

"Anything you want me to send you?" she called out.

He shook his head, then called back, "Yes, as a matter of fact there is. Take a picture of the harbor at Wonsan."

"We'll be visiting Buddhist monasteries along the way. They're probably from the same period as your . . . the pavilion we visited . . ." she broke off, embarrassed by this too personal reference, but Banning replied matter-of-factly. "Monasteries aren't my style, but I hear the harbor's quite unusual."

"It's also quite strategic," Gifford said thoughtfully as they pulled out into the middle of the river.

"What do you mean by that?" she demanded as she waved good-bye, pretending it was the river breeze that made her blink so often.

"Just what I said. That's a strategic harbor."

"So?"

"So, I just wonder what he's going to do with a picture of it—frame it? Not likely," Gifford mused. "Banning was acting quite strangely. I got the distinct impression he was anxious to get us out of there, which was why I insisted on staying another day. I just wonder what he's up to." Sensing his silent companion was speculating too, Gifford hazarded, "Perhaps he wanted us out of there because Natasha Waeber is due to arrive at any minute."

"Don't be silly, Giff," Marigold retorted. "Natasha would never brave those rapids and you know it. That's ludicrous!"

"You know what they say about the mountain and Mohammed. When Mohammed won't come . . ."

"I know," Marigold answered irritably. "But it's still a ridiculous idea."

"Maybe he's got a little Korean filly hidden away—that little piece who came storming in this morning, for instance."

"How can you! She was just a child."

"That's the way some men like them. I notice he's speaking the language now. They always say the best way to learn a language is on the pillow."

"I speak Korean," she snapped. "Are you implying . . ."

"Not you, of course I didn't mean you."

"But Mark's fair game, that's it."

"So it's Mark now! Things seem to have altered between you. He was fair game with you until just recently. I don't know what happened last night . . ."

She broke in quickly with, "I find all this criticism of him uncalled for, especially after his hospitality to us. He got the boat back into shape, restocked our money supply as well as our food, not to mention the wine. He even insisted on sending his man, Lee, along to help get us upstream . . ."

"I've no doubt you would champion him now even if it turned out he was trafficking opium," Gifford sneered.

"How can you take his hospitality and then make accusations like that!" Marigold was angry as well as shocked.

"If you weren't so taken with him, you'd know that he's just the type to get involved in something underhanded. He's always on the make and he wouldn't be too discriminating about the product. A gold-mining operation would be the perfect cover, and Wonsan would make a perfect port to ship out a load with no questions asked. And remember that day in Seoul—he asked us not to tell anyone he had been there—not even the love of his life. I suspected then that he was up to something, and now I'm convinced of it."

They made their way up river to Paik-kui Mi, where they were to pay off Hong and pick up ponies for the continuation of their journey across the mountains. The sampan had to be poled and dragged through the ever-increasing rapids. Even with the extra man aboard, both Gifford and Marigold had to set to and assist, leaving little time or energy for further speculation about Mark Banning.

But though nothing more was said, inward speculation ran rampant. The sparks Gifford had noticed before in clashes between Marigold and Banning had again ignited during their brief stay at the mining camp; of that he was sure. He had witnessed the looks exchanged between them, the way their hands touched, her anx-

iety when the men were carrying him back to his hut, the way she
had nursed him. She had even stayed alone with him all night on
the flimsy pretext of his illness, and afterwards she, who had been
so insistent on going to Wonsan, had not wanted to leave. Now
she jumped to his defense at the slightest criticism. Gifford noted
everything and felt satisfied. It was just a matter of time before that
flame erupted into a conflagration. And when it did, Sully would
come to him for consolation and their friendship would, once
again, be just as it had been before Marigold had come between
them.

Marigold wished she could dismiss her concern that Mark's
wound might become gangrenous. He could swear by ashes and
spittle all he wanted, but she had no faith in that remedy. The
wound must be kept clean, the dressing changed frequently, and
those stitches she had put in must eventually be removed. He
might be as self-sufficient as he claimed to be, but how could he
possibly do all that for himself? Yet if he didn't who would? Was it
possible that Natasha would venture there from Seoul when she
heard? Who was Teuk-sil, the girl he didn't want her to mention to
anyone? She was young and innocent, but was it possible . . . no!
Anyway, Marigold was glad the girl was there. She was obviously
concerned about Mark, she would take care of him. His recovery
was all that mattered. As for the nefarious schemes Gifford laid at
his door, they were, she supposed, entirely possible. He certainly
hadn't been anxious for them to stay. But apart from all that, she
was troubled by the change in her own feelings toward Mark Banning from the time they had first arrived at Chum-yol—and perhaps even before. She went to some pains to forget them and, as a
result, thought of nothing else. It was as well he would not be
returning to Seoul, she thought, as they pulled into Paik-kui Mi.
By next summer everything would be different.

As Queen Min had promised, a string of ponies, with a mapu, or
groom, at the head of each, was awaiting them at the village. Like
everyone else on the river, the mapu must have known of their

arrival for they stood ready to load their supplies onto the ponies. They seemed anxious to depart immediately.

Hong and his silent assistant were paid off. Though they had often been lazy and stubborn, Marigold felt a reluctance to part with them and the sampan that had been their home.

She tried to pay off Lee, the man loaned to them by Banning, but he refused to accept anything.

"Buy something for Teuk-sil if you don't want it for yourself," she suggested hoping she might learn something about the girl.

"I know of no Teuk-sil," he answered abruptly.

Expecting Lee to return to Chum-yol with Hong, she gave him a hastily written note for Banning, advising him of their safe arrival. She included the address of Chu-sun's parents, where she would be stopping, in the hope Banning might reply and tell her how he was doing.

Lee returned her note, saying "I'm going on with you through the Diamond Mountains."

"But Mr. Banning will expect you."

"I will stay with you," he insisted.

Lee spoke little, but when he did, she noticed he was well spoken. His clothes were poor, yet he carried himself proudly. Maybe he was a scholar who had fallen on hard times and, in the manner of distingushed travelers, wanted to see Keum Kang San, the great Diamond Mountain, before he died.

So to Banning's note she added a postscript notifying him that Lee would be going on with them and gave it to Hong to deliver.

The mapu gathered together, fascinated by the English saddles that Marigold and Gifford had brought along for their own use. But the man holding the bridle of the lead pony pointed at the late afternoon sun and ordered them to start.

"No travel after dark—tigers," he said in explanation of their haste.

Marigold no longer scoffed at that idea, yet she did comment to Gifford, "A man for each pony seems extravagant."

"Since we're not paying, I don't see why we should care."

So they bade farewell to Hong and set off along the road to Wonsan. As they climbed into the mountains, Marigold looked back toward the river. It was her river. She had learned what to expect from it. Ahead lay the unknown.

8

Do not fail to write down your first impressions as soon as possible, Lafcadio Hearn observed in *Glimpses of Unfamiliar Japan,* for they are evanescent; they will never come again, once they have faded.

That phrase, from the book Banning had given her, came to mind frequently as Marigold made her journey through the Diamond Mountains. But though there was ample opportunity to drink in the dramatic views that unfolded before her, hour by hour or sometimes minute by minute, it was difficult to concentrate on finding the right words to describe them.

From morning to dusk, she struggled to encourage her hard-mouthed, stubborn, and often savage mount to continue along the narrow track through the mountains, through the dense woodlands of pine and maple that, now and then, gave way to glimpses of distant gray and pink granite ravines with rushing emerald torrents and deep mountain pools. On grassy summits, plums, cherries, and pears were ready to harvest; in the woods were lichen-covered rocks and ferns. No words seemed adequate to describe those mountain peaks scraping a limitless sky, so perhaps it was just as well that she lacked the time and opportunity to record any.

At times, when the path became all but impassable, Marigold dismounted. Leaving the pony to the care of the mapu, she made her own way, leaping from boulder to boulder, clambering around rocky promontories, splashing through mountain pools. She soon discovered her leather shoes were totally inadequate for the dangerous terrain but, like a guardian angel, Lee appeared with Korean string shoes that created a perfect foothold.

Lee, she discovered, was never far away. He had discreetly moved from the back of the pack until he assumed the leading position. He tested every bridge they came to by crossing it first with his mount, heavily loaded with their supply of *cash*. Only after assuring himself of its sturdiness, would he wave them on. When the mapu lingered at the frequent devil posts—piles of stones where each traveler would throw one more on for luck—Lee was the one who made them move on.

"Heathen habits. Don't set a bad example," Gifford grumbled when Marigold, too, paused to add a stone to the pile.

But what Gifford most objected to were the trees and bushes that were said to contain human spirits. The branches of these spirit-trees were hung with fly-infested rice, fish heads, pieces of meat, or rags and strings. These were offerings for the spirits of men taken by tigers, of women dead in childbirth, of those dead before completing their sixty-year cycle—their appointed time on earth. The mapu would stop to add whatever offering they had to these branches, in hopes of appeasing these unhappy spirits and, as Gifford pointed out, taking their own sweet time about doing it. To make use of these frequent breaks in their journey, Gifford took to preaching his own word to the mapu. He would take a position immediately beneath the spirit tree, taking care to avoid the rotting fish on the lower branches, with Marigold at his side as translator. He saw himself as David before Goliath, pleased to see Marigold doing justice to his elegance as she conveyed his words in Korean for the mapu listened, transfixed. They never took their piercing dark eyes from the woman who, single-handedly, had killed a Siberian tiger, the size of which escalated with each retelling of the tale.

"At last—progress," Gifford breathed in satisfaction. "I'll have them giving up this heathen muck before we're through these mountains."

But when they came upon ancient dolmen, huge monoliths up to fifteen feet in height, even Gifford gazed upward in awe, wondering who had erected them, and why, for there seemed no logical accounting for their origin.

At night, when there was time to write down impressions of the day, there was no conducive place to do so. Until they reached the monasteries, they had to put up at inns that at best were crude, at worst filthy. The garbage-strewn, hole-ridden courtyards were a confusion of black pigs, snarling yellow dogs, chickens, bulls, ponies with their loads, and their mapu. Inside it was not much better: there would be a large common room with ondol floors covered with dirty paper into which everyone crowded to eat and sleep. In the stalls outside, the ponies kicked and fought one another viciously. Sometimes the mapu were forced to string them up, wrapping straw matting around their bodies to make a sling, then hauling them up to the crossbeams where their legs flailed to no avail. Then the animals were forced to give vent to their anger through cries and bellows that kept everyone awake.

Marigold was allowed to use the women's quarters, often called "clean rooms" though they were just as filthy as the common room, filled with vermin and stiflingly hot, since the shutters were firmly closed for fear of tigers.

Lee, who seemed prepared for every eventuality, always preceded Marigold. On the floor he would lay oiled paper covered with cotton boiled in linseed oil.

"To stop fleas and bed bugs from biting," he explained. And it worked.

He would also hang up a drape to give her some privacy, though this was not as successful as the floor covering. Curious women would break through to touch or pull a hair from the head of this Western woman who had no fear, even of tigers; again it was Lee who came to her rescue and drove them away.

A night of respite came when they reached Tong-ku, for this was the home of Chu-sun. Marigold had looked forward to meeting Chu-sun's family ever since they started on the mountain trail. She hoped, too, having told Banning of their stop there, that word of his condition might be awaiting her. Their arrival was anxiously anticipated, for servants awaited them miles from the village to escort them to an imposing walled home on the outskirts. Bright roofing tiles and newly constructed high walls signaled recent renovation and expansion.

They were ushered into a large inner court where a welcoming committee had been assembled by Chu-sun's father. It consisted of his sons and fellow yangban from the surrounding area.

With a short, stiff bow, he began. "The Lady Chu-sun is grateful for the knowledge that you have imparted to her." Hands clasped behind, he strutted back and forth as he continued, "The Princess Chun-mae appreciates all the help you rendered during the recent birth of her child. It is regretted that child was a girl, and born in the year of the horse, too—no man willingly chooses to marry a girl born in the year of the horse. But we beg you to attach no blame to yourself for that misfortune."

Marigold's returning bow served to conceal her smile. "She is a lovely baby."

"We thank you on their behalf," he concluded stoutly, seeming to resent any interruption of his obviously rehearsed statement.

Marigold would have preferred less eloquence and more spontaneity. But it was a foretaste of what was to come, for during the visit she had ample opportunity to observe that his daughters' ties to the palace had made their father a personage of great importance, in his own eyes as well as in the eyes of his neighbors who fawned over him while he exulted in their praise. From all Marigold had learned from Chu-sun, she was sure her father hadn't always been this pompous autocrat. But Chu-sun hadn't seen him since he had come into possession of derived power, and his mantle of borrowed plumes ill suited him.

But still more shocking and distressing to Marigold was his mention, not once but many times, of an impending marriage in his family that would soon eclipse that of Chun-mae.

"I have to correct you if you refer to Chu-sun and . . ." she began, but was cut short by an angry hiss.

"Say nothing of what you know or suspect. Nothing. It is a royal secret."

"A royal secret," was the obsequious echo from his neighbors.

"I am quite sure your daughter can have told you nothing," Marigold commented with asperity.

Chu-sun's father was obviously displeased. He drew himself up to his full height and glared at her. "I know of this through other sources, impeccable sources at the palace. My daughter has nothing to say in the matter. It is for those concerned to make the choice and for me to give approval." Then, when a clamor for information arose from his company, his anger abated in a complacent laugh. "All in good time. I am not at liberty to say more now, but you may be sure the celebration will be even more lavish than the hwang-ap we are preparing for my mother." He turned to Marigold. "Next year my mother will have completed her zodiacal cycle of sixty years—hwang-ap. She was born in Ul Mi, the year of the sheep under the earth sign of cow. That cycle begins once again next year. In Korea a child is one year old at birth, so, according to your manner of counting years, she will then be sixty-one. Hwang-ap is a time of great celebration."

"A splendid occasion, indeed. Will your daughters attend?" Marigold asked.

"It would dishonor their grandmother if they did not."

Marigold smiled. "Then I think it truly wonderful."

She felt she could forgive almost anything at that point. Everything suddenly seemed to be falling into place. Even if she was in disgrace over refusing to marry the crown prince, Chu-sun would have a legitimate excuse to leave the palace. Marigold would forewarn Tuk-so when she saw him; if he were the noble man Chu-sun had described, he would surely be able to arrange it so that she need never return to the palace. Then the hwang-ap might well turn into a joint celebration: the completion of her grandmother's life cycle and the beginning of Chu-sun's happiness.

Marigold was anxious to meet this venerable woman. But as soon as Chu-sun's paternal grandmother laid eyes on her, she burst into a fit of giggles.

"What an odd shape her eyes are. Round! Who ever heard of round eyes! And look at their color!" One hand covering her mouth, she peered into Marigold's eyes. "They're green. I'll swear they're green. Eyes are supposed to be brown. Who ever heard of green eyes!" These comments were flung at Chu-sun's mother, who dutifully agreed. "And aren't her eyebrows strange, so straight—and thick as a man's. But her hair, oh what hair!" At this point Chu-sun's grandmother clasped both hands over her mouth and collapsed with uncontrollable laughter. It was impossible to speak to her of anything because, Marigold knew, she would never be taken seriously. Her hopes of discussing Chu-sun and her future rested with her friend's mother. But in the presence of her mother-in-law, the women barely spoke.

The next morning, however, Marigold managed to see Chu-sun's mother on her own. Even then, she showed the same unwillingness to say anything of significance. Realizing how rapidly the visit was drawing to a close with nothing accomplished, Marigold abruptly took the initiative and broke into her pleasantries with, "Your husband tells me he has news of a marriage for your daughter, Chu-sun."

She bowed her head in acknowledgment.

"If it is the marriage of which I have heard, a royal marriage, I must warn you that your daughter is decidedly opposed to it and with good reason. The young man in question is not only very young but he has a sickly body, a sickly disposition, and a sickly mind. She despises him."

Chu-sun's mother remained unmoved, causing Marigold to repeat, "Chu-sun despises the young man in question."

"What has that to do with anything?" Chu-sun's mother asked, without looking up.

"But it has everything to do with everything. It's not possible to marry someone that you despise. Besides which, she loves another. I believe you know him—Kim Tuk-so . . ."

But at this Chu-sun's mother held up a hand to silence her.

"You must never say that name again—nor use that word."

"What word?"

"Love. We do not speak of love. Love is an emotion that waxes hot and cold, it comes, then it goes. It brings no happiness. We have no use for love in this country, most especially where marriage is concerned."

"I don't believe that. The song 'Arirang' that I hear everywhere is a love song. And the sijo that Chu-sun has taught me, most of those are about love."

"'Arirang' is a song of rejected love. No?"

"True—but the sijo."

"Can you remember any that she has taught you that connect love with marriage, or even love with happiness?"

Marigold thought, then shook her head dubiously.

"I knew that, for these I taught her myself. Our sijo contain the seeds of truth and the truth is there is no happiness in love. You must promise me not to give my daughter any more foreign ideas or . . ." her voice broke, "or false hopes."

"I'm sorry. I cannot promise that."

"Then you are not her friend," Chu-sun's mother said, and left the room.

It was a sombre Marigold who left the village of Tong-ku. Her last act had been to request the family to gather together for a photograph for their daughters. Father, sons, and grandmother posed readily for her camera, but it was only when Marigold refused to take the picture unless Chu-sun's mother joined them that, with some resentment, she was sent for.

Chu-sun's father was obviously displeased as he bade them farewell.

"Under what sign were you born?" he demanded of Marigold.

"I was born in the year of the tiger."

"It is as I thought." He pursed his lips, nodding his head vigorously. "Horse—dragon—tiger, all very bad years for a girl."

From Tong-ku they began the ascent to the great Diamond summit of Keum Kang San and came upon the first of the Buddhist monasteries. The same invisible grapevine that had preceded them along the river must have continued into the mountains, for without prior notification, their arrival at the first monastery was expected.

The monks were friendly, curious, and at times even jolly. They gave up their bare but clean cells for their visitors, and shared their vegetarian meals of tea, rice, home-grown honey, and freshly picked pine nuts. Marigold was lulled by the clatter of the windchimes, the toll of the great bell throughout the night, even the great chiming of all the bells at four announcing that prayer was better than sleep. Even Gifford found this degree of piety to be unnecessary; he would go back to sleep until a more civilized hour, when he paid homage to a more civilized god.

As the monasteries were located in the most scenic areas, it was no hardship for Marigold to get up at four and watch the sun rise over the mountain peaks. The air was fresh, the day was new. It was a time of enchantment, a time for quiet reflection. She might have written then, for she had the time and place at last to put her thoughts into words, but now she wondered at the wisdom of doing so.

For in those early hours she thought of many things and many people: of her homeland, her father, her sister, of Queen Min, Herbert Farquhar, of Tuk-so and Chu-sun and what lay ahead for them. She was disturbed to find how rarely Sully came to mind. If she closed her eyes, she could barely remember what he looked like, for invariably Mark Banning's dark countenance superimposed itself over Sully's pink, blunt features. She knew she shouldn't think about Banning. He didn't think of her; no message had awaited her at Tong-ku even though she'd told him she would be there. Yet while she knew she should not think of him, and she tried hard not to, his image persisted, continuously intruding upon her thoughts.

At the approaches to the final ascent of Keum Kang San, they crossed an ornate red bridge to the huge monastery of Yu-chom Sa, with its high curving roofs. This was the largest monastery they had yet visited; it comprised seventy monks, twenty nuns, and more than two hundred lay servants, many of whom were young boys with shaved heads, given up by their families, who were unable to support them. Among the many ornate tombstones at this monastery was that of Queen In-mok, whom Queen Min had referred to as a paragon of maternal love. Queen In-mok had spent her final years at this monastery, paying silent tribute to her murdered son.

The abbot endeared himself to Marigold from the very first by greeting her with, "The beauty of the heavens lies in the stars; the beauty of women lies in their hair." After all the disparagement she had received on that subject, Marigold was delighted to find her hair an object of admiration.

The abbot settled Gifford down with his senior monks, chuckling, "Even though a little wisdom may prove a stumbling block on the path to Buddhahood, let them try to learn something of the beliefs of others." Then he whisked Marigold off to see Queen In-mok's relics and to relate the story that had gone down in legend of her sufferings along with her son, Prince Yung-chang, murdered at the hands of his wicked half-brother, Kwanghae-gun.

"The palace, I fear, has never been a happy place. But, queen or beggar or abbot, we must accept our lot in life," he concluded with a beatific smile.

"I can't agree," Marigold responded. "That would mean to accept the unacceptable, to lie down like a dog, to give in without a fight. Life may be a struggle, but it is meant to be lived fully."

He examined her curiously, before answering her. "It is because life is for living that we must accept and experience each moment as it is given to us, whatever that moment may contain. In the West you think you have liberty and choice. That is just an illusion. Your choices are limited to tiny decisions—will you eat rice or bread—or both? Will you rise early or lie abed? But the big decisions—such as this journey you have embarked on through our Diamond Mountains—those choices have already been made."

"But it was I—and Gifford—who made the decision to come here," Marigold protested.

"Was it?" His gaze was long and steady, causing Marigold to think back. They had waited for the kwan-ja; it had been a fluke that Queen Min had suggested that they go on to Wonsan. Or had it been a fluke? He seemed to divine her thoughts, for he laughed, "I see you think you begin to understand."

"Perhaps," she replied, wrinkling her brow.

"But you don't understand, of course, any more than I do. To expect to truly understand even the simplest of things is vainglorious. We see only through a crack in the great curtain of the universe. But we are sent here to do whatever it is we are capable of doing, just as well as we can do it, that is all. We must relish each moment of our experience, be it great or sad or even ordinary."

"That seems to be expecting a great deal," Marigold objected. "So much of life is habitual, like washing your face in the morning. To ask that we relish even perfunctory tasks doesn't seem reasonable."

"But suppose your face were dusty and grimy and there were no water, would you not relish washing it then?"

"In that case, I suppose I would."

"When you wash your face, you should experience it as though you were washing it for the first time, or if that is not possible, as though you had been deprived of water to clean yourself. Do it as though it is the most important thing in the world, for at that moment there is nothing else. Experience the texture of the washcloth on your skin, the water on your face, the motion of your hands. Feel your nose, mouth, cheeks, chin, forehead. Think about what you are doing at that very moment, not what you will do next. And never do more than one thing at a time. To try to wash your face and piss at the same time means you are unlikely to end up with either a clean face or an empty bladder." He laughed at Marigold's look of surprise at his blunt language. "You mustn't mind my words, but listen to their meaning. The mouth, I fear, is a gateway to great misunderstanding. I was once a poor boy, like those you see here. A flower always goes back to its roots."

And suddenly, without being asked, Marigold found herself going back to her own roots, telling him about her own beginnings in England, about her father and his death, about her journey to Korea, about Chu-sun, finally explaining why she was going to Wonsan.

"Chu-sun's father expects his daughter to marry as the queen decides. And I know that according to Confucian precept, a girl must obey her father. But only Chu-sun knows her own heart."

"And you, also—you must listen to your heart, for the fallen blossom can never return to the branch," the abbot observed. "Though I suspect that is what you have been trying to do in coming to Korea. Of course, the true reason behind your coming is something quite different, something you may or may not yet have encountered."

Marigold paused to consider this remark before she said slowly, "I think, perhaps, that I have encountered that reason." And she told him about Mark Banning. "I am engaged to marry Sully—Dr. Sullivan—yet I scarcely think about him. I can barely remember what he looks like, yet Mark's face is as clear to me as yours is at this moment. I try to blot it out but it won't go away."

"To talk of trying is foolishness. Nothing is ever solved by grim determination. We do, we don't do, that is all. Life is like a lamp-flame before the wind—you can't direct its course. The insects of summer must fly to the flame—there is no point in torturing the body by refusing the desires of the heart."

"But don't you, as a celibate, think it wrong? Though perhaps . . ." she broke off awkwardly.

"First of all, I am a celibate, but not because I think sensual pleasure right or wrong—such words have no meaning. It is a matter of where you choose to place your energy, and how. Like that pony you're riding—such strength, such vigor, but of what use is it if unharnessed? You must listen to that wild colt of a heart of yours, but at the same time you must keep a tight hold on the reins."

She frowned, "I don't understand. You seem to be saying that I should follow the dictates of my heart, yet also that I should hold them in check. That seems to be a contradiction."

"Life, itself, is contradiction. All joy is the source of sorrow, all sorrow the source of joy. But what is this word *should* that you use so often? It seems to me to belong with *right* and *wrong*. You must dismiss such words from your vocabulary."

"I only wish I might sit at your feet until I could make some sense of the obscurity of your words," Marigold replied wistfully.

He laughed, "My dear, my words are not obscure, they are simplicity itself. But to become an abbot one must begin as a novice. We are all on the path, but at different points along the way."

Though Marigold might not fully understand the abbot's words, she found peace and strength in them. She would have liked to have stayed on at Yu-chom Sa, but with rain threatening, Lee warned that they must leave quickly or the road to Wonsan might well be washed away.

"I wish I didn't have to go," she told the abbot as they departed.

"All meetings are but the beginning of separation," he answered. "But have no concern. Ambrosial times lie ahead. Wait, you'll see."

"Ambrosial times, indeed!" Gifford muttered after his pony slipped and he tumbled into the mud for the third time. The rain had started falling almost immediately after they left Yu-chom Sa, and soon they were deluged by sheets of water. In an effort to save what was left of his shoes, Gifford held up his feet to protect them from the mud. In so doing, he only succeeded in consigning the rest of himself to a rain-filled gully. He rose, mud-covered, blackened, and bruised.

"I'll be dashed if I'll bother to climb that sacred mountain of theirs. We'll take the most direct route to the next monastery."

"That will be Pyo-un Sa. Then I'll meet you there."

"You're going on alone?"

"No. Lee will come with me," Marigold affirmed, certain that Lee would accompany her.

And so, together, a wiry Korean man and a red-headed Western woman ascended Keum Kang San on foot, for it was impossible to take the ponies along the tortuous paths that led to the top. Supplies were cut to a minimum, though Marigold insisted on taking her camera. Together they climbed above the forest, up to the jagged central ridge. When they reached the yellow granite pinnacle, a sudden clearing of the skies allowed Marigold to capture on photographic plate the majesty of the twelve thousand peaks of the range that lay beneath them.

Lee's face was blissful. "Now, I can die a contented man."

"But not yet. As long as we take the same precautions going down as we did coming up, neither of us need talk of dying."

He threw her a pitying look. "We don't choose our time. Children of karma accept the goodness that is returned for goodness, as well as the evil that is returned for evil."

It was the longest speech Lee had ever uttered. Overlooking the half-rebuke, Marigold sensed that at long last she was about to learn something about this mysterious young man. "So you are Buddhist, Lee?"

"I am nothing," he muttered and, as though he regretted having spoken, he swung around and began the descent.

When they reached Pyo-un Sa, it was literally a return from the sublime. They found Gifford in a state of shock. At first Marigold, knowing Gifford's propensity to catch colds, thought his tremors resulted from influenza or even pneumonia. She wiped his brow and fed him warm broth, but he remained listless. Then he suddenly slumped back in the cot, pulling the single blanket over himself, forming a cocoon as he muttered over and over again, "It was awful! Bloody awful. Oh my God!"

"Oh, Giff! What happened? What was so awful?" Marigold asked, realizing that he was suffering from much more than a bad cold.

He sat up. His hollow voice was shaking, but he made an effort to speak. "I've seen something so brutal, something so horrible, something I never thought . . ." The words caught in his throat, momentarily gagging him.

"What did you see, Giff? What was it?"

Marigold waited until at last he began to breathe more evenly.

"It was on the Wonsan road, before we reached the monastery. From the mountain you wouldn't have come on it for you didn't approach from the same direction. Lucky for you! It was my misfortune to have come here directly." Marigold refrained from pointing out that had been his choice. She remembered the abbot's words: "The small decisions we may make, but the big ones are made for us." This division in their routes, which had seemed of little significance at the time, had clearly had major repercussions. "Lucky you!" Gifford repeated. "If you'd seen what I did, you wouldn't be able to sit there so calmly. We must return to Seoul by the first available means. Nothing you do or say can possibly convince me to continue."

"I'm not asking you to do anything. I'm only asking what you saw."

Gifford leaned forward until his thin face was within inches of hers. "Because on the road out there is a man who's been . . . been . . . been crucified!"

"Crucified," Marigold repeated in shocked consternation. "You mean . . ."

"I mean crucified. Nailed on a cross—with a sign over him. His feet bound with red rope. A black bag over his head. There's scarcely anything left of him, his flesh is torn or rotted away . . . nothing but bits of his vestments."

"Vestments. You mean he's . . ."

"A man of the cloth. A missionary! RC by the looks of the clothes, but even that doesn't call for such persecution."

"What did the sign say—did it give his name?"

Gifford shook his head. "It was in Korean—all I could gather from the mapu was that the territory was forbidden to Christians by order of Min Tae-jon. I tried to maintain order, but they were terrified. They turned back, taking everything with them—our money, everything—except for your useless photographic stuff. All I have is what I had on me and what was strapped to my pony. I could have gone with them if you'd been there, but I could hardly leave you behind."

"Thank you, Gifford. I appreciate your concern," she said awkwardly, thinking how wrong Banning had been in saying Gifford wanted to be rid of her; he had that opportunity, yet he had stood by her.

"We must get out of here as quickly as we can, by the shortest way. Since we're now so close to the coast, I suppose travel by boat is still best."

"That means Wonsan, then, which was our destination anyway."

"But we're not going marching into town and up to Min Tae-jon's palace. We can't allow him to find out. And in this country our faces are a dead giveaway." Gifford thought for a moment. "We must go in disguise. You know those mourning costumes they wear here—the long white robes and huge hats—there's no telling who's underneath the brims of those things. Maybe Lee can get hold of some for us. Then when we get to Wonsan, he can get us information about sailings and help us slip aboard."

"What makes you think he will? Maybe Lee will turn back too."

"He's been watching over you like a mother hen all the way," Gifford pointed out. Then he shrugged angrily. "If he wants to go, let him. He's probably the same as the rest. Anyway, it's just as well those mapu took off—mean bastards they turned out to be, when it came to putting what I'd taught them into practice. They pretended to listen to the word but when the chips were down, they ran faster than mice chased by a cat. If you'd been there, you might have stopped them. They listened to you. As it was, they wouldn't allow me anywhere near them. You'd have thought I had the plague."

So Gifford hadn't remained behind for her sake after all, Marigold realized. But she said nothing: he had been through an unnerving experience, he had suffered enough.

"One good thing about them making off like that," Gifford said, "is that when it gets back to Min Tae-jon, as it undoubtedly will, he'll be under the impression we turned back along with them. I suppose that's what he wanted. That must be why he put that ghastly thing on the road in the first place"

"Or to put the fear of God into us," Marigold observed factually.

Gifford sighed heavily. "I'm glad you can be so calm about all this—but you didn't see it. I did. And oh, Marigold, it was a terrible sight. For as long as I live, I'll never forget it."

Marigold's heart went out to him. "It must have been awful Giff." She got up. "I'll talk to Lee and see what he can do about the clothes."

At the door of the cell she turned back, "If the abbot here is anything like the one at Yu-chom Sa, it might help you to talk this over with him."

Gifford gave her a withering glance. "How could one of these heathens, with all their claptrap and gongs and bells and chants, help me, an ordained priest of the church! Don't be ridiculous!"

It was, perhaps, ridiculous to compare the complicated and exacting rights and ceremonies of Gifford's church with the simplicity of the abbot's life at Yu-chom Sa, Marigold reflected.

"Have you got any money?" Gifford asked.

"About thirty-five Japanese silver yen. Mark thought we'd be able to change them quite easily at Wonsan since it's a major port."

"Anything else of value?"

She still wore around her neck the kokok Mark Banning had given her so long ago. He had promised it would bring her luck, and she had never been parted from it. Perhaps it was superstitious of her, but she didn't offer it now.

"My camera," she said hesitantly.

Gifford was cheered. "Good! That should be worth something— let's see what Lee can get for it."

"But don't you think Korean mourners trying to peddle expensive photographic equipment would be a dead giveaway?" Marigold hesitated to sell her camera, feeling that would be tantamount to giving up part of herself.

"I suppose you're right," Gifford agreed disconsolately. Then his face suddenly brightened. "But what about your ring?"

"My ring?" Marigold looked down at her left hand. "But of course, I'd forgotten all about that." Without hesitation, even with a sense of relief, she pulled the ring from her finger. "I'll give it to Lee and ask him to sell it. With that and the yen, there should be enough to pay for our tickets."

9

Three mourners in sangbok—white hempen gowns topped by huge round hats like inverted baskets with wide brims that all but covered their faces—made their way along the main street of Wonsan. It was a busy street, its houses more substantial than any they had seen since leaving Seoul; it led to an even busier wharf dominated by offices of NYK (Nippon Yusen Kaisha) the Japan Mail Steamship Company, a Japanese bank, and a large customs building.

"Civilization, at last," Giff sighed. "Maybe now Lee can sell your ring and change those Japanese yen. Then we'll get out of these ridiculous togs."

"They were your idea," Marigold reminded, not particularly kindly. After Lee had managed to find the clothes, there had been the trouble of getting Gifford to wear them properly. He had adamantly refused to dispense with his black trousers and shoes underneath the yellow-white hemp turugami.

"You might as well not go in disguise at all if you're going to keep those on," Marigold had argued.

"But it's indecent. I'd feel half naked without my trousers."

"It's a question of whether we go into Wonsan as we are or whether we go in disguise. I'm all for taking the risk of sticking to our own identity. But you can't have it both ways."

Gifford scowled. "All right. Leave me and I'll take them off."

It was a red-faced Gifford who emerged, legs encased in white hempen paji, the ankle strings of these loose white trousers attached so clumsily that they kept slipping down around the komushin, the flat slippers upturned at the toe that he had put on at last.

"I feel ridiculous. Absolutely ridiculous!" Sensing the quiver of a smile on her lips, Marigold pulled down the brim of her hat to hide her amusement. The disguise did have its advantages.

"Did you notice that yellow road as we came into town?" Marigold asked as they walked along the wharf, checking on ships in the harbor. "Lee says it leads to Min Tae-jon's palace. Yellow is a royal color in China. He says it's the fashion there to pave the way to their palaces in yellow clay."

"For a coolie, he seems to know a lot."

"Lee's far from a coolie," Marigold observed. Lee remained a mystery. Throughout the journey, his support had been unfailing, yet coming from a man who scarcely knew them, such loyalty was unexpectedly puzzling. It could hardly stem from a wish to assist Christian missionaries, for he was not a Christian. But apart from that, he had vouchsafed little of his own background.

"Whatever he is, let's heed the warning," Gifford said. "We'll avoid that yellow road as though it were the yellow plague. What we need to find is an inn and then send Lee out for information on sailings."

Their inn, chosen for its obscurity, was close to the waterfront and sufficiently busy to allow them to mingle with other travelers without undue suspicion. They sat down with relief and Lee ordered them hot water with ginger before he left for the shipping offices, pocketing the ring and all Marigold's money.

"You shouldn't have given him everything," Gifford argued, kicking the komushin off and gently rubbing one foot against the other.

"There wasn't enough to argue over. Either he gets the tickets or he doesn't. Did you get blisters?"

"These things must have been made for ballet dancers—no heels. I felt as though I was falling over backwards the whole time. I can't wait to get back into my own clothes. It's been a ghastly journey. And I don't even feel as though I've accomplished anything."

For once Marigold was in full agreement with Gifford. She had accomplished nothing either. To get all the way to Wonsan and then not to be able to see Tuk-so was to have failed in her mission. And yet perhaps there was still a chance; she knew where he could be found, if only an opportunity would present itself.

Lee provided that opportunity. Time and again, either purposefully or inadvertently, he had come to her aid. Now he returned with tickets on a boat that would not depart until the following morning. Time, at least, was still on her side.

As she followed the wide yellow clay road that led to Min Tae-jon's palace, Marigold did not follow the abbot's advice of living in the moment, but constantly concerned herself with what lay ahead of her. She was disappointed that Lee had not offered to accompany her. She had told him, though not Gifford, where she was going, thinking that the man who had willingly clambered up to the peak of Keum Kang San at her side would surely go along with her to the palace. But far from offering to go with her, Lee had stringently opposed her plan.

"That is no place for you. Min Tae-jon is evil. He is cruel with the power to indulge his cruelty. He respects no one, most certainly not Western woman who is nonperson, sangnom."

That remark, together with Banning's earlier warning, served as a clear forboding of the nature of the man whose palace she was approaching, a palace almost as large and considerably more ornate than Kyongbok, the royal palace in Seoul.

"Miss Wilder. Come in. His Excellency is expecting you." She heard the voice before she saw the indigo-blue brocade-robed figure, his high, black, horsehair hat tied under his chin. He had appeared from inside, apparently called by a guard who must have seen her approaching. That this man recognized her and knew her name was not entirely unexpected. She had changed into her own clothes, the official purpose for her visit being to deliver the queen's letter to the governor. From Chu-sun, Marigold knew that the queen had already sent a letter in that regard, and so she breathed more easily at this sign of welcome. She remembered the words of the abbot: Ambrosial times are ahead. It seemed they were.

As they passed through endless corridors, the official who had greeted her explained that His Excellency the governor was observing an inquiry the magistrate was conducting in the courtyard.

How fortunate, Marigold thought; she didn't even have to ask to see Tuk-so. She was being taken to him.

Just then she heard the distant shriek of a bird or animal. She hesitated, but either the official hadn't heard it or else he recognized the sound as quite ordinary, for he kept on walking, commenting as he did, "I am convinced the inquiry will soon be over and then the governor will speak with you. He looks forward to the opportunity."

There came another shriek, louder, closer. This time Marigold stopped, convinced it was no animal cry but a human cry, a dreadful cry of pain that shattered her courage.

"What is that?" she demanded.

Unconcerned, the official waved her on, then slid back the door to the courtyard, knelt, bent to the floor in a bow, and finally indicated that she step out onto the raised dais.

Seated, with his back toward her, was a resplendent figure in stiff black and gold brocade; over the high topknot on his head, which stuck up like a single horn, he wore a tall manggon decorated with gold and jade. She had never seen even the king wear anything quite as splendid.

But that moment of contemplation was shattered as another terrible scream rent the air. Her eyes flew beyond the regal figure to the courtyard, where three guards in cone-shaped helmets stood over a bound figure crumpled in the dust. In between his legs, which were tied together, two long sticks had been inserted. Gripping the ends of these sticks, the guards were twisting them, turning his legs like a corkscrew while his body was held securely in place. The scream of pain extorted by this barbarous act was joined by another scream, this one of horror.

"Stop it! Do stop it. I beg you. Put a stop to it."

The figure in front of Marigold held up a hand to silence her, then said pleasantly, as though she had just inquired after his health, "It's almost over, Miss Wilder, almost over."

The crumpled figure and guards were facing another official, a younger man who raised himself to his full height to demand in gutteral, official tones: "Are you now willing to relinquish the girl?"

There was no movement from the crumpled figure, not a cry, not even a whimper when the question was repeated. The official raised his hand to signal the guards to continue, but the figure in front of Marigold interceded: "Magistrate, find out whether the fellow has fainted. There is no point in applying pressure to one who can't feel it. He's old. He may even be dead. Don't waste the efforts of the guards on a dead man." Then he arose and turned to Marigold with an expansive smile on his thin lips. "Miss Wilder, I am Min Tae-jon. Welcome to Wonsan and my humble abode."

Queen Min was a handsome woman, and Marigold could detect a similarity in her brother's features, indicating that he, too, had once enjoyed that same favor of nature. But time had not served Min Tae-jon as well as it had served his sister. His head seemed too small for his thick body. His face was bloated, his eyes dull and yellow. His expression, even wreathed by that welcoming smile, was one of consummate evil.

Marigold attempted to still her trembling body. Her fists, clenched white at the knuckles, were pressed against her teeth to prevent herself from screaming.

Min Tae-jon seemed to expect no reply. He waved back toward the scene in the courtyard. "I am sorry you arrived just at a time when we were conducting a little business. But luckily it seems to be all over now. Shall we go inside? Come. Come."

The perfect host, he stood at the door, waiting until Marigold turned back inside; he then led the way into a splendid room with gold-painted screens on the walls, a low table in the center, and large cushions strewn on the woven straw matting on the floor.

"It's Japanese tatami," he explained, flinging himself down on several cushions that formed a low settee. He bent one leg, clasping its ankle with both hands, and surveyed his visitor with interest. "I find it more comfortable than our ondol floor covering. Sit down. Tell me what you think. The Japanese have a few ideas worth copying—not many, but a few." He rang a bell and a servant immediately appeared. "Let me see, you're English. You would probably like tea. What kind do you prefer, green tea, jasmine, Ceylon? You have only to ask."

The words might have come from a waiter in a London tea-room. Marigold, her hand still pressed against her mouth, was struck by the incongruity as well as the horror of her situation.

"Green tea? Will that do? And bean curd cakes? But no—a ship just came into port with a cargo from Scotland—whiskey, of course, they also presented me with some sort of sweet bread. You must sample it," smiled her genial host.

Marigold could still not bring herself to respond.

"I suppose you might prefer to sit on a chair, but I dislike people to look down upon me. Sit! Sit!" he enjoined.

She took a place on a cushion, but could make no reply.

"You are my guest. I want to please you. What can I do?" He thought a moment. "My young magistrate, Kim Tuk-so, that's it! I'll call for him. He's a great favorite with the ladies."

One of the worst blows Marigold had suffered was finding Kim Tuk-so, the man she had journeyed so far to see, officiating at that incredibly brutal ceremony. She had to remind herself not to condemn him. He was acting under duress—he *had* to be acting under duress.

She regained sufficient composure to ask, "That man, what had he done? What crime had he committed?"

"Man?" Min Tae-jon queried, his small head cocked to one side in consideration. "What man?"

"The man in the courtyard. The man they were torturing."

"Torturing—certainly not! But I see you mean the man being questioned. He is unworthy of your concern."

"But I am concerned," Marigold cried out, her voice rising. "I must know what terrible thing he did to deserve such punishment."

"My dear Miss Wilder. You seem overwrought." He tutted sympathetically, then turned at the sound of an arrival. "Ah, here comes our fine young magistrate. We'll let Kim Tuk-so tell you all about it, since the little matter seems of such interest to you."

The door slid open and Kim Tuk-so entered. He knelt down and bowed to Min Tae-jon, clasping his hands together and bending from the waist until his forehead almost touched the floor. Then he knelt down on a cushion opposite his superior without so much as a glance in Marigold's direction. Even in her agitation, Marigold studied him eagerly. His face was oval, with a smooth olive complexion; his eyes were deep brown, soft, and soulful. Beside the dissipation of Min Tae-jon, he glowed with vitality.

"This is Miss Wilder. She has journeyed all the way to our humble city from the capital, where, I understand from my sister the queen, she has been teaching English to a young lady of your acquaintance at the palace, the Lady Chu-sun."

Kim Tuk-so looked at Marigold for the first time and bowed, a much abbreviated version of the bow he had extended to Min Tae-jon. His shoulders under the brocade of his turugami were broad and powerful. His features under the brim of his high crowned kat were distinct and strong, though there was a looseness to his mouth that prevented him from being entirely handsome. Still, from his appearance it was easy to understand why Chu-sun had fallen in love with him.

"The Lady Chu-sun?" he repeated, drawing his brows together in puzzlement, "Chu-sun? I don't believe I remember the lady."

Marigold gasped, then caught her lip between her teeth. Obviously, he would have to deny any interest in Chu-sun in the presence of the queen's brother. She began to sympathize with the terrible position in which this young man had been placed, under the command of a tyrant of such monstrous proportions.

Min Tae-jon laughed, commenting to Marigold. "This young magistrate of mine is such a one for the ladies, I don't believe he remembers which he has from one night to the other." He looked at Tuk-so with a mixture of envy and pride. "And who is to be the lucky one tonight, eh? Don't keep me guessing. That new kisaeng that arrived from Seoul, the one with the freckle on her left cheek. You know which cheek I mean." He laughed and slapped his hip, enormously pleased by his own wit. "This is a young man of great fortitude," he explained to Marigold. "Even in my youth, I don't believe I possessed quite as much vigor."

Marigold ignored these sexual innuendoes; her concern lay in the scene she had just witnessed. "The man you were . . . questioning just now. What had he done?"

Kim Tuk-so looked over at Min Tae-jon for guidance.

"Tell her. She wants to know, so tell her."

Kim's voice was low, even; his gaze was direct. "This is a simple, old man cursed with the misfortune of having only daughters. His Excellency, in all the goodness of his heart, had relieved him of the burden of the older girls, but, quite astonishingly, when he offered to do as much for the youngest, he was refused. His Excellency's gesture was a kind and generous one, but unaccountably the foolish man not only refused, but spirited the girl away in a fruitless effort to hide her—as though anything can be kept from His Excellency."

The servant arrived with tea, served in low cups painted with golden cranes, beautiful, delicate pieces. Marigold held hers between her hands, waiting for Tuk-so to finish.

"This is the bread from Scotland," Min Tae-jon said. "I am

happy to be able to offer you something familiar to your taste. Try it! Tell me if it is good."

There was nothing to do but to take the proffered piece, nibble at it, and pronounce it good. As she did so, Marigold kept her eyes pinned on Tuk-so. He was munching on the shortbread and was far more effusive in his praises.

"Such texture. Not too sweet. A very fine choice, Your Excellency. And it goes so well with tea. I should like to order some for myself—that is, if Your Excellency would not consider it presumptuous of me."

"Not at all, Tuk-so. I admire your prowess, and I am always pleased to repay those who serve me well."

Marigold, who could wait no longer for this exchange of mutual admiration to end, blurted out, "I must know this man's crime."

"But he explained that to you." Min Tae-jon's tones were moderate and reasonable. "The man refused my request. That was impolite."

"But you can't torture someone for being impolite!"

"Torture! Why must you call it torture? The man was being taught to obey."

Noting Min Tae-jon's displeasure, Kim Tuk-so quickly enjoined, "It is wrong to refuse any request made by the governor. In fact, it is a crime to do so. This man knew better. Not only were his other two daughters assisted, but he, too, benefitted. So he knew it was to his advantage as well as the girl's to send her along to the palace when asked. But he was an obstinate old man, who added insult by sending the girl far away in a vain attempt to hide her. That was wrong."

"But you're talking about his daughter—not a piece of furniture!" Marigold exploded.

"It makes no difference. Once the governor makes a request, it must be honored. To have a request—any request—denied, just for some whim, sets a bad example. Who knows where it might lead if it became known that someone had succeeded in withholding property when asked to surrender it? People might refuse to pay taxes or be conscripted. The result could be anarchy! Rebellion of any kind, no matter how small, no matter what the reason, must be squelched immediately." Kim made it sound so reasonable.

Then Min Tae-jon like a senior advocate presenting the same case, leaned forward to add, "You see, Miss Wilder, I could simply have taken the girl from him." His tone was again that of purest reason. "But I prefer to do what is right. I asked her father to give her to me. It was a perfectly reasonable request. He would have been amply rewarded for the gift, he knew that. He had been paid for the others. Like her sisters, the girl would have had the pleasure of living in the palace, for a time at least, while she remains young and pretty. But out of sheer obstinacy, he refused. It was unfair to himself as well as the girl."

"It was sheer insubordination toward His Excellency," Kim Tuk-so put in forcefully. "But I believe he has learned his lesson. Both legs are broken. I doubt he will ever walk again."

"Oh my God!" The shortbread fell from Marigold's hand. She picked up the crumbs, one by one, concentrating on each as though her life depended on it.

"Miss Wilder!" Min Tae-jon pleaded. "Don't worry yourself. The servant will take care of that." He turned to his magistrate. "What kind of entertainment do you suggest for our guest's pleasure, Tuk-so? What do you think she would enjoy? A little music, dancing, food, wine. Tell us what you would like."

"Nothing," Marigold swallowed in an effort to hide her horror and disgust. "I want nothing. I came to deliver a letter, that is all." She reached into her pocket and pulled out the queen's letter and handed it to him. "I have to return to the inn. We leave early tomorrow."

"Nonsense." Min Tae-jon waved aside the letter without opening it. "Our laws of hospitality prohibit that you be allowed to leave. Besides, why should you? Your friend, the Reverend Partridge, may depart, but you—you must plan to stay on here with us for a while." His dull eyes surveyed her from head to toe before he turned to Tuk-so. "Don't you think it might be amusing to have with us a woman so . . . so . . . not pretty, of course, but different."

Marigold's heart quickened, as the full extent of her precarious position dawned upon her.

"Reverend Partridge won't leave without me."

"But he's already gone aboard ship. They sail at the morning tide," Min Tae-jon's thin lips puckered as he watched her reaction to this news.

Was it possible that Gifford had deserted her? It was true that she hadn't told him where she was going, convinced he would try to argue her out of it. But even so, would he leave her so callously? Min Tae-jon seemed to fathom her thoughts as he went on smoothly, "As he was put aboard your friend said that he had warned you against following the yellow clay road; he said you were asking for the yellow plague. Now what could he have meant by that? I am told he was most cooperative about leaving. In fact, he seeemed anxious to get on board."

Marigold recognized the words as Gifford's. Though her heart sank at hearing them, she kept her response strong. "I must point out to Your Excellency that I am a British subject. I am traveling on an official kwan-ja issued by your government. Your sister, the queen, knows me well. I am a frequent guest at the palace."

Min Tae-jon's brow wrinkled in puzzlement. "Of course. But why do you tell me these things that I already know?"

"Simply to warn you that I am not unprotected. If any harm were to befall me, there would be questions, official questions that your government would have to answer."

"Harm? But my dear young lady, who would want to harm you?" He looked over at Kim Tuk-so. "If you fear that this young man has designs upon you, I can assure you he already has too many women on his hands as it is. As for me," he raised his hands in a gesture of despair, "I would it were possible, but alas!"

She flushed. "I didn't mean that exactly."

"Then what did you mean?"

"I . . . I have delivered the letter that was the reason for my visit. It is now time to go." She began to rise, but he motioned her to stay seated.

"It would be inhospitable of me to let you leave. My sister would never forgive me. You must stay and dine with me at least. You will not, I trust, refuse this small request."

Marigold had already seen what happened to those who refused; her host left little room for argument.

"Besides, you are of particular interest to me for my sister tells me you are a photographer. You took some excellent photographs of the crown prince that she sent to that fat old woman who sits on the throne of England."

Marigold jumped at what seemed a golden opportunity for escape. "I should very much like to take a photograph of Your Excellency, if you will permit it."

He nodded. "A fine idea. I like it."

"But I shall need my camera. It is at the inn where I am staying. Let me go back for it, and . . ."

He laughed amiably. "There is no need. I have had all of your things brought here, including the camera. Tell me," he suddenly leaned forward, his jaundiced, narrow eyes boring into her own, "why were you taking pictures of the harbor?"

Was there anything he didn't know? Marigold wondered as she quickly responded, "A traveler likes to record places of interest."

"And a spy likes to record strategic areas."

Marigold was taken aback. "A spy! Are you implying that I am a spy!"

"It is entirely possible, Miss Wilder. You are a friend of Mr. Banning, are you not?"

"I am, but I don't see what that has to do with it."

"Such innocence! I suppose it was he who asked you to take a picture of the harbor."

"As a matter of fact it was." Her hand flew to her mouth. "But you can't mean . . ."

"Your Mr. Banning is a spy. A clever but evil spy for he is a spy without a conscience. He spies on the Russians, on the Japanese, on us. He befriends the Tong-hak and foments rebellion. That Lee he sent with you is a Tong-hak. But of course you knew that."

"No, I didn't," she denied, realizing that had the ring of truth for it would explain many things about Lee.

"I have had Mr. Banning under surveillance for a long time."

"If you believe he is a spy, why haven't you reported it to the queen? He is mining gold in partnership with her."

"Women are very foolish. My sister, at times, succumbs to the weakness of her sex. Besides," Min Tae-jon smiled, "Mr. Banning is mine. He has attempted to thwart me in a very personal and unforgivable way. I want him. But I can afford to bide my time. I have no intention of taking him until he leads me to everything I want to know. It would be useful, for instance, to know the code he uses. Did he, by chance, confide in you?"

"Spies! Codes! This is really ludicrous! The stuff of *Boy's Own* or, or . . . *Treasure Island*."

"*Treasure Island?* What is this *Treasure Island?*"

"It's a boy's adventure story. I can't believe that anyone whose reading goes no deeper than *Treasure Island* could turn out to be the nefarious character you describe. Mark Banning is an adventurer, but he is no more a spy than I am."

"But you are a spy, Miss Wilder, whether you admit it or not. Banning is a clever man who knows how to use women well. For him you shoot not only a camera but also a gun. He has taught you well. Your prowess has earned you fame in the capital. My sister, by the way, is delighted with that tiger skin. And that woman at the Russian legation, on her pillow he has learned all their secrets— secrets I shall, undoubtedly, get from him when the time is right." Min Tae-jon smiled speculatively. "He is a man after my own heart. I look forward to meeting him. It is a pity our acquaintance will not be a long one. But enough of these matters of business. For now you are my guest. You must rest and refresh yourself. Then at dinner we will discuss this matter of photography."

A servant conducted her to a room that was heavy with lacquer and brocade hangings and far too warm. Despite her anxiety, Marigold felt tired. The pervasive smell of some heavy perfume filled her nostrils as she sank down onto the bed on the floor and closed her eyes.

The scene was an amphitheater with a scaffold in the center on which stood the tall figure of a man, his head in a noose. A woman warrior, in a helmet of shining bronze, was sitting in judgment. The executioner, a fat tabby with the head of a man, stood waiting.

"You must choose between me and the Russian?" the warrior said.

"I answer to no one for my choices," the man replied.

"Then you'll answer to me with your life."

She signaled to the hangman with a gun. But before he had time to perform the execution, she fired, hitting the man right between the eyes. He fell, dangling from the noose, swaying to and fro.

Then the abbot from Yu-chom Sa appeared, smiling. "Didn't I tell you ambrosial times lay ahead?"

Marigold awoke with a start. Someone was shaking her. Sweat was running down her body, from the heat, from the memory of the dream.

A maid with a bowl of warm water, holding a deep green and gold chima and chogori over her arm, stood above her.

"His Excellency is waiting," she said.

Marigold entered the long banquet room hesitantly. She had refused to put on the Korean gown, much to the maid's distress. The grubby, creased skirt and blouse that she still wore seemed the only way to maintain her Western identity.

She was immediately aware of a sweet, cloying smell. It wasn't the perfume of the room she had just left; it was even more suffocating and sickening. Min Tae-jon reclined on a bank of cushions, drawing on a long-stemmed pipe attached by a flexible tube to a large curved bowl. His eyes were glazed yet, at the same time, his gaze was piercing.

"Come, Miss Wilder. Come in." His voice was slow yet insistent. She did not move, and he rasped, "Come, come."

He looked at her clothes. "These are such sad garments."

When she said nothing, he addded, "And you are so sad." He held out the pipe to her. "Here, you would like this. It is pleasant. It will gladden your heart."

"No," she said sharply, then swallowed and, like a child at a birthday party refusing a treat, added, "No, thank you."

"You are hungry? Eat." He indicated a low, carved table where a variety of foods were set out: delicately fried fish, soup, rice, pickles, kimchi, pancakes, beef strips. In the center of the table was a bowl of fruit. It was a large and appetizing display, but she noticed that only one place was set.

"Please, sit down and eat."

She sat down, wishing she weren't so hungry. But it was useless to pretend when her stomach growled at the sight of the food. She lifted the soup bowl and drank.

He watched her as she ate, seeming to savor the food with her as she swallowed each mouthful. Occasionaly, he drew on the pipe, but he did not speak until she was finished. Then he began slowly, carefully enunciating each word.

"I've been thinking about those photographs of yours, Miss Wilder. There are some subjects in which I am interested."

"Of course," she agreed readily, then paused before asking suspiciously, "What are these subjects?"

"Things I find very pleasant to look at."

"If you think I would ever take pictures of people being tortured . . ."

"No. No. That is a thought, but no," he laughed. "In fact what I am going to suggest is quite the opposite. I should like some photographs to add to my pillow book."

"A pillow book?" she prompted, for his voice had faded; had his eyes, with their odd glint, not been pinned on her so insistently, she could have sworn he was falling asleep.

"I have been ruminating on likely subjects. Do you not think that Kim Tuk-so is a handsome man?"

Marigold's relief was enormous. A photograph of Tuk-so was precisely what she had hoped for. Even though her original enthusiasm for the man Chu-sun loved was now clouded, Marigold could sympathize with his predicament. He was even less able to escape than she was. If she had the opportunity to photograph him, then she might have the opportunity to talk openly to him as well.

"Kim Tuk-so would make a handsome subject for a photograph," she agreed. "I should very much like to take a photograph of him. I prefer being alone with my subject. I find that produces a truer result."

Min Tae-jon drew on his pipe without speaking. Then, as he exhaled, he said slowly, "That can be arranged. I want the result to ring true. I have a resident artist who makes scenes for my book, but they are too . . . too . . . how shall I say it, too pretty."

Marigold nodded. "I understand the importance of realism. You want to see people just as they are."

"Exactly!" His glazed eyes suddenly glinted brightly as he studied her. "So the camera for you is like this pipe to me. It, too, helps me to see people as they really are. The results are sometimes astonishing, are they not?"

Though she hated to acknowledge that she had anything in common with this ogre, Marigold was forced to agree.

He drew on his pipe, then sat without speaking for so long that although his eyes remained fixed upon her, Marigold wondered whether he had drifted into some hazy beyond. When at last he spoke, his voice was clear but ominous.

"Since the skin of the tiger you shot in the mountains was put on display at the royal palace, they are calling you the White Tiger of the West. They say you are without fear. I see you are not afraid of me—yet. But you will be. Everyone is eventually, even my sister." Then his lips drew into a thin smile. "I like the idea of having my own photographer. Tell me if there is anything you need?"

"I have the plates and the materials for developing the prints. But I shall need an enclosed area in order to process them, as well as space to hang the prints to dry."

"You shall have everything, you have only to ask. The pictures for my pillow book must be the best you have ever taken."

"What is a pillow book?" she asked.

"What does it sound like to you?"

"I don't know—I suppose a book you might take to read in bed."

"That is precisely what it is." A strange glint came into his eyes. "Tell me again the name of that book Mr. Banning reads in bed?"

The swift change of subject caught Marigold off guard. She thought for a moment before answering, "Do you mean *Treasure Island?*"

"That is it, *Treasure Island.*" He reached for a scroll and ran his finger down a list of items. "There it is. *Treasure Island.* It was noted when the contents of his room were examined. Always look for the item that doesn't fit. That must be it." His expression was Mephistophelean. "Thank you, Miss Wilder, you have been very helpful."

"I don't know what you mean. It's just a book. A boy's book."

"That's it. It is a book for boys. Mr. Banning is not a boy, yet the book is obviously much used. We should have thought of that. We considered everything but a book code. Now we have you to thank, Mis Wilder, for helping to solve the puzzle for us."

He extended a half bow in her direction.

Could Mark Banning really be a spy? Did *Treasure Island* contain some secret code? Marigold remembered the seriousness that underlay Banning's remark, "I'd appreciate your never mentioning that book again." In sudden distress, she thought of her dream. Had she unintentionally put a noose around his neck? She had to get away. She had to warn him.

"I will take the photographs for your book, if you promise I may leave as soon as they are finished."

"As soon as they are satisfactorily finished," he corrected.

"You told me your sister has found my work satisfactory. I see no reason why the photographs I take for you should not be equally acceptable."

"Good. It is settled then." He clapped his hands and ordered that the equipment be brought in.

Having set up her camera opposite the bank of cushions where Min Tae-jon was seated, Marigold asked, "May I take a photograph of you to begin with?"

"But of course." She had expected he might move the pipe and was glad that he did not. In the haze of smoke, the relaxation of his facial muscles brought out the stark malevolence of his features. It was a perfect portrayal, and, as the shutter clicked, she felt a sense of pride in having captured the essence of his man. Yet now that she knew him better, she was scarcely encouraged, for the reversed image of the lens had revealed an infinite cruelty that bordered on sadism.

"Now, I should like you to take a photograph of the newest addition to my household."

A wave of revulsion swept over Marigold as the new subject was brought in. Dressed as a bride, she was small, slender, lovely, and terrified beyond measure.

"Teuk-sil!" Marigold gasped.

"Exactly. As I suspected, you've already met. Teuk-sil. An apt name—special fruit, just ready to be plucked."

"She's only a child," Marigold protested in horrified dismay.

"She's at the brink of womanhood," Min Tae-jon responded with some satisfaction. "But still intact. I had her examined to make sure Banning had not tampered with her. Luckily, his taste runs to older . . ."

"He is not depraved!"

"This a matter of opinion." Imperiously he tapped the cushion beside him. Teuk-sil glanced pleadingly at Marigold before sitting down. As Min Tae-jon put a proprietary arm around her, she drew back in fright, at which he pulled her to him and forced the pipe between her lips. She choked on the smoke and he laughed.

Marigold could stand by no longer. Storming across the room, she flung the pipe to the floor, breaking the bowl. Then, with a protective arm around Teuk-sil's narrow shoulders, she pulled her from her tormentor.

"How dare you!" She shook with cold fury. "She's only a child!"

"So you've said," Min Tae-jon snapped, angrily tapping the cushion beside him. His gesture only made the girl cling more tightly to Marigold. "A child must obey or else be taught to obey."

"By her father, perhaps. But you're not her father."

"She knows what's become of her father. He's broken, he no longer has any hold over her. It's me she must obey from now on."

"She's an innocent child, not some woman of pleasure. Call on the kisaeng you drooled over earlier if that is the sort of amusement you want."

"In due course I shall. That kisaeng is one of the subjects you will take photographs of for my pillow book."

"For your pillow book," Marigold repeated hollowly as the true meaning of the term sank in.

"For my pillow book," he repeated, reaching to pick up his pipe from the floor where Marigold had flung it. "Everything worth anything demands its price. While this pipe has allowed me to reach untold heights, I have had to pay for it with my vital juices. My pleasures with women have become limited to vicarious enjoyment, or initiating innocents like this—this Teuk-sil."

As he stabbed the stem of his pipe toward the young girl, Marigold's voice rose in hot indignation. "If you expect me to photograph these women in . . . in indecent situations, you must be mad. I refuse categorically to do anything of the sort. There's nothing in this world that could make me."

He held out his hands in an attitude of hurt surprise. "But Miss Wilder, I explained what I wanted. I asked you to take the photographs for my book. Having seen what happens to people who refuse me, like the sensible woman you are, you readily agreed to my request."

"I had no idea you wanted . . ." Words to describe what he wanted failed Marigold. "I only agreed to take a photograph of Kim Tuk-so—"

"But he, too, will be in the photographs. I am delighted with the service he has rendered here. He has proved a splendid addition to my household."

"You're depraved, as well as mad, to imagine I would ever contribute to this dirty little book of yours!" Marigold raged, holding the trembling Teuk-sil to her.

"Why all these protestations, Miss Wilder?" Min Tae-jon's voice was calm. Then he sighed. "As I said just now, everything worth anything demands a price. Knowing I want these pictures, I presume this is an attempt on your part to extort some vast fee for them." This reasoning seemed to satisfy him, and he leaned back. "I'm a generous man. Ask it."

"You filthy lecher! I've already told you there's nothing in the world that would make me take pictures like that."

He raised his eyebrows, studying her anger, studying too the young girl who clung to her.

"No price, Miss Wilder?"

"None whatsoever."

"That sounds final."

"It is final."

He shrugged. "Very well, then. You may go." He waved an impatient hand at her camera. "Take that thing and leave."

She looked at him uncomprehendingly. "I may leave. Just like that."

"Just like that." He beckoned to the young girl, tapping imperiously on the pillow at his side. "As for you, my Special Fruit, come over here. Now."

The girl's arm tightened around Marigold and she buried her head in her skirts, whimpering with fear. Marigold's predicament suddenly dawned upon her.

"Come here," he commanded. "You need to be taught obedience."

Marigold tried desperately to disguise both her rage and her disgust as she pleaded, "No, Your Excellency. Please. I beg of you."

"The girl is mine. She will do as she's told or learn to take the consequences, which I can assure her she will not like. As for you, Miss Wilder, I've already told you to leave."

Her arms held Tuek-sil close to her. "You know very well I can't walk away from this child."

"Then make up your mind. Leave, or comply with the very small request I made of you."

The decision required little thought, yet she waited, protectively stroking the young girl's dark head as she did so.

"I want Teuk-sil," she said at last, in defeat.

"She's yours."

"I want her father, too," she added.

"But of course—what's left of him. I told you you had only to ask." Min Tae-jon rubbed his hands together in satisfaction. "Now for the photographs."

10

Taking the photographs was not the impossible task she had imagined. A numbed calm came over Marigold as she began to work. She became an instrument, just as the camera was an instrument. At home, in England, she had been able to remove herself when photographing scenes of hunger and poverty. And when she had photographed the king of Korea, she had forcibly been banished behind her black drape. Now, she did the same, removing herself from these naked bodies. She had neither seen nor known the women who came before her, one after the other, or sometimes in groups of two or three. Whenever their plight threatened to intrude upon her conscience, she remembered that young girl clinging to her for protection, she felt the trembling young body against her own, the smoothness of that hair beneath her hand. There was little she could do to help the women who came before her; but she could—and would—save Teuk-sil.

Through the lens the images were upside-down, removed, and unreal. Still, it was with great relief that she inserted the twelfth plate from the magazine into the camera, noting crisply, "This is the last."

As before, the women grouped together, but Marigold could not suppress her cry of disgust as Kim Tuk-so took a place in their midst, caressing the kisaeng prized by Min Tae-jon for the distinctive mark on her anatomy.

With an air of finality, Marigold released the shutter on the image of Kim Tuk-so.

"Done," she said briskly, deliberately refusing to dwell on Chu-sun and her dashed expectations. Then, hidden by the cloth, she covered her face with her hands. It was disgusting, distasteful, depraved—but, as always, she had done what had to be done.

Yet as she gathered her things together, keeping her back to those in the room, Marigold blinked to force back tears. How had the daughter of an Anglican clergyman been prevailed upon to make such a record for the pleasure of an oriental despot? How could she have done such a thing? Then she thought of Teuk-sil and her broken father. How could she possibly have refused? Mark Banning had already stuck his neck out in an effort to save her; he would not have hesitated to do the same in her situation. That thought comforted her.

Marigold refused to develop the photographs until she had seen the pair on their way. The old man, crushed and broken, had to be carried out of the palace grounds on a makeshift stretcher. Neither had any money and Marigold had given them the only thing she had left—the kokok that Banning had given her for luck. This antique piece could, perhaps, be exchanged for medical help and food. But as she watched them go, she had the terrible feeling that her own luck was departing with them. The kokok had been with her ever since Banning had pressed it into her hand at that London station. She hadn't thought she believed in its power while it was in her possession, yet without it, she felt bereft.

She returned to the darkened room that was illuminated by a single candle to develop the plates. She immersed them, one by one, in the developing solution. As soon as the images began to emerge, she plunged the plate into the fixing bath of hyposulphite soda and water. She worked quickly, methodically, efficiently, examining the reversed negative images for intensity and density. She worked as one who knew and understood what she was doing and what she wanted from her work. It wasn't until she began to make contact prints from the negatives, until the images sprung out at her in positive shades of black and white, one woman after another, forcing themselves into her consciousness, leaping out to accuse and shame her, that she faltered, realizing what she had done. When she came to the last photograph with Kim Tuk-so amidst the women, the depth of her degradation became complete.

She hung up the prints to dry, humiliated by their clarity. In recording these women she had outdone herself as a photographer. She had captured their bodies with the utmost precision. Every detail was in clear focus, down to and including the freckle on the anatomy of the kisaeng being fondled by Kim Tuk-so. Of all the photographs she had taken in Korea, she was taunted by the fact that, in form though certainly not in content, these were her best.

Yet had the results not been clear, she might have been forced to take the photographs again. She had used up her supply of photographic plates; it would have meant weeks of waiting at the palace to get more. She must leave this place, not only to preserve her own sanity but also to warn Mark Banning of Min Tae-jon's conviction that he was a spy. And she knew the only way she could leave was to satisfy Min Tae-jon. At least she knew she had done that with these photographs. While, at that moment, she might loathe herself for having perfected her craft with that particular commission, she was prepared to live with that on her conscience.

While the prints were drying, she went outside into the deserted courtyard that earlier had been the scene of the old man's torture. She shuddered, imagining she could see blood on the stones, but though the night was clear and the air quite still, she suspected it was only shadows. The air was cool and clean and fresh. She breathed deeply in an attempt to purify herself. A beam of moonlight shone across the courtyard, so vivid she felt she could climb its golden path and leave behind all the degradation and disgust she had thrust herself into in coming there.

Chu-sun's sijo suddenly came to her mind:

> O moon, O shining moon,
> Is he sleeping there alone, or does he clasp
> some other girl . . .

Chu-sun must never know, Marigold resolved. And yet, if she did not learn of Tuk-so's true character, she would go on loving a man completely unworthy of her.

Across the courtyard a door slid open, and a figure emerged to glance cautiously in both directions and then cross toward her. She recognized the person and turned away in revulsion.

"Miss Wilder. Wait!"

"What is it you want?" she demanded.

Kim Tuk-so lifted his finger to his lips to silence her.

"I had no choice," he said softly.

"Of course you had a choice," she upbraided. "We all have choices." She broke off, thinking of what the abbot had said— small choices you make, but the great ones have been made for you. Had all this been ordained? But she didn't believe in fate, and as though to convince herself, she repeated, "We all have choices. What you did tonight, and seem to have been doing all along to please that tyrant, is scandalous, disreputable, vile, indecent . . ."

"You can't say anything to me I haven't already said to myself. But there is no choice. Everyone obeys him. You obeyed him," he pointed out.

This simple truth struck Marigold forcibly. "I did," she admitted, "but I had a reason."

"There is always a reason," Kim Tuk-so responded.

"Then what is yours?"

"I want to live," he said simply.

"Have you no pride, no sense of decency, no sense of shame?"

"What are these things beside life itself? Live here for a day, a week, and you, too, will do anything." He drew himself up angrily. "I don't know why I should explain or excuse myself to one who is sangnom. In just one afternoon he made you just as much the voyeur that he is. Worse, in fact, for you not only looked at his women but photographed them. That is even more scandalous and reprehensible."

"I did it to save the life of that old man you had tortured," she argued violently. "I did it to prevent his young daughter from falling into the hands of that lecher. That's why I did it."

He shrugged. "So you got something you wanted. That's his way. He gives, but only what he is prepared to give. And he always gets exactly what he wants."

"And what has he given you?"

"I've told you. My life."

"And a very comfortable life it is too. You've been made magistrate. People now fear you as much as you fear him. Don't you see what's happening? You're becoming just like him."

"How dare you!" He raised his hand as though to strike her, but then let it fall. "I am not like him. I am not. I am not."

He shook his head, repeating this last phrase over and over, as though to convince himself of its truth. He was so shaken that Marigold almost felt sorry for him.

"Why did you come?" he asked her at last.

"I came to see you."

"Me? But why me?" He looked at her eagerly. "Have you a message for me?"

She nodded.

"From the king? Does he want me back at court?" His face lit up with excitement. "The capital, the royal palace, that is where I belong. I have shown what I can do here under the most adverse circumstances. I have survived here—no mean feat—I have even advanced to the magisterial level. My value has been recognized, that is it! I am now ready to assume my position as state councilor at court. Is that the message you have for me?"

She shook her head, and his face fell.

"I have not come to further your ambitions. I think you can take care of that well enough yourself."

"Don't scorn me! It is very difficult to survive the friction and intrigue that pervades court life between the king and queen, the queen and her brother."

"'Let who will be king, I'll still be vicar of Bray,'" she quoted.

"What is this vicar of Bray?" Tuk-so demanded suspiciously.

"A simple churchman. He lived in England in Henry the Eighth's time. The king had two daughters: Mary, a Catholic, and Elizabeth, a Protestant, who, in due course, succeeded him on the throne. Depending on who reigned, the vicar of Bray turned from Protestant to Papist, Papist to Protestant—but he was still vicar of Bray."

Kim Tuk-so nodded his head in approval.

"He was no simple man. He was most astute this vicar. No wonder his name has gone down in legend."

Thinking of Chu-sun's love for the ignoble man who stood before her, Marigold sighed. "Perhaps he was."

"But if the message you brought was not from the king, who sent it?"

For a moment Marigold considered saying nothing of the purpose of her visit. Kim Tuk-so was so utterly undeserving of Chu-sun. Yet she could imagine the questions Chu-sun would ply her with when she returned, the questions of lovers the world over: Did you see him? How did he look? Was he well? Was he happy? Did you tell him I love him? What did he say?

"Chu-sun." She watched the look of shame descend on his face. There was no longer any question of denying that he knew her.

"You know Chu-sun, then?" he asked.

"She is my friend," Marigold replied.

There was silence.

"What did she say?" His voice was hoarse.

"That she loves you."

"I love her," he replied. "Tell her for me."

"Do you? Is it possible that you really do love her?"

He drew himself into a magisterial posture. "How dare you question my sincerity, my honesty. Don't be insolent!"

"I asked the question by way of information only," Marigold explained. "The queen is forming a match between Chu-sun and the crown prince. Chu-sun loves you and no other . . ."

"The crown prince! Chu-sun and the crown prince!" There was awe in his voice and a note of excitement. "That is wonderful news."

"But I've told you, she loves you," Marigold interrupted, thinking he had not understood.

"Of course she loves me. What has that to do with marriage?" he demanded, echoing the earlier words of Chu-sun's mother. "She will marry the crown prince and eventually become queen. Then she will make me her chief state councilor, and together we will rule. This is wonderful news. Wonderful!"

He began to give her messages for Chu-sun, messages Marigold didn't hear. In the moonlight, Marigold saw only his face, flushed at the thought of the power he would derive through Chu-sun, just as Chu-sun's father had basked in the reflected glory of his daughters. Both were only too willing to make a tool of Chu-sun, to use her. Marigold felt she would just as soon see Chu-sun married to the queen's dimwit son as to this servile protege of Min Tae-jon. Chu-sun's strength of character could make up for the weakness of the crown prince, but she doubted her goodness could ever overcome Tuk-so's scheming ambition.

She left Tuk-so in the courtyard, still building castles in the air, and returned to finish the contact prints. Then, one by one, she broke the plates, all except the one for the portrait of Min Tae-jon and, on an impulse, she saved the last plate of Tuk-so amidst the harem. It seemed important proof of his character, yet she doubted she could ever bring herself to show the picture to Chu-sun.

As she had expected, grunts of appreciation and satisfaction greeted the photographs when she showed them to Min Tae-jon.

"These are good. These are very good. Excellent! Oh, but this one is even better!" And so it went as he interleaved the prints into his book.

She said nothing, waiting only to escape. She wondered whether Lee might still be waiting nearby. Perhaps she could find him and send him on to warn Mark Banning. And perhaps he might be

willing to help her find passage—she had to get far away from
Wonsan as soon as she possibly could.

Min Tae-jon was smiling. "Excellent work, Miss Wilder. I want
to thank you, to show my appreciation."

"I have done as you asked. You gave me what I wanted. Nothing
more is necessary, except my departure." She indicated her packed
belongings.

"Fascinating," he murmured, still studying the photographs.
Then he looked up, "May I examine that apparatus of yours?"

She passed him the bulky camera.

"How does it work?" he asked.

"It is a method of light passing through the lens onto a sensitized
photographic plate," she began, but he stopped her.

"No use telling me. I am an artist, not a mechanic. I ask simply
because these are so good, I should like others . . ."

Her voice rose in anger. "Our agreement was for these pictures
and these only. With them I have used up all my plates, every last
one."

"But surely it is a small matter to procure more."

"You are reneging on our agreement." She could feel her cheeks
redden in fury. "I said I would take these in exchange for allowing
the young girl and her father to go free. That is all I agreed to . . ."

Imperiously, he held up his hand to silence her. "Listen to what
I have to say. You need take no more pictures since, for some reason, it seems to upset you. But now that I have seen the results, I
am fascinated by this process of recording things exactly as they
are. All you need to do is to train someone else to use this thing."
He raised the camera. "I can assure you, I'll make it well worth
your while—I will give you whatever you like. You're a missionary.
Perhaps it would please you to have a mission here at Wonsan. That
can easily be arranged. You have only to ask."

A mission procured at the expense of distasteful photographs!
Marigold was rendered speechless at the thought and at the real-

ization that Min Tae-jon's satisfaction with her work had had such a negative outcome.

"How dare you go back on your word! In that case . . ." She rushed at Min Tae-jon, seized the camera from his hands, and did what she could never have imagined herself doing—with deliberation, she dashed it to the ground. It shattered. Her eyes filled with tears as she looked down at the pieces.

She was saved from Min's immediate retaliation by a discreet cough. Kim Tuk-so had entered the room.

"Your Excellence. I apologize, but I . . ."

"Take this . . . this woman . . ." Min Tae-jon spluttered, but the usually unctuous and obedient Kim Tuk-so didn't wait for him to finish. He hurried over to whisper something in his ear.

"He is here?" It was the first time Marigold had seen Min Tae-jon show surprise. "You brought him?"

Kim Tuk-so was crestfallen. "He came of his own volition, Excellency."

"He did? Then send him in."

Kim Tuk-so looked at Marigold. "Did you wish me to remove the woman first?"

Min Tae-jon thought for a moment, then shrugged. "No. Let her stay. She may find it amusing."

"I can't imagine finding anything amusing in this place," Marigold said caustically.

"That is because you lack a sense of humor."

"The only thing that will restore it is allowing me to leave."

"All in good time," Min Tae-jon said, his genial countenance returning as the visitor was shown in by Kim Tuk-so. "Mr. Banning. This is such a pleasure. Your visit is most opportune—it saves me a great deal of trouble. How kind of you to come."

"Mark! Oh, my God." Marigold's hand flew to her lips. She was elated to see him—he had never been far from her thoughts—but her elation was mingled with a fear greater than any since her arrival. "You shouldn't be here!"

"Neither should you." He put a comforting hand on her shoulder for an instant. "But neither of us ever does the expected."

Her eyes searched his.

"Why did you come?"

He studied her, as though to convince himself she was all right. "I rather thought you'd be glad to see me."

"I am. You know I am. But you really shouldn't be here."

"I didn't have a great deal of choice," Banning said.

"I don't understand . . ."

"What is all this," Min Tae-jon interrupted angrily. "Speak in my language or not at all."

"Tell him I've come for a prize beyond worth, for which I'm willling to give a prize beyond worth," Banning told Marigold.

"But he thinks you're a spy," Marigold whispered.

"Just tell him what I say. You may not like or approve of some things," Banning warned, "but tell him what I say exactly as I say it."

Marigold turned to Min Tae-jon and, in a strained voice, translated Mark's statement.

"I don't see that a spy has any opportunity to make demands, Mr. Banning," Min Tae-jon responded. "You don't deny being a spy, do you?"

He shrugged. "For a price, I will supply anything."

"Information to your government?"

"If it comes my way."

Min Tae-jon seemed as disappointed by this terse admission as Marigold was flabbergasted by it.

"For God's sake, Mark, what are you saying?" she said in English.

"Just tell him everything I say," Banning repeated tersely.

"And you see that it comes your way with remarkable regularity, don't you, Mr. Banning?" Min Tae-jon responded.

"I don't let grass grow under my feet. Nor, from what I hear, do you."

Min Tae-jon looked him up and down speculatively. "I begin to see why you are such a favorite with the ladies."

"My love life's fine, thanks," Banning answered. "Sorry to hear yours isn't so hot."

"Mark! What are you trying to do, get yourself hanged, drawn, and quartered? You're speaking to the right person if that's what you want," Marigold intervened sharply.

"No, Maggie, I'm not ready for that yet. Just tell him what I said."

Against her better judgment, Marigold translated.

"You may consider yourself a Casanova, you with all your women —the Russian and this Englishwoman—but I can assure you your amorous adventures ended the moment you stepped inside my palace." Min Tae-jon's grip on the book in his lap tightened, showing whitened knuckles. "You tried to steal that young girl away from me, a foolish act, one I cannot forgive. Miss Wilder obtained her release—temporarily. I can get her back whenever I choose. Nothing, no one escapes me. I would have taken you when I was ready. Your most foolish act was to come here of your own accord."

"I think not. My purpose in coming is to collect Miss Wilder. And in appreciation of the hospitality you've shown her, I've brought you something you desire more than anything else in the world."

Min Tae-jon snorted. "You think you can come here, confess you are a spy, and then expect to leave freely, Mr. Banning?"

Banning nodded. "I do."

"Your audacity is interesting but quite foolhardy. If the position were reversed, you would never allow me to go, now would you?"

"I beg to difffer. I most certainly would if you'd brought me anything as desirable, as beneficial, and as precious as the present I have for you."

"Ridiculous!" the governor snapped, yet his curiosity was clearly piqued. "I shall have whatever it is you have brought, with or without your giving it to me."

Mark Banning looked surprised. "But then it wouldn't be a present, Your Excellency." His voice sounded hurt. "A stolen gift would lose a great deal of its value, its efficacy. Quite apart from that, if you're as pleased with this small token as I believe you will be, you'll undoubtedly want to know where to obtain more. And a man whose gift has been forcibly taken is not likely to be willing to give out that sort of information."

Min Tae-jon gave Banning a thin smile. "Ask Miss Wilder. She will tell you that I get whatever information I want whenever I want it. You have heard of the leg screw."

"A thoroughly nasty practice. There are a lot more enjoyable ways to screw. Still, maybe for those incapable, watching the leg-screw applied to some poor wretch may provide an alternative, though far inferior amusement."

Min Tae-jon flushed angrily.

"You're mad! Absolutely mad!" Marigold, too, flushed, but in embarrassment and dismay. "Don't you realize you're committing suicide? Is that what you want? Do something. Give him whatever it is, for God's sake—though I don't know what you could possibly have that would please him enough to overlook all these insults."

"He's got to ask me for it," Banning said in a lowered voice.

"What is it?"

"It's the only thing he wants that he can't have and if it's even half as effective as it's reputed to be, he'll be pleading for more and we'll be home free."

"I won't have a sangnom speak to me in that fashion. Worse than sangnom, you're an admitted spy," Min Tae-jon roared. "I can do whatever I want with you without any fear of reprisal. Even your government would not step in to help you. To admit to having sent a spy to our country would be a great embarrassment to them."

"They didn't send me here. I came for my own purposes—to

mine gold. Whatever I've done, whatever information I've passed on, I've done entirely for my own reasons."

Despite his anger, Min Tae-jon seemed impressed. "Your candor does you credit, Mr. Banning, but it will not earn your freedom. Now you are my prisoner, to do with exactly as I choose. The crane's dance, perhaps."

Marigold turned white, but Banning showed no reaction to this threat.

"I prefer to think of myself as your guest. I must warn you, if I don't like the way I'm being treated, you can forget about ever getting more of the token present I've brought for you."

Min Tae-jon stood up. "Who do you think you are to make such demands? And what could you possibly have that I don't have already?"

"This." Banning reached for his coat pocket, but he had scarcely moved before he was seized by Kim Tuk-so.

Roughly, Banning freed his arm from the hold, wincing as he did so. Marigold realized that he was far from recovered from the tiger's mauling.

"I'm unarmed, you know that!" He turned to Min Tae-jon, "Call this goon off if you really want to know what I've brought for you. If not, it's okay by me."

His curiosity overcoming his anger, Min Tae-jon motioned to Kim Tuk-so to step back.

"That's better," Banning said, rubbing his injured shoulder; in indignation he brushed and straightened the sleeve Kim Tuk-so had grasped.

Marigold closed her eyes and shook her head. What was he doing? And why was he doing it? He was going to be killed and he wouldn't even try to help himself.

From his pocket Mark Banning had brought out a small vial. Marigold groaned as he began, "Ever since I first learned of your unfortunate predicament I had intended to give this to you. I had hoped to bring it under more auspicious circumstances, to make the presentation with greater ceremony, for this is truly a gift above price."

"What is it?" Min Tae-jon demanded suspiciously.

"It was given to my by a sheik in Arabia who, like you, had beome too fond of the poppies. After suffering the incapacitating consequences of prolonged use of opium, he issued a proclamation offering half his fortune to anyone who could restore his potency. This remedy was the result. It was taken from a recipe discovered, he claimed, in the *Perfumed Garden,* a secret work of Sheik Nef-zawi of Tunisia—with some important additions."

Despite himself, Min Tae-jon held out his hand to examine the small bottle. "What is in it?" he demanded.

"A mixture of galanga, an Indian root, pounded with surnag, a root from Morocco, bound together with oil of fruit from the mastic tree. A little honey and ginger not only add to the effect but also disguise the bitterness. This mixture, the sheik assured me, has never failed him."

Min Tae-jon's lips turned down. "How could this be any better than our own panax ginseng? My apothecary kisaengs have prepared it specially, adding the roots to snake soup. Another advised using it with bird nest soup."

"Bird nest soup! That's useless."

"But with powdered deer antlers," Min Tae-jon stressed.

Ludicrous! Marigold thought as she translated. They sounded like Harriet and Prim exchanging recipes.

"And without appreciable result, I'll bet. As an aphrodisiac, your ginseng is vastly overrated."

"It was the finest panax ginseng, red ginseng," Min Tae-jon complained. "Nurtured for seven years in specially cultivated ground."

"Even so, it didn't work. Whereas, I have it on the authority of the sheik himself that a spoonful of this potion could make a Lothario of a eunuch."

Min Tae-jon held the vial up to the light. "How do I know it isn't poison?"

Banning shrugged. "I've brought only a very limited quantity, just a sample, otherwise I'd take some myself." He turned around. "We could, of course, try it on Kim Tuk-so—though from all I hear of his exploits, he has no need of it. I know full well that if anything were to happen to you, I would be a dead man. And I can assure you, I'm not yet ready to die."

"No man ever is," Min Tae-jon rolled the vial between his hands distractedly yet thoughtfully.

"However, if you don't want to take the risk . . ." Banning reached for the vial, but Min Tae-jon held it back and with the air of having reached a momentous decision, he rose and left the room.

As soon as he was gone, Marigold said fiercely, "How could you! That was perfectly disgusting! Besides, it was quite useless."

"I warned you you wouldn't like it. But before you dismiss me as some kind of American aberration, let me remind you that sexual prowess, or the lack of it, is one of the main topics of discussion in your most exclusive St. James's clubs. Still, I'm really sorry you had to translate something . . ." A smile flickered on his lips as he concluded, "that's unsuitable for missionary ears."

After all she had been through, this was too much. She turned on him in fury. "Do shut up about my being a missionary!"

He held up his hands, as though to ward her off. "Sorry, Maggie. I didn't mean to hit a nerve."

"You know very well you did," she fumed. "But let's not quibble about that now. Don't you realize you've walked into a trap? If your reason for coming was to rescue Teuk-sil, she's safe—for the time being, at least."

"Lee already told me that. You're the one I came for—I had to."

"I don't see why you *had* to," Marigold said, crestfallen that he had come out of duty.

"I just can't go on being in your debt. You know how it is in this country—the life you save belongs to you. Well, you saved me from the tiger, and that left my life in your hands. Being an independent type, I couldn't let that go on. So I figured if I got you out of this mess you got yourself into—all because you wanted to deliver your girlfriend's message to a most undeserving beau—that would even the score."

"I see." His explanation sounded so calculated, Marigold thought in disappointment. "But who told you that's why I came here?"

"It wasn't hard to put two and two together from the things you'd told me at the old pavilion."

"As a spy, you've always got to keep your mind on your work, even when you're amorously involved. I suppose that's how you get the secrets out of your Russian friend, too." Marigold was still stung by Min Tae-jon's comment linking her name with Natasha's.

"Maggie! Don't let's quarrel."

"I'm not quarrelling," she exploded. "And as for that revolting potion you gave him, how could you possibly want to give that horrible lecher something to make him worse than he already is?"

"Do be reasonable, Maggie! You're a sensible woman. There's only one thing that man wants that he can't have, that he'd give anything for—and the promise of that little vial is it. Instead of arguing, we should both be praying that the Arab huckster's cure-all can produce a miraculous erection."

At her scorching look, he began pacing up and down. Then he stopped and picked up the book Min Tae-jon had set aside.

"Don't!" she entreated, but too late. He had opened it and had already seen the first photograph; then he looked down and caught sight of the broken camera on the floor.

"Oh Maggie! Dear, sweet little Maggie! Why didn't you tell me? My dear one!" He came to her and put his arms around her. "Maggie! I'm so sorry, so very sorry. No wonder you're upset. What a devil of a man, to make you do something like that!"

She clung to him as he spoke. She had wanted him to hold her

like that, yet as he pulled her closer to him, she pushed away.
"Don't—don't touch me."

His arms dropped. "Maggie, look at me. Look at me, I said." He
waited until she looked up. "I told you you were a sensible woman.
You need that common sense of yours now more than ever. I know
you. You did what you obviously had to do—just as always—just
the way you came to collect that errant young sister of yours in
London. You always do what has to be done, but once done, it's in
the past and forgotten. You must do that now—put this in proper
perspective. Just because this man's depraved doesn't mean that all
contact between men and women is depraved."

"You're a fine one! Just listen to the way you played upon that
depravity of his! You're as bad as he is."

Unceremoniously, he grasped her wrists. "Look at me and tell
me you really believe that."

"All right," Slowly she looked up into his eyes, then almost immediately looked away again. "But you must admit you were playing
upon his depravity."

"Of course I was. Because that's the only way we're going to get
out of here. Can't you understand that? I only wished you'd listened when I told you not to come here. I wish Lee had stopped
you."

"He tried. He's a Tong-hak, or so Min Tae-jon said."

"He's a good man."

"And you?" she asked.

"I'm not a good man, not if you mean the sort of good man Sully
is."

"Don't bring Sully into this. I meant, are you an American spy?"

He hesitated before replying, "I'm a sometime spy."

"Do you really do it for money?"

"Why? Does it make a difference? I'm not some kind of hero,
Maggie. I said it before, we're a lot alike. I, too, do what needs to
be done—or at least what I think needs to be done. Sometimes I

take money, more often I do it just for the fun of it—it prevents life from becoming a bore."

She shook her head. "I don't believe your life was ever boring. I don't think you know what a boring life is."

There was silence, then she said, "I'm afraid I gave away your code—the *Treasure Island*," she explained. "I'm sorry."

He laughed. "I'm not. I never felt comfortable with that idea of Doug Andrews's. It was bound to be discovered."

"You knew Mr. Andrews before you met him at the Russian legation dinner?"

"Of course. Doug and I are old drinking buddies. He recruited me, if that's the right expression to use for someone in my less than professional capacity."

"I wish you hadn't come," she said.

"Let's not go over that again."

"But he uses torture—terrible torture. Teuk-sil's father—I saw it."

He put a comforting arm around her and kissed the top of her head. "My dear. I'm so very sorry."

"It was terrible, even though I didn't know who he was. But how much worse, if it were . . ." She changed the "you" she started to say to "someone I knew."

"I made you translate things that, in light of what had gone on before I got here, must have seemed particularly ugly. But you must realize I had no choice."

She put her cheek to his hand for a moment. "I was just so thankful to see you, it really didn't matter what you said."

There were footsteps, then the sound of the door sliding back. It was Kim Tuk-so. His bow was curt, certainly not the grovel he had extended to the governor.

"His Excellency sends his thanks for the gift. He is graciously willing to accept more of this elixir."

"Hallelujah!" Banning whispered under his breath, gripping

Marigold's arm in a signal of triumph, but aloud he said cautiously, "It might be arranged—for a price."

Kim Tuk-so drew himself up and frowned. "No one bargains with His Exellencey."

"In America, everyone bargains. And from what I've found, it's not so different here or anywhere else in the world for that matter," Banning answered tersely. "I want thirty thousand Japanese yen."

"Thirty thousand . . ." Tuk-so spluttered.

"Silver yen, that is. And the stipulation that I, myself, be allowed to get the . . . the elixir. Naturally, Miss Wilder goes with me."

"That is impossible," Kim Tuk-so began, but Banning cut him short.

"A lackey doesn't decide anything. Take the message to your master. Let him say whether it's impossible or not."

After Tuk-so had left the room in a fury, Marigold asked, "Do you think it was wise to make him so angry?"

Banning shrugged. "Do him good. At least it will get him to convey the message with feeling."

"There's no doubt of that. Do you really have more of that . . . that stuff?" she asked.

Silently he shook his head.

"Then why . . . ?" she began, but he silenced her.

"We must be together on this, Maggie, all the way. Let me do the arguing, let me make the decisions, knowing you'll follow me. Do you trust me?"

Though she nodded, she didn't understand why he hadn't taken the first opportunity to leave and why he constantly protracted the negotiations that ensued. He yawned at Min Tae-jon's offer of ten thousand yen, and adamantly refused fifteen. But when, after further haggling, the fifteen thousand was promised unconditionally, with another fifteen to be given after the remaining potion was delivered, Banning sighed. "That boss of yours drives a hard bargain. What do you say, Maggie?" And before she had the opportunity to say anything, he went on, "I suppose it's the best we're going to get."

"That is absolutely His Excellency's final word," Kim Tuk-so muttered malevolently.

"Very well," Banning agreed at last.

"Then you may leave—under armed escort, of course," Kim Tuk-so said. "I myself will lead it."

"How fortunate to have your protection! We have to go into the mountains and I'll be damned if I want to run the risk of being mauled by tigers again. Don't you agree, Maggie?"

Though she nodded assent, Marigold couldn't imagine that their position would be much improved once they were outside the palace, placed under the guardianship of a man whom Banning had infuriated and who obviously detested her.

11

The closed palanquin, which was no more than an enclosed box, bumped and swayed along the mountain road. The windows were sealed from the outside, and Marigold had no idea where she was. But even without the aid of a watch, she estimated that it was four hours since they had left the palace.

Mark Banning was in a separate closed palanquin—how uncomfortable he must be with his long legs and no place to sit—at the head of the party, with Kim Tuk-so riding alongside. He had been warned at the outset that if he tried to escape, or if the party were set upon, he would be run through.

"You need have no fear. Cold steel on the inside of my gut is not something I crave," he had said.

"So much the better. Then cooperate to the fullest if you wish to remain unscathed and able to enjoy those things you obviously do crave," Kim tuk-so snarled.

All Marigold could think of as she bumped and swayed with the palanquin was that they were surrounded by guards, heading into the mountains to obtain something for Min Tae-jon that did not exist. If Mark had a plan, he had made not the slightest indication of what it might be.

Her nerves were frayed and taut from the experiences of the past twenty-four hours. And Mark's arrival had only added to her tension, for now she worried about his well-being as much as—yes, she had to admit to herself—even more than her own. She had been so glad to see him, yet she was so afraid for him, afraid that he underestimated the evil of Min Tae-jon. He had spoken to him fearlessly, in a foolhardy manner that seemed guaranteed to bring harm—if not now, then at some future time. That tyrant wouldn't let anyone tweak his nose and get away with it. She shuddered at the thought of Mark, alone, in front, in a similar conveyance, with Kim Tuk-so alongside, only too ready to put a sword through him— perhaps these were his orders.

She watched the light fading on the window screens, signaling the approach of night. Surely they wouldn't ride through the night. Even these guards must have the same superstitious fear of tigers as the others.

Yet it was some time before they halted. She could hear voices conferring about setting up camp. Then she heard Banning demanding in pidgin Korean to be let out.

"Damn it all! This is ridiculous. If you don't open this door and let me out, there'll be the damnedest mess to clean up." At last, she heard a door swing open, and an aggrieved Banning's "About time!"

"Don't get any ideas," Kim Tuk-so said.

"I've only got one pressing idea at the moment. If you want to come watch, you're welcome!"

She heard Kim Tuk-so shout to one of the guards to accompany Banning, before he went back to issuing orders for setting up camp.

She waited. There was a lot of activity outside, but no one came to let her out.

Then suddenly a shot rent the air.

Immediately all around her there were shouts and scuffles. Someone wrenched open the door of her palanquin and she was seized. She tried to cry out but something was thrown over her head so that she could neither speak nor see her assailant. Her heart pounded madly as her wrists were grasped behind her and she felt herself being dragged, pushed, and carried through brush.

When, at last, she gathered her wits and began to struggle in earnest with her captor, she found herself abruptly set down.

"That's enough gallantry for one night. If you won't cooperate, you walk from now on. Or how about carrying me the rest of the way."

She pulled the cloth from her head.

"For God's sake, Mark. Why didn't you say it was you? Why carry me off like . . . like a sack of flour?"

He grinned. "That's exactly what you felt like—a dead weight."

"Why didn't you say it was you?" she demanded for a second time.

"I didn't say anything because I didn't want them to hear our voices. If they'd heard us speaking in English, they'd have nabbed both of us instantly. And talk about a red rag to a bull, I had to cover up that head of yours." Lightly, he ruffled her hair, before seizing her by the hand. "Come along, we can't stay here."

"Where are we going?" she asked as, hand in his, he guided her up the mountain.

"To a safe house up near the top."

"What were those shots?"

"The Tong-hak."

"You mean it was arranged?"

"Uh huh."

"You might have told me." She was out of breath, trying to keep up with the terrific pace he had set.

"And warned that flunky while I was at it!"

"He doesn't understand English."

"I preferred not to give him the benefit of the doubt. Here we are. I think this must be it."

They had come upon the high wall of a house built close to the summit. Only a local dignitary could have afforded such an establishment.

"Are you sure . . ." she began, when there came a cry to halt. She drew close to him.

"Mal bok," a gutteral voice nearby named the lunar holiday for the last heat of summer.

"Paeng no," Banning answered, indicating the first frost.

Without another word, they were ushered inside the wall, where another dark figure met them and spoke quietly to Banning. Then, avoiding the large house, they were led to a small pavilion some distance away.

They removed their shoes and stepped onto the ondol floor. It felt warm and comforting underfoot. A candle burned on a table already set with food.

Marigold was relieved yet puzzled. "What is this?"

Banning had thrown off his coat. He sat down cross-legged, then, saying, "I'll never get used to sitting on my haunches," he lay full-length on the floor. "This feels better. You're no light weight, Maggie!"

"What is this place, anyway?" she asked again, more hesitantly as she observed the bedding on the floor in the corner of the room.

"I don't know the name of the owner, nor do I want to. All I know is that he's a Tong-hak sympathizer."

"How do you know? It might be a trap," Marigold pointed out.

Banning's eyes had closed. "Lee told me to come here," he said, as though that closed the issue.

She sat down, but when he didn't speak, she supposed he had fallen asleep. However, at the sound of a light footstep outside, he sprang up and reached for the pistol at his belt.

The door opened and, with a tray of hot tea in hand, a young girl entered.

"Teuk-sil!" Marigold cried. "What are you doing here?"

"Lee brought us here, my father and me." She sank to her knees at Marigold's feet. "I'm so happy to see you again, to be able to thank you." Then she looked over at Banning. "And to thank you, too."

"I'm only sorry they found you and brought you back."

"I should have listened to you and stayed out of sight. It was my fault," Teuk-sil responded shyly.

Marigold leaned down and pulled the girl to her feet. "What matters is that you're all right. But what about your father—how is he?"

"His legs are broken, but because of you he will get well. We gave the kokok to an apothecary who was then willing to set the bones. Now he may be able to reach his full life cycle and celebrate hwang-ap. When he is well, he will serve you—both of you. He will do anything you ask." She smiled shyly. "I, of course, am yours always."

"All we want is for you to grow up strong and free," Marigold replied.

"What a delicate little thing she is," Banning commented as she left the room.

Marigold shuddered, remembering the sight of that little figure in Min Tae-jon's hands. "Do you think she can ever be kept safe from that ogre?"

"I'm pretty sure Lee will see to it that she never falls into his clutches again." He put the pistol away. "You were brave to help her, Maggie, and generous to give up all you had."

Her hand reached for the place where the kokok had been as she spoke. "It's silly to value things, you told me that. But I can't help feeling lost without the kokok. I've worn it ever since you gave it to me, though I don't really believe it had any power to bring luck," she added, as though to convince herself.

"Things don't bring luck. People do." Mark looked at her for a long moment.

She tried to diffuse the intimacy of that moment by observing, "These Tong-hak are your friends."

He took her cue, replying factually, "I'm never sure who my friends are, but I know I'm their friend. They want something decent for this country. And from the little I've seen, it sure needs it. 'Korea for the Koreans' is their cry, but with both the Japanese and Chinese—not to mention the Russians—baying at their coast and borders, that cry may be no more than the mournful note of a train whistle in the night."

As they began to eat, the warmth she felt outside was met by an inner warmth and Marigold's taut nerves relaxed. Then the full realization of everything that had happened suddenly overcame her. Quite without warning, tears filled her eyes and coursed down her cheeks. Banning said nothing, watching her as though waiting for a sign. But when she began to sob, he waited no longer. He pushed aside the low table between them and took her in his arms.

Almost immediately, she pushed him away. "Don't touch me!" she said sharply, adding more softly, "Please don't touch me."

"I promise not to do anything you don't want me to," he said holding his arms out to her. She hesitated before allowing him to embrace her.

Slowly she relaxed, trusting the comfort of his arms around her, the large, consoling hand that pressed her head against what, she realized later, was his wounded shoulder. Then all the tears she had held back were loosed like the breaking of a cresting wave. Koreans cry even when they love, Chu-sun had once told her. Now Marigold cried as she had never cried before, and Mark allowed her to, not saying anything, not even a word of solace. But then, with his arms around her, no word was necessary.

As her sobs subsided, he kissed her throbbing eyelids, smoothed back her damp hair, and kissed her brow. He kissed her wet cheeks, her throat, her eyelids again and then her lips. First they were light, fluttering kisses, kisses that made her long for more, so that when at last he pressed his lips to hers, parting her own as he did so, she was the one who clung to him and never wanted him to stop.

But when he touched her breast and she felt her nipple harden beneath his hand, she pushed him away.

"Let go," he said softly. "Let me touch you where you want to be touched—don't be afraid."

But she was afraid. He waited, until at last, reassured, she leaned toward him. Then he unbuttoned her blouse and touched her bare breast. She sighed a long-drawn sigh, as though she were about to reach somewhere she had long desired to go without knowing where it was.

In the flickering light of the candle, she watched as he undressed her. But at the sight of her own naked body, she drew back as a sudden wave of shame overcame her. Recalling the women of her photographs, she pulled away, crossing her hands over her bare breasts.

"No. I can't. It's wrong."

"I told you once before, nothing between us can ever be wrong, Maggie." He leaned across and kissed her breast. She didn't stop him then, because she knew she couldn't.

He drew back to look at her. "It's not going to be ugly or degrading like those photographs you had to take. I want to show you that this is life's most beautiful experience. Don't be afraid, Maggie. Don't ever be afraid with me."

The candle fluttered and went out. She felt him beside her, his bare skin against hers. His hands stroked secret places, evoking unknown sensations, moving without haste, sometimes rhythmically, sometimes nimbly, then rapidly, alighting here and there, then stopping and waiting for an assurance that what he did was pleasing to her. Then she found herself kissing him, knowing that in all the world he was the only one who mattered to her.

She had been his long before he entered her. Later, when she had time to think over what happened, she realized that in some sense she'd been his from the moment he winked at her in the church at Barleigh. He had seeped into her spirit then, as surely as he entered her body now.

As he had guided her up the mountainside earlier, now he

guided her until her movements followed his instinctively. And as he moved inside her, she moved around him, pulling him deeper and deeper into herself. She wasn't sure exactly when that unknown, unexpected seizure, that ecstatic tremor that radiated from the middle of her being to the soles of her feet, to her fingertips, to the crown of her head, came upon her. She only knew it threatened to tear her apart, tear them both apart, for he, too, was overcome.

For a long time afterwards, they lay together, still clinging to one another but without the same desperation. It was a closeness such as she had never known, something she had never realized existed, yet something for which she had always waited.

Her arms tightened around him.

"I love you, Mark," she said, feeling suddenly shy for having said aloud what she'd been thinking ever since she'd left him at Chumyol.

His lips moved against the soft skin on her neck, as he whispered, "That was the best coming I've ever known, Maggie."

She was glad he was happy. It wasn't until later that she realized he hadn't said he loved her too.

When Teuk-sil came to remove the dinner dishes and to tell them a bath had been prepared, she studiously ignored the uneaten food and crumpled bedding.

The bath was a wooden tub of very hot water in an adjoining tiny room with a window looking out onto the night. They washed one another down before stepping into the water, inch by inch. Then they sat together, holding hands, until they became used to the heat. She touched the deep scar on his shoulder.

"Did Teuk-sil get all the stitches out?"

"I told you, I take care of myself."

"But how did you do it?"

"Snipped at them with scissors and picked out the thread."

"Even if you can take care of yourself, I wish I'd been there to do it for you." She leaned over and kissed the wound. "Does it hurt?"

"How could it, with you kissing it?"

She leaned toward him and kissed him and then, once again, he touched those secret places that he knew pleased her. But now she, too, had discovered what pleased him. With the air of a conqueror, she reached over to him.

Afterwards, as they dried off together, in one big tent of a towel, he held her close to his warm, wet body, brushing back the damp curls on her forehead.

"You're a beautiful woman, Maggie."

"You didn't think so when you met me," she reminded him.

"I always thought so," he maintained. "Though you were never as beautiful as you are now, at this moment. You're not only beautiful, you're the possessor of supernatural powers."

"Why?"

"I didn't think it was possible to have the stamina to make love in scalding water."

There was no scaffold, no warrior, no hangman, no victim in her dream that night. She dreamed of what had happened just as it had happened, but this time, with Mark beside her, she wasn't always dreaming.

He was up and dressed when she awoke. He had been out and had brought in a riot of red and pink wild cosmos blossoms. They were strewn around her on the bed, beside her on the floor. There, too, was a pot of green tea.

He knelt beside her, poured the tea, and handed it to her.

"You should have woken me," she said, feeling suddenly shy. She brushed her hair back from her face and wondered, for the first time in her life, what she looked like in the morning.

"I wanted to but you were sleeping so beautifully. You looked so thoroughly happy, so at peace with the world, I couldn't bring myself to."

"Have you been awake long?"

"Hours."

She sat up, holding the cup in both hands as she sipped the hot tea.

"What have you been doing for hours?"

"Walking mostly. Lee arrived about an hour ago. He brought your things from the abandoned palanquin."

"What happened to Kim 'Tuk-so?" she asked.

"He got away."

She studied his face. "Is that why you look so serious?"

He turned away from her scrutiny.

"Are you worried Min Tae-jon will send out more troops?"

"Min Tae-jon's going to be looking after his own skin, not mine, for a time at least. Lee brought some disturbing news. The Japanese have landed at Chemulpo and here at Wonsan. The Chinese are said to be moving south. It's war, Maggie."

"War?" She repeated the word as though it were foreign, unknown.

"You have to get out of here before those armies clash."

Her brows furrowed as she realized he'd said "you," not "we."

"What about you?"

He got up and put the teapot on the low table.

"There are things here I have to take care of, loose ends to tie up."

"What things?" she demanded. "What could be important enough to make you stay and risk your life?"

"My life's at no more risk now than before. Min Tae-jon's occupied with both the Japanese and the Tong-hak rebels. As for the Japanese, they're convinced I'm on their side."

"Are you?"

"I'm on my own side. I have to go back to the mine, and then to Seoul."

"For God's sake, Mark, why go back to Seoul! The queen now knows you're a spy. You won't be welcome there. As for the gold, surely your life's worth more than yellow dust!" She pulled a robe around her and got up. "Still, if you insist on staying, then I'm staying with you."

"That's not possible." His voice was firm, distant. "I've already sent Lee to arrange for your passage to Japan. You can stay with

Lafcadio Hearn there—I've written a note to him. You'll be secure with Hearn and his family until this blows over. For now, you'll be safe here."

"And afterwards?"

"Then you can return to Seoul, if that's what you want. Or, if you'd rather, Hearn will book passage for you to England."

She stood stock still, looking at him in disbelief. He turned from her unblinking stare.

"It's for the best, Maggie—for you, and for me."

She couldn't speak for a moment as the significance of what he had said sunk in.

"What about you?" She swallowed, trying to disguise a break in her voice. "After you've got your gold and gone to Seoul—to see Natasha, I suppose—what then?"

"I've . . . I've got to get back to America."

He made no attempt to deny her innuendo.

She paced up and down, unable to believe that he was sending her out of his life after their night together.

"But why!" she asked. "Why must you go there?"

"There are things I have to . . ."

"Loose ends to tie up," she supplied. "I know. Just as you've taken care of me and tied me up like a piece of forgotten baggage. I suppose that's what last night was all about."

"Not exactly. It wasn't planned, if that's what you mean. But it's true I didn't want you to remain afraid or ashamed of making love to a man. After what you'd seen, I thought . . ."

"You thought you'd cure me," she said harshly. "Cure me and send me back to Sully, while you go back to take care of Natasha, or whoever's next, is that it?"

"Sully's a good man, Maggie. You said so yourself."

"Leave Sully out of it!" she exploded.

"I didn't bring him into it. You did. But the fact of it is, Sully's a marrying man and I'm not. You know I'm not. You told your sister as much. To be quite honest, Maggie . . ." he spread his hands in a gesture of frankness and sincerity that only added to her fury. "Last night scared the hell out of me. I felt myself falling into an abyss—the abyss of you—and I was scared to death I would stay there forever, because it was so good. I woke up early and had to get away from you to prove that I still could. I don't expect you to understand, but I can't afford to lose myself like that. I must leave you now, while I can, while I'm still my own man."

"I understand, all right," she said bitterly. "This was a convenient little war for you, almost as though you'd arranged it."

"I didn't arrange it, but I knew it wouldn't be long in coming."

"I was right when I said you deliberately choose women who belong to someone else."

"You probably were," he admitted. "Responsibility is not my strong suit and marriage is an institution I've never understood. Maybe it's because I've never run across much to recommend an arrangement that seems to cause nothing but grief. After the bloom wears off—and it never seems to last long—men find themselves bound: legally, physically, economically. I guess I'm not ready for it—or not right for it."

"I don't remember asking you to make an honest woman of me," she bridled. "Even if you were to make such a terrible slip, you need have no fear of my ever accepting you. I haven't made marriage my goal in life."

"I'm sorry, Maggie. I . . ."

"Don't keep saying you're sorry!" she snapped.

"I want you to know I—I took precautions." He hesitated, suddenly awkward at her lack of comprehension. "You're not likely to find yourself pregnant. If you were, of course I'd . . ."

"Tie up the loose ends," she said bitterly. "I know."

"I'm really sorry . . ." he began, but at her infuriated look broke off.

There was silence.

"I should never have made love to you," he said at last. "It was wrong for you, and yet, if the truth were known, it was even more wrong for me. I've never been drawn to any woman in the way I'm drawn to you. In so many ways we're alike, yet you give me what I lack . . ."

"Spare me these protestations!" She picked up her clothes. "If you don't mind, I'd like to be alone."

"Maggie . . ." he began.

"If you're going to say you're sorry again, I won't be responsible for my actions."

"Trouble with you, Maggie, you're too damned responsible. You were responsible for your father, your sister, now it's your friend at the palace and Teuk-sil. You're responsible for everyone but yourself, for your own happiness. You deserve . . ."

"I deserve to be left alone. Get out!"

He slid the pavilion door open, but turned back.

"Maggie. The truth of it—and the hell of it is that I do love you. I think I loved you from the first."

"Liar! You didn't even look at me. You never have when there's been any other woman around. Damn it, get out! Leave me alone." To add emphasis to her invective, she took up the first thing that came to hand, which happened to be the teapot, and hurled it at him. It sailed past—at some distance from his head, through the paper covering of the unopened screen.

"Maggie! Maggie!" He shook his head. "I'll just never understand how you managed to hit that tiger."

THE
RED PHOENIX
OF THE SOUTH

1

"It is written that the people of Korea once commissioned an artist in China to carve a life-sized wooden statue of Kannon, the Goddess of Mercy. But when the work was completed and carried to the harbor for shipment, the statue had become so heavy that no human effort could move it from the beach. When it was decided that, since it could not be moved, the statue must remain in China, it returned to its normal weight. It is enshrined in the Kaigenji Temple in Ming Chou. Why did this statue of Kannon refuse to come here to Korea?"

To find the answer to this koan had been the task set by the abbot of Yu chom Sa for his latest novice.

Marigold Wilder had arrived at the gates of the monastery one morning, dressed as a boy, her head shaved, asking admittance. The abbot had received her without question or comment, as though she were any ordinary novice. She had been assigned space in the nuns' quarters, but, at her request, she was allowed to follow the routine of the monks. Though she was relieved of the duty of going about the country to beg, where her obviously Western features would have attracted too much attention, she took her share of the monks' load, neither asking nor being offered favored status.

She worked very hard that fall and winter. She was up each day at the call of the morning bell at four, and after a hurried toilet went on to the main hall to chant, meditate, and drink a ceremonial cup of tea made from plum seed, then to the dining hall to breakfast in silence on soup made from whatever scraps the monks had gathered and a drink of honey water. After this, the day's work began: chopping wood, scrubbing, cleaning, cooking, tending the vegetable garden and apiary.

At midday came their most substantial meal of vegetables, rice, and occasionally a treat of mashed bean curd or a paste of sesame seeds. Before any food was eaten, a five-part vow was ritually chanted:

To think only how much had been accomplished and how the food had been received.

To accept the food only because of having performed deeds deserving of it.

To take only enough to satisfy needs, always leaving hunger not quite satisfied.

To partake of the food as nourishment to maintain the health of the body.

To find in the food a means of furthering the way towards nirvana.

Work continued in the afternoon unless it was the allotted day for discourse with the abbot on their chosen koan, set for study in an effort to gain enlightenment. Then came the hour of meditation, spent either together or alone, walking or sitting.

Supper was usually made up of leftovers from the midday meal.

The only unstructured time of the day was between supper and the evening bell, which was struck 108 times to signify the number of man's delusions. That was their own hour, to do with as they wished. Then to bed, on a single mat on the floor folded to form a top covering.

Though the abbot had accepted her unquestioningly, Marigold had caused some consternation among the other nuns and monks. But when she proved her willingness to perform the same tasks, accepting whatever was required of her, rigorously following their routine, they gradually came to accept her. She was gratified by the disgruntled comment of one crochety, senior monk who wondered aloud, "How is it possible for this foreigner, with a mind like a bee flitting from flower to flower, to be capable of such obedience to our rules?"

But it was those rules and her strict adherence to them that became her salvation. When Marigold had knocked at the gates and begged admittance to Yu-chom Sa, she was emotionally spent. Following the degradation and disgust of her experience at the palace of Min Tae-jon, she had reached the height of fulfillment and passion. She had given herself to a man completely, without reservation. She loved him. There was nothing she would have refused him. His subsequent rejection had shattered her and left her in despair.

When Mark Banning left her that morning, Marigold felt indecisive for the first time in her life. No matter what difficulties she had faced in the past, she had always instinctively picked up and gone on. Now she was consumed by a destructive anger, directed as much at herself as at Mark; that was soon followed by an even more destructive lassitude. Nothing seemed to matter.

She knew she should leave Korea—the country was at war and return to Seoul was impossible—but paradoxically, perhaps because she knew Banning was staying on, she didn't want to go. So she wavered, awaiting Lee's return with a ticket she did not want to use. Without the comforting presence of Teuk-sil, who stayed with her, Marigold was sure she could not have survived.

Lee came, at last, with news that the Japanese were swarming ashore at Wonsan and had put Min Tae-jon under house arrest. Despite the confusion, he had managed to arrange for her passage to Japan and proudly displayed the ticket. The sailing was almost a week away, and since Lee was anxious to rejoin the Tong-hak, now aligned with the king against both the Japanese and Chinese invaders, he offered no more than perfunctory argument when Marigold told him that Teuk-sil had offered to see her to the boat.

In the ensuing week, Marigold pulled herself together and tried to consider her alternatives realistically. She remembered the abbot at Yu-chom Sa. "Ambrosial times are ahead," he had said. In a sense, he had been right—she had known ambrosial times, but had not expected them to be quite so fleeting. Nevertheless, the memory of that gentle man enabled her to reach a decision.

She learned from Teuk-sil that the girl's sisters, after being discarded by Min Tae-jon, had been sold into prostitution. Marigold presented her with the ticket.

"Go and sell it. It should be worth enough to gain your sisters' release."

Teuk-sil was tempted, but then she shook her head. "I can't! You have given so much already—too much."

Pointing out that it was for her sisters' sake, not her own, Marigold managed to persuade her.

"But what will you do?" Teuk-sil asked.

"I'll be all right."

"I wish I could do something for you in return. If you do not go to Japan, I shall worry. You are not safe here. You may be found . . ."

"Perhaps not, with your help. There is something you can do for me."

"Anything," Teuk-sil agreed readily.

"Find me some boy's clothes—old ones—and shave my head."

"Shave off your hair—all of it?" Teuk-sil drew back in horror at the thought.

"All of it," Marigold said firmly.

"But only monks shave their heads!" She stopped abruptly. "Oh, no!"

"Yes. But if Lee—or anyone—should ask, you must say nothing. Just that you took me to the boat as arranged. Promise?"

Reluctantly, Teuk-sil promised. "But life in a monastery is difficult. I think you will not like it. The work is hard, the discipline strict. You are even told what to think."

"Then that is exactly what I need."

The discipline and asceticism of the monastic life had turned out to be exactly what her dejected state demanded. Being a victim of lost love was bad enough, but what confused and upset Marigold most of all was that despite Banning's rejection of her, she still loved him. And no matter how hard she tried, she couldn't stop loving him. In fact, the more she tried to forget, the more vividly she remembered every moment they had spent together. She was a fool—as bad as Natasha—and she knew it, but she was unable to help herself.

"God help the fool," her father used to say with a touch of derision in describing some witless parishioner, as though only the wise were worthy of divine assistance.

"God help this fool," Marigold repeated to herself, frightened by the intensity of her own passion. She was in love in a way she had never imagined possible. Deep in her soul she had discovered an emotion that robbed her of self-will and, in return, gave her nothing but confusion and heartbreak.

She tried to reason this feeling away. It would not go. She tried to mitigate the force of her love by comparing it with others: in England, that of Harriet for John Keane, or her sister's feelings for Algernon—satisfactory, perhaps, but quite devoid of passion; in Korea, the Gardners, the Allens—such matter-of-fact marriages— and of course Natasha and Boris Waeber. But she didn't want to think of Natasha.

Chu-sun had come closest to describing the passion she now felt, but that similarity gave Marigold little comfort. Ignoble Tuk-so had begrudgingly accepted Chu-sun's love as though it were his due; Mark, on the other hand, had unequivocally rejected hers. The two men were an unworthy pair, she thought in despair, and she and Chu-sun were foolish to love them as they did. She resolved not to succumb. She must redeem herself in her own sight and, when she had, she would help enlighten Chu-sun so that she, too, could be free.

Yet as she grappled with her koan on the immovable statue of Kannon, her thoughts invariably returned to Mark Banning—he was planted in her heart and mind as firmly as the statue on the beach, equally incapable of being dislodged. Just as the statue had grown heavier and heavier the more they tried to lift it, so his image persisted in her thoughts the more she tried to forget him.

Each week the abbot received her. It was bliss to have someone who would listen to whatever she had to say but who never scolded her for being foolish. He still spoke in riddles that eluded her, but he never berated her for not understanding.

"I've never felt like this before—so aimless, so lost—I don't know where to go or what to do," she confessed as they walked together in the monastery grounds. "Please, help me find my way."

He pointed up to the Great Diamond Mountain, Keum Kang San.

"When the mountains close in on you from every possible direction, choose the pathless way."

"All the ways before me are pathless."

"Good!"

"But don't you see, that's just the trouble. I don't know where to turn. You know why I came here."

"Life's vicissitudes dictate our fate. If we do not expect anything, if we do not try to establish a path of our own, different from the path established by nature, all will be well. Be glad you found that moment of fulfillment with this lover."

"I'm sorry I ever laid eyes on him," she said bitterly.

"It is a matter of truth, not regret. Love is the ultimate reality. Love is dynamic. Love is personal and also universal. Awakening comes in many ways. To you it came through this man. You cannot hate him."

"I only wish I could. Instead, I end up hating myself for still loving him, for not being able to put him from my thoughts, for not seeing reason."

"Such passions! Such senseless passions! Hating yourself is like burning down your home to get rid of a rat. Hating for loving is even more futile. As for reason," he shrugged, "awakening comes in many ways, but never through reason."

He stopped abruptly, to quote a favorite poem:

> *Alone, cup in hand*
> *I view the distant peaks.*
> *Even if my love came to me,*
> *Would I be any happier?*
> *The peaks neither speak nor smile;*
> *But what happiness, O what joy!*

"Consider becoming one with nature. Don't be like other Westerners, a victim of intellect and logic. Don't let the reality of life, as you perceive it, confuse you."

"But how can I become one with nature when I remain consumed by this overwhelming passion?"

"Meditate upon it."

"I do. It's all I think about."

"But you only seek to rid yourself of it. You have told me so a hundred times. Instead, accept that through this lover you reached a moment of awareness, a moment of pure reality."

"Is that all there is—a glimpse, no more?"

"You have experienced that verge, that crest of the wave, that point of absolute immediacy. Think yourself blessed. Some, in a lifetime, never attain it."

"I would prefer never to have found a passion that has only led me into the depths of despair. How can I ever replace this turmoil with your detached serenity—that is what I want to know."

"Truth is beyond words. Don't be in a hurry. You have the saying, Rome wasn't built in a day. It may take one lifetime—or many."

The abbot's reply was hardly encouraging, but he smiled consolingly.

"Serenity will seek you out, when you are ready. To attempt to find it is to put the cart before the horse. You make no progress. You turn and turn, churn and churn; meanwhile, that which you seek stands aside watching, laughing."

"If serenity is so cruel, perhaps I don't want it after all," Marigold averred stubbornly.

The abbot smiled. "Good."

And Marigold felt, as she did so often, that they had traveled in a circle and she was no wiser than before.

"That verge, that crest of the wave—how will I ever find it again?"

"Pissing is a small thing to do, but I have to do it myself."

"I understand—and yet I don't understand."

"There," he triumphed. "You have it!"

Their hour finished, she left, with the same confusion, the same longing. Would she always be prisoner of this senseless passion that grew rather than diminished? But when she began to give up all hope, release came, though not from the expected source.

It did not come through discovering the ultimate truth behind her koan, nor did it come during her talks with the abbot, though maybe, in some mysterious way, both were behind the communication she received from Lafcadio Hearn.

Knowing that he was awaiting her arrival in Japan, she had written to tell Hearn that she had decided not to leave Korea after all. She begged him to keep her whereabouts secret. There were things she had to resolve; she was in the best place for that. She had closed her letter by saying how much she enjoyed *Glimpses of Unfamiliar Japan*. On an impulse she added that she felt like the bereaved Japanese woman he'd written about who sought to remain forever loyal to memory by cutting off all her hair.

The letter required no reply, yet one came and surprisingly quickly, perhaps because, with the Sino-Japanese war raging, communication was speedy between Japan and the Korean peninsula. Hearn was immediately sympathetic. He understood not only what she said, but he seemed to grasp what she had not said as well.

"Never be frightened of anything in your own heart," he wrote. "Love is rarely given to us in the most suitable form. I do not know your religious persuasion. For myself, I am not a Christian, but there is an Unknowable Power that I rely upon. He who relies upon his own strength cannot conquer.

"I live in a world where eleven gentle people depend on me for Love and Light and Food—my dear little selfless Japanese wife and all her family, and our son, Kazuo. I am able to supply their needs through my teaching and writing. I offer as much to you, should you ever be in need."

Just as her original letter had required no reply, nor did his answer. Yet she was immediately drawn to this kind and generous man. She had written to Herbert Farquhar, assuring him she was all right; now she asked Hearn to do her the favor of forwarding the letter to Farquhar from Japan. It would allay his fears to think her there in safety. If there was anything she could do in return . . .

"Your letter is gone, as you requested. In return, you may tell me about this Land of the Morning Calm," Hearn wrote. "I have an avid curiosity. Tell me everything, from sky-blue to indigo."

And so she began to recall her experiences ever since her arrival so long ago at Chemulpo. She wrote about life in the streets of Seoul, of the men's white garb and described the women's unending labor to keep that garb spotless. She wrote of life in the palace and the royal ladies who never left those walls. She wrote of the grip of the yangban nobles on the peasantry, of life on the river, of shooting the rapids. It was, she wrote, a land of paradoxes. People boasted of their gold-laced mountains while living in abject poverty. Tigers roamed, filling the populace with both terror and pride.

"I'm enchanted," Hearn replied. "You have great powers of observation, and you obviously love this Hermit Kingdom of yours. Why not enlarge upon these scenes you have painted for me? Gather together those photographs you spoke of by way of illustration. Do not be afraid to give too much detail, even when describing those things that seem ordinary to you—perhaps, most especially, describe those as minutely as you can. I can assure you, from my own experience, that deluging yourself in such a demanding task will allow you to think of little else." How did he know that hard work was exactly what she wanted, she wondered, before reading on. "Send the resulting manuscript to me. If you maintain this clear concise prose style, with your permission I should like to send the manuscript on to my publishers for their opinion. I gather that, like myself, you are dependent on your own means and would not be averse to some additional income." Then, perhaps for fear of sounding overly optimistic, he concluded cautiously, "Of course, there is not a great deal of profit in literature, unless one happens to please a popular taste. I make no promises."

She wanted no promises. She began writing immediately. She didn't care whether her work would be published or not. During periods of meditation, she ceased dwelling on her koan, choosing instead to take up this task that demanded and received all her attention.

They were now in the dead of winter. The ground was covered with snow; there was no longer any outdoor work. Rather than writing inside, where the heat of the ondol floors sapped her energy, she set up a tall desk on the veranda where she stood, wrapped in many layers of clothing, her hands in woolen mittens. At first she handled the pen clumsily, but soon devised a method of gripping it that allowed her to write clearly.

At first, too, she was a figure of fun to the other inhabitants of the monastery. Both nuns and monks thought it mad to brave the elements rather than taking refuge inside, but they soon got used to seeing her standing before her high writing desk. They would pass by, as though bound somewhere else, but peering in her direction. Soon they stood openly watching her. She didn't even seem to notice. Gradually, like squirrels to a nest, they brought her presents—drinks of ginger or honey with hot water, nuts, dried persimmons. She accepted these with only a nod, not wanting to speak and break her train of thought. This they seemed to understand. Sometimes she paced up and down along the veranda, or else she set off, briskly walking across the frozen paths, returning with her cheeks red, her eyes bright, to settle down again with resolve and write until the last light in the northern sky.

Occasionally, because of her involvement in her work, she was late for her appointment with the abbot. He refused to listen to her apologies.

"I don't mind. Be late. Don't come at all. It does not upset me."

"But it is wrong to waste even a minute of my time with you, which is so limited."

"Nothing is wrong. If you're short, be short; if tall, be tall. That is reality. You are doing exactly what you are supposed to be doing. You were chosen to do this work, to bring Korea to the attention, not of other governments—regrettably we are at present suffering the consequences of that—but to the attention of ordinary people on the other side of the world. Not for anything would I disturb this task you have been given."

"But this is the most important hour of my week."

"Who can say which hour is more important than another, which minute even. Through this writing, you may achieve more of what you seek than I, or anyone else, can ever give you."

"It doesn't give me that placid, calm mind that I want. My mind remains in turmoil."

He smiled. "Yet I sense it has become a sort of orderly turmoil."

And as she smiled back at him, she was forced to agree, "I suppose it has. I am so occupied that even when darkness forces me to stop, my mind goes on composing; and I have to confess that during morning meditation, my mind often strays to what I will write about in the afternoon. It is strange the way this happened—all because I wrote to Lafcadio Hearn."

He held up his hand, "Nothing is strange. We may not understand, but it is all as it should be."

"He says even the fortune-teller doesn't know his own fate."

"A wise observation."

"My life is no longer aimless. I feel almost . . . almost happy," she observed with surprise.

The thunderous beating of the abbey's great drum and a special meal of rice and vegetables ushered in the Year of the Sheep in the depths of February's cold.

The new year brought two surprises for Marigold. One was a package from Hearn in Japan containing a small folding Kodak camera, the most compact she'd ever seen, and a quantity of roll film.

"Don't thank me," he began. "I am merely forwarding this gift to you. It came from Mark Banning. Now you can add some photographs of daily life at the monastery. I suggest—and it's only a suggestion—that you conclude your book with those. By the way, how's the work going? I'm looking forward to reading it."

Marigold put the camera aside. She had vowed never again to use one, after her last photographic experience. However, she did begin to go through her negatives, looking for photographs to accompany her text. She had been afraid of finding the one she had saved of Kim Tuk-so among the women. She couldn't imagine what had prompted her to keep it, but now, to her great relief, she discovered that it was gone. She didn't know how it had disappeared. She was just glad that unpleasant reminder was no longer among her possessions.

Curiosity eventually got the better of her. The new camera was so small and compact that when folded it would even fit inside her pocket. It had a built-in spirit level to indicate with precision when the camera was straight. Its most remarkable feature was a view-finder through which scenes could be framed; it was actually equipped with a mechanism that allowed images to be viewed right-side up rather than upside down. The shutter could be set for a bulb release that allowed for time exposures, letting it stay open for as long or as short a period as desired.

Altogether, this was a remarkable instrument and the more she examined it, the more she wondered about the sort of pictures it would take. She decided to try one roll of film, just to see how it would work and whether the film produced as clear and fine an image as a plate. Just one, that was all.

So she kept the camera with her as she went through her daily rounds in the monastery. As she looked for composition in the scenes of daily life, she became more and more excited. Soon she had finished the first roll and couldn't wait to develop it.

Lafcadio Hearn had been right, she realized as she examined the finished work. These were going to provide a perfect conclusion to her work.

The next surprise for Marigold in that new year was the arrival of Teuk-sil at the monastery.

She, too, brought a present with her. It was the kokok Marigold had given her.

"Mr. Banning wanted you to have it back. He gave Lee gold for me to take to the apothecary so I could exchange it for the kokok. But I discovered the apothecary had sold it to a Japanese sea captain, and I thought I would never find it. Then Lee came to my aid. He found the Japanese captain had been drinking in a bar and had given the kokok in exchange for whiskey. The bar owner had given it to a kisaeng for favors. And she had used it to . . . it's a long story. Anyway, it was found at last and here it is."

"Teuk-sil, you shouldn't have—such a lot of trouble." Though Marigold shook her head, she held the kokok lovingly. It felt even more precious now that it was back in her hand.

"It was more trouble for Lee than for me," Teuk-sil's eyes lit as she mentioned his name. Then she quickly lowered them. In these

few short months Teuk-sil had become a woman, Marigold realized, and this man had obviously become dear to her.

"Lee is a very good man—and a very brave man."

Teuk-sil agreed without looking up, her cheeks flushing.

"Please thank him for me."

"I shall."

"Is there anything else you want me to know?" Marigold asked.

Teuk-sil hesitated. Then she said, "Your hair is growing."

Marigold touched her short hair. "I had to grow it in the cold.
Anyway, it was much too difficult to keep it shaven."

"It's like a burnished halo," Teuk-sil observed.

The last time Marigold had considered her appearance was the
morning she had woken up in a bed strewn with flowers. She was
surprised to find herself thinking of that morning without
bitterness.

"Did . . . did anyone ask for me?" Then, afraid she had sounded
too eager, Marigold added, "Did you tell Lee I was here?"

"You told me to tell no one, so I did not. But I did not want to lie
to him. I said I would see that you got the kokok; that is all."

"How is everything going—the war? I hear nothing."

"The Japanese are overwhelming the Chinese. Lee says the Chinese fight with paper fans and umbrellas while the Japanese have
armed themselves with deadly rifles. He hates both of them, scrap-
ping like dogs for a country that belongs to neither. He fears things
will never be the same as they were."

"Better perhaps." Marigold dared not voice the idea that things
might be worse.

Teuk-sil frowned. "Lee thinks not. I am sorry to say this to you,
but he wishes we could close off our country again to all who are
not Korean, just as it used to be."

"And you?"

"I agree with him—except for one thing," she looked down, adding softly, "for then I would never have met you."

As Marigold walked back to the gate with Teuk-sil, she found the courage to bring up Mark Banning's name. "I suppose Lee does not like Mr. Banning, then, since he is a foreigner."

"Some people call Mr. Banning our Blue Dragon. They believe he wants Korea to be free, not a vassal to a foreign power. Lee calls him kunja."

"Kunja—a superior man—that is indeed an honor."

"You think him deserving of being called kunja?" Teuk-sil asked curiously.

"The important thing is that Lee does," Marigold replied evasively.

"Lee had no rest until he had carried out this task for Mr. Banning."

"Is your Blue Dragon still in Korea?" Marigold could not hold back her question.

"Lee says he went away. He did not tell Lee where he was going, nor did Lee ask. He said it is better not to know."

"Of course." It was better that she, too, did not know. Even so, she found herself saying aloud, "I wonder whether he plans to return?"

"Lee says he should not return. It would be most dangerous if he did."

Marigold was amazed that she had been able to speak of Mark Banning without anger or bitterness. Her conversation with Teuk-sil had also made her realize what was happening in the country around them. The monastery was isolated in the mountains. Occasionally the mendicant monks, going from house to house with their begging bowls, wooden gongs, and rosaries, brought back some news of the Japanese invasion, but their reports were vague and unsubstantiated.

One day, soon after Teuk-sil's visit, an unusual feast was set before them thanks to these mendicants: sinsollo, a regal casserole of vegetables and eggs mixed with pine and gingko nuts, kimchi of course, then bean curd cakes and refreshing sujonggwa, a drink made with persimmons and ginger. Everyone marveled at the unexpected luxury. Later, Marigold learned that the monks had called at the home of Chu-sun's father at the time of the hwang-ap, the celebration for his mother's sixtieth year. In exchange for their blessings, they had been suitably rewarded.

"Such extravagance!" they said. "Food, so much food! They must have eaten their house—how could they afford to live after such a celebration? And music, and dancing, a circus even. And so many dignitaries—you should have seen it. They had come from everywhere—all the way from Seoul even—the Royal Princess Chunmae and her sister, the Lady Chu-sun."

"They were there?" Marigold demanded. "Was Chu-sun really there?"

"We just told you."

She had been so very close, Marigold thought; if only she had known.

"Not only that, but the governor of the province came with his retinue. Such an affair!"

"Min Tae-jon was there, too!" she exclaimed. "But I thought he was under house arrest."

"Not Min Tae-jon. He is long since dead."

"But how?" she demanded.

"He died mysteriously in his own palace. No one knows for sure what killed him, and it is better not to ask too many questions about it."

"Then who is the new governor?"

"Kim Tuk-so."

Like a true vicar of Bray, Kim Tuk-so had advanced, even under the Japanese occupation. And at last he and Chu-sun had met again.

A sudden desire to see Chu-sun, to know what had happened during that meeting, gripped Marigold. She realized that she was no longer the same person who had begged admittance to the monastery. She was calm, measured; she had gained a new perspective. She knew she was ready to go back into the world.

The abbot knew too.

"You were destined to come back here, and now you are destined to leave again."

She had always objected to the notion that she would one day leave. Now she did not.

"You once said all meetings are but the beginning of separation," she reminded him.

"But after that separation, the meetings do not merely go on as before, they are enriched by the crossing of paths. In this respect, you are more fortunate than most; with your book, you will have the opportunity to share your experiences with people you may never ever meet."

Marigold nodded, but her face was downcast.

"When I walk through those gates for the last time, that will not be a happy day for me."

"Happy, sad, these are things of our own making. Each day is absolute, therefore each day contains the potential for happiness if we can only reach out and grasp it."

"I'm not sure if I'll be able to get along in the confusion of the world. I'm afraid the peace I have found here will desert me when I leave. I only know I must go."

"Don't speculate with all these 'ifs.' A cracked mirror never reflects back an image in the same way as one unscarred, but it has its own special place in the world. You will find you may live quite as full a life outside these walls as you have lived within them, but it will be a different life." He chuckled. "Worrying and fretting do no good. Remember how you thought you would never see your path. Now look before you. There it is!"

She was about to leave when she remembered her koan.

"I never found the answer. Why did the statue of Kannon refuse to come to Korea?"

"But of course you did." The abbot laughed. "The statue did not have to come here because the miraculous powers of the goddess Kannon were here already. Those same powers manifest themselves everywhere. To go to the statue in Ming Chou in search of truth and compassion is to return empty-handed. You have only to open your mind and heart to find them, as you have done."

2

Marigold landed at Chemulpo with the beetles and locusts in the heat of summer.

She looked out on the still barren landscape from the deck of the steamer that had brought her from Fukuoka. The dull port had been transformed into a Japanese settlement. The largest building, the Japanese consulate, was surrounded by guards. Barracks covered the hillsides, and platoons of troops strutted up and down the streets while white-robed, black-hatted Koreans dejectedly looked on.

She hired a chair, and as she bumped and jostled along the rough path that still passed for the main route into Seoul, she considered that other Marigold, the dutiful daughter bent on fulfilling her dead father's wishes, who had made the same journey two years earlier. Now she belonged to no one but herself; she answered to no one but herself. And because she knew that, others did too, and she began to attract attention by nothing more than simply being herself.

The final step in freeing herself from her past had come when she stopped in Japan to meet Lafcadio Hearn.

From his letters, she felt she already knew him well. She looked forward to meeting him and was unprepared for a reticence on his part to receive her. But when, after several attempts she was finally admitted, she sensed from the awkward way he sat, never looking at her directly, that he was sensitive about the disfigurement of one side of his face.

"I am like the moon," he joked deprecatingly in a soft Irish brogue. "I show only one side of myself. The other, I fear, is not pleasant. You, on the other hand, are even more pleasing to look on than I had imagined. You arrived at an opportune moment. This just came for you."

He indicated a package. When she opened it, she gasped with delight. It was a book—*Life in the Land of the Morning Calm*—and there on the cover was her name, Marigold Wilder.

She opened it tenderly, admired the reproduction of the photographs, and then, hugging the volume close to her, she said, "Without you this would never have been possible. I'm forever in your debt."

"That is something I never allow. There are too many people who live in a perpetual state of indebtedness to others, especially in Japan. You can absolve the debt immediately by staying to dine."

At dinner Marigold met his wife, Setsu, and his two-year-old son, Kazuo. The boy was a charming combination of West and East but Setsu neither spoke nor understood English. Since Hearn's Japanese seemed minimal, Marigold thought that so little communication must make for an odd marriage.

Perhaps surmising this, Hearn said, "Setsu is charming, infinitely unselfish, and quite naive in all things. A perfect wife. From my observation of Occidental marriages, they can be an awful damper on the affections."

"Mark Banning is of a similar opinion, though possibly he got that idea from you."

"That I doubt. From what I've seen, he tends to make up his own mind—although no man ever knows the soul of another. Only a woman can learn what is in a man's heart." For the first time he looked directly at her, forgetting to hide the disfigured side of his face. "Do you know what is in Banning's heart?"

"I thought I did, but I don't seem to any more. Perhaps no one—man or woman—can ever know another completely."

"Perhaps not," he said thoughtfully. "Though I have a feeling that you know me, just as I feel I know you. We're kindred souls."

"I sense your compassion and your strength. I thank you for them," she replied quietly.

Kazuo bowed good-night to his father, and Hearn reached over to ruffle his young son's brown hair. He watched as the boy left the room with his mother.

"I keep wondering," he hesitated, "I keep wondering whether, at my age and being in such indifferent health, it was wrong of me to have a son."

"But wouldn't it be impossible to consider the world without Kazuo?" she asked.

"Quite," he said, then looked directly at her and smiled. "Quite."

From then on he never again turned his face away from her.

"And where are you off to now?"

"To Seoul, for a short visit, then back to England, I suppose, though I'm not sure I belong there any more, nor what I'll do when I get there."

"What sent you off to Korea in the first place?"

"I went as a missionary—don't shudder, I've read your opinion of missionaries. I have to confess I was not a believer, but I went hoping to carry on my father's work. For obvious reasons, I was not very successful at it. Now I've spent months at a Buddhist monastery, finding peace, becoming convinced that there is an Unknown Power, yet I'm unable to subscribe completely to the tenets of Buddhism. So here I am, with both Christian and Buddhist elements firmly entrenched in my soul, yet unable to fully accept either doctrine." She shook her head. "I just don't belong."

"You belong to yourself. I knew that as soon as I saw you. As for religion, it's wrong to think there must be only one way, the right way. If we pray for anything, it should be for the joining together of all faiths—that would be the greatest miracle of all."

He studied her face, thoughtful in the candlelight. "If the publisher were to want you to do another book on Korea—a companion volume to this one, updating recent happenings, would that be of interest?"

"Oh, yes," she replied without hesitation. "But do you really think they'd want it?"

"They will want it," he assured her.

She reached across the table to touch his hand in gratitude. "You are so very kind to help me achieve this independence. I haven't much of a head for business."

"I happen to think all matters of business a horror—a nightmare and torture unspeakable—yet, in the end, we are all forced to make a living one way or another. I know for a fact they like this book a great deal. I'm sure they're going to like the next even better."

"I have to admit I'm not so sure I can write another book. This one was written . . . almost as a purge."

"Of course you can. Just remember that all the best work is done the way ants do things, in tiny but untiring, regular steps."

On an impulse, as she was leaving, she asked, "Do you like Mark Banning?"

He nodded thoughtfully. "I've liked him ever since I first met him. He's the only person I know who never noticed my disfigurement, and when I mentioned it, he examined me and said, 'Damned if you're not right.'"

Though the road to Seoul was rough, the coming of the Japanese had brought progress, for both telegraph and railroad lines were being constructed to link Chemulpo to the capital. Marigold's chair was forced from the path several times by oncoming Japanese who were very much in control. The yangban she had encountered on her other journeys were nowhere to be seen.

They crossed the river into Seoul and entered by the South Gate. As her chair jostled through the busy thoroughfares—past the oxladen carts, the mangy dogs and grimy children, the women in changot with only their eyes and hands visible, still washing in the conduits—apart from the Japanese presence nothing seemed strange. She felt she was coming home.

She noticed Japanese soldiers alongside the haet'ae outside the Kyongbok palace. Her first duty would be to call on Chu-sun, who had been constantly on her mind. Dear Chu-sun, how she longed to see her again. She smiled at the thought of their meeting, though not at the thought of what she must tell her.

Unwittingly, Marigold had smiled directly at an old gentleman in a tall, horsehair hat. He was shocked at this overture and pointed an accusing finger at her, nudging his companion who immediately recognized her.

"It's the White Tiger of the West!"

The cry was taken up by several people along the way. This was the woman who had shot the great tiger, the skin of which had been displayed in the streets. Her chair was taken by members of the crowd and she was held up high and carried quite precariously to the monstrous red-brick house on Nam-san.

There, with some relief, she got down and thanked the swarm, who gathered around her like bees around their queen. She was glad when the front door opened and the tall, black-robed figure of Herbert Farquhar appeared on the step.

"Marigold! My dear, Marigold!" His eyes filled with tears which he hastened to blink back. Then he blew hard on that beak of a nose. "My, my! I wondered what all the commotion was about. Come in. Come in, do."

The hall still contained the mahogany umbrella stand and coat rack; the living room, the same sofa with its faded chintz covers, the same bookcases, the same upright piano.

And as soon as she sat down, Tiffin jumped into her lap.

"It's like coming home," she said, rubbing Tiffin's ears to produce a paroxysm of purring.

"This is your home, or home away from home I suppose you

would call it." Though she had written to tell him that she could
no longer serve the Anglican cause, he had insisted that she come
and stay with them. "But it can't be home without tea. Halmoni!
Tea! Miss Wilder is here. Tea!"

Halmoni came running in to see for herself. She pointed at
Marigold, her old face wrinkling with joy. "White Tiger!"

"They never stop talking about that tiger skin. Gifford received
quite a bit of reflected glory when he got back as well. He says you
brought the animal down with one shot from a pistol. How on earth
did you do it?"

Marigold repeated what she had said at the time. "It was a
miracle."

"Ah, yes, a miracle." He sighed. "Needless to say, I'm sorry
you're not coming back as a missionary."

"I should never have come as a missionary in the first place. I
was never suited to it, Gifford knew that." She paused. "I suspect
he also knew I didn't believe."

"My dear, it's deeds that count, not words. You showed what
could be done by listening and understanding. You served our cause
well, whether intentionally or not. We'd really fill the pews of our
Church of the Advent if you came back to us now. But I can understand . . . you're a famous author."

"I'm not a famous author," Marigold protested. "I have written a
book and I'm in the process of writing another, but I'm far from
famous."

"You're famous here in Seoul, and that's what counts." Herbert
grew serious. "I'm afraid Sully thinks that's why you've called off
the engagement."

"Oh, dear!" Marigold sighed. Still, that was yet another reason
she had come back, to tie up loose ends, just as Mark had done.

Just as they had on her first day at the mission, Sully and Gifford
arrived together when tea was about to be served.

"You must have heard the kettle boil," Herbert Farquhar
accused.

"Actually, all we heard was 'The White Tiger's back! She's here—the White Tiger!'" Sully announced, glancing at Marigold, glancing quickly away, then turning back to stare. "Marigold! You've . . . you've . . . you look so different."

"Sully!" She smiled, holding out both hands in welcome. "You look just the same." Then she turned to Gifford who, the last time she saw him, had been clad in hempen paji. "Giff! It's been a long time. Glad you got back all right."

If he was grateful that she said nothing about his deserting her at Wonsan, Gifford didn't show it; on the other hand, Sully was openly happy to see her back.

"I dare say you enjoyed basking in Japan under the cherry blossoms while we were embroiled in war," Gifford said defensively.

"But Marigold wasn't in Japan, Giff. She's just been telling me that all the time we thought she was there, she was staying in a Buddhist monastery in the Diamond Mountains. That's where she wrote that marvellous book of hers. And she's come back to write another." Herbert Farquhar beamed with avuncular pride. "I couldn't be more proud of her, even if she were my own daughter."

Marigold smiled, thinking how much she loved and respected Herbert Farquhar as a friend, but how grateful she was to be freed of obligations to anyone but herself.

"You're so changed," Sully echoed her thoughts when, after a great deal of maneuvering, he managed to get her alone. "I suppose that's why you left me all these months without a word." He glanced down at her bare left hand and commented bitterly. "Gifford told me you sold my ring. That really hurt me."

"I'm sorry Sully. I sold it because it was the only thing I had to sell."

"Giff said you had your camera, but you chose to sell the ring," Sully accused.

Marigold sighed. Sully hadn't changed at all. Nor had Gifford, it seemed.

"To some extent, that's true."

"I gather it means you no longer wish to be engaged to me—now that you're famous and making pots of money, a poor doctor can scarcely hope . . ."

"Sully, it's not that I'm rich and famous—I'm neither—and you're a good doctor, not a poor one. It's just that I'm not going to marry anyone."

"That sounds definite. Still, you can't blame a chap for continuing to hope." Sully paused, then went on, "Giff told me you saw quite a bit of Banning—he said you two were quite thick."

"I don't know what he means by being quite thick." There was more than a touch of acerbity in her voice.

"Well, you know—he thought Banning was sweet on you."

"Mark Banning's not a sweet man. I doubt he's ever been *sweet* on anyone in his life. And I don't see much point in discussing him. He's gone and not likely to come back."

"Rumor was rampant last year that he'd been spying for the Americans—embarrassed that sacrosanct lot at their legation, I can tell you. Of course, Allen denied everything—he had to—and he may not have known anything himself. Banning always travels alone. I'll bet he only did it for the money—that seems to be all he cares about."

Marigold ignored the innuendo. "He's probably sorry to have had to give up on the gold. He had quite a lucrative operation going from what Gifford and I saw."

"Trust Banning—he wasn't about to lose out on that," Sully pontificated. "He sent over some old geezer who used to mine with his father—Jeremiah Crump, or something of the sort, a thoroughly uncouth fellow. 'Just call me JC,' he tells Edith Allen. You can imagine how that went over." Marigold couldn't help but grin at the thought. "Anyway, he reopened the mine in April and from all accounts he's been hauling the stuff out of the ground, quite to Her Majesty's satisfaction. I think the gold was the only thing that saved Banning's hide. He came back here after the war started in spite of the rumors of his involvement with the Tong-hak. We all expected him to be picked up, but he wasn't. And where do you think he stayed?"

"I've no idea."

"At the Russian legation—the gall of the man! Everyone knew he and Natasha were sleeping together, except old Boris—though I dare say he may have known, too."

"I dare say," was Marigold's only comment.

Marigold was received back into the community with some pleasure and also with a touch of envy. She had succeeded in broadening her sphere, while theirs had been encroached upon by the Japanese.

The first thing Natasha Waeber noticed about Marigold Wilder was her hair—short, crisp curls around her face. A woman with short hair, how daring, how unusual—and how pretty! Next she noticed how much taller Marigold seemed, but perhaps that was due to her commanding posture. She would have liked to have dismissed her appearance as being disgustingly masculine, but there was a new softness about Marigold Wilder—the sort of softness that a man gives to a woman—that had not been there before.

The first thing Marigold noticed about Natasha was the large gold nugget that hung from a chain around her neck. Her fingers constantly strayed to touch it, just as Marigold's own so often touched the kokok she wore.

We're both his women, she thought with a sense of shock. His gifts hang from our necks, marking possession like padlocks and chains. Yet there was no bitterness in her voice as she congratulated Natasha on the splendid piece.

"It was the very largest nugget Mark found."

"I believe it. It's quite magnificent."

Natasha eyed her from head to foot. "Your hair—what a terrible shame!"

Marigold knew from the look on Natasha's face that she had inadvertently scored a triumph. She tossed her head and laughed. "I really don't mind it at all. It's so easy to take care of."

"It will grow back," Natasha consoled.

"I'm not sure I'm going to let it."

Young Miss Gardner, who'd just put her hair up, looked longingly at Miss Wilder's short curls.

"Do you think I might, Mother," she began.

"Certainly not!" Mabel Gardner answered sharply. She had also been scrutinizing Marigold's head, allowing her imaginary shears to prune a little here and there. But really, all in all the symmetry was quite perfect. It was most provoking.

"Poor Dr. Sullivan," Miss Gardner whispered dreamily, half to herself. "Just look at the way he moons over her. I only wish he'd look at me like that just once."

"Dr. Sullivan's Irish," her mother cautioned. "Your time would be far better spent looking in Gifford Partridge's direction. He's from a fine English family."

"But Gifford never looks at girls, Mother."

"That would scarcely be proper in a man of the cloth."

"But if he's not interested . . ."

However, her mother had already turned to listen to Mrs. Allen, and they were commiserating with one another on their favorite subject, the incompetence of servants.

"Just when I finally get the tennis club organized and my lawn is ready, our houseboy keeps rushing into the midst of our first game, dashing after the ball in play. I had to have him pulled aside quite forcibly in the end. He gave some flimsy reason for his conduct— said he was trying to save us all that trouble. I attempted to explain that it was a game, and do you know what he said to that?"

"No," said Mabel Gardner, though she knew what she was going to hear anyway.

"He said he couldn't see why anyone would work so hard if they were playing. Such impertinence!"

Mabel Gardner shook her head. "These people have no idea. Why only last week I instructed Hong, who knows our ways—he's been with us forever—to serve cocktails at five, and what do you suppose . . ."

"I'll bet he went out and caught the rooster and served up its tail feathers!" Mrs. Allen burst in triumphantly.

"Yes, as a matter of fact." Mrs. Gardner seemed almost as aggrieved with Mrs. Allen as she had been with Hong. "And we had important visitors from the Foreign Office. I was mortified!"

"I knew because the same thing happened to me—not that I approve of cocktails at all, but Harold has convinced me that as official hosts, we have to serve them. For my part, I don't see why they can't be content with drinking sarsaparilla . . ."

Overhearing their conversation, Marigold decided that war or no war, nothing had changed.

"Splendid to have you back," Dr. Allen beamed, coming to her side. "Just splendid! From what Gifford told us, you two had quite an adventure. I guess you must have been glad to have him along— he sure helped you out a time or two."

"He told us about the time that yangban's servants threatened to confiscate your sampan and how he was forced to threaten them at gunpoint," Mrs. Gardner smiled fatuously in Gifford's direction. "I always say that education at the proper schools will show. You have to give the English gentleman his due . . ."

"I don't think we can afford to overlook Yankee ingenuity," Mrs. Allen put in.

"Speaking of which, has anyone heard from Mr. Banning?" Mr. Gardner asked, much to Dr. Allen's annoyance. Having assiduously avoided all mention of that name, he was sorry that his wife had brought up a subject guaranteed to bring Banning to mind.

"I don't believe he's in our hemisphere," he said, trying unsuccessfully to keep a note of relief from his voice. "As you know, he sent someone else to reopen the mine—Jeremiah Crump, I believe is his name."

"A nasty old miner left over from the California gold rush. He drinks whiskey like water and has no manners whatsoever. I do think they should vet these people before allowing them to come over," Edith Allen carped. "People like that awful old man tend to put all of us Americans in a bad light."

"Oh, I wouldn't say that," Mabel Gardner demurred, while her small, deep-set eyes glinted their agreement.

"Didn't he claim he was a partner with Banning in his share of the mine?" Gardner put in. "If I know anything about Banning and his love of the almighty dollar, I'll bet he got the old codger to come out and work for him for next to nothing and he'll be pocketing all the proceeds."

Dr. Allen cast a discomfitted look at his wife, who rushed in to his rescue. "There's Mr. Partridge. Do come over and join us. Mrs. Gardner has just been reminding all of us of the advantages of an English public school education."

Mrs. Gardner smiled at Gifford again. "I was just remarking that rising to the occasion is the sign of a true English gentleman."

Gifford's cheeks flushed slightly. He assiduously refrained from looking at Marigold.

"But I know how you gentlemen hate to talk about yourselves— unlike others who are always boasting," Mabel Gardner gushed on. "I was saying as much to my daughter. She's developed quite a soft spot for you, Gifford, though I suppose I shouldn't tell tales out of school."

Gifford turned his back on Mrs. Gardner's effusions to demand of Marigold, "What was the name of that young woman you used to teach at the palace?"

"Do you mean Lady Chu-sun?" Marigold's tone was one of concern. She had received no reply to the note she had sent Chu-sun, but that morning a message had been delivered from Queen Min, granting her an audience, for which she had not asked, on the following day.

"That's it." Gifford was relieved at the change in subject. "Lady Chu-sun. It has just been proclaimed that she and the crown prince—that dimwitted fat one—what's his name?"

"Prince Sunjong," Marigold supplied in a whisper, stunned at the thought of what was surely coming.

"That's it. It's just been announced that they are to marry."

3

Queen Min sat on the dais in the Imperial Throne Room where Marigold had first seen her. Her appearance was more regal than ever, if that was possible. Her face was white, immobile, impassive, yet Marigold could sense rather than see her anger.

Marigold's attention was divided between the queen and the lady who sat on her right hand, in a position of honor only before occupied by the crown prince. True, Lady Chu-sun's chair was slightly behind the throne, yet clearly she had been singled out from the other ladies of the court. Marigold waited for her friend to acknowledge her, but by not so much as a movement of her eyebrow did Chu-sun give any indication that she knew Marigold or that she had ever seen her before.

This inexplicable rejection, which both hurt and dismayed Marigold, was underscored by the queen's welcoming remarks.

"I am pleased to be back. I am also honored that Your Majesty was willing to receive me so soon after my return," Marigold began.

"We hear you have passed many months in a Buddhist monastery in our famous Diamond Mountains. Also that you have visited Japan." The last word was spat out in anathema.

"I did, Your Majesty, though only for a very short time."

"Have you, like your friend, Mr. Banning, come back to spy on us? If so, be warned that we do not deal kindly with spies, even those who seek to ingratiate themselves with magnificent presents."

With a wave of her long hand she indicated the tiger skin which hung on the wall behind her.

"I assure Your Majesty that I am not a spy. I have no interest in spying—for anyone. Very frankly, I feel more Korean than English, though I accept that in your culture I am forever sangnom. I have only the interests of Korea at heart and, if it were known," Marigold found herself adding, "I believe that Mr. Banning did also."

Queen Min pressed her thin lips together. "Not according to my dear departed brother."

Marigold was reminded that she had brought along the portrait of Min Tae-jon for presentation. She handed it to a lady of the court who passed it up to the queen.

The queen looked down on her brother's likeness and, for one unforgettable moment, Marigold thought she was going to see her cry. Her eyes narrowed, her mouth wrinkled and turned down, but that was for a moment only. Then her face became impassive again.

"It is a good likeness," she said at last.

"I find it so myself," Marigold agreed.

"He was a fine man, cut down in his prime, by Japanese devils." Her voice grew in volume and she stopped using the royal "we" as invectives against the Japanese poured from her lips. "I shall hate them until my dying day. I curse them. I have ordered Chilyongun to conduct a kut every week for that purpose. They sense her power and it frightens them. They order us to stop these practices, but I shall never stop until the last one is ejected from my kingdom. This envoy of theirs, Count Inouye, he seeks to gain power through that worthless uncle and father-in-law of mine, the Taewon-gun. Has he no eyes to see the Japanese, who bring with them torments of the modern world, are opening a veritable Pandora's box. Telegraphs, railways, paved roads—we want none of these unless they are decided on by myself—or my husband." This was an obvious afterthought. "All day, every day, they issue proclamations—banning the long tobacco pipe, ordering the planting of pine trees, abolishing our system of punishment, calling together the geomancers to decide when the king will worship at the ancestral tablets. How dare they! What right have they to usurp our authority?" Her voice had been rising, and here she shook with anger. "They even threaten that all men must cut off their topknot. My husband, the king, will never agree, not while I am his queen." She shot a sharp glance at Marigold. "Do not think he is weak because of those announcements in the Official Gazette refusing to accept resignations of government officials. He orders them back to their posts in order to preserve the government at all costs."

"I understand, Your Majesty," Marigold sympathized. There had been an epidemic of government officials feigning "official sickness" and threatening resignation; it was freely bandied about that the Japanese, discovering that the inertia and insolence of the yangban were harder to overcome than the Chinese, would have welcomed their departure.

The queen abruptly changed the subject. "We understand you have written a book."

"I have requested a copy for Your Majesty, but it has not yet been received. As soon as it comes, I would welcome the privilege of presenting it to you."

"Yes, yes," the queen said impatiently. "We understand you have come back because you will write another book about our country."

"In part, that is so," Marigold agreed, looking at Chu-sun, willing her to show some sign of their friendship. She longed to be alone, to talk with her, to let her know that she, as much as any publisher's request, was the reason for her return.

"You will journey to many places, take many pictures with that apparatus of yours?"

"As long as I am granted a kwan-ja," Marigold said.

"We do not expect you will experience any difficulty in receiving one."

"Thank you, Your Majesty."

"In return we have a small favor to ask of you."

"Anything."

She motioned Marigold to approach the throne and leaned forward to say softly in her ear, "You say you feel more Korean than English—now you may prove it. In the royal palace we are cut off. As you journey about this land of ours, you could provide us with useful information. What is the spirit of the people? Are these Japanese in control as they would have us believe? We do not know whether the information we receive is true or censored. In order to get rid of the Japanese and the Taewon-gun, I must know the people are behind me. I must know my strength."

Marigold realized she was being placed in the awkward position of being recruited as a spy. Was this how it had happened with Mark Banning, she wondered? Had he been drinking with Andrews and then had a seemingly reasonable request made of him just as this was being made of her now? Korea was in need of reform. Queen Min and those who surrounded her were conservatives, interested only in preserving the established order. They were, indeed, cut off from the people and the people's needs. Would the queen act differently if she knew how the people really lived and what they really thought? Perhaps this was a chance to make that point.

"On my return I shall be glad to give you my observations," she began guardedly. Then, seeing a way out of her dilemma, she added, "and also give you copies of the photographs I take, so you may see your kingdom for yourself."

The queen indicated her approval with a curt nod. She turned back to whisper something to Chu-sun, who got up immediately and left without a backward glance. Marigold looked after her in dismay.

"I had hoped to be able to extend my congratulations to Lady Chu-sun on her forthcoming marriage," she said.

"You will have that opportunity. She has gone to prepare a letter we dictated before your arrival. You will be able to deliver it to a relative of mine in the town of my birth, Yo-Ju."

Now that she was recruited, Marigold could see she was no longer to be consulted on whether she would or would not perform tasks. Still, she didn't argue. At least she would be able to talk to Chu-sun.

"You are to remember, however, that the Lady Chu-sun is no longer a simple lady of the court. She is to become a royal princess—a crown princess. For that reason, your relationship can no longer be as it once was."

Could this be the reason for Chu-sun's coldness, Marigold wondered as she waited an interminable time for the letter. She feared Chu-sun might send someone else with it, but at last she appeared. Her eyes remained fixed on the floor at her feet as she handed the envelope to Marigold.

"My reason for coming back was to see you, Chu-sun," Marigold began. "Why did you not reply to the note I sent you?"

"Because I did not wish to see you," she muttered.

"But why?" Marigold demanded. "What have I done?"

Chu-sun was silent. But as Marigold repeated her demand, she replied sharply, "You know very well what you have done."

"But I don't. You must tell me," Marigold pleaded.

"I have spoken to Kim Tuk-so," Chu-sun said at last.

"Ah!" So that was it.

"He told me everything. I thought you were my friend." Chu-sun looked up for the first time. There were tears in her dark eyes.

"Oh my dear. I am your friend!"

"I am no longer your friend, and now I know you were never mine."

"What exactly did he tell you?" Marigold demanded.

"You were there; you know full well what passed between you."

"I do—but I cannot be sure he told you exactly what was said."

"Now you call him a liar! He said that he tried to help you, but that you hated him. You were rude to him, you called him unkind names. He is fine and decent. At last he has been rewarded by a position in which he can benefit the population."

"He will serve any master, Chu-sun."

Angrily, she stamped her foot. "There! That is exactly what he said you would do—find him unworthy and try to besmirch his good name. I said that would never happen while I had breath in my body."

"I'm sorry, Chu-sun. I want to believe he was a good man once, and that he fell under the evil influence of Min Tae-jon . . ."

"He survived Min Tae-jon! That is what matters. You would give him credit for nothing, yet your own actions there were far from creditable."

Marigold was astounded. "Did he really tell you that? Did he tell you why?"

"He would only say it was something that no Korean lady would ever have done; she would have taken her own life first. He was kind to you. He said certain things must be overlooked in a barbarous foreigner."

"I will tell you what happened, but before I do, I must warn you that Kim Tuk-so was involved in a far worse way . . ."

Chu-sun clapped her hands on her ears. "I will not listen to anyone who speaks unkindly of him."

"Then you will not listen to the truth."

Chu-sun tossed her head. "He has become governor. That is wonderful—but I suppose you don't think so."

Marigold shook her head sadly. "For your sake, I wish I could say that I did, but I don't." Her eyes narrowed in sudden suspicion. "You see him, talk to him, you obviously still love him, but then you come back and agree to marry the crown prince! Why?"

"I am marrying the crown prince because that is what Kim Tuk-so wants me to do," she answered stubbornly.

"So that he can eventually become first minister when you are queen." Marigold leaned forward urgently. "Don't you see his am-

bition, Chu-sun? Don't you see how he's using you? He'll use any-
body who'll give him power."

Chu-sun stepped back. As she did, she changed to become every
inch as regal as Queen Min herself. Imperiously, she raised a finger to indicate the door.

"Yobo! Leave this minute, or I'll have you thrown out!" Chu-sun's
use of this term to one who had been her friend was a shattering
blow. Marigold was suddenly glad to be leaving Seoul. She wanted
to get away.

Throughout that summer, as Marigold journeyed the length and
breadth of the poets' "land of three thousand li," she remained far
more vexed by her parting from Chu-sun than by the suspicious
Japanese who followed her everywhere. She pondered how she
could make Chu-sun understand the kind of man Kim Tuk-so
really was; she had to do that, even if it would kill all hope of
redeeming their friendship. If Chu-sun were someday to become
queen, her continued deception by Kim Tuk-so could harm not
only herself but the nation.

While wrestling with this problem, Marigold decided to do the
one thing she could do for Korea; she could give Queen Min an
accurate record of the lives led by her people. So she eschewed
pavilions and temples to train her camera on farmers in the rice
fields in Chollanamdo, roof thatchers in Hahoe, screen paperers in
Chonju, kimchi makers in Taejin, fishermen in Uisangdae, and
women wherever she could find them. The most visible were
washerwomen and those who had been sold into slavery; and then
there were children everywhere. She showed the people just as
they were—hungry, tired, dispirited. The pictures were not pretty,
nor were they meant to be. They might, however, help the queen to
better understand the plight of her people.

Marigold retraced her journey down the north branch of the
Han River, taking a sampan at Ma'chai. Every bend in the river
carried memories. En route to Yo-Ju, where she was to deliver the

queen's letter, she found herself at Chum-yol. Could Banning possibly be there, she wondered, noticing the activity on the bank and mountainside. Her heart jumped as she ordered the sampan to pull in, reasoning that the queen would surely want to know about progress at the mine.

She had hardly stepped ashore when a thin, wiry figure approached from the direction of the camp. He walked with a stiff gait, rocking back and forth from side to side like a sailor just set ashore. As he drew nearer, he pulled a hand from the pocket of his mud-caked overalls, and his narrow, weather-beaten features wrinkled into greeting.

"God damn but it's good to see a round-eye again! Pardon my French, ma'am, but I ain't been around a lady in so long."

The hand Marigold shook was dry and hard and deeply encrusted with grime; the nails were black with dirt.

"Jeremiah Crump, or is it Cragg?"

"Neither. It's Jeremiah Crowe—but just call me JC. All my friends call me JC and I can see you're a friend—not like that fat American woman back there in Seoul. She don't like me, and that's a fact."

"Mrs. Allen is a bit of a fuss-pot . . ."

"That's puttin' it mild. There's other things I'd like to call her— but I won't."

He was still pumping Marigold's hand in greeting and didn't drop it till she introduced herself.

"I knowed as much. Soon as I spotted you way up river—bet that's the gal that saved his life, I says to myself."

"How . . . ?" she began.

He pointed to her head. "That mop of yours is a dead giveaway. He told me you was a redhead with a temper to match."

"Mark Banning?"

"Course! Who else? Said if you was to come, I was to be sure and make you welcome. So the beefsteaks is on the fire, and the beer's out. It's not cold but leastways it's cool."

So many memories of the last time she was there came rushing back. It wasn't only the sight of the hut, but the fact that JC's conversation centered almost entirely on Banning.

"I knowed his daddy when first he came out to the goldfields. A regular greenhorn he was—talked funny, took a lot of razzin' because of it, but I liked him from the start. Took him under my wing, you might say, showed him the ropes. But he was quick—he soon caught on. But that young'un of his, he was like a son to me, too. Talk about smart! I knew he'd make his way in the world, all right. And he has. I'm right proud of him."

"What's his mother like? Do you know her?"

He nodded as he lit a stubby, yellow pipe. "I know her, though she don't know me. She never did cotton to me—most ladies don't, like that bunch down there." He took the corncob from his mouth and poked it in the direction of Seoul. "Jack Banning'd made and lost three fortunes, four maybe, by the time he met up with her in a 'Frisco saloon—she wasn't no bar-girl, mind. Her daddy was *alcade* in the valley—he threw her out 'cos some young dude got the hots for her and she let him have his way. Still she wasn't no loose piece and she didn't belong in no saloon. Jack knew that. Two days after they met, he took her off and married her as much to save her from that life as anything."

"Didn't he love her?"

"He was crazy about her, but that's no reason for marrying her, now is it?"

"A lot of people would agree with you," Marigold said, thinking of what Chu-sun's mother had said, as well as Banning's thoughts on the subject of marriage.

"Sounds like you don't think so, but truth of the matter was Jack Banning wasn't no marrying man. He was free and easy, like that boy of his. She led him a dance with that temper of hers, I can tell you, always wanting him to settle down, while him and me and the boy were always hot to be off prospecting. Did she ever get mad!" He laughed, shaking his head from side to side. "And that poor kid'd get torn both ways, wanting to come with us and yet wanting her to be happy. But he always came with us in the end. He was curious, he wanted to be on the move, adventuring, discovering things. 'Mark'll never make anything of himself,' his mother'd yell at Jack. 'If he hangs around with you, he'll turn into a bum like that worthless friend of yours.' But young Mark did all right for himself—and for her. He give her the home she always wanted— set her up back at her old family place. She holds court there now like a duenna. She's the only woman he ever paid attention to and even to her he don't pay overmuch. She's still at him, nagging him to settle down, but I'd sure like to meet the filly that could tie that one down. Jack Banning's life would've been a lot happier if he'd never gone and got soft-hearted over that gal."

"But then Mark would never have come into the world," Marigold pointed out, much as she had to Lafcadio Hearn.

And JC responded much as Hearn had. "Ain't never thought of that! Sure couldn't imagine the world without him. Treats me just fine, just like I was still young and frisky 'stead of an old codger going on seventy. He never lets on, but he's always looking out for me. He knows I won't take nothing for nothing, so he puts jobs in my way. I earn a bit, then lay back for a bit. It ain't a bad life."

"Sounds like a pretty good one to me." She nodded toward the men working by the river. "Looks like you've got things in hand here."

The old man drew hard on his pipe. "JC's good! I won't deny that. Not for a minute. But not too many men my age get offered a partnership in a mine like this when the hard work of finding gold and getting set up's already been done. Still, modesty's no virtue of mine, nor of any man worth his salt. I got to hand it to myself, I know how to work these Chinks, I know how to get on with them. This lot's as tough as I've come across. Bad as a bunch of Irishmen, they are. But they always let you know where you stand. I like that. And I think they like me pretty good, too." He took off his hat and scratched an iron-gray thatch. "It's a god-forsaken place this, and no mistake, but give it its due, it's the one place I been where it pays to be old and gray!"

Not until she was leaving did she ask the one question she'd been longing to ask from the start. "Mark—do you hear from him?"

He shook his head. "I'm not one for writing. Nor is he. Don't know where he is. Don't know when I'll see him next. Not here, I hope. From all accounts, this ain't too good a place for him to be."

"He shouldn't come back to Korea," Marigold concurred.

"With that guy . . . well, you just never know. He goes where he wants, when he wants. And no one tells him what to do."

4

On the way back, Marigold thought a lot about JC and all he'd said. She'd liked the old man for his honesty, for his loyalty, and for himself. Far from feeling exploited, he loved his work. Marigold wished she had JC's vitality; although she looked forward to working again, she was tired after her long journey and now there was so much to be done. She had to develop and print her pictures, decide on an approach, and make a layout for the new book. She sought peace and seclusion, but arriving back in the capital she found an uproar.

The cause of the turmoil was the rampant rumor of a hair-cropping edict. To the Korean man, the topknot was an indication of his manhood; it signified nationality, antiquity, and sanctity. A boy's coming of age was marked by the elaborate investiture ceremony of the topknot. He was given his long white coat and black hat; then a circular spot was shaved at the crown of his head and his long hair was drawn together at that point, tied into a firm twist, and pulled forward to stand upright like a horn. This topknot was then covered by a richly decorated manggon which was secured under the chin. Only when so invested could a Korean offer sacrifices to his ancestors. Without a topknot, he was only half-man, so any mention of cutting it off was tantamount to threatening castration.

Count Inouye had been replaced as Japanese envoy by Viscount Miura, a far less tractable man who sought to impose his stamp of authority. His announced reasons for the edict—preservation of health and greater convenience in business transactions—were ludicrous, but Viscount Miura was insistent. Every member of the government must have his topknot cut off, beginning with the king. The king was to set the example by appearing shorn before his people at a Kur-dong, the only occasion when he ever left the palace, to make sacrifices at the tombs of his ancestors.

In the midst of this uproar, Marigold went to the palace to report to the queen. She took a sheaf of photographs with her.

"This hair-cropping edict, can it be true?" she asked.

"Miura will try to force it down our throats."

"I am sorry. Can nothing be done? Can the king not refuse?"

"My husband listens to that worthless father of his. Taewon-gun is Japan's puppet," she said contemptuously. Taking the photographs Marigold handed to her, she began, one by one, to examine them.

Marigold started to speak but the queen motioned her to be silent until, at last, with an air of disdain, she threw the photographs aside.

"I do not like them," she said.

"I didn't mean for you to like them, Your Majesty. I meant to show you what your country is like."

"Why did you choose only peasants?" she demanded.

"Because these are your people."

"I am of noble stock. The yangban are the people who count. It is their mood I wanted to know, it is their mood that matters—not these peasants'!"

"The yangban are few in number . . ."

"But strong in power."

"Power lies in the people, Your Majesty," Marigold averred. "If only you will look to the needs of the people, they will support you."

"What do you mean, they *will* support me? They have to support me. I am their queen!" She stood up and Marigold, sensing the interview was at an end, rose too. She couldn't resist one parting shot.

"No ruler can afford to overlook the needs of his people, Your Majesty. Louis XVI of France discovered that, as did King George III. You have an opportunity . . ."

"I don't need opportunity. Only commoners need opportunity!" the queen shouted.

Chu-sun entered the room. She bowed low to the queen and didn't approach the throne until the queen signaled to her.

Whatever she whispered made the queen's eyebrows rise and fall. Without a word to Marigold, she swept from the room.

As Marigold left, she discovered Chu-sun waiting outside.

"I'm so glad you're here. I've been so anxious to see you," Marigold began.

Chu-sun said nothing, and Marigold tried again.

"I'm afraid I've annoyed the queen. I tried to show her what her country is really like—a picture cannot lie, it speaks more clearly than words, but I'm afraid mine spoke too clearly." Sensing she had struck a sympathetic chord in Chu-sun, Marigold went on in a rush of words. "I've been so terribly upset by what happened last time I saw you. I don't want you to be angry with me, but I do want you to understand. May we talk—please."

Chu-sun hesitated. "I have to translate now for the queen."

"Let me wait for you, then. Afterwards we will talk."

Chu-sun seemed to be waivering. She motioned Marigold to follow her, saying, "Come. This may be something to amuse you."

They crossed the courtyard to the Imperial Throne Room, climbed the dais, and took their places behind the screen.

"I've thought of you so often," Marigold began, but Chu-sun held a finger to her lips, silencing her. She kept her eyes down though it was some time before there were sounds of people entering the hall, then the step of the queen herself climbing the dais.

How ridiculous this was, Marigold thought, to be hiding once again behind a screen. She felt like jumping up and announcing her presence, but at the first sound of the visitor's voice, she clasped her hands together in fear. She threw an accusing look at Chu-sun.

"Amusing! How can you think listening to Mark Banning put his head in a noose will amuse me?"

Defiantly Chu-sun raised a finger to silence her.

"I did not expect you to come back to Korea, Mr. Banning. My brother gave me a full report of your activities. You must realize that by coming here, you place your life in jeopardy."

"I had to come back, ma'am. There are things I have to take care of. There are also things I have discovered that you must know."

"You admit you know so much? How?"

"Your Majesty knows very well I have friends in a number of places who give me information."

"You admit to being a spy."

"I've never denied that I receive information." At this admission, Marigold shook her head, then covered her face with her hands. "What I have learned is important. Your life may depend on it."

"You amaze me, Mr. Banning. A man with any cunning would have made a staunch denial of being a spy in this country."

"Cunning has never been an attribute of mine. As for spies, they have their uses, ma'am."

"Only if they do as they're told." The queen's severe comment was, Marigold suspected, directed as much at herself as at Banning. "Not when they take matters into their own hands. I suppose you will swear you only did it out of patriotism for your country."

"Hell no! Patriotism is the most abused of sentiments. Whatever I do is for hard cash—or else for the challenge."

"You seem surprisingly honest, Mr. Banning—or surprisingly stupid. I don't know which."

"Having done business with me, ma'am, you should know exactly how honest and stupid I am. You know how far you can trust me, just as I know exactly how far I can trust you."

"Which means?"

"I trust you to cheat some on the amount of gold due me. I'm

here to see that you don't take too much advantage of my old partner and friend who's been running that mine. I want to make sure
he gets everything that's due to him."

"You call me dishonest!" The queen's voice quivered with indignation. "How dare you! Men have died for less."

"As you've said, I may be surprisingly stupid, but I trust you not
to take my life since it's really not to your advantage."

"I shall decide that. What is this that you know that you want me
to know?" she demanded.

"There are forces at work that want you out of the way."

She laughed. "That is nothing new. There have always been
forces that wanted me out of the way. I've outwitted them every
time."

"The stakes are getting higher, the play's getting tougher. You've
surrounded yourself with sycophants and phonies. You talk to the
wrong people, you refuse to listen to the right people. You don't
know who your friends are."

"I suppose you've come to tell me they're the Americans."

"I've come to tell you they're not the Russians," he broke in
swiftly, causing a sharp intake of breath from the queen. "You're
making overtures to the Russians because they've promised you
they'll get the Japanese out."

"And they'll be as good as their word," the queen responded.
"Haven't they given proof of their intentions by forcing the Japanese to return the Liaotung Peninsula, seized by them in the war,
to China? They're helping weed out pro-Japanese elements in the
Cabinet. I shall certainly not listen to a word against such a
staunch ally, Mr. Banning. Anything you say to impugn the motives
of the Russians stems, no doubt, from your own self-interest."

"You're playing a dangerous game—one that may end up costing
you your life. The Russians are enticing you to their side only
because they intend to use Korea as a pawn in an even bigger
game."

"Are you speaking for your government, Mr. Banning?"

"I'm speaking for myself, to someone I hope will be smart enough to listen. You've turned your back on a lot of idealistic and brave young men . . ."

"If you mean the Tong-hak, they are tools of the Japanese—just as I suspect you are either working for the Japanese or allowing yourself to be used by them. The Tong-hak rebellion was a way for the Japanese to implant themselves here in the role of protectors. I hate them, Mr. Banning, and I hate spies!"

Her voice had risen to a virtual scream, but his shouted response drowned her out.

"You hate and you don't listen—and that's exactly your trouble— ma'am. Listen to the Tong-hak, listen to what they're saying. They see the plight of the people. They want a Korea that's for the Koreans. They want their Blue Dragon to rise and hold its own. What's wrong with that?"

"They want things their way."

"Their way was not so wrong. If you'd only listened—if you'd only tried to meet some of their demands, there would have been no rebellion, and Seoul would not now be overrun with Japanese hairdressers calling the tune. These brave young men—and women, too . . ."

"Women! How dare women interfere in such matters!"

"If you'll excuse my saying so, ma'am, your condescension toward your own sex is the one less than admirable trait you share with your English counterpart. Queen Victoria regards herself as superior to other women—so do you. The few women she can tolerate she believes to be incompetent, or, if she has any respect for them, she thinks of them as honorary men of some sort. Neither one of you promotes the advantages given to those of your sex. Instead of appealing to the strength in women, you ignore them. Worse yet, here in Korea, you allow them to be taken into slavery. You might listen to that White Tiger of yours—she's straightforward. She'll tell you what she thinks. She's honored in your country because she is a woman, not in spite of it . . ."

"Aha! So that is why Miss Wilder thrust those objectionable photographs of my people on me. I should have guessed that you two are in league. She, too, has been spying for you."

"I can assure you she has not," Banning said sharply. "I've had no contact with Miss Wilder since . . ."

"Since you slept with her at Wonsan. I, too, know a little of what's going on, Mr. Banning. Ah, good! I see by your face that you are angry. You won't have Miss Wilder's name sullied, is that it?"

"If you attempt to tarnish her reputation, you'll bring as much discredit on yourself as on Miss Wilder. Whatever happened between us is all in the past. No recriminations should fall on her; she is entirely blameless."

"So, now you have finished with the Englishwoman, you have undoubtedly returned to your Russian lover, yet you come behind her back to warn me that I cannot trust the Russians. You are a disreputable man, Mr. Banning."

Marigold glanced up to catch Chu-sun's look of triumph as he agreed, "Thoroughly disreputable, Your Majesty. But disrepute is not confined to commoners."

"What do you mean by that?"

"Min Tae-jon, that opium-addict brother of yours in Wonsan, for instance."

"How dare you so much as mention his name! All foreigners are rude and insufferable, but you are the worst of them. I shall have you forced to do the crane's dance until you apologize to his memory."

"Do you enjoy the same vicarious thrills? The victims of his pleasures are to be found throughout the province."

Queen Min clapped her hands together, calling to the guard. Marigold pressed her clenched fist against her teeth. Why must he say things that were calculated to infuriate the queen? Why couldn't he be more diplomatic? His bravado may have succeeded with Min Tae-jon, but he ought to know it wouldn't with the queen. She could easily have him tortured as a spy to prove her power, and there was no guarantee that Dr. Allen, who so clearly wanted him out of the way, would ever come to Banning's aid.

"If you want to be an enlightened nation, you can't go on using these evil, inhumane tortures," he was saying.

"They are our way, as you are about to learn, to your great discomfort, Mr. Banning."

"They may have once been your way, but your barbaric methods can no longer be supported if Korea wishes to join the rest of the world. You can't continue to put friends and relatives into office if they gouge and steal and threaten with complete impunity. You quashed the rebellion brought on by one brother who supplied the troops with rice laced with sand; you turned a blind eye to another's opium-addiction. Min Tae-jon was murdered by one of his aspiring proteges, who was named governor for his efforts."

Chu-sun had stopped abruptly, refusing to translate this last sentence. She cast a malevolent glance at Marigold.

"You put him up to this," she hissed.

"How could I? I didn't know he was here," Marigold whispered angrily. "You made me come here, you forced me to listen."

"You have shown no compassion for Tuk-so. Why should I show any for you?"

"I can't stay silent any more," Marigold said, rising.

"No, don't!" Chu-sun pleaded. "She will blame me."

"Finish, Lady Chu-sun!" the queen commanded. "Tell me exactly what he just said."

Had Marigold not been there, she was sure Chu-sun would have altered the meaning of Banning's accusation.

"Please sit down," Chu-sun whispered, before she haltingly complied with the queen's request.

"How dare you say such things!" the queen spluttered.

"I dare because I say no more than the truth."

"That is not the truth. It was the Japanese, not Kim Tuk-so, who were responsible for the murder of my brother."

"You'll insist on blaming them for everything. You'll allow your

hatred to blind you to what's really going on. They wanted Min
Tae-jon removed, and they got Kim Tuk-so to do their work. If ever
there was a tool for use by the highest bidder, it's Kim. I advise you
to get rid of him—and soon. He's dangerous, not just because of his
vices, but because he has no loyalty—he'll serve any master."

"Just like you."

"I serve only one master—myself. We're alike in that respect."

"You, a sangnom. How dare you liken yourself to a queen!"

"Just put it down to ignorance, ma'am. But what I'm going to say
is the truth, and you must listen. There's a plot afoot to get you out
of the way. Viscount Miura, who is in no way as reasonable a man
as his predecessor—or as smart—is behind it. And, as you might
suspect, so is Taewon-gun. The Russians know about it, but don't
count on them stepping in to save you. Your death can be used to
their advantage, leaving Korea with a weak leader and themselves
in a commanding position. I advise you to get out of Seoul now.
Find a refuge for a time, at least until this plot blows over."

"The Japanese and my dear father-in-law want me out of the
way, and you are advising me to step aside, leaving the field clear
for them, is that it?"

"If you don't leave temporarily, they're going to force you out in a
very permanent way," he warned.

"I will not move an inch to accommodate them. I hate the Japanese with a passion that you cold-blooded Westerners can never
understand," she fumed.

"Passion must be tempered with reason. You could use them
instead of letting them use you. Take advantage of them. Let them
build their roads and telegraphs. Korea will benefit in the end, as
long as you are working on making the nation strong from within
and making the right alliances without."

"They expect me to keel over like that foolish husband of mine,"
the queen fumed. "If he cuts off his topknot, then he is no man. I
want no more of him. I don't know why I even talk to you. You've

shown me how impossible it is for a sangnom to understand the importance of our traditions."

"If I were you, I'd be working up more of a sweat if he were threatening to cut off an essential part of his anatomy instead of his hair, but to each his own. We Americans put more store by the democracy of the living than the democracy of the dead."

"Korea wants no part of democracy."

"Now that's too bad. There may come a time when it would be useful to know what democracy's about, even if you don't intend to put it into practice. You're a strong woman. You could save Korea—you have the strength and the ability to do it. But you can't do it from some ancestral tomb."

There was a sharp clap. This time the queen wasn't calling the guard, but rather opening her fan to indicate the audience was at an end.

"I begin to think I've been mistaken about you, Mr. Banning."

"No, ma'am, I believe we understood one another perfectly, right from the start."

For the first time since the audience began, Marigold relaxed. She felt sure, now, that Banning would be allowed to leave unharmed, and she realized that he must have developed as quick a sense of nunchi as the Queen.

"Say no more if you value your head."

Banning sighed. "I have grown quite fond of my head."

"Then I suggest you leave while it is still on your shoulders."

5

The first time since her return that Marigold saw Mark Banning face to face was when he entered the reception room at the new French legation. Madame Duvall, the wife of the French representative—who gave every evidence of challenging Natasha Waeber as the arbiter of fashion, in her chic velvet-banded silk blouse and sunray pleated skirt—hurried across to greet him.

"Monsieur Banning, is it not? I knew it must be. I am charmed you could come. I have heard so much of you from Madame Waeber." She used her hands extensively, and her smiling lips curved enticingly over short, even teeth as she over-aspirated the H's unused in her own language. "How sweet, but you shouldn't," she gushed, as he handed her an oblong package.

Marigold caught the accusatory stare Natasha directed at their hostess and Banning. Then, very deliberately, she trained her glance on Marigold before turning her back on all of them.

Dr. Allen looked as though he would have liked to turn his back on Banning as well, but he wavered, unsure whether to acknowledge a man who was accused of having done illicit work for his government. Madame Duvall saved Dr. Allen from this quandary by taking possession of Banning's arm and leading him to the table, where champagne was being dispensed.

It had been several days since Banning's audience with the queen. He had surfaced in Seoul, then vanished, apparently without contacting anyone. However, rumors of his return had spread rapidly.

"Looks as though he's swimming in fresh waters," Sully whispered to Marigold, cocking his head in the direction of Banning and Madame Duvall, "and is Natasha peeved!"

"She doesn't appear to be too happy," Marigold agreed, not feeling particularly happy herself as she recalled Banning's remarks to the queen.

Just then, Mark Banning's eyes caught hers, only for a moment, yet it was as though he had reached across to touch her. The memory of his hands on her body turned her cheeks a flaming pink.

Marigold had wondered how she would react when she saw him, for she had realized it was only a matter of time before their paths would cross again. Once she was certain that the queen would not persecute him, she had had time to dwell on the way Banning had dismissed their relationship. That had hurt. She knew it was over, yet she also knew she still felt deeply for him. She had rehearsed their inevitable meeting countless times, imagining herself cool, calm, and in control as she greeted him. But in none of these carefully planned scenarios had she blushed and simpered like a schoolgirl.

Sully noticed the color in her cheeks and blustered, "You didn't blush like that when you laid eyes on me."

"It's hot in here." Marigold fanned herself with her handkerchief, knowing this to be the flimsiest excuse in the world. Sully seized upon the heat as a pretext for taking her out onto the terrace.

"Something did happen between you two, then," he insisted once they were outside. "I suspected it before. Now I'm sure of it."

"My dear Sully, whether it did or it didn't, it's really no business or concern of yours. Besides," she added, "it's over—finished."

"But I would like it to be my concern. I dearly would. Oh, Marigold, if only you would reconsider . . ."

Before she realized what was happening, Sully had dropped to his knees at her feet.

"Sully, please . . ." she began, attempting to pull him up.

"Oh, my heavens! We interrupt, I fear." Madame Duvall stood at the terrace door, Mark Banning at her side. "But what a charming picture! France is noted as the land of lovers, so how fitting to inaugurate our new mission with a declaration of love."

"The scene is depressingly familiar," Banning observed dryly.

"How intriguing! Would you give us leave to announce the good news?" Madame Duvall gushed.

Sully scrambled to his feet, his "You may as far as I'm concerned," coinciding perfectly with Marigold's "There's nothing to announce."

Madame Duvall must have taken this as an assent for she laughed genially, "But how silly of me! How could I announce something when I don't remember the names. Naughty of me, but I am so new. You must excuse me."

"Miss Marigold Wilder and Dr. Timothy Sullivan," Banning supplied.

"Wilder—Marigold Wilder. Why does that name, how you say— ring the bell? No, no!" she shook her finger playfully at Banning. "I remember now. The book you just presented to me—was that not by Marigold Wilder? Can this be the author?"

"It is," he said gravely.

"Now I am doubly *h*onored." Madame Duvall aspirated even this silent *H*. "Such talent! Such charm! How clever to write a whole book. I wish I could," she sighed prettily, "but my attention—how do you say it—hovers."

"Wanders," Marigold corrected, "like Mr. Banning's."

"I shan't object if monsieur's attention wanders my way from time to time," Madame Duvall observed with a tinkling laugh.

Marigold glanced quizzically at Banning before remarking smoothly, "I don't doubt it will. He's managed to lighten the hours of so many of us. He has a marked preference for married ladies, so undoubtedly your turn will come."

"They don't call Maggie 'The White Tiger' for nothing," Banning noted as Madame Duvall bridled.

No one attempted to stop her as she flounced back into the reception room, mumbling something about matters needing the hostess's attention.

"Afraid Marigold's taken the steam out of your sails," Sully remarked to Banning, though he was the one who was peeved at Marigold for having intervened. Banning, on the other hand, didn't seem to care. "Hope she hasn't scotched anything for you."

Banning turned to him. "Do you do this all the time or is there something about my arrival that brings it on?"

"Do what?" Sully demanded.

"Propose to Maggie." Then he turned to Marigold. "Or maybe it's your fault, for not making your position clear to this gentleman."

"My position?"

"On whether you are or are not a marrying woman."

"I'm as much a marrying woman as you're a marrying man, Mr. Banning," Marigold answered easily, then, noticing Sully's downcast face, "I really don't mean to hurt your feelings, Sully."

"All women are marrying women, Marigold," Sully insisted sullenly. "It's ordained by nature. If you don't realize it now, you will one day. And when you do, I may not always be waiting in the wings."

He stalked off with an air of defiance.

"Dear me! That sounded rather final. I'm afraid you upset him —or was it me?" Banning said. "I didn't know whether to come out here or not. I was afraid you might throw something."

"I don't throw things anymore."

"Don't you? Pity!"

There was a moment of stillness as they studied one another.

"You've done something very nice with your hair," Banning said at last.

"I cut it off."

"That's it. So you did. And all this fuss over cutting off the topknot. If I'd known, I'd have pointed you out to Queen Min as an example."

"But her point is that it's a tradition they're being forced to break. It's all very well for you to say you put more store by democracy of the living over democracy of the dead . . ."

Her hand flew to her lips as she realized she had betrayed the fact that she'd listened in during his audience with the queen.

"I had a suspicion you might be there," he said, "though I rather hoped you weren't. Some of the things that were said . . ."

"You needn't worry. As you so rightly pointed out, all that is in the past."

He studied her face, until she looked away. Then he said, "I suppose it is."

"Do you really believe the queen is in danger?" she asked, anxious to change the subject.

"I know she is," he replied quietly.

"Do you think she'll heed your warning?"

"I very much doubt it. She's a stubborn woman." With a very deliberate look, he added, "There's another woman I'd like to caution, but she's stubborn, too, and I doubt she would listen."

Marigold became thoughtful. "That would place Chu-sun in danger."

"I wouldn't expect anyone in the palace to rest easy. I hope your little friend wasn't too undone over the revelations about that miserable toad, Kim Tuk-so. She was holding a candle for him, as I remember it."

"She still is, though she became terribly upset when I tried to forewarn her about him. She refused to believe me, so I wasn't altogether sorry you corroborated my view of Kim. Still, I hated to see her so hurt. She wouldn't listen to what I had to say since he'd filled her with his own version of the truth. She believes him, of course, because she loves him."

"Such fidelity, even for a scoundrel—he's lucky. What a nice sort of love to have," he mused.

"But, in this case, it's a love sadly misplaced."

"Something none of us can afford, can we?" He fixed his dark eyes on hers.

"We can't," she agreed, looking away as she continued, "I only wish Chu-sun would realize I wasn't simply trying to blacken his character."

"How can you blacken something that's already as black as the ace of spades?"

"What I want is for her to be aware of what he's really like, but I don't know how to tell her so that she'll listen."

"Too bad you don't have some truer-than-life photograph of that young man in action. The ones you showed the queen seemed to have affected her more strongly than any description."

"I wouldn't use it, even if I had. She doesn't deserve to be hurt like that," Marigold said, thinking of the photograph she had taken of Kim Tuk-so amidst that harem of women. That had clearly shown the debased person he had become. It was just as well that photograph had disappeared; Chu-sun would have been devastated by it.

"Was she upset by what I said?" he asked.

Marigold nodded. "She won't speak to me, she won't answer my letters. I don't think things will ever be the same between us again."

"She's a little fool if she forgoes your friendship," Mark said. "Someone—or something—must eventually make her see the light."

"I only hope so."

"Time is the cure—trite but true. Forgiving, forgetting is just a matter of time."

"I expect you're right."

There was silence again. Neither of them moved. Even the air seemed still.

"Thank you for the camera," she said awkwardly. "It was kind of you to think of it."

"Thank you for making such good use of it. Your book's really splendid. It's been widely reviewed."

"I haven't seen any." She waited and when he said nothing, she asked cautiously, "Are the reviews . . . favorable?"

His eyes twinkled as he spoke, "Monotonously so." He reached into an inner pocket for a sheaf of papers and handed them to her. "See for yourself."

She unfolded the papers to read on the uppermost:

Miss Wilder has studied the Koreans with a clear but sympathetic eye. Her account, along with her own admirable photographs, is a triumph in bringing to light the truth about this Hermit Kingdom.

"I dare say it's because so little is known about this country," she said, refolding the reviews. "No one can possibly contradict what I've said."

"Do you *seriously* think that's why they're so good?" he asked.

She thought for a moment, then said, "Seriously speaking—no."

"Thank God! If we don't take what's owed us, no one else is going to see we do."

"JC said something like that."

"You met him?"

She told him about their meeting at the mine while she was collecting material for the next book, concluding, "I can see why you appreciate him so much—though not half as much as he appreciates you."

"Glad to hear someone appreciates me."

"Your *hostess* certainly does," Marigold said, overaspirating the *H* in imitation of Madame Duvall.

He smiled, but said nothing beyond, "She brought me out here to show me the garden." They both looked out at the formal garden laid out in front of the legation building. "It's rather silly, isn't it? Incongruous and out of place in this setting."

"I've been thinking the same thing," Marigold agreed.

"I've missed you," he said, still looking out at the garden.

When she made no answer, he turned to her. "How have you been?"

"I've survived rather well."

"I believe you." He studied her face, then asked, "Is what you told Sully really true—that you're no more a marrying woman than I'm a marrying man?"

"You taught me quite a lot in that short time we were together. Marriage is just some futile attempt at establishing a permanent arrangement in a transitory existence, so it doesn't make much sense, does it?"

"Those sound more like your abbot's words than mine."

"Perhaps. But the ideas are yours."

"Perhaps." He grew serious. "Maggie. Promise me you'll be careful. I couldn't bear for anything to happen to you . . ."

"I've fended for myself before. You didn't seem too worried when you left me alone in Wonsan."

"As I remember it, I arranged for you to go to Japan where you would have been safe. You wouldn't listen . . ."

"I was safe at Yu-chom Sa. How could anyone be safer than at a monastery?" she demanded.

"You're still not listening. You heard me warn the queen. She wouldn't listen either. Given your connections with her court, the best thing to do now that you've collected material for your new book would be to leave Korea—go back to England for a while, or back to Japan."

"Don't keep telling me what to do!" she cried, angrily flinging the sheaf of papers at him. They floated across the terrace and formal garden like giant snowflakes.

"Thank God you still throw things, Maggie," was all he said, leaning down to retrieve some of the reviews that had fluttered to the ground at his feet.

"I don't know what it is about you, but five minutes with you and I lose the serenity I found at the monastery and start screaming like a banshee!"

He stood up, smiling, "I'm awfully glad to hear that! You looked so calm and collected earlier, I thought my wild and wonderful Maggie was gone forever."

"But I don't want to be wild."

"How about wonderful?" he asked, catching hold of her hands as she went to retrieve the papers he held out.

They were interrupted by a voice at the terrace door. "I always knew that one day that spark between you two was bound to ignite." It was Natasha.

"Don't worry, Natasha—it may have ignited, but there was no conflagration," Marigold said, snatching the papers and her hands from Banning's grasp.

"So that's where you've been?" Natasha railed as Marigold left the terrace without looking back. "I've gone out of my mind waiting for you, and all the time you've been with her."

Banning did not return to the reception, nor did Marigold see or hear of him in the days ahead. She was glad to have a book to prepare and an approaching deadline. She had to concentrate on her work to the exclusion of all else. Because she was so busy, because she only left her room to take long, solitary walks and think, she was completely unaware of the pall that had fallen on the mission. She was unaware of the accusatory glances thrown in her direction by Gifford and of Herbert Farquhar's obvious concern until one day he came and knocked softly at her door.

"Marigold, may I—could I, eh, have a word with you?"

"Of course. Oh, Herbert, I'm sorry. I'm an awful guest. I do apologize."

"Well, yes, I mean no, you're not an awful guest. And I don't think there's anything to apologize for. At least, as far as I know there isn't."

He stood awkwardly in the middle of the room, studying the piles of papers and photographs spread out everywhere, looking at everything except at Marigold.

"Is there anything wrong?" she asked, at last.

"No, why should there be?" he answered defensively.

"I don't know. You said you wanted a word with me."

"Yes. Yes, I did." He sniffed soniferously, then cleared his throat.

"What is it, Herbert?"

"You haven't taken any photographs that were . . . I don't know how to put it! I shouldn't even ask it of you, I know you couldn't have done it, and yet they're saying . . ." He broke off, thoroughly miserable.

"What are they saying? And who are the 'they' that are saying whatever it is?"

"They're saying you took some terribly depraved photographs. One of them's been circulating through our own community, and now Gifford's just discovered numerous copies of it being passed among Koreans here in the capital. Everyone's saying that you took it. I know it isn't so—it couldn't be, but they're using it as a reason to malign your good name. It isn't true. It couldn't possibly be true," he repeated, as though to convince himself, then struggled on, "but I do think there's only one way to put the matter to rest and that is for you to publicly deny it." When Marigold said nothing, he finished miserably, "I hate to have to ask you to even mention such an awful thing, but in the light of the gossip and rumors, I think it's the only way."

Marigold's knuckles were white as she gripped the edge of her desk. "What kind of photographs are they talking about?" she asked at last. "You can be quite frank with me."

"There's only one that's been making the rounds, though there is talk that there were others."

"You've seen it?"

"Yes. Gifford showed it to me. It's . . . Oh, Marigold, it's disgusting. I know you couldn't have had anything to do with it because it's—it's a picture of, of women without . . ."

"Without anything on," Marigold finished for him and he nodded abjectly.

"And there was a man in the midst of the group," she described factually.

Again he nodded, then his face shot up.

"You know the picture? They've had the audacity to show it to you, then? How dare they bring that sort of filth to your notice. That disgusts me as much as anything. Who did it? Was it Gifford, for if it was, I'll have words with that young man. I fear he's been doing more than his share of gossiping about this whole business."

"No. It wasn't Gifford. And no one has shown me the photograph—but I'm quite sure I know the one you mean and—and the truth of the matter is that I did take it."

"Marigold!" He slumped down onto a chair. "Oh, Marigold, no! I don't believe it. No! No!"

"It was under duress. I couldn't help it. It was that or . . ."

"Or what! I can think of nothing and no one that could persuade a decent Englishwoman of genteel background to do such a thing! No! No!" He rose from the chair. "Nothing can excuse it. I am shocked beyond belief."

"I am sorry. I wish you would allow me to explain so that you can try to understand my position in this. I don't care about the rest, but you're important to me—I want you to understand how it happened."

Herbert Farquhar was shaken. Marigold made him sit down, then she pulled out a chair and sat opposite him before telling him the whole story. At first he wouldn't look at her, but as she continued speaking in a calm steady voice, describing Teuk-sil, the torture of her aged father, and the lecherous governor, Farquhar cried out, "Oh, no, Marigold, no! How terrible, for them—for you. But course, what else could you do? They must be told. You must explain this to everyone."

"I don't care about everyone. You are the only one who needs to know the truth." Then suddenly she realized that if this photograph was making the rounds, undoubtedly a copy would have reached the palace, and Chu-sun would have seen it. "Oh, no," she cried. "She is going to think I did it on purpose!"

"Who?" Herbert Farquhar asked.

"Chu-sun," Marigold said distractedly. "The photographic plate disappeared from my luggage soon after I took the picture. Do you know where these prints have come from?"

"I gather they were sent here from outside Seoul, but from where, I really don't know."

Marigold began pacing the room. "I suppose it is possible that Mark Banning could have done this."

"Does he know about it then?"

At her nod, a frown of disapproval crossed his face. "Do you know where he is?"

"No."

"He's so strange, the way he comes and goes. There was all that talk about him being a spy, but when he came back, I thought it must be untrue," Farquhar ruminated.

"I dare say he's gone back to the mine to make sure JC's all right."

Herbert Farquhar pursed his lips dubiously. "There's a lot of talk of Banning taking great advantage of that old man."

"JC's not complaining," Marigold assured him. "He's delighted to be there and says he's getting more than his fair share."

Farquhar frowned again. "It doesn't seem quite right to call him that."

"They are his initials," she pointed out.

"Yes, yes, but still . . . you were saying Banning might be responsible?"

"What I meant was, he's the only other person who knew about the photographs. He came to Wonsan, to Min Tae-jon's palace. He was the one who helped me get away afterwards. We stayed together . . ." she broke off.

"You stayed together," Farquhar prompted.

"For a short time. He could easily have taken the plate. He considers Kim Tuk-so, the man in that photograph, to have been wrongly appointed. He's disloyal and dishonest. Banning wanted to get him removed from office. What better way than this? But how could he! I'd only just told him I never wanted Chu-sun to know!" Marigold cried out in anguish.

"He knew all about the photographs, then." The dubious expression on Farquhar's face deepened into distrust. "Had he seen them?"

She nodded.

"And he was aware you had taken them?"

She nodded again.

"It sounds rather—rather reprehensible—on his part, at least." He paused before adding hesitantly, "Was there . . . is there? . . . Think of me as your father. Is there anything you want to confide in me?"

"I don't understand what you mean."

"Did he—did Banning try to take advantage of you in any way? Did he . . . dear oh dear, I am making a mess of this. Forgive me. Never having had a child of my own, it's difficult. But you are the daughter of my dear friend, and you must feel free to tell me if he . . . if he did anything improper."

"Anything improper?" Marigold stared at him uncomprehendingly. She thought back to the night they had spent together. She supposed he would think it improper, she supposed all of them would think it improper. Without quite knowing why, she began to laugh.

"Oh my poor, dear girl," Farquhar said awkwardly, going to put his arms around her. Then he seemed to decide against it, his arms falling loosely to his sides. "My poor dear! How terrible of him. He must be brought to account. If necessary he will be forced to make an honest woman of you . . ."

Marigold shook her head, yet she couldn't stop laughing. Perhaps it was from hearing Farquhar repeat words she had flung at Banning, perhaps it was because she was exhausted, perhaps it was because of the underlying sense of panic that gripped her.

"Oh dear, this is terrible. Worse than I thought. I liked him, and now I find he has deceived all of us. I'm beginning to think I'm no judge of human nature after all."

Marigold's first thought, after she had calmed herself and calmed Herbert Farquhar, was that she must, if necessary, force her way into the palace. She had to find Chu-sun and make her understand she wasn't responsible for what had happened.

She had expected this to be difficult, but surprisingly, after bicycling up to the palace gates and asking for Chu-sun, though she had to wait for a considerable time, Marigold was eventually told that the Lady Chu-sun would receive her.

She followed the courtier past the Kungjong-jon, where she had photographed the King, past the Hamhwa-dang, where she had first given lessons to Chu-sun, past the pleasure pavilion by the lotus pond, back to the private women's quarters, behind the orchid door.

The courtier pushed back the paper-covered door, and Marigold went in, sliding the door shut behind her.

It was dim inside. At first she thought it was a trick, that the room was empty. Then she made out a heap on the floor that looked like discarded clothing. She knelt beside it and stretched out her hand; she was startled to feel the fragile, tiny form inside, not moving, barely breathing. Though she couldn't see her, Marigold knew it was Chu-sun.

"I'm sorry, Chu-sun, deeply sorry. You must be thinking I'm responsible for circulating that photograph," her voice broke. "I'm not. I swear I'm not."

"But you did take it," Chu-sun's reply was muffled. "Can you deny taking it?"

Marigold swallowed. "No, I can't deny that. I wish I could. I have to confess I once thought of showing it to you, because I thought you should be aware of the sort of man Tuk-so is. I thought you might not believe me and that a photograph would convince you . . . but I knew I couldn't do that. I realized how much it would hurt. Believe me, I'm not the one who's behind this. I'm not responsible."

"But the photograph came from you."

"No, it didn't. The photographic plate disappeared, months ago, right after I took it, in fact."

"If you didn't do it, then that friend of yours did, that Mr. Banning," Chu-sun accused.

"I wish I could deny that," Marigold answered miserably. "You don't know how much I wish that. If I knew where he was, I'd confront him. If he's responsible for this—and frankly, I don't know who else could be then . . . then I hate him for doing something I'd told him I would never do. I hate him for hurting you this way. I can only say I'm sorry, Chu-sun, for the harm this has done to you, and beg your forgiveness."

Chu-sun sat up. Her hair hung, loose and dishevelled, around her shoulders. Her face was puffed from crying.

"What about the harm done to Tuk-so? Do you beg his forgiveness, too? Don't you realize that he has now lost face? There is nothing left for him but to commit suicide. And there is nothing left for me but to do the same."

"Chu-sun, you mustn't," Marigold said urgently. "You mustn't take your life—certainly not over this." Her voice hardened. "I very much doubt that Tuk-so is likely to do that. You have seen for yourself the sort of man he is—I wish I could have spared you . . ."

"You wish you could have spared me! You have done nothing but tell me how vile he is. Even now, I don't believe you. I love him.

You know what it is to love a man—I could see it in your face the other day when you feared the queen would harm your friend."

"It's because I do understand that I feel for you. I may love Mark Banning, but I'm not blind to his faults. If he is responsible for hurting you in this way, I should find it hard to forgive him. I believe I know why he might have done it—he distrusted Tuk-so, he felt that people should know what he is really like. Perhaps I did, too, but I would never . . ."

Chu-sun's voice rose in anger. "How dare you continue to malign one who is my very existence! Without him, my life is nothing."

"Chu-sun, you mustn't say that. Your life is important. It was given to you by God."

"How dare you talk to me of God! You . . . you . . . self-confessed hypocrite!"

Marigold winced at this scornful indictment. "I may not be a good Christian, but I have learned that God is in my heart. I do believe—in a more personal way."

"Then why has this God you claim now to believe in not taught you compassion? What right have you to stand in judgment on others, to persecute them even?" Chu-sun charged. "But how could I expect you to understand! You have your lover—the queen let him go, even though he has caused so much trouble. You say Tuk-so has no loyalty, but what loyalty has Mark Banning?"

"He is loyal to himself," Marigold replied quietly. "I used to think that everything he did was merely for personal gain, but that's not so. In his own way, he is an honest man. He does what he believes to be right, even when it's not comfortable. I dare say he thought it was right to circulate that photograph. But I don't, because it has harmed the innocent as well as the guilty."

"Look at the way you are loyal to this man you love," Chu-sun scorned. "But when I do the same, you crush me with lies and half-truths. What right have you to condemn Tuk-so after your own immoral behavior?"

"Chu-sun!" Marigold held out her arms, but Chu-sun pushed

her aside. "I'm sorry. If there were anything I could do or say to undo what has been done, I would."

"To save your own skin! Tuk-so told me you had done some reprehensible thing when you were there. He was too kind to you—he didn't tell me what it was. How could you!"

"I was forced to," Marigold said quietly.

"Just as Tuk-so must have been. I know he would never have willingly taken part in that . . . that debauchery." Chu-sun broke off, her anger giving way to pleading, "Please, tell me he did not."

Marigold was silent. She would have given anything to find the words of a comforting but honest response, but she could think of none.

"Tell me! Tell me!" Chu-sun gripped her by the shoulders and began shaking her.

"I wish I could tell you what you want to hear, Chu-sun, but I can't lie to you."

Chu-sun dropped her hands. Her voice was cold, distant. "Don't say anything more. I've had enough of your half-truths, your slander. I only received you so as to tell you to your face how shameful I consider your conduct to be. As the future crown princess, I have discussed this with the queen. Her Majesty, too, finds your behavior scandalous. At my request, she is issuing an order for you to leave the country immediately."

Marigold sat back, stunned. "Chu-sun! I don't believe you."

"You will have to believe it. You have three days in which to leave Korea forever."

Marigold stared at Chu-sun. "Why," she began, then swallowed, for the words would not come out. "Why did you *really* allow me to come in and see you?"

Chu-sun looked at her for a long time, tears streaming down her face. "I wanted to try and remember you as you once were—when you were my friend."

Marigold could feel her own tears, warm and wet as they ran

down her cheeks. "But I am your friend. I would do anything for you—anything."

"Then deny everything you and Mark Banning have said about Kim Tuk-so," Chu-sun hissed. "Tell me it is all falsehood. Tell me the man in that photograph is not Tuk-so—or that somehow you falsified it. Tell me he did it under duress. Tell me something, anything that will give me back hope and respect for the man I love. Tell me. Tell me."

She had again gripped Marigold, her fingers digging into her shoulders as she repeated over and over again, "Tell me it's not true!" Chu-sun shook her back and forth, like a rag doll.

But Marigold said nothing. Finally Chu-sun let go and collapsed back onto the floor. "Go. I never want to see you again. And I never shall."

Marigold rose, but when she hesitated at the door, Chu-sun screamed, "Go! Go!" A courtier came running and roughly escorted Marigold from the palace.

Marigold picked up her bicycle and rode blindly, oblivious to where she was going, unaware of the strange glances thrown at her, until suddenly something hard struck her and she was thrown to the ground. She lay there a moment, wondering what had happened, feeling her bones to see whether they were broken. Her left wrist had taken the brunt of the fall; it was throbbing, her cheek was bleeding.

She got up and looked back. Behind her, a group of washer-women were gathered together menacingly. Their eyes, the only visible feature under their changot, glared at her. She saw they had been at work, pounding clothes on a rock to iron them; one of them must have flung her wooden roller at Marigold for there it was, at her feet. No wonder they were called women's weapons, Marigold thought, wincing at the sharp pain. She bent down, picked up the roller, and held it for a moment before tossing it back.

"No White Tiger! White Devil!" they cried. "Shame!"

But the shame of that day did not end there. When she returned to the mission house, she found Herbert Farquhar pacing the floor, clutching a piece of paper.

"Marigold, it's . . ."

"I know." Her voice was quiet with fatigue. She pushed her hat off her head and hung it squarely on a peg of the hall rack. "I'm being ordered to leave the country."

"But your cheek—it's bleeding!"

She pressed an already soiled handkerchief to her face. "It's nothing. I'll go up and start packing. I'll have to find out about sailings."

"You don't need to worry about that. Gifford's already found there's a boat leaving Chemulpo the day after tomorrow, so that's going to work out." Despite his solicitude, there was relief in Farquhar's voice. Marigold couldn't blame him. Her presence there could only bring further embarrassment to his mission.

"That was good of him. Where is he?"

"He's comforting Sully—Sully's pretty broken up by this whole business. Poor old Sully!"

"Poor old Sully," Marigold repeated, though she couldn't help wondering why Sully deserved sympathy when it was her life that had been shattered.

In her room she pulled out her steamer trunk and began moving things from one place to another; she told herself she was getting things ready to pack. But when it grew dark and there was no reason to pretend any more, she lay down.

She remembered Chu-sun saying, "You English say birds sing, we say they cry. We are a sorrowful people. We even express our love in tears more than laughter. You can never be a Korean unless you know how to cry."

And though at that moment she felt neither particularly English nor Korean, Marigold Wilder cried.

6

That night, Marigold was awakened by the sound of footsteps running down Nam-san in the direction of the city. She got up, and peered out into the darkness. She could make out lights, moving in the direction of the palace.

She dressed hurriedly. She could hear people beginning to stir in the house, but before anyone had time to get up, she ran downstairs.

She took a large black coat of Gifford's from the rack in the front hallway and put it on; it enveloped her, which was just what she wanted. Next she found a heavy muffler and swathed it around her head, covering everything but her eyes. Forcing her hands into the deep pockets of the coat, she ran out into the night air. She decided against taking her bicycle. Instead, she joined the crowd that was running toward the palace.

She heard disquieting shouted orders.

"Deal with the Fox as you see fit!"

"Get her, dead or alive!"

"Better dead."

"Put an end to the Min rule forever!"

Marigold ran even faster. As she arrived at the palace, the crowd had already forced its way in through the Kwang-wha gate. Inside the walls, chaos reigned.

Marigold pushed and shoved her way in one direction only, toward the women's quarters. She was dismayed to find that the main body of the heavily armed marauders was following that same route.

She ran and stumbled. She was pushed, prodded, and, when she fell, almost trampled on. By some superhuman effort, she managed to scramble back to her feet.

A section of the crowd broke off and headed toward the king's quarters, forcing him to appear before them. He wore no head covering and everyone could plainly see that he had been shorn of his topknot.

The mob stared at this humiliation in disbelief. Marigold hoped they would stop there, but despite bitter cries of "Shame!" no one seemed intent on doing the king bodily harm.

"The Fox! Let's get the Fox!" the repeated cry rang out.

They turned and forced their way on toward the queen's apartments, with Marigold in their midst.

"The queen! We want the queen!"

Surely the guards wouldn't let them in! But guards were nowhere to be seen; the marauders gained easy access.

Marigold knew where the queen slept, but there was nothing she could do to save her. The mob might have listened to the revered White Tiger, but not to a former Western missionary who had now fallen out of favor. She could only hope and pray that she would be able to reach Chu-sun in time.

But as she turned in the direction of the orchid door, she heard a familiar voice cry out, "She is your queen and mine. You shall not have her."

Marigold swung around. To her consternation and horror, there, before the queen's door, stood Chu-sun with her arms outstretched.

"You shall not touch a hair on Her Majesty's head." she cried defiantly. "Not while I have breath."

The mob hesitated for a moment, then surged forward. Clawing her way through, Marigold yelled, "Get out of the way, Chu-sun!

Get out of the way. There's nothing you can do to save her. Move away or they'll kill you!"

Chu-sun raised her eyes, looking in Marigold's direction for a moment, but she did not acknowledge her. She didn't move.

"Kill me if you must have blood," she said, "but don't harm the queen."

"But they don't want you!" Marigold sobbed, "And the queen's beyond saving."

Chu-sun responded to Marigold then. "You never had faith in your heart, did you?"

As the first blow was struck, Marigold slumped forward, feeling it as sharply as if it had been directed at her. She was helpless, trapped. There was nothing she could do to save Chu-sun. Penned in by the mob, she couldn't even reach her. Marigold was forced to be a helpless witness to her slaughter. At that moment she longed to have a gun in her hand—that was the only thing that might stop these demons.

Through the melee she occasionally caught a glimpse of Chu-sun. She was bleeding profusely, but was still standing, despite the numerous blows she had sustained. She had made no attempt to escape through the door behind her, nor did she so much as raise an arm to ward off the rain of blows.

"Chu-sun, this is suicide . . ." Marigold's voice broke off. She suddenly realized that was precisely what Chu-sun was doing—committing suicide!

Swords flashed; time after time, they were lifted and came down, but not a single cry escaped Chu-sun's lips.

The assailants soon pushed her hacked and broken body aside, but as they were about to smash down the door behind her, it slid open and a sudden hush fell on the mob. Towering before them, clad in regal garments of state, her tall, gold crown on her head, was Queen Min.

The crowd fell back, momentarily overawed.

"Where is my son?" she demanded harshly. "You may have me, but you must promise to spare my son."

"He is safe," someone murmured. "The crown prince is safe."

She looked down at the body of Chu-sun.

"She would have made a worthy crown princess. I knew it from the first."

No one dared raise the first sword.

But then a guttural voice from the back of the crowd cried out, "Fools! Are you going to get the Fox now, or let her outwit you again?"

It was spoken in Korean, but the voice did not belong to a Korean. There was a scuffling, but no one moved. Then the man who had spoken pushed his way through, sword upraised. Taking deliberate aim, he brought it down on the queen's head. She reached out, clutching an iron screen at the window in an attempt to remain standing. Now the crowd was moved to action. Screaming revenge, her assailants wrenched her away from the screen and began to shower her with blows.

Everyone wanted to strike her. Blood gushed from the queen's wounds, covering her body, covering her attackers. The taste of royal blood inflamed the mob. Not content with killing the queen, the crowd began to hack her body to pieces.

"Let her burn! Let there be no remains to bury!"

"Get the tiger skin! Wrap her in her precious tiger skin."

"Be sure to burn every particle—the skin too. We want nothing left to entomb and worship!"

"Build the fire out by the Lotus Pond. This is the end of Queen Min!"

The acrid fumes of kerosene being poured onto the tiger skin filled Marigold's nostrils as she tried to force her way through. Buffetted and mauled from all sides, she was still hoping and praying for a miracle—that there might still be life in Chu-sun. But it wasn't until the mob had shouldered their gruesome burden and carried it out toward the pine grove by the pond that Marigold caught sight of Chu-sun—or what was left of her.

She had either crawled or been pushed into a corner of the ante-room, where she lay in a pool of blood. Blood poured from her wounds; both hands had been severed.

"Chu-sun! Oh, my God! Oh no!" Marigold pulled off the coat she wore and wrapped it around the maimed and wounded body. Then she cradled her friend in her arms, holding her close, crying, crooning over and over again in Korean.

"Chu-sun. Chu-sun. My dearest friend! I love you, how I love you."

Light from the rising bonfire came in through the broken paper window screens and illuminated Chu-sun's barely recognizable face. Her eyes flickered for an instant.

"Marigold?" she murmured. "It is you, Marigold."

It was the only time Marigold ever remembered Chu-sun calling her by name. She held her close.

"Yes, it's Marigold. It's me, Chu-sun."

"I knew it must be you. I saw you. The queen, is she . . . ?"

"I don't know," Marigold lied. "You were so brave and loyal. I'll never forget it."

Chu-sun's eyes closed.

"Don't die, Chu-sun. Say you forgive me. Say you are still my friend."

Chu-sun eyes flickered again, but did not open.

"You were always my friend. But tell me none of it was true—tell me Tuk-so is a good man. Tell me he loves me."

Marigold put her head down on Chu-sun's shoulder, her lips close to her ear, repeating, "None of it was true. He's a good man, he loves you,"

A smile flitted across Chu-sun's lips. "I knew it."

As her friend's breath faded, Marigold suddenly thought of one of the sijo that Chu-sun had taught her:

In the blood that was spilt
A woman is soaking her hair.
Could weeping regain what was lost
She might weep for a hundred years.

"Oh, if only it might, Chu-sun!" Marigold sobbed, though she knew her friend could not hear her.

She stayed there, holding Chu-sun's lifeless body in her arms, rocking it as though she were a mother comforting a child. Yet it wasn't Chu-sun, now past all comfort, whose fears she sought to allay, but her own. She could hear the roar of the mob outside, and, for the first time, Marigold felt alone and helpless.

She heard footsteps in the anteroom. They had come back for Chu-sun—she had known they would. She threw herself over the body, screaming, "You can't have her. You shan't have her."

She felt a hand grasp her shoulder and turned, lashing out at the face above her with her nails. "You shan't take her. I won't let . . ."

"Maggie!" It was Banning. His face was bleeding where she'd scratched him. He took one look at Chu-sun, then put his arms around Marigold. "Come away, Maggie. She'd dead. There's nothing anyone can do for her now. We've got to get you out of here."

"I don't care about me. Look! Just look! You did this as surely as if you raised the knife yourself. You're responsible. How could you! How dare . . ."

"This isn't the time or place for an argument," he said tersely, roughly pulling her to her feet.

"You were the only one who knew about that photograph. You stole it from me. You took it out of my luggage that night. You always kept your mind on your work whatever you were doing, didn't you?"

"Shut up!" he said fiercely. When she cried out as he tore her away from Chu-sun, he slapped her face.

"Damn it, Maggie! Don't you realize you'll be next!"

"I don't care," she whimpered.

"Well I do. I'm not having any heroic deaths on my conscience!"

"You already have," she sobbed, struggling to free herself. He took off his coat and threw it around her, then tied the sleeves together, encasing her in a strait-jacket.

"Tie me up. Do what you want. I won't go. You can't make me," she screamed.

"I'm warning you, Maggie . . ." He broke off. Something had caught his attention. Her eyes followed his. Stuck in the iron screen at the window was a finger. Its talon nail clearly identified it as the only piece of Queen Min's body that had escaped the mob.

Banning reached up and extracted it with the care of a biologist gathering a prized specimen. He wrapped it in his handkerchief and put it in his pocket. Marigold watched him in silence. She knew that without some part of the queen for burial, there could be no tomb, no place for her descendants to worship her memory.

"Come on. We must go," he said urgently.

"But Chu-sun—she deserves a proper burial, too," she argued.

"We can't wait any longer, Maggie."

"But she's deserves to be buried . . ." She didn't finish her sentence, for he'd found the muffler she had been wearing. He wrapped it around her hair and covered her mouth saying, "There's nothing else for it, if you won't keep quiet."

Then he flung her over his shoulder, muttering, "You're still no light weight, Maggie," but when she struggled against him, he struck her, saying sharply, "This isn't a game—it's life and death. These antics of yours are going to endanger both our lives. I'm not willing to be a martyr to any cause, even if you are."

She knew he must be staying close to the walls, since she grazed them so often. Sometimes, at an approaching sound, he stopped perfectly still, holding her tightly against him. Then he moved on again. Gradually the noise of the crowd receded, but even when she was sure they must have passed the palace enclosure, he kept walking, then climbing. When, at last, he set her on her feet unceremoniously and loosened the covering from her head, she realized they were at the mission.

"As I said, you're no light weight . . ." he began, pushing back the hair from her face and looking at her for the first time. "Oh, Maggie. My darling Maggie! I never wanted to see such pain in those lovely eyes of yours."

She struggled to free herself of the coat, and slowly, very slowly, he began untying the sleeves. "I'd have given anything to have spared you this. In time, I hope the horror of this day will fade, but you must always remember that nothing you or anyone else could have done would have prevented this from happening. Only the queen herself could have prevented it. She could have saved herself by going into hiding but she wouldn't. The king and that precious son of hers chose flight over valor. They disguised themselves as women and made their way to the Russian legation." Banning's voice was grim as he added, "The king even took along his favorite concubine to comfort him in his trials." He patted his pocket. "But at least the queen won't be forgotten. In her way, she was a great woman. She deserves to be remembered."

When at last he removed the scarf covering Marigold's mouth, harsh accusations poured from her lips. "You thought about the queen, because she was your business partner. What about Chusun's body! Her death lies at your door—don't you owe her a decent burial, too? Unlike the queen, she didn't have to die—but she chose death because you circulated that photograph of Kim."

She waited, hoping for a denial, but none came.

"Don't you have anything to say?" she demanded.

"Only that I suppose, ultimately, I am responsible. I'm sorry Chu-sun died, but there's not much that can be done for someone who is determined to die. Her country will view her as a heroine who gave her life for her queen, instead of as a foolish woman taking her own life over a worthless lover."

"You're cold-blooded—heartless! Don't expect me to thank you or feel indebted to you for my life."

"I never expect anything from anyone."

The quietness of his response surprised her. She hesitated, then remembered he'd denied nothing. He had caused Chu-sun to kill herself, and he wasn't even sorry.

"When you admitted to the queen that you were thoroughly disreputable, I was prepared to champion you just as foolishly as Chu-sun championed Tuk-so. I thought you meant well, even when you did things I thought were wrong. Now I realize you spoke nothing but the truth. You *are* a thoroughly disreputable man."

He winced at her scorn but didn't reply. "I'm glad I'll never have to see you again."

"You're right, it's unlikely we'll see one another again. You're returning to England. I only wish you'd gone sooner—then you might have been spared."

"Spared from knowing what sort of man you really are—from loving someone every bit as worthless as Tuk-so? No!" She shook her head vehemently. "No. I'm glad I stayed to see you just as you are. My love for you was the last thing I needed to be rid of. Now I'm free."

But as Marigold entered the mission, she didn't feel free, only drained of all feeling. Herbert Farquhar came running to meet her.

"Marigold! My dear girl! This is terrible!" He looked in horror at her puffed eyes, her tear-stained face, her clothes covered with blood. "But the main thing is that you're back—safe and sound. We've been so worried! Terrible rumors have been circulating about bloodshed at the palace. We were so afraid you might be involved. They say the king and queen have fled, but no one seems to know where—no one seems to know anything for sure."

"The king and the crown prince are at the Russian legation. It was the queen they wanted," Marigold said wearily. "They found her. She is dead."

"You look half-dead yourself, Marigold. You need tea. Tea will put you right," Herbert said, drawing her over to the fire and sitting her down in an armchair.

Nothing, not even tea, would put her right, but Marigold saw no point in arguing.

"Gifford, tell halmoni to bring tea," Farquhar called out.

Gifford came into the room.

"Have you seen my overcoat, Marigold?"

Dazedly Marigold looked from Gifford to Farquhar, trying to understand this ludicrous discussion of tea and overcoats after all the pain, the bloodshed, the horror she had witnessed that day.

"Chu-sun bled to death on your overcoat, Gifford. I wanted to keep it because it was soaked with her blood but Ma . . . someone forced me to leave. Probably by now that mob has thrown her body on the fire where they burned the queen, and your coat along with it."

"How bloody awful." It was unclear whether Gifford's comment applied to the loss of his coat or the events surrounding it.

"That describes it exactly, Gifford, bloody awful." There was an unrelenting note in her voice that had never been there before.

"Marigold's very upset, Gifford," Herbert said in a loud whisper.

"So they did away with the queen." Gifford's voice lacked any sympathy. A thought struck him that was obviously less than pleasing. "I suppose this means since she issued the order for you to leave, now you won't have to go."

"Can't you understand anything!" Marigold cried out in despair. "There's nothing—absolutely nothing—left to stay for."

7

What difference does it make whether or not it's a lot of hocus-pocus? What difference did it ever make? Why did I torment myself over it? Marigold Wilder wondered, her hands clasped before her face, her head bowed as her brother-in-law's intonation of the great litany began.

"*O God the Father of Heaven: have mercy upon us miserable sinners,*" Algernon Reid-Banning, his once slender figure now inclined to corpulence, raised his voice to resound throughout the gray walls of St. Swithin's.

Four years earlier, Marigold had knelt in the same pew wrestling with her doubts, attempting to please her father without being true to herself. She never thought then that she would have to cross the world and live in an alien culture in order to see beyond the dogma and ritual and find God in her heart. The love of Christ wasn't confined within the wall of St. Swithin's any more than the truth and compassion of the goddess Kannon was confined in the Kaigenji Temple in Ming Chou: like Lafcadio Hearn's Unknowable Power, they were everywhere. She supposed the abbot at Yu-chom Sa would have said that her journey of discovery had long since been decided.

"*O God the Father of Heaven: have mercy upon us miserable sinners.*" Primrose Reid-Banning, now a very proper young matron, led the response. Though already midterm in her third pregnancy in as many years of marriage, she was still lovely; there was, however, a petulant line to her mouth that Marigold had not remembered. She was never troubled with my doubts, Marigold thought, so that couldn't be the cause. Prim now had what she wanted—a comfortable home, a respected husband, and lovely children—or had she?

"From all evil and mischief;"

Three-year-old Esmeralda played happily with the plume on her aunt's hat, then she undid the bow under her chin. Her Aunt Maggie smiled, kissed her niece's chubby little hands, but made no attempt to stop her. Esmeralda liked this newly discovered aunt of hers. She never got angry, like her mother, no matter what she did. Only when she tugged at that funny piece hanging on a chain around her neck did her aunt remove her hands, but then she reached into her pocket and pulled out a clothes pin she'd made into a doll and gave it to her. Aunt Maggie was full of surprises. Esmeralda smiled up at her, thinking of the story she'd told last night abut the swinging games played by girls in Korea. She intended to try them out on her own swing.

"From sin, from the crafts and assaults of the devil; from thy wrath, and from everlasting damnation."

As Algernon ceremoniously encircled the altar, the candlelight glinted on the gold embroidered orphreys of his chasuble, and Marigold was reminded of the pulsa kori that the Queen's mudang used to perform. How shocked Algernon would have been if he knew she was comparing his ritualistic movements with Chilyongun's shamanistic magic.

"From all blindness of heart; from pride, vainglory, and hypocrisy; from envy, hatred, and malice, and all uncharitableness."

Marigold still received regular news of the Seoul community from Herbert Farquhar. Sully had proposed and been accepted by young Miss Gardner, though her mother had insisted they wait until she was eighteen before they could marry. A whole year— Miss Gardner thought she would die waiting. Gifford thought he would die, too. "He is particularly fond of Sully," Herbert wrote. "He's convinced Sully's making another tragic mistake; I rather think he has hopes of convincing Sully of that fact during the waiting period."

Diplomatic hospitality flourished, for Natasha Waeber and Madame Duvall constantly sought to outdo one another in every respect.

"There is talk of the Waebers being recalled to Petersburg—a promotion, no doubt, for having delivered Korea into the Russian camp. Dr. Allen has been upset by the move in that direction. I understand he did everything possible to persuade the Koreans to turn toward the West.

"Again, many thanks for your contributions, which are gratefully received," he always concluded, referring to the money Marigold raised at the various talks she gave. "Though you refuse to admit it, you are the best representative our cause has ever had."

Since her return, Marigold had been much in demand as a speaker. What had begun as a short address to the women of the St. Swithin's parish had soon turned into a speaking tour: church groups, general audiences in town halls, and, finally, an address before the Royal Geographic Society in London. That invitation was extended only after heated discussion concerning rumors of certain unmentionable photographs; the society had reached the conclusion that no Englishwoman in her right mind could possibly have committed such a deplorable act. Though the members could not bring themselves to ask her directly about the truth of this unsavory report, their meeting with Miss Wilder had convinced them that she was definitely of sound mind. In fact, she made such a favorable impression on them that she was assured, had she not been female, she would have been invited to join their ranks.

Primrose was puzzled by her sister's success and more than a little envious. She didn't know what to make of the special treatment Marigold received; even her own husband no longer argued with her. It was strange—it was almost as though he didn't dare.

Lately, in fact, Marigold found her brother-in-law more congenial than her sister. Primrose had welcomed her back with the preconceived idea that she would take up her position of maiden aunt, caring for the children or doing what needed to be done around the house. But Primrose had made a great mistake in allowing Marigold to talk to the women of the parish. Just look at the result—she was bustling around all over the country, and the publicity that surrounded her was deplorable.

"Father would never have approved," she contended, invoking a dictum that had never before failed to move Marigold.

"Don't you think so, Prim?" her sister responded, sipping her tea. "I rather believe he would have enjoyed it. Anyway, it doesn't make any difference. We'll never know. And the fact of the matter is, I enjoy doing it. That's what counts."

Primrose had been overwhelmed by this argument. The very idea of a woman doing something just because she enjoyed it! Marigold used to have a sense of responsibility; they'd always been able to rely on her knowing what needed to be done and then doing it. What good was it to have a sister who acted just as though she were free? And even at the advanced age of thirty, Marigold looked more attractive now than when she had left home. When she measured her own widening girth with her hands, Primrose felt that life really hadn't been fair.

But the crowning blow had come when Marigold received a letter from her publisher suggesting a book on Afghanistan.

"You can't do it. You must say no, that's all there is to it," Primrose had said firmly. Seeing the lack of concern on her sister's face, she had appealed to her husband, "She can't, can she, Algernon?"

"Who can't what, my pet?" Algernon had asked, carefully cutting around the yolk of his fried egg. His habit of separating the white from the yolk before eating his eggs had seemed adorable when they first married; now it irritated his wife beyond endurance.

"Marigold can't go to—to Arabia."

"I don't know that I have any say in the matter," Algernon said cautiously. "I can advise, of course, and my advice would be that it would be a difficult place for a woman."

"A very difficult place," Primrose seconded. "And if you don't have a say, I do. I may not be the elder, but I am married, which gives me precedence. I forbid you to go to Arabia, Marigold, and that's that."

With an air of determination and defiance, she eyed her sister across the breakfast table. Marigold seemed completely unruffled by this ultimatum.

"I'm not thinking of going to Arabia—not yet, anyway."

"Good! So that's settled then."

"But I have agreed to do the book on Afghanistan. In fact, I'm already making inquiries about sailings."

"How long would you be gone?" Algernon asked, since Primrose was speechless.

"I really don't know. It depends how things are when I get there. I've found it best not to plan too much in advance—things so often don't turn out the way you expect them to."

Algernon cast a telling look at his wife. "A very wise observation." Then, as though for solace, he reached for another slice of toast, layered it with butter, and generously spooned marmalade on top. Without being asked, Primrose refilled his tea cup. In silence, both sisters watched as he dispatched toast and tea.

"*From fornication, and all other deadly sin; and from all the deceits of the world, the flesh, and the devil.*"

Marigold bent forward in the pew, burying her face in her hands. Algernon's words had inadvertently conjured up the memory of the steam bath she had shared with Mark Banning. The more she tried to dismiss the thought, the more it persisted. She felt the warmth of blood rising to her cheeks and buried her face even more deeply into her hands. When, she glanced up at last, she caught Algernon beaming with pleasure at her piety.

Marigold was sure she would never see Mark Banning again. She could never forget the bitterness of their parting and the accusations she had made—accusations that turned out to be not only unjustified but disastrous. Mark had brought magic into her life. Would she ever feel for another man the emotions he had evoked? The secretary of the Royal Geographic Society had been most attentive to her when she was in London. He'd even called at the vicarage on the pretext of being in the vicinity, though later it became clear he had made the journey for the purpose of seeing her.

He was a nice man, well-mannered, well-spoken, well-educated . . . well-everything. Algernon had liked him tremendously. Perhaps that's why Marigold hadn't. No, that wasn't it exactly. She did like him, but she could never imagine him making love to her, particularly in a steam bath. In fact, he hadn't aroused ideas of love at all. She had felt she knew all about him within ten minutes of meeting him. Mark Banning, on the other hand, was like the dragon that writhed around Korean vases and bowls and could never be viewed in its entirety—even if she'd spent a lifetime with him, she could never have known all there was to know about him.

"From all sedition, privy conspiracy, and rebellion; from all false doctrine, heresy, and schism; from hardness of heart, and contempt of thy Word and Commandment."

She buried her head in her hands again, remembering the anguish she had suffered when, after her return, she had learned from Lee that Mark Banning had been imprisoned. After parting from her at the mission, he had returned to the palace to take Chusun's body for burial and the mob had captured him. No one knew where he was being held—worse yet, no one seemed to care. The Western community had turned its back on him; even Dr. Allen, his country's representative, refused to become involved. Lee had turned to Marigold, even though she was so far away, because he knew of no one else who would be willing to help. He did so with a sense of shame, since he had been the one who had taken the photographic plate of Kim Tuk-so from her luggage. He had had copies made and eventually had them circulated.

Lee's letter explained a great deal, but it filled her with fear for Mark's fate—and with shame for her unwarranted accusations of him. Lee wrote:

But the worst thing is that Mr. Banning is being blamed for my act, even though he knew nothing of it until afterwards. People here say he did it to besmirch your good name. Perhaps that is why no one will come to his aid.

My intention was to make Kim Tuk-so lose face and force him out as governor of our province. I did not realize that you—or others would suffer. For that reason, I now regret very much what I did.

The photograph did cause Kim to be removed from office. However, he has since ingratiated himself with the Russians in Seoul and is now carrying out their wishes, which makes Mr. Banning's position even more precarious. I beg your help.

After that letter, Marigold's life became a nightmare; her imagination ran riot envisioning the tortures she knew Kim Tuk-so was capable of inflicting with Mark as his victim. She realized, with considerable anguish, that she was responsible; she had goaded Banning into returning to the palace for Chu-sun's body. But wallowing in recrimination was of little use. She had to do something. Her first inclination was to appeal to Natasha on Banning's behalf, but she remembered their last encounter and doubted that plan would work. Boris was probably gloating. Dr. Allen, Mr. Gardner, Sully, Gifford, even Farquhar, because of her previous accusations that Banning had circulated the photograph, were unlikely to help him.

But perhaps public opinion would! Marigold sat down and wrote her first political piece on Korea, denouncing the queen's murder along with that of the future crown princess, the domination of the king by the Russians, the power given to men like Kim Tuk-so; more urgently, the article deplored the wrongful imprisonment and probable torture of a Westerner, an American, Mark Banning.

She sent the article to the *Times* in London, and cabled a copy to the *New York Times*. Since Marigold was already regarded as an authority on Korea the article was printed verbatim. It caused little stir in London, but in New York the matter of an American citizen being held against his will was immediately raised in Congress.

She did not have to wait very long before learning that, on behalf of his government, Dr. Allen had lodged an official protest with the king and that Mark Banning had subsequently been released. Newspaper accounts were sparse, since Banning adamantly refused to be interviewed and turned down large sums to tell his story. From Lee, Marigold learned that while the king claimed to have no knowledge of the affair, he had been prompted to offer a reward to anyone who could locate the Westerner who had been able to save the only remaining relic of his consort. Shortly thereafter, Kim Tuk-so had "discovered" Banning's whereabouts.

In the same letter, Lee also informed Marigold of his marriage to Teuk-sil. "We expect to have many children," was the closest his tradition would allow him to come to confessing that he loved his new wife. Yet Lee reported sorrows amid his happiness:

Mr. Banning suffered greatly while in captivity, though he has made light of it. He has now left Korea, for his own country, I believe, though his plans were as indefinite as ever.

Regrettably, Kim Tuk-so continues to exert influence, pocketing large bribes from those who want to advance under the present administration.

Will nothing rid Korea of such men!

In reply, along with a generous gift of money and her congratulations to the newlyweds, Marigold tried to console Lee. She pointed out that such people were not confined to Korea; regrettably, they were everywhere.

"*Good Lord, deliver us,*" Marigold echoed with the rest of the congregation, fervently wishing that the world might be delivered of all such self-seeking, power-hungry tyrants.

"In all time of our tribulation; in all time of our wealth; in the hour of our death," she sent up a silent prayer for Chu-sun. The memory of her final lie on behalf of Tuk-so while her friend lay dying still made Marigold uneasy. She wondered whether Chu-sun could see her now, still struggling with that conflict between compassion and honesty. Thanks to Banning's generous gift of gold, the geomancers had been able to find an appropriate burial place where Chu-sun's body had been ceremoniously entombed.

"And in the day of our judgement," Algernon finished. Marigold had never been able to imagine such a day, not as a final point in time. But she supposed each person was held accountable for his—or her—own actions; the Buddhists called that karma. She bore responsibility for what had happened to Banning; in looking back, she realized how unimportant the burial of Chu-sun's body had been, compared with the suffering he must have had to endure since then. She had hoped to hear from him so she could relieve her conscience by telling him how she felt, but no word came. That silence was her penance.

"That it may please thee to keep and strengthen in the true worshipping of thee, in righteousness and holiness of life, thy Servant Victoria, our most gracious Queen and Governor.

"We beseech thee to hear us, good Lord."

Baby Algernon gurgled and was hushed by his mother, who held tightly to his leather reins. Marigold leaned over and offered to take him. Primrose passed the child to her with obvious relief. A little over a year old, he was a sturdy fellow, but much despised by Esmeralda who, quite rightly, suspected her father of liking him best.

"That's not so," Marigold had assured her when the little girl pointed this out. "How could anyone help but find you the sweetest, most lovable, most adorable girl in the whole wide world? It's only because he likes you so much that your father has to be particularly attentive to little Algie, just so he won't feel left out."

Primrose had come in just as Esmeralda asked, "And what about the one that's inside Mummy's tummy? Won't they both like that new one the best of all?"

"Marigold! What have you been telling this child? Come here, Esmeralda." Glaring at Marigold, Primrose had taken her daughter's hand and hurried her from the room. "Come along with Mummy. She'll take you out to the cabbage patch and explain these things to you."

"That it may please thee to rule her heart in thy faith, fear, and love and that she may ever more have affiance in thee, and ever seek thy honor and glory."

Marigold put Esmeralda between herself and Harriet Keane, holding Algie in front of her.

"Little Algie's a dear, but I'm just as glad Dr. Keane and I never had any," Harriet had confessed. "I could never have coped."

John Keane glanced over his wife's bowed head at Marigold and smiled. Though Marigold smiled back, she was glad that Harriet's eyes remained tightly closed. John had been unusually attentive to Marigold since she'd been back; she had the uncomfortable feeling that Harriet suspected her husband of liking her more than he should.

"That it may please thee to be her defender and keeper, giving her the victory over her enemies."

King Kojong was still ruling the country from the Russian legation, undoubtedly under Russian guidance. People said he was considering naming himself emperor and renaming Korea the Empire of the Great Han. This was grandeur, indeed, for a king virtually without a kingdom to call his own.

Still, there must be some money left in the royal coffers—the king had refused to move back into Kyongbok palace and was having another palace built near the South Gate; and he was still paying geomancers to search out a proper burial site for the finger of the queen that Banning had found. It was to be a tomb of magnificent proportions, a high mound encircled by stone images with a polished marble table placed in their midst for sacrificial offerings—a tomb specifically designed for the finest of women, a true consort.

Had she been more of a consort and less of a queen, she still might be alive alongside the king and their son, living in luxury at the Russian legation. But even after her death, Queen Min was reaching out to claim her due. The treasury was being rapidly depleted by the geomancers' search for the perfect tomb site: a hill facing the sun, the phoenix, flanked by equally proportioned hills for protection—the dragon to the east, the tiger to the west, with an advancing dragon, or mountain line that curved back onto itself to ensure that no other peak could command a view over such a sacred place. The eventual funeral for that one finger was sure to be of such lavish proportions that it would threaten to bankrupt this poor nation, but tradition demanded it for the consort of the king.

While the king preserved the myth of Queen Min as perfect consort, Marigold took steps to preserve the myth of Chu-sun as loyal servant and martyr to the queen. She would see that Chu-sun lived on, not only in her own memory but in the memory of others. The final chapter of her second book on Korea, *Turmoil in the Land of the Morning Calm* had been devoted to Chu-sun's valor. Marigold never gave a speech without mentioning her story.

"That it may please thee to illuminate all Bishops, Priests, and Deacons, with true knowledge and understanding of thy Word; and that both by their preaching and living they may set it forth and shew it acordingly."

Algernon's chant became particularly sonorous on this exhortation. He virtually bowed like Tuk-so in the direction of the mitred bishop who sat on his red plush throne beside the altar. Algernon was under consideration for the position of chaplain to the bishop, and his future rested on the outcome of this service.

He had been interviewed twice and had invited the bishop to dine at the rectory. Or rather, the bishop had invited himself, saying it was important for the whole family to be suited to life within the cathedral close.

In preparation for this event, Primrose had outdone herself. she had bought a new dress for the occasion—chic, but not too chic—with a braid-trimmed bolero that disguised her condition, and an exceptionally high collar that gave a wonderful arch to her neck. The table had been set with her finest lace cloth and her very best silver. She had fretted over the lamb cutlets, peas, and raspberry sorbet until the cook had threatened to leave if she stepped into the kitchen one more time.

But then Marigold had spoiled everything. She had originally offered to stay with the children, but Algernon decided it would be best for the nursemaid to present them to the bishop and then immediately whisk them away. So Primrose had instructed Marigold to ensure that the food came to the table hot and was suitably served; she expected her sister to pass things and generally make herself agreeable. But Marigold had abysmally failed to follow instructions, mainly because the bishop had refused to allow her to leave his side. He asked about her travels and her writing and her talks; he knew Herbert Farquhar and discussed at length the Korean mission. He didn't appear to notice what he ate or drank and spared not so much as a passing glance for the children or Prim's new dress.

Primrose could not have been more provoked.

"The bishop was supposed to judge whether we were suitable for life within the close. How can he tell, when he didn't say more than two words to anyone except Marigold, and she won't even be there?" she had wailed. "It isn't fair. She didn't even dress properly for the occasion—those gaudy Korean blouses she wears are simply hideous!"

"I agree, my dear, but don't carry on so," Algernon tried to mollify her. "My lord bishop was satisfied, quite pleased, in fact. He is to come to the service Sunday, and if all goes well, the position is mine—I mean, ours. And who knows where it may lead—a deanship even."

"Or even a seat in the House of Lords. Oh, Algernon!" Primrose exclaimed.

So there sat the bishop, crook in hand, surveying Algernon and his congregation, in turn, and only occasionally nodding off.

"That it may please thee to preserve all that travel by land or by water, all women laboring of child, all sick persons and young children; and to shew thy pity upon all prisoners and captives."

When her inquiries elicited that the RMS *Oceanic* had a cabin available amidships, Marigold had booked passage to Afghanistan. This time Primrose raised no objections.

Marigold found England confining; she was anxious to leave. She had tasted the wider world and found it to her liking. She would miss the children, but it was wonderful to be free and independent. She earned a comfortable income. She could come and go as she pleased without answering to anyone. She was a very lucky woman, and yet, sometimes, when she was alone, she had a sense of emptiness, a suspicion that her life lacked something vital.

"That it may please thee to have mercy upon all men." And women too, Marigold added silently.

The litany was finally drawing to a close. Perhaps that was what had caused the bishop to look up from his dozing with renewed interest. For the first time, Algernon stumbled in his delivery, his expression neither happy nor particularly holy.

Esmeralda stood up and looked toward the back of the church. Primrose nodded sharply to Marigold to make her daughter kneel down again and turn toward the altar.

It was such a long service for a little girl Marigold thought, as she put her arm around the child and pulled her plump knees down onto the cushion. But Esmeralda refused to look back at the altar, something had caught her attention.

"Is that a jewel, Auntie, or just a shiny piece of glass?" Esmeralda whispered.

"Sshh . . ." Marigold began, but Esmeralda's question struck a familiar chord. Abruptly, she, too, turned around.

At a nonchalant, leisurely pace, advancing down the aisle between the pews came a figure known to them all. Among all the black-clothed men, he was conspicuous for wearing brown—his boots with their three-inch heels were brown, too. In his cravat was the object of Esmeralda's attention, a huge, shiny red stone.

"*We beeseech thee to hear us, good Lord.*" Prim's intonation was deliberately cast in Marigold's direction in an attempt to prevent this disruption of Algernon's big day.

Mark Banning paused as he reached the end of their pew. He returned the bishop's stare, then glanced across at Algernon, as though deciding whether they were going to provide him with sufficient amusement. Then he sat down at the end of the pew and leaned back.

Primrose was horrified. "Tell him to kneel," she hissed. The hiss carried to the altar, where the bishop clearly heard the command, as did Algernon. Marigold turned toward Banning; over John Keane's bowed head, he solemnly winked at her!

Infuriated, Algernon put special emphasis on the next exhortation, "*That it may please thee to forgive our enemies, persecutors, and slanderers, and to turn their hearts,*" but then omitted the last two to go directly into the *kyrie eleison,* as though he suddenly couldn't wait for the service to be over.

"He's ruined Algernon," Primrose whispered to Marigold in cold fury. Not even the ten-pound note Banning dropped in the plate saved him from her wrath. "That's what he wanted, of course. You suspected it from the first, and you were right. I imagine he's never forgiven me for having chosen Algernon over him; now he's deliberately come to ruin his chances."

Marigold's mind was racing. She was as stunned by his unexpected arrival, his complicit wink, as she had been the first time he had appeared.

"He could scarcely have known the bishop would be here today," she pointed out to her sister, attempting to regain her own composure through logic.

"Perhaps not. But even so, he can see that the bishop is here now," Primrose correctly observed. "He's paid him no more deference than Algernon. He didn't even bow his head when the bishop passed down the aisle and bestowed his blessing."

Marigold wondered whether Banning had winked at the bishop, too, but she didn't dare voice that thought aloud. Primrose, in her delicate condition, might have been overcome.

8

Banning stood at the end of the pew, waiting as everyone filed out. Marigold's heart raced; as she drew close to him, she noticed scars on his face, and she sensed deeper changes in him, beyond the obvious. As though to ward off her scrutiny, he turned his attention immediately to the children.

"I brought a present for little Merry here," he said, tousling Esmeralda's blonde hair, then leaning down so she might kiss his cheek. "But I didn't even know about this little fellow." He took Algie's reins from Marigold with, "He's not a horse, but I'll just bet he'd like to ride one," and there, in the church, hoisted him onto his shoulders. Algernon gurgled with delight as he was trotted down the emptying aisle.

Primrose hurried forward in an attempt to cut Banning off before he could reach the bishop on the porch. But Banning resolutely refused to accompany Prim outside by way of the side door.

"Algie's going to be slighted if I don't say hello to him right away," he pointed out.

"But he mustn't be disturbed or upset today, it's a very special day," Primrose explained in the measured tones she used with Esmeralda when the child misbehaved. "Algernon's being considered as chaplain to the bishop—it could mean a deanship and eventually even . . ."

Words failed her; she didn't dare announce too publicly her ambition to have a husband who sat in the House of Lords and commanded his own palace.

"Algie, a bishop!" Banning concluded for her. "My God! He'd be perfect for the part."

Just as though it were a role in a play! Primrose closed her eyes in dismay as Banning, with little Algie still on his shoulders, said, "I'll have to put in a word for him," and trotted out onto the porch.

The bishop peered at him. "Now who is this gentleman, that is what I've been wondering."

Algernon did no more than give his cousin a weak smile, leaving Banning to respond, "I'm Mark Banning, Algie's cousin from America." He shook the bishop's hand heartily, without deference for the purple, just as though he were any ordinary cleric. Then, clasping little Algie's chubby ankles again, he demanded of his cousin, "I'd heard about Merry, Algie, but you sly dog, you! You didn't tell me about this stout lad, nor the one that's on the way. I see how you've kept yourself occupied since I last saw you. I'd never have thought you had it in you! Congratulations!" And taking Algernon's limp hand from his side, Banning wrung it with equal heartiness.

"Is this the present for me?" Esmeralda pointed to the box under Banning's arm.

"That's for this lady," Banning said, handing the box to Marigold. Apart from his solemn wink inside the church, this was his first direct acknowledgment of her presence.

Marigold took the present, examining his face, the scars over his eyebrow and on his cheek. Again, disturbed by this scrutiny, he demanded, "Well, aren't you going to open it?"

"Yes. Yes, of course."

Inside was the gray-green celadon bowl decorated with the writhing dragon that Sully had sold to Banning.

"What a nice little pot," Primrose remarked as Marigold held it up for all to see.

"It's not a nice little pot—it's a piece of royal celadon, very special, very rare." She ran her fingers over the dragon, saying to Banning, "Teuk-sil told me they called you their Blue Dragon."

"And you were their White Tiger," he replied.

"I never expected . . ." she broke off, feeling a lump in her throat.

"The piece of celadon," he concluded for her. She'd been about to say she never expected to see him again, but she decided it was better to leave it at that. "Let's say it's yet another attempt to even the score. If you hadn't written that article, I'd still be in prison, or worse. My life seems to be constantly in your hands."

"Ah, now I have it." The bishop beamed, glad to have finally placed Banning. "This must be the American gentleman you wrote about in that spirited article I read in the *Times*."

"But what about my present?" Esmeralda pouted. "You said you brought something for me."

"This," Banning reached into his pocket and held aloft a string of pearls, "is for you."

"Those look like real pearls." The bishop observed the luminosity of the pearls as they spun and twisted in the sunlight. "And very fine ones, at that."

"Of course they're real. Merry couldn't wear anything else."

"Then they must be worth a great deal of money. Aren't they— too grand a present for a little girl?" the Bishop wondered.

"She may not appreciate them now, but she soon will. Won't you, Merry?" Banning asked, bundling them up and casually putting them into the little girl's hands.

She ran them speculatively through her fingers, then bit one of them, at which her mother intervened with, "My lord bishop was perfectly right. Mummy had better take care of those for you, Esmeralda," and promptly pocketed the string.

"But what are we going to do about this little fellow—little Algie, is it? I thought as much. I know." Banning reached up and removed the red stone from his cravat.

"That's a very pretty piece of glass," Esmeralda commented solemnly.

"It's a ruby," Banning corrected.

"Is it possible—a ruby that size?" the bishop asked with increased interest.

Banning nodded. "It was given to me by Amir Abdur Rahman as a token for a small service I was able to render. I've since been investigating the mine it came from, somewhere east of Kabul."

He was talking in much the same way as when he had first come to Barleigh, saying the sort of things that had made Marigold accuse him of bragging. Yet now it seemed so different to her. Perhaps it was because she knew him better, perhaps it was because she understood that these priceless objects were worthless to Banning in themselves. It was only the pursuit of them he relished.

"Finest stones I've seen," he concluded.

"Just shows how effective Algernon's sermonizing was this morning. He's made me see the wisdom of divesting myself of everything. That was the most meaningful sermon I've heard this twelve-month."

"This is quite a compliment your cousin pays you," the bishop commented to Algernon, who, guessing it was probably the only sermon that Banning had heard in the past year, could only smile a weak assent. "I found it quite . . . quite thought-provoking, but that it could produce such results speaks for itself. I must say, Reid-Banning, I had no idea you had such interesting and resourceful relatives. I'm surprised you have never mentioned them to me before. I was simply enchanted by Miss Wilder's stories at dinner the other night, and now you've arranged for me to be similarly entertained at luncheon today. Or perhaps it's Mrs. Reid-Banning I have to thank."

He smiled at Primrose for the first time. She positively beamed in response, even allowing her smile to encompass her husband's cousin.

"Most resourceful indeed," the bishop reiterated, looking at the ruby little Algie was clutching. "You know, Mr. Reid-Banning . . ."

"Banning—just Banning."

"Ah, yes, Mr. Banning. I happen to have one or two pet charities that I believe would be of interest to you. After all, as the sermon indicated, and as you have so rightly observed, it does no good to lay up treasure on earth. Might I invite you to join me in my carriage on our way to the rectory so I may tell you about them?"

"I never ride when I can walk," Banning said, and turning to Marigold, he added, "Nor, I believe, does Miss Wilder."

"In that case, Mr. and Mrs. Reid-Banning may ride with the little ones and we shall walk together."

"A fine idea." Banning set little Algie upon his father's shoulders, much to Algernon's discomfort. How could a prospective canon of the church maintain his dignity with a toddler aloft? But having discovered the joy of riding piggyback, Algie was not to be easily dislodged.

Esmeralda adamantly refused to let go of her aunt's hand.

"Come along, then. Come along!"

So they set out, the bishop in his frock coat, with Banning, Marigold, and Esmeralda.

Esmeralda looked at Banning in awe, then whispered to Marigold, "Is he an uncle?"

"A sort of uncle," Marigold replied.

"Should I call him uncle?"

"You'll have to ask him that."

"Call me whatever you like," Banning responded, "but I'll never call you anything but Merry."

"I like that," the child smiled. "I really like being Merry." Then to Marigold, she whispered loudly, "What funny shoes he has on, they've got high heels."

"They're the kind of boots cowboys wear out West," Banning explained. "Can't beat them for comfort."

"My bunions would appreciate that, but I'm afraid they wouldn't suit this regalia." The bishop indicated his stock and gaiters. "So, you are just come from Kabul, Mr. Banning."

"No, I arrived from America."

"You are quite the world traveler, then, just like Miss Wilder."

"Mr. Banning has traveled far more extensively than I have," Marigold put in. "Still, I'm doing my best to catch up."

"Do you expect to be with us for long?" the bishop asked.

"I never stay anywhere too long, unless forcibly detained."

"Ah, yes. That must have been a nasty business." The bishop looked as though he would have liked to have heard more about it, but Banning made no response. Noticing Marigold's obvious concern, the bishop added, "I begin to think you two know one another rather well."

"We were in Korea together," Marigold said, then added quickly, "I should say we were there at the same time."

"I see. And where will you go next, Mr. Banning?"

"I've been asked by the Amir to look into alluvial deposits along the Oxus River and at Kandahar."

Marigold glanced up at Banning in astonishment, while the bishop was ruminating, "Kandahar . . . Kandahar. I regret my sense of geography is rather vague. Kandahar is . . . ?"

"In Afghanistan," Marigold supplied.

The bishop turned to her. "Well, bless my soul, Miss Wilder, isn't that a coincidence! Didn't you tell me you were going to Afghanistan?"

"I am."

"Really!" Banning commented. "That certainly is a coincidence. I have passage on the *Oceanic*."

"So do I." Marigold was certain from his expression that he was already well aware of that. "Another coincidence, Mr. Banning."

He smiled. "It's getting to be a very small world."

"So, that means you will be in Afghanistan together—I mean, at the same time," the bishop corrected himself.

"I wish I could go, too," Esmeralda said.

"No doubt you will, one day, Merry," Banning told her. "You know, Miss Wilder, they have some of the oddest marriage customs in Afghanistan. They say if a girl takes a man's fancy, all he has to do is to cut off a lock of her hair and declare her his bride."

"Then it's as well for a woman to keep her hair short."

"Just like you do, Auntie," Esmeralda put in.

"Seems they've thought of that, Merry. If the man can't catch hold of a lock of hair, then he throws a sheet over his chosen one and carries her off."

"I seem to remember something of that sort happening already, though not in Afghanistan," Marigold responded enigmatically.

"Pagans!" the bishop lamented. "But I've no doubt we can count on you two to set these heathens straight on such serious matters as matrimony, which cannot be entered into lightly."

"My thoughts exactly," Banning agreed. "As I've told Maggie— Miss Wilder, more than once."

"I was of the opinion you thought it shouldn't be entered into at all," Marigold responded.

"What I meant was not without due consideration."

"Very wise," the bishop put in. "Marry in haste . . ."

But Banning went on, without waiting for the bishop to conclude. "I've had ample opportunity in these past few months to consider any number of things, Maggie."

"Such as?"

"Such as the way my life keeps getting into your hands."

"But we're even. Remember you saved mine that day at the palace." She shuddered at the thought. "You shouldn't have let me go on thinking it was you who had circulated that photograph."

"A circulating photograph?" the bishop prompted with interest. "What was it of?"

"It was a picture of a thoroughly nasty fellow—you wouldn't approve of him at all," Banning said.

"Then I don't understand why you circulated his picture?"

"It was Lee who circulated it," Marigold explained.

"I see," said the bishop, who didn't.

"You can imagine my feelings when Lee wrote to tell me that he was the one behind it—I wanted you to know how sorry I was for wrongly accusing you, but I didn't know where you were. I just don't see why you took the blame for something you didn't do."

"But I was ultimately responsible. I know and understand Lee— I know what drove him to do it. Had I had that plate, I might have used it as he did. He didn't foresee the results and he shouldn't be blamed."

"I don't blame him. I'm just sorry—terribly upset that I ever blamed you." She blinked, feeling dangerously close to tears as she went on to say what had been on her mind for so long. "Not a day has gone by that I haven't remembered goading you about Chu-sun's burial and realizing what happened to you because of that. You went back to take care of it, and . . ."

He shrugged. "Kim had it in for me. It happened then, but it would probably have happened eventually anyway."

"Did he—were you harmed?" She could not bring herself to use the word "torture."

"Don't I look all right?" he demanded.

"Yes," she agreed dubiously. But looking into his eyes, she saw greater depth and also greater vulnerability, and she knew he had changed. "He did harm you, didn't he." It was a statement of fact, not a question.

"He didn't have that power. Whatever was physically done has healed. My mind was always my own," he replied brusquely. "But while I was undergoing . . . while I was in his clutches, I had time and occasion to think about a great number of things I hadn't seriously considered before. The question I kept asking myself was, what do I have to live for? And I got only one answer."

He had stopped. Marigold, still holding Esmeralda's hand, stopped, too. The bishop hovered awkwardly in their wake.

"You, Maggie. You're all I want to live for. That's why I came— to see whether, since my life keeps falling into your hands, and you keep saving it . . . Oh God!" he said in exasperation. "I'm making a far worse mess of this than Sully ever did. But then, I haven't done it as often. The thing is, Maggie, I got to wondering whether you might consider the possibility of just letting it stay there for good."

Marigold was flushed but thoughtful. "I seem to remember once hearing you say that fusing the Blue Dragon with the White Tiger produces supernatural powers." Then she added with a slight smile, "That being the case, I don't see how I can possibly refuse."

"I don't see how you can either," Banning replied lightly, though his relief was evident.

"That seems to settle the matter, then." The bishop rubbed his hands together. "Now you two will certainly be able to set the right tone out there among the pagans."

"Maggie, perhaps, but for myself, I can make no promises." Banning took Marigold's hand, turned it over, and bent to kiss the palm. She clung to him for an instant. He raised his head. "Come to think of it, Bishop, I'm not so sure I can give you any guarantees about Maggie either."

Author's Note

In the late fifties and again in the mid-sixties I lived in Korea, a Korea not so different from the Korea described in *The Blue Dragon* as from the industrial nation it has since become. At that time, particularly in regions distant from Seoul, it was possible to see life as it had been lived long before the Hermit Kingdom opened its doors. I came to know and appreciate the country, its people, and its culture.

Though *The Blue Dragon* is a work of fiction, its background—Korea in the last decade of the nineteenth century—is drawn from accounts of a particularly turbulent period in that nation's history.

Many of the events actually occurred; some of the characters are based on real people. Queen Min played a vital role in her nation's history and her murder was one of the more dastardly acts to befall an already troubled nation. The scramble for power over Korea, most particularly between Russia, China, and Japan, was ongoing once trade and religion had forced open the Hermit Kingdom, while King Kojong, without the guidance of his queen, was no match for his adversaries. Japan annexed Korea in 1910 and forced the king to resign in favor of his weak son; nine years later the king died and the monarchy went into decline.

Lady Chu-sun and her sister, the Princess Chun-mae, are creations of my imagination, though events in their lives, such as the kantaek at which they appeared, have been described in *Women of Korea: A History from Ancient Times to 1945*, edited by Yung-Chung

Kim, and *Virtues in Conflict: Tradition and the Korean Woman Today,* edited by Sandra Mattielli.

In many instances I have used actual names of foreign residents of Korea during that period, creating fictional characters around those names. Insight into the lives they led so far away from their respective homes came from accounts such as *The Passing of Korea,* by Homer B. Hulbert, a missionary, educator, and diplomat; *Choson—The Land of the Morning Calm,* by Percival Lowell, counselor to the first Korean mission to the United States that took place after the Hermit Kingdom opened its doors; and *Things Korean,* by Dr. Horace N. Allen, U.S. minister to Korea.

For the story of Marigold's journey up the Han River and into the Diamond Mountains, I am entirely indebted to Isabella Bird Bishop's *Korea and Her Neighbors.* Mrs. Bishop, a Scotswoman, became an indefatigable world traveler quite late in life. She made four trips to Korea—a country that she said grew on her—between 1894 and 1897.

My appreciation for the sijo came from Richard Rutt, a bishop in the Anglican church whose work I came to know through his regular contributions to the *Korea Times,* an English-language newspaper in Seoul. His articles were later collected into book form in *Korean Works and Days.* In *The Bamboo Grove: An Introduction to Sijo,* Bishop Rutt has not only given a lucid account of this unusual form of Korean poetry, but has translated a wide selection of sijo, both ancient and modern.

Among others instrumental in giving me an understanding of Korea was Paul Crane, an American surgeon, son of missionary parents, who, having lived in Korea for most of his life, was often prevailed upon to share his insights with the foreign community at forums conducted by the Royal Asiatic Society. His talks have since been compiled in *Korean Patterns.* I also appreciated the work of Lee O-Young, a journalist whose collection of essays, *In This Earth and*

In That Wind, helped me picture Korean society through commonplace events.

Last, but definitely not least, I owe a debt of thanks to the eminent writer who first awakened my interest in the Far East. At the end of the nineteenth century, Lafcadio Hearn, a remarkable man of Greek-Irish parentage, went to Japan for a brief visit and never returned to the West. He puts in a brief appearance in *The Blue Dragon* where, for the most part, his words are taken from his collected works.

—Diana Brown
San Jose, California
October 1987